BLINDSIDED

Blue Blooded Brothers Book 2

Sofia Aves

Dedication

Jo & Neen - because cuppas together make all the difference

Jacinta - because coffee is life

never drawl. From what I'd gathered, Mandy had always lived in cities and never strayed far from her high-priced hairdresser or nail technician.

I nearly snorted. Rule one — *never* ask a man what he's thinking. I glanced out the window, but the runner I'd been watching was long gone.

Stalker, much?

Peering around the thick window frame, I jumped when I was poked again, this time banging my head on the glass.

"Ow." I clutched the same spot as before, looking back at Mandy. She sat there, attempting to look sexy — or sweet, I couldn't tell which — dull hair hanging limply around her face with those razor-sharp talons that had cost me the best part of a week's wages, and I said it. Honestly, it was meant to come out kinder, as a compliment, something.

But really, I was as brutal as they come.

Still rubbing my head where I'd banged it on the window, the words just slipped out.

"Mandy, I can't do this anymore."

It was like she'd been waiting for it. Tears on tap, they erupted from her in waves. I tried to reach out — pat her, wasn't that what you did when faced with emotional trauma?

Remnants of mascara quickly tracked her cheeks until she resembled a washed-out panda.

Tears always put me on my back foot. Widow's tears, even parent's, I could deal with. Anything to do with the job. But not personal ones. And when you'd fucked a girl seven different ways on your couch —and hers — things got classed as pretty personal.

She slapped her hand flat on the table, glaring at me as she knocked over her coffee, then scrambling to dry her claws on her skimpy top. She whacked me with her dripping phone on her way out the door. The place was silent, and I realised everyone was looking my way. Social anathema? Only for me. She'd gotten away with that one scot-free. Hell, she could probably blog it, and make a mint.

My throat burned with self-disgust, which quickly moved to self-loathing. I gave it a few more seconds before I made my move, just to put a little distance between us, hoping to god I wouldn't find her waiting at my truck.

Rising, I tossed money on the table, taking care to slip a few extra notes down. The waitresses had to deal with the fallout from this morning's domestic disaster — pretty much the story of my life.

I nodded sharply to the patrons at the next table. A tiny lady hidden beneath a swath of purple curls glared at me, and I made my exit in haste.

I was still shaking my head when the elevator doors pinged open to the office. Slightly dazed, I was halfway through the bland reception area when I realised the place was absolutely silent. Steph wasn't at the reception desk. Peering into the fishbowl that represented our Incident Room and general office area, I noticed a frazzled head of red hair in front of Cal's desk. Steph was rigid — whether with anger or shock, I couldn't tell.

After the mess with her last boyfriend — who turned out to be the younger brother of a murderous lunatic — it was unsurprising to see her at Cal's desk. What was surprising, was that he'd taken several weeks to get around to firing her.

Maybe my boss was a good guy at heart, after all. Or maybe Mila had softened him up. I fervently hoped for Steph's sake that it was the latter. She hadn't done anything wrong, really — no more than having poor taste in her love life — Cal and I were both guilty of that.

The elevator doors pinged behind me again, but I was too busy trying to read Cal's lips — though he was turned away from me — to notice the only other occupant in the room.

"That's not going to end well."

My head snapped sideways at the feminine voice. Professionally treated blonde hair flowed to a white business suit and a pair of the longest, tanned legs I'd seen in ages. Still dressed in the singlet and running shorts I'd donned early this morning, I felt distinctly underdressed. A hand was proffered at waist level.

"Ally Sinclair. You must be Danny." A warm smile accompanied brilliant blue eyes. I snapped my mouth shut before I drooled on her.

"I am." My brain kicked into gear. "Uh...what are you doing up here?"

"I'm her replacement."

"What?"

Her smile dimmed a little, possibly with her assessment of my IQ, but that wasn't a problem.

"I'm the new receptionist."

"Cal hired you before he sacked Steph?" Internally, I cringed but kept my face smooth as my eyes slid between the two women. Though only a thin wall of glass separated them, they were worlds apart.

Way to run off your mouth, Danny. You're out of practice.

"Liam sent me down." She shifted a small box in her arms. I took the hint and liberated it while she shook her arms out. The box was heavier than I'd expected.

"What have you got in here, a bowling ball?"

"Conscience of the men upstairs," she bantered, the sparkle back in her eye. I laughed, placing the box on Steph's — *Ally's* — desk.

"Surely they wouldn't all fit in something so small."

"Coffee machine and thirty pieces of silver." Startled at her humour, I laughed again.

"Time and a place, Danny." Cal's piercing gaze caught me as he escorted a despondent Steph through the office, making me feel like a school kid waiting outside the principal's office. Her head dropped as she collected her handbag, not making eye contact with any of us.

I wanted to make her feel better, but what do you say to the girl who got your boss' girlfriend tortured? Cal looked briefly at Ally with a small nod as he passed, his hand between Steph's shoulder blades as he propelled her into the elevator.

"He'll be back in a moment." I gestured to the office. "Want a tour?"

Ally frowned after Cal as the doors closed behind them. "He shouldn't be touching her." Her voice was soft, but her tone brittle. I noted it for later, unable to help myself.

Always watching, never stopping.

It was the curse of any decent undercover cop. Even in the office, or at home, I couldn't just switch it off. Always on edge, waiting for them — or me — to make a mistake. It wasn't logical or rational. But it was part of me — and something in our new receptionist brought out the old paranoia. Time to test the waters.

"Well, you know what she did, right?" I turned away but watched Ally's mirror image in the reflection of the fishbowl.

"Ooh, no. Tell me." A swishing sound drew my attention to those long, slender legs swinging over the edge of the desk. She tilted her head back, perched on the desk, a speculative look in those bright eyes as she surveyed me.

I gave Ally an easy smile, leaning my back to the desk next to her, not answering. If Liam hadn't told her, then she didn't need to know. I relaxed, close enough to be in her space, but not touching her. Especially not after that comment aimed at Cal.

I might not always get along with the man, but he was my boss, and he'd earned my respect more than once in recent months.

I just hoped I could earn his back.

"What'd you do to catch Liam's eye? Guy's a machine," I commented, not looking at her. She gave a soft cough.

"He works hard," she acknowledged, but there was a pause in her voice I didn't like. Something seemed off about this girl who had just walked into our office, and how she got here. I needed to know more.

"But...?" I pushed. She shrugged, flipping blonde strands over her shoulder.

"I don't know. Just... He's got an agenda." She shrugged it off, flipping her sheet of straight blonde hair over her shoulder in a practised move.

The stairwell door creaked. I turned to look straight at Ally as Cal walked back into the office, running a hand over his shaved head. A clear face and clear eyes stared back at me. I knew that look, because it was mine, every time I was in a situation with work. My mask.

"He does. Us." I pushed off the desk, waiting for Cal. "You alright, boss?"

Cal nodded, shadows shifting beneath his skin as energy seemed to leave him, though it wasn't yet midday.

"That never gets easier." He threw a forced grin at me and turned to Ally. "Thanks for coming down so quickly."

Ally smiled, never moving from her spot on the desk.

"Thanks for having me in here. This one's mine?" She stroked the desk beneath her. Cal followed her hands, gaze sharpening.

Not the right guy to flirt with. Not now.

Especially after he just had to have *the talk* with one of his staff. My estimation of our new receptionist was sinking with each moment. Cal nodded in her direction, and she simpered at his attention. I hid a grin, knowing what was coming.

Hell, I was becoming as jaded as Cal and Liam. Was it possible I was growing up? I snorted. Never going to happen.

"After what I've just had to do, let's keep everything professional and above board, shall we?" Cal raised an eyebrow at our new receptionist until her head bowed under his sharp gaze. She hopped off the desk, fiddling with the box of things she'd brought with her. Cal's eye caught mine. "Got a job for you."

I nodded. "Thanks," I held Ally's gaze as she caught mine for a brief moment, "good luck."

"You, too." She smiled thinly, but I couldn't help thinking there was more to what she wasn't saying.

Cal squeezed my shoulder, and I headed into the incident room. Four terminals took up the space, with a blank wall at the far end, and a new sheet of blackboard wallpaper spread across it. Cal had taken the old one down right after we'd closed out Operation Niffler and given us all time off.

It had been a hell of a case, and we'd earned the downtime. All of us. I rubbed my neck where I'd been jabbed with horse tranq and woke up after — all the action done with. I winced — we'd all gotten complacent, but I'd let my guard down.

I couldn't afford to let it happen again.

I flicked my terminal on, slumping in my chair. I always felt odd sitting at the tiny desk, too bulky for it, by far. Not as bad as Micah — the man dwarfed everything he touched. The glassed door to the office rattled as Cal came in. I sat up straight.

I wanted to be part of his unit, but unless I could give him something more than I had in the last case, I wouldn't last long. Elite meant being elite — the best — *all the time*. I needed to up my game.

"She seems nice," I nodded to Ally setting up her desk on the other side of the glass. Books emerged from the box, followed by a stationary caddy with lots of sparkly accoutrements. At least there wasn't anything fluffy in there.

"Keep your eyes in your head, Danny. Haven't you got enough to deal with on that front, right now?" Cal glared at me. Not the best start. It took me a minute to work out what he was talking about.

"Whoa– dude. We broke up. And I'm not after an office affair. Too bloody messy." I held up both hands in mock defence, grinning to de-escalate. "Besides, you said you had something for me?" The thought of a new job revved me up—nothing worse for a cop than boredom.

"Good." Cal hefted a file from his desk. The thing looked like a bible, post-its and tags dangling from all sides. He canted his head and tossed the file to me. I caught it — just.

"What's this?" Cal nodded, and I opened the cover, looking at a much younger picture of myself. "Cal?"

"You're up for professional development. I've booked you in with a coach. You start tomorrow, and it will run as long as it needs to."

"No."

"No?"

I closed the file.

"You're wasting both my time and yours. Put me in undercover or get me a hacking job. Somewhere I can be useful." I waved the file. A pink post-it fluttered to my feet and settled on industrial-grade carpet. "Do something, more than just sitting around."

Cal grinned. "You sound like Liam."

That caught me off guard.

"What about Liam?"

"He's on leave until further notice.'" Cal grimaced, "Until we get a new caseload. Something decent. I'm working on it, but he's...not taking downtime well. Selena's babysitting him."

"Ouch."

"So, until then...you're on PD. The coach is–"

"I told you, I'm not doing this." I could barely keep the desperation out of my voice. "Just put me somewhere I can do something. Please." My voice had a whining quality I instantly hated.

"You need this," Cal held up a hand, "to specialise. You can't work undercover forever, and you need a career path if you want to stay here." His gaze connected with mine, and I slumped back into my chair.

And there it was. What I couldn't get past. If I wanted to stay, it was Cal's way, or I wasn't on the team.

A few months ago, I'd decided to sleep with Cal's — my boss's — ex. Very recent ex, who was now *my* recent ex. If that wasn't enough, I'd decided to top it off by sucker-punching the arrogant bastard. He hadn't deserved it, not really — my own insecurities shone through, chafing about authority when I thought I could do Cal's job better than him.

Cal pulled out the chair at Micah's desk opposite me, scooting forward.

"Danny, you're the smartest guy on this team. Hell, you're always going to be the smartest guy in the room, apart from maybe Liam." I smirked at that. "I know you work hard at looking like an idiot–"

"Gee, thanks, boss–"

"*But* you need direction. So, let's find where you're going. All the info for your coaching is in there. You just have to turn up. Tomorrow. Plus, Liam insists."

Awesome. If Liam had his hand in this, there was no way I was getting out of it. I rose, gripping the file, so it bent in the middle despite its girth. Cal leaned back but didn't stand.

"Is this the part where I say I'll have your job?" I gritted my teeth before I said anything I'd regret. "Guess I'll see you when you have real work for me."

I strode out of the office, making sure the door didn't bang on my way out. I'd lost my temper, and Cal had seen it — again. Damn it, I needed to get a handle on this. Glad I'd worn my running shorts in — the gym wouldn't cut the edge off my energy, but a few laps around the lake might.

"Leaving so soon?" Ally popped up from behind her desk, a tangle of phone and computer cords in her hands. I gave her the same easy grin from before, slipping comfortably back into my mask. Shoulders relaxed, stride turning to a strut. *Hide everything.*

"Gotta keep the guns big." I flexed, and she giggled. It was a pathetic routine, but at least I didn't have to go into the argument I'd just had with my boss. Besides, it was in me to flirt just because I knew it would irritate Cal further. I winked. "See you 'round."

"Bye, Danny." She waved as I got into the elevator, her facade as fake as mine, I was sure.

CHAPTER TWO

DANNY

I messaged Micah on my way to my truck. As much as I wanted to belt out my anger on my own, it was more fun to torture my friend with a form of exercise he hated.

Me: Running the circuit. You in?

Micah: You piss Cal off again?

Me: Why you always assume I'm on the wrong side?

Micah: It's you. That alpha dog thing.

Me: I'm insulted. Get your ass down to the lake.

Micah: Doing weights

Me: Do any more weights and you won't fit through the door. Pick you up in ten.

Micah: Hell no. I don't fit in your mini machine.

Me: Fine. Get your ass to the lake.

I swung up into my Jeep Gladiator, taking stock of its size. The damn thing wasn't that small. Despite his whining, I knew he'd be there. Even when I'd punched Cal — and been dressed down by him pretty drastically — Micah always had my back.

I tossed the fat file Cal had given me onto the passenger seat without looking at it, but the flutter of pages told me something had come loose. I settled into the truck I'd saved and scrounged for until I could afford it a year ago. Spending so much time in undercover work, I didn't often get to spend what I earned.

The open cab suited me — the rush of air clearing my head by the time I arrived at the lake. Micah had beat me there. No surprise, as he only lived a few blocks away. I parked next to his blue monster — literally a roadworthy monster truck he used for competitions. His truck did dwarf mine, I admitted ruefully, but that and bodybuilding were the man's main hobbies.

"Tiny thing like that makes you slow, old man." Micah leaned against the driver door, looking bored, though I knew he was anything but. Probably working on schematics for a new chassis. The intricacies of the man's mind blew me away. His thought process was like nothing

I'd ever come across. Only last week he'd put down plans for an enhanced fuel distribution system for his truck.

"We'll see who's slow on the first lap."

"You gonna make it more than one?" Horror etched Micah's face. I laughed, patting his shoulder.

"You know I'll keep pushing you." Still grinning, I pulled my arms over my head, beginning to stretch out the tension I'd carried with me from the office.

Micah grumbled all the way through our warm-up. It was good to move my muscles, but I really wanted to run, and push. Nerves jumped in tiny movements beneath my skin. I needed to get moving.

I shuddered when we jogged past the cafe I'd broken up with Mandy at this morning. But then again, screwing up relationships was my superpower. Was it only this morning? I shook my head. Too much had happened in such a short period of time — no wonder I'd pushed Cal so hard for an assignment. I was as on edge as a hooker on a Monday night. Micah glanced sideways at me.

"Tell me."

I sighed; the man might not be mainstream, but he read emotions like no one else.

"Cal and I–"

"No. It's not Cal." He shook his head, looking away as we hit the edge of the lake, feet pounding in sync. "Mandy?"

"Broke up." It was all I got out before he took off on me at a pace I hadn't expected. I gave a short laugh as I caught up. "What the hell was that?"

"You need to get it out, right?" We were both covered in a sheen of sweat. I was always astounded that despite his whining, he could run flat out for a quarter mile and not be out of breath. No mean feat for a guy built like him.

"Yeah."

We were halfway around by the time my lungs felt ready to explode, but I refused to slow down. Hell, if the day came I couldn't keep up with Micah, I may as well hand my badge in. Puffing too hard to speak, I reigned back, matching the huge man's step on the pavement. The lap was ten kilometres — we still had five to go. I refused outright for this to be the slower five.

Pushing harder, I zoned out, letting my body work out the stresses I'd put on it. In just a few words, Micah had pinpointed the guilt I hadn't known I was carrying. I had never been in love with her — nor her me. I was pretty sure I'd been with her just to annoy Cal — well, mostly.

She still had great curves, but there was little more there to attract me. I wondered how much her side of the relationship had been rebound or revenge on her ex — who was my boss.

I shook my head at my own stupidity. What was it Mila had said during my last case — make sure I dated someone at least as smart as me?

Smarts had different definitions, and when it came to relationships, I was well in the red. Nothing lasted long, and I had never really cared. Or maybe I had, and just hid it behind a mountain of work. Doing stints undercover never really allowed time to develop friendships or anything more.

The few flings I had were good fun, and we usually ended amicably. Maybe it was time for more. But that meant giving up undercover work, which I loved too much. Wasn't that what Cal had been trying to tell me?

By the time we returned to the carpark, I was surprised to find my head reasonably clear of the junk that had been weighing me down. Micah puffed beside me, hands on his knees. I grabbed water from my truck.

"Thanks, dude. Really. That was..." I shrugged, not knowing what to say.

"Helpful?" Red-faced, Micah grinned at me, white teeth gleaming against olive-dark skin. With a Spanish heritage, he had muscle definition I could only dream of. He upended the bottle over his head, looking like a damned sports mag model. Shaking his long, dark hair out, he eyed me. "Don't you go getting all familiar on me."

"Like you'd reject this." I flexed, just to get a rise out of him.

"Don't even try, bro." He tossed the water back to me. "I'm out. Gotta find out what the Big Guy wants."

"Cal messaged you?" I frowned. "Did he say what for?"

"Just to get in for a team meeting. See you."

There was a team meeting — and I wasn't invited. Awesome. That professional development thing must be bloody important — or I was on my way out. Unease churned in my stomach. I wished I hadn't drunk so much water.

I remembered the file I'd tossed onto the passenger seat of my truck, loose pages sliding out at the negligent behaviour. I hadn't thought of the open cab — and hoped nothing important had floated away.

Twirling the water bottle in my hands, I tossed up working through a cool down — Micah and I had powered through the run — or risk lactic acid building in my muscles from the pace we'd set. Tomorrow, I could be brutally sore.

Mind, I was impressed Micah had managed to keep up with me at all, let alone outpace me in the beginning. Guy's head was certainly wired something crazy.

I stared out at the water, movement near the cafe catching my eye. Slim, long legs in black tights sparked my memory. I drifted closer, watching the woman I'd spotted this morning as I'd broken up with Mandy — fine, dumped my girlfriend — pack up a laptop and a bunch of folders into a slim, rose gold case.

Like Ally, she sported long, blonde hair and a tan, but where Ally was high maintenance salon-ready style, this girl was a class above, and I could bet every inch of her was natural.

Not something I usually valued, but this girl had caught my eye — twice. That definitely made her worth more attention.

I stood behind her for a second, channelling my inner stalker with no idea what to say. Her head lifted, and she swivelled to face me. Aqua eyes pierced me until I was a butterfly pinned to a paper. Or maybe a moth. My mouth emptied itself of the first thing that came into it.

"You're still here? I– I mean, I saw you running this morning. Or maybe it was yesterday morning?" I turned my stammer into a question to deflect my discomfort. *Creeper.* Man, I was out of practice. My time with Mandy had clearly reduced my intelligence. She eyed me warily, no doubt wondering what sort of psychotic stalker she'd attracted.

"I run every day," she said neutrally, a long, silvery-blonde ponytail hanging down her back. "But I had some work to organise. You've been here that long?"

The wariness in her didn't dissipate, eyes travelling over every inch of me before they returned to mine. I grinned, not used to having someone check me out to my face. She paused, dappled sunlight enhancing high cheekbones — dark lashes framed eyes I could get myself lost in. *Wanted* to get lost in. I jumped to fill the silence.

"I was here– here in the cafe this morning. Went to work, needed to come back for the run I didn't get earlier." I stumbled over the words, tongue-tied. Her blonde ponytail bobbed slowly.

"You have to get that run in each day, huh." She continued packing up, and I thought for a moment I'd lost her — my conversational skills clearly not at their peak. Head down, she continued, "You and that big guy — who knew someone that huge could run that fast."

"He usually doesn't." I grinned, then started, as I made the connection. "Wait, you were watching us?"

"You. I meant I didn't think someone like you could run that fast." Her eyes sparkled when she smiled, taking my breath away.

I raised an eyebrow, a laugh huffing from my chest. "Is that a challenge?"

"Maybe. Not sure I can keep up with that," she teased. I loved it, and dove right in.

"Take you up on it tomorrow morning?"

Her laughter was like a shower of rain on a spring day. Everyone in the area looked around at us — at her.

"I have a new client starting tomorrow, and I'll be stuck in an office building for who knows how long. I wanted to enjoy some air, sunshine."

Looking at the perfect tan that covered toned arms, I'd say she'd got plenty of sun. Pity though. I would have loved a running companion like her.

A flash of her, sweating, panting beside me on the path, quickly changed to her sweating and panting beneath me on the grass. I shook my head to clear it and found her staring at me.

"What about you?" she prompted.

"Running off excess energy. Boss and I clashed...again. I didn't want to take it out on anyone else." Why was I telling her all this? I never shared my professional life — never had anyone to share it with. "I want to do...a different sort of work than he's tasked me with. I'm good at it, too. Just frustrating. Sorry, didn't mean to go all D and M on you."

She tilted her head, assessing. Amazingly, it didn't feel invasive — as though she was truly considering what I'd said, turning it over.

"Find something in common with him. Something important. Develop your relationship so he can see the world from your point of view — and you from his." She collected her laptop bag, sliding files under her arm. "I hope you sort it out." She smiled, eyes still thoughtful. "It was nice to meet you."

I watched her cross the carpark and get into a silver coupe before I realised I hadn't asked her name.

The drive home was quick, and my muscles were already beginning to ache. Regretting not cooling down properly, I messaged Micah as soon as I pulled into the garage beneath my apartment block.

Me: Already sore. Thanks for the run. You faring any better?"

Micah: ...

Micah: ...

Micah: In meeting. Where are you?

The elevator had a sign hanging off it. I didn't bother to stop to read it — the thing was notorious for breaking down. It was a far safer bet to use the stairs.

I wondered if he was texting on the table — Cal hated phones in meetings. And if the boss hadn't told anyone why I wasn't there, then I wasn't about to explain if Micah could just ask for himself. By the second stairwell, a dull ache blooming across the tops of my thighs, I realised that I was the reason I wasn't at that meeting. It hit me hard — I'd had a tantrum at my boss and walked out on him.

For the second time in one day, I wondered if Cal hadn't been right to send me to PD. Gritting my teeth, I fought with the wonky fire door that led to my landing. A solid cool down and a protein shake might help me get back on track.

I was at my door when I realised I'd forgotten the damned file.

By the time I returned to my apartment, my legs were screaming, and my phone had buzzed half a dozen times. I couldn't be bothered answering the thing and tossed it on the kitchen bench. Turning the air con on to a setting that would have made an abominable snowman proud, I drowned myself in protein shakes and flicked on a sports channel while I stretched out my tortured muscles.

My phone rang. I flicked it off the counter with one hand, still gripping my toes with the other.

"Yeah?" I grunted into the speaker, hoping like hell it wasn't Mum.

"That was attractive." Micah sounded amused. I cringed a little, but at least it was my mate, not my boss. "Where'd you go today?"

"Didn't think I was invited," I griped, switching legs. Damn, that stung. I curled my toes backwards, hunching over my leg. I could barely touch the floor the tendons were so tight.

"Cal expected you to be there."

He had? Shit. Micah's tone was mildly rebuking, and I knew there was more to it. The churning pit of parasites was back in my gut. I sat up straight.

"What happened?"

"There's a new operation. When are you back?"

"Back from...?" I played dumb, but it was a bad idea.

"Don't be a dick. When you're finished your motivational — uh, professional thing." Micah changed course mid-sentence.

"Sounds like you don't have any more an idea what it's about than I do." Starting on my arms was a worse idea than doing my legs. Pain ricocheted across my shoulders, giving me an instant headache.

"Dunno; met the instructor. She came looking for you. Think you'll like her." Was that a hint of a laugh in Micah's voice? Cheeky bastard. Then my brain connected with my ears.

The PD coach was a chick? Awesome. I'd get fuck all done and some wishy-washy hippy nonsense that wouldn't make a whit of difference to my career. My phone creaked in my hand. I placed it on the floor and put it on speaker.

"You think?"

"She's your type, man."

"What the hell do you know about types?" I laughed, the idea of Micah — very much *alternate* Micah with his demolition's magazines and monster truck paraphernalia — knowing what someone's *type* was, sat oddly. "I don't have a type."

"You do. She's sitting at the front desk." Micah's reply was short. "Gotta go. Think there's work here for you when you're ready to pull your head out of your ass."

He hung up before I could say goodbye. I hit the end, flopping onto my back, and stared at the ceiling. Great, now I'd pissed off my best mate, as well. The edge of the folder hung over the edge of the sofa.

I wiggled my toes, letting my circulation recover and grabbed the floppy, cardboard sheath, sending a shower of my personal data and photos floating over my head. Cursing, I rolled to collect them, putting some semblance of my history back into order.

CHAPTER THREE

LAURA

My routine was the same every morning: a quick breakfast after yoga on the deck to greet the rising sun, followed by a homemade chai and a morning run around the lake. There was no spiritual reason that motivated me; I just liked allowing the quiet of the day to set my brain in order.

I threw water at the orchids draping themselves over my kitchen window, collected my files for today, and shot out the door for my run, everything packed into one laptop bag over my shoulder.

"Morning, Mario!" I waved to the coffee shop owner as I jogged the first few hundred meters from the carpark. He waved in return as I slipped my earbuds in, wondering if I would see the man I'd met yesterday. I was still mulling over whether he was a creeper — but the way that body was carved said he worked on it every single day.

Not that that precluded him being some psycho stalker, my brain argued as I found my stride — it just meant he was an attractive one.

While he had a bit of an arrogant attitude — *who wouldn't if they looked like that?* — that physique screamed pure determination; someone not scared of a little pain or of pushing themselves. I loved those things in a man; if he had the brains to match, he'd be hellishly hot.

And the way he and his friend had paced each other — twenty bucks said they worked together in a high-stress environment or they'd known each other for a very long time.

Maybe both.

Surely, they weren't lovers? The thought sat weirdly with me before I discarded it, remembering their antics after they'd finished their run. And he'd definitely flirted with me. Those brown eyes were something a girl could melt into, I mused, lengthening my stride.

And those shoulders. I wondered if they were hard enough to dig my nails into... I was well immersed in a daydream that involved my nails and those same shoulders when I realised someone was running beside me. Very close beside me.

I squeaked, pulling out my earbuds to find those shoulders right there with me. I looked at them longingly for a moment, then dragged my eyes up to his face. Short, dark hair slicked back from his face, his body shone in the morning sun, a light sweat already beading his skin. He grinned, dark eyes creased just a little at the corners, and I knew he'd caught me looking. Damn.

"Hi," I croaked softly. He kept pace with me easily.

"Lost in your thoughts? Or a daydream?" He teased. I looked back at those shoulders for just a moment, beaded with sweat. Ink decorated his forearm from elbow to his wrist. Blacked out squares contained chess pieces — a queen on her side, with a knight standing over her. Cleverly drawn, the lines of the chess pieces enhanced the muscles tensed beneath. If I could just touch...

Get your hormones together, Laura.

"Daydream," I blurted and cringed. He snorted a laugh beside me. I elbowed him, stretching my legs a little further but he matched me, stride for stride. I wasn't used to anyone keeping up with me, in anything really. I couldn't decide if I liked it, or not.

"Want to share?"

"Share what?"

"Your daydream." His eyes were laughing at me again. I focussed forward.

"No." I needed to get off this conversation. "Did you fix things with your boss?"

"No."

Same short answer I'd given him. Fair enough.

"That sucks." I sucked air through my nose, upping the pace a little more. As before, he matched me.

"A bit. So, new client today, huh?"

"Yes." I wasn't sharing anything more about my business with a man I'd met yesterday. He was still a stranger, albeit one I was far too comfortable with. I glanced down, looking for a distraction and was accosted with a pair of the brightest trainers I'd ever seen. "You should be careful with those. Something might take a liking to them."

"Gotta have some personal touch. Pink's my colour." He grinned. "What you listening to in there?" He nodded to my earbuds hanging out the front of my shirt. My cheeks heated.

"Um, Chris Voss." I hedged my answer as we hit the last curve on the path, "Did you expect it to be K-Pop?"

"The FBI negotiator?" He looked at me, surprise widening his eyes. I hid a grin as his pace slowed. "You're a cop?"

I laughed. "No, just interested in his strategies — de-escalation, how to get someone to understand your point of view or vice versa." I'd said as much yesterday when he'd mentioned his disagreement with his boss.

"Mmmhh."

"What was that?" I looked at him sideways.

"Interesting podcast to listen to on a run." He raised his eyebrows, and I realised neither of us was breathing hard. *Damn.* This was what I got for letting myself get distracted by a pretty face — and some seriously good muscles. My gaze drifted back to his shoulders; droplets of sweat rolling off them. I wanted to lick them.

I yanked my eyes back to him but knew he'd caught me looking. Again. I was worse than a horny teenager.

"I have to get to work," I murmured, not looking at him, aiming towards the carpark.

"Got time for a coffee?"

I closed my eyes, wanting to say yes, but I knew this man would be a huge distraction from my work.

"I don't drink caffeine."

"Me either," he spoke softly behind me. I turned to face him. Something sad and puppy-like sat behind that enormous physique, though his physical size didn't intimidate me at all. In fact, I liked it far too much. He shrugged. "Water and protein shakes. My jam."

"Chai or turmeric tea," I responded, then wished I hadn't. I wasn't interested in this man. I wasn't.

Liar.

He looked me over, gaze drawing down and back slowly. *Would he take it that slow in bed?* I shook the thought away. "I have to go."

He stepped back, giving me room to breathe. His eyes returned to my face. I nodded, walking quickly to my car when I heard his soft comment behind me.

"See you tomorrow."

I stopped, but by the time I turned around, he was already in the huge, safari Jeep-thing he drove. I bit my lip and tried not to think about the next time I would see him.

The office was cool and far too bright. I placed everything quickly on my desk, dimming the lights, so the large screen on one wall became the feature of the room. In a small adjoining room off the main office, I grabbed my work clothes, heading for the gym showers downstairs to wash and change before my newest client arrived.

Part of the advantage of being housed in the bottom floors of the police building was that it put me in the centre of the CBD — and close to my clients. Liam had given me a heads up there was a decent sized going begging for cheap rent on the lower floors which admin and filing services usually occupied. I'd jumped at the chance, and he'd listed me under essential services.

I replayed yesterday in my head, trying to get back into the right state of mind. This morning's meeting with the hot runner had flustered me, and I didn't have time to analyse that — now, or ever. Cal had given me a stack of information yesterday, but I hadn't had a chance to look through the file yet either.

Life gets in the way sometimes.

Too often. I'd spent hours looking after my sister through her latest break up and countless hours of drinking. I'd even had to drive her to work, worried she was still over the limit by the time her shift started at the local pub. Not that they cared.

I was more worried she would lose the job altogether, and she couldn't afford to pay her rent without it. Washing as efficiently as I could, I hoped I'd get back to my office before my appointment showed up. I only needed a few minutes to skim the file.

Rushing, I threw my hair up in a damp bun, used the minimum amount of makeup I could get away with while still appearing professional, and swapped my runners for high heels. A black pants suit was my standard work attire, especially when I had regular meetings with executives at Cal and Liam's level.

I'd recently specialised in police work, though my earlier clients were smaller, local business owners. Lawyers and the occasional wannabe judge added to the mix, though anyone aiming to work at a higher level would get something worthwhile out of a session with me.

Sorting my workout clothes into a neat pile, I stored them in the side room and headed straight for my desk. The file splayed open, a very familiar picture in the centre staring up at me. Younger by a few years, but those same honey-brown eyes, the same dark, wavy hair.

"Hi, Laura."

I spun around to face him. Dressed in a black, tight, Under Armour tee and dark blue jeans, short hair slicked back, he looked nothing like the runner I'd met at the lake. Totally off guard, I didn't even know his name.

He stepped forward, extending his hand. I took a moment to grasp it, my mind reeling as I tried to catch up and process everything. Him.

He caught my hand and pulled me into him, just a little. My heart sped up.

"Danny Woods." He squeezed my fingers when I didn't respond. "My name," he added softly. Too softly for my office, especially with the lights dimmed. Soap, clean sweat, and something male filled the air around me.

Focus.

I drew my hand away, though he released it only reluctantly, still in my space.

"Laura."

"I know."

That set off some bells. I narrowed my eyes, hands sliding to my hips. "How long have you known?"

The young man cocked his head. "Found out this morning when I spotted you dashing to the showers in your gym gear. Asked a few questions, got enough answers."

"Oh." Breath left me. He hadn't been playing me after all.

"I didn't know who you were — not yesterday, not this morning. Just knew I wanted to see you again." The words came out so smoothly, I was caught off guard. Again. Body heat radiated from him, the dim lighting and his dark shirt doing nothing to tone down the atmosphere — his presence — in my office.

I stepped away, fumbling for the light switch. The room flooded bright white, and even though I knew it was coming, I blinked.

"Whoa," Danny shook his head, "you could light up half of Melbourne with that thing."

I ignored the smile that raised the corners of my lips and grabbed his folder, leaning on my desk as I flipped the pages. Scanning quickly, I watched a younger man grow into a career police officer, with highly sought skills in hacking and undercover work. Leadership was heavily underlined, but there was a question mark right next to it. Looking sideways, I wondered if he felt the weight of it hanging over him.

Scanning the comments from Cal, I strained to read Liam's tiny, angled notes beneath. They wanted clear career progression for him, but he had to show interest in it first. Liam had outlined exactly what he wanted, while Cal was far more reserved in his comments.

"Interesting." Danny leaned over my shoulder, flicking the corner of the page I was reading. "Mine didn't have any comments at the bottom."

I snapped the folder shut sharply, and he snatched his hand back.

"What do you mean, your copy?" I turned to look up at him. "Cal gave you a copy of your own file?" *Why would he do that?* Danny stared at me blankly. Apparently, both of us were a little in the dark. I placed the file on the desk behind me. "Okay. Let's start with why you're here. Tell me what's going on."

Danny winced, his mouth remaining firmly closed. I tapped my foot, swivelling so I could see his face properly.

"Come on, anything? You told me more at the lake yesterday. This morning, even." When he didn't respond, I shook my head. "Danny...this isn't a phone call I want to make."

He lifted his hands in surrender, then slapped them down onto his — rather huge — thighs.

"Cal and I clash."

I nodded; he'd said as much at the cafe yesterday. Danny pushed away from the desk, pacing a few steps, and turned back to face me — pain, or was it embarrassment? — written on his face. I was still trying to decipher which, when he solved the problem for me, throwing his hands in the air.

"Fuck it. I have a problem with being told what to do when I can see the answers in front of me, especially if they aren't the ones I'm getting. I can hack. I love undercover work, and I'm damned good at it." He paced the steps back, stopping right in front of me. "I slept with his ex and punched him in the face. And I let Mila get taken away when I was supposed to be protecting her."

Mouth hanging open, I shook my head.

"You what?"

"You heard me." He backed away, waiting for my reaction. "And until a few minutes ago, I didn't want to be here. Doing this."

"That's what you argued with Cal about yesterday. That's why you weren't at the meeting." I blinked, realisation beginning to dawn.

He nodded; mouth set in a hard line. "Laura — that team's important to me. I want to keep my place there."

"Then you'll need to work bloody hard to stay on it," I snapped. I closed my eyes for a moment. "Danny, we're going to have to really work at this to salvage it. You."

"Gee, thanks. Totally motivational, there."

"I'm not about motivation. I'm about building your fucking career, Danny," I snapped. Tapping my toe, I took a deep breath. I never lost my temper, let alone swore at a client. "Right. Rules. No more undercover. No more policing, until I sign it off with your boss. Got it?"

Danny straightened, saluting military style. "Yes, Ma'am."

It hadn't been in their notes, but he must really be something special if they wanted to get him moving higher. I studied him: back rigid, shoulders high and straight. Intelligent eyes that saw far more than he'd admit to. He caught me looking, and the change was instantaneous.

He stepped back, his face smoothing to a blank canvas. Nothing — not the slope of his shoulders or tight muscles around his eyes — said we'd just snapped at each other. I was presented with an apparently calm man.

I stared, seeing how quickly he'd retreated: a smooth, perfect expression that displayed not a skerrick of the anger or disappointment in himself he'd shown a moment ago. It was like looking at my sister — all the lies, hidden beneath the surface. I stamped my heel, annoyed.

"Don't you do that." I walked towards him. "Just because someone told you to pull your head in, doesn't mean you get to shut down, to hide it all."

He arched one eyebrow, staring down at me, all arrogance.

"It doesn't?"

"It doesn't. Not here. Not with me." I stepped into his space, watched his eyes narrow the tiniest amount. I knew I only saw it because I had half expected it. If this was his undercover face, then he must be good. Or I was about to waste a lot of my time — and his. "Not after I've seen you push yourself with Micah. Not after you've run with me. Promise me. Promise me you'll give me a chance to help you sort this, to be an important part of that team you love so much."

I bit my lip, wondering if I'd let that get too personal.

I'd met Micah yesterday in the meeting with Cal and hadn't been able to place him until I got home. Considering how memorable his build was — nearly double the size of Danny, who was no slouch in the muscle department — I'd glossed over him. Glossed over all of them, during the meeting, my mind totally elsewhere. It had set off flags on how attracted I was to him. And far too distracted. That was something I had to stop.

I stepped back, but Danny's hand caught my waist, drawing me back to him. My hands hit his arms, pressing back, but he didn't let go.

"I promise," he murmured, so close I could smell the sweet-smoky scent of his breath. I inhaled, but that swirled more of him around me. I couldn't think straight.

"This isn't appropriate," I murmured, unable to break my gaze from his. "I'm meant to be–" But what I was meant to be doing had left me completely as my hands curled around his arms — well, part of. His biceps were too large for my fingers to meet even part-way around. I took a breath and pushed again. "Danny–"

He pulled me closer until our bodies almost touched. For just a moment, I forgot how to breathe.

"Damn what's appropriate." His voice was like black velvet, dark and rich, the hairs on my arms standing up at his words. Something in his eyes read more than desire, though. I looked deeper, picking out something I couldn't quite figure out — that was it. Triumph.

I slapped his arms away, wrenching myself from his grasp and stumbled backwards. He reached out to help, but I waved him away and took a breath to steady myself.

"Don't you touch me again." I swallowed the cold words down, chest heaving. This was why I never got involved with clients. It was a stark reminder — the young cop had been in my office for less than half an hour, and already things were spiralling out of my control. I reigned in a grin; that wasn't going to happen.

The victory in his eyes darkened into something else. A new shiver worked its way up my spine as he smiled, showing teeth.

"I'll take that as a challenge."

I stood still, letting his words settle inside me. A threat? More a promise. His bulky form became fluid, like a wild cat, stalking me. Prowling. How many faces did this guy have? Despite the reservations of a moment ago, my heart raced. A million thoughts tumbled about in my mind — some more attractive than others — but I couldn't let this get any more out of hand.

I tilted my head back, planting my heels into the carpet.

"Do I need to make that call, Danny?"

My words hit their mark; his body stiffened, drawing to his full height. It was meant to be intimidating, except that he wasn't. Not to me. I smiled — a professional, brittle thing — and turned my back to him.

Work. Focus, Laura. You have a job to do.

The file was thick in my hands as I flicked past the earlier information, getting into Danny's more recent assignments. There was the report on Mila. He'd been shot with a dose of tranquiliser. Not a human one, by the looks of things — my mouth dropped as I read the amounts — yet he'd been up and working only hours later.

I flicked back to reports he'd filed on hacks he'd traced, undercover assignments — the man had more than one strength. By the look of it, Cal and Liam were tired of waiting for him to work out which one he wanted to focus on.

"Mila wasn't your fault," I said softly, closing the file.

"What?" Warm breath hissed against my neck.

I jumped; he was right behind me. Spinning around, my heel caught in the carpet. I caught a hand to the desk behind me, so I didn't topple over, and tapped the folder against my leg.

"Mila wasn't your fault," I repeated. Danny growled; a deep rumble that began in his chest, rising higher. I tapped my foot, too, already tired of the ego show. "I've read the file. The guy was mad. What he knocked you out with should have kept you down for at least a day. At *least*. I don't know if that was courtesy of your ridiculous metabolism or just pure determination–"

"I should have known there was something wrong with him."

"When Cal had told you to let him into his house? I don't think so. You did your job." Danny growled again. "Stop being Mr Alpha Wolf and listen, for a moment. This file says you're an excellent cop."

Danny snorted — a minor upgrade from the growl — and began to turn away, but I wasn't having a bar of it.

"I wouldn't have been sent here, to you," all the niceties dropped as he sent me an emotionless stare, "if I was that damned good."

"*And*," I continued as though he hadn't interrupted me, "the comments from Liam and Cal — Cal especially — say you're the best man on their team."

"It does?" Danny revolved on his heel, surprise wiping the faux arrogance from his face.

"It does. We're going to work on some acceptance issues and EQ — emotional intelligence, with you. That's what I want." I folded my arms. "So. My question to you, Danny Woods, is what do you want?"

Danny's mouth opened, several times as he worked it through. I was still. Anything I did now could detract from what might come out of his mouth next — and whatever that was, I had the inkling it would be important. This was Danny's moment of truth — and we were negotiating on his future.

He shook his head, running a hand over his head in a very familiar gesture. I wondered if he knew he'd picked up Cal's habits. It was common enough when you spent hours with other people — a shared living space or workplace — and I knew Cal's team were as close as they came. These guys lived in each other's back pockets.

I doubted anything Danny did now was a conscious action. We were getting to the gritty stuff much faster than usual, but if the process worked, I was all for it. Whatever got us the best results.

"I don't belong on that team," Danny ground the words out until they were raw and frayed at the edges. He plopped himself onto a seat, facing the screen. Looking straight at me, he smiled, completely lacking in humour — life — any semblance of the passionate man he'd been before. *Soulless.* The thought whispered its way along my spine. "I shouldn't be there. I– I want to be part of something special, even though I don't deserve it."

It was my turn to stare with my mouth open, wondering what in the hell I was going to say to the suddenly-very-vulnerable mountain of a man taking up most of the space in my office.

CHAPTER FOUR

DANNY

Laura stared at me. I could see the desire in her eyes to *fix* me when there was nothing broken. Well, nothing I couldn't fix myself anyway.

Music blared from my hip, breaking the moment. Laura jumped sky high, but I grinned.

"Saved by the bell." I sent her a jaunty wink.

Laura frowned. "Your ringtone is *Beverly Hills Cop?* Seriously?"

"Kudos to you for knowing what that is." It was Cal. I picked the call up. 'Sup."

"I need you back up here. Ten minutes." My boss sounded resigned, but my heart leapt.

I slipped the phone back into my pocket, heading for the door.

"Where are you going?" Faint footsteps followed me across the industrial-grade carpet. Her voice rose at the end. I grinned; glad she was as annoyed at me as I had been with her earlier.

"Sweetcheeks, I have to work. I'll be back later." Just to round my exit out nicely, I gave her a pat on that pert ass and shot up the fire escape stairs before she could roast me for it.

"Jack. Fucking Jack." Nick the Prick swirled his ice, coating it in dark brown liquor before he tossed it back. I inclined my head, gesturing to the bartender for a refill for my drunken mate.

Black stared at me from dark eyes, filling Nick's glass with watered-down Jack Daniels, reminding me of the fiasco in the bar with Liam and Selena only a week ago. Black paused in front of me before he walked away to the other end of the bar.

"Oi!" I called him back. May as well make a show of it. "Me too, mate."

Cal's old partner glared at me, taking a bottle of tequila filled with water from the middle shelf and sloshing it liberally into my glass. It had taken us the best part of the afternoon to talk the local publican into letting us take over his pub for the evening. Though I had an idea that Cal had made a donation for our services.

I gave Black a dopey grin and turned back to the contact Cal had set me up with for the night.

It was a small pub; just one room, a bar and a door, and it stank of stale beer and piss. Though there wasn't really that much of a difference between the two.

After he'd pulled me out of Laura's office — for which I was grateful — Cal had asked me to set up an information exchange using an old profile we'd created when I'd first joined his team.

Danny Miller was a gym junkie and an above-average hacker who had little in the way of morals. There wasn't much he wouldn't do for a quick buck either. Which included moving information from one interested party to another.

In this case, the interested party was my boss.

"He's not bad," Nick the Prick slurred, waving at Black who leaned with his back to the small bar, completely ignoring the clientele.

"I've had better."

Black was meant to watch the back of the bar — and my back, to boot. Getting clubbed over the head because I was neck-deep in character wasn't my favourite way to end a stint undercover.

And Laura wouldn't be impressed.

My stomach curdled at the thought of her — I'd just promised her I wouldn't do any of this sort of work until I got my headspace right, and here I was, breaking that promise on the first night.

It wasn't the best way to begin a relationship.

I scratched the back of my head. Where the hell had that thought come from? Laura was a class A distraction. She was a class A something else, too, but I wasn't going there, right now.

Class A distraction. That's all. Focus.

Nick dropped lower to the bar. If I didn't get what I'd come for soon, the small-time crook was likely to pass out on me.

And I'd be in the red with more than one person.

"So, Nick," I prompted, turning to face him. Nick leaned his cheek on his glass.

"Danny. You're still a hacker, right?"

"Always, my man." I might be laying it on a bit thick, but there was a solid chance Nick wouldn't remember a bloody thing in the morning, let alone that he'd seen me or what he'd said. "A damned good one, too."

"Yeah, yeah, they all say that. Right, right. But," he leaned toward me, tottering on his stool; I pressed my foot against it to prevent any drunken misdemeanours. "There's this dude, right. Says he's got a big job. Needs some boys to do some work for him."

"Yeah?" I twirled my glass on the bar. Globs of fluid stuck to the bottom and I desisted. "What job?"

"Wouldn't say."

"You don't know what job."

"Mebbe banks."

"Banks? How? What?"

"Dunno."

I smirked. "Okay, let's go for who called you." Nick leaned over his stool a little too far. I kicked his shin. "Oi, fucker. Wake up."

Nick swayed, leaning on the bar. "Logan something. Lincoln. Maybe."

My bloody froze. "Logan. Wayde Logan?" If it was him, Cal would be over the moon. Though how Logan was

53

sorting jobs through four walls with a little barred window, I had no idea.

"Lucas!" Nick shot upright, a gleam in his eye. My heart rate slowed. *Damn.*

"Okay, Nick. Give me some details so I can call this bastard."

I typed the information into my phone. Black sauntered over, holding the bottle of tequila. I nodded, and he topped up my glass. The place made me sweat.

"What 'bout me?" My contact gripped the bar with a limp hand. I watched as Nick the Prick slid off the barstool into a boneless heap on the floor.

Black folded his arms on the bar, leaning over it to look at our sleeping friend.

"Get what you needed?"

"Yeah."

"Good. Keep Cal happy, yeah?"

"You wanna keep me around that much?"

"Nah. Recruiting's a fucking bitch."

"Gee, thanks. You know you're supposed to be all supportive, oldest in the unit and all. What are you, fifty? A mentor." I gave him shit, just for giggles, sipping my tequila water.

Black levelled me with a glare. "Forty-eight. And it's Senior, you little..." he trailed off as a small bar brawl broke out at the door. "Fucking..." He slid a throwing knife from his belt, tossing it with as little care as if he were playing cricket. The slim blade thudded into the door frame. Several sets of eyes from around the pub turned to meet his dark stare.

The fighting patrons drifted apart, throwing nervous looks to each other as they crept out from under Black's glare. "Keep it down, eh?"

With a raised eyebrow, he turned back to me. The patrons returned to their conversations, chatter filling the small room.

I kept typing on my phone, adding in a few extra bits, and sent the whole thing to Cal. I looked up. "I wouldn't do that." I nodded to the surface of the bar.

Black looked down, pulling his arms away with an oath.

"Fuck's sake," he grumbled, dabbing at his arms with a wet rag.

My phone beeped. I read the text from my boss with narrowed eyes.

Cal: Is this it?

Me: You got a contact. That's what you wanted, right?

Cal: Black could have gotten more.

Ungrateful prick. It was the word of the night. I sucked my cheek into my mouth, chewing on it. I was determined not to lose my shit in a public place.

Me: I'm sorry it wasn't Logan.

I pocketed my phone, seething, and sent Black a feral grin. *Time to poke the bear.*

"So, nearly fifty." I picked up the conversation where we left off. "Jenny notice the age difference?"

Black growled. I laughed at him.

"I can tell why Cal hates working with you so much," he groused.

Well, that got up my nose. Mind, I'd been dealing with him too. But I'd be buggered if I'd let him have the last word.

"Yeah. Well. You make a shit bartender."

Cal's old partner laughed.

I knocked on Laura's office door, fighting nerves. I was so uncertain about how to approach her after the debacle yesterday — and it could only be called that — especially after the way I'd left her. Hell, I'd taken it *way* past flirting.

I raised my fist, thumping it solely on her door before I could overthink it any further.

The door opened quickly. Laura held it completely open, standing in the shadows of her dimmed room as she ushered me inside, closing the door with a sharp click.

Something unusual uncurled in my stomach, and it took me a moment to recognise it — doubt. Not something I came across very often, and even then, it was usually around Cal.

I took a moment to study that as I strode into her office. Did that mean I thought of her as an authority figure I fought against? I smiled at her, internally shaking my head. No. That wasn't it.

It took another moment before it all came together. Laura's opinion of me mattered.

Just like Cal's.

That had taken far too long to click. I hoped to hell she wouldn't ask me anything important today.

"Danny." Laura met me in the middle of the room.

"Laura." I sent her a winning smile, ducking when she threw something at me, but I caught it by reflex anyway.

"What's this?" I turned the file in my hands, studying it. Not quite as thick as it had been the last time I'd seen it spread across her desk, she'd thinned it out and highlighted different parts.

"Your future." Laura sent me the same, smug grin I had when I'd left her yesterday, and I knew I was in deep shit.

I held my life in my hands and watched her step toward me. Her hand came down on top of mine.

"Laura, I don't need to see my file to know what's wrong with me," I growled, letting the nerves, the angst that meant I actually cared what happened in this office, turn to anger — fully prepared to sabotage it. This chance.

Laura stilled, her fingers pressing lightly on the back of my hand. Tiny electric currents spasmed beneath my skin wherever we touched.

"So, tell me. What's wrong with the big guy who thinks he can hide, can fake it with me, and run away?" Her voice broke on the last word. "I'd actually thought you were better than this. I thought you were worth my time. And theirs." I knew she meant Cal and Liam.

She tugged the file from my hand, banging it against her leg in an already-familiar gesture.

I shrugged.

"So," I mimicked her, "now you know I'm not."

CHAPTER FIVE

DANNY

I knew I'd shocked her, but the words tumbled out before I could stop them. Seemed like an overshare type of day, already. Not that I'd really been thinking much at all — Mila's face kept swimming before my eyes. My failure. I'd let Cal down that day, and there was really no coming back from that, no matter how many jobs I did, trying to rectify it.

But I didn't expect Laura to understand.

I was pretty certain that was how it worked. It had left a hole where my heart was meant to be, that made me feel hollower than ever. I remembered Laura's comment on my file from yesterday. That he and Liam had given me a glowing report came as a hell of a surprise.

"Are you kidding me?" Laura gave that odd smile again, her hand tightening on the folder she kept banging on her leg.

My fingers splayed over my thigh. I'd spent over an hour putting it all back together, only a few nights ago. If there was any chance of those papers ending in a mess on the floor, I was prepared to dive across her office to save them.

"So, we've covered that you don't think you're worthy," *Was that a note of derision I detected?* Noted that one, for later. "of being on the team, but you want to be there. Come *on*, Danny. What do you want to do there? What's keeping you from moving away?"

"Ha." I barked. At least that was an easy one. "They're the best. There's only one way to go from here." I made a downward sliding motion with my hand but refrained from making a swooshing noise. I had a feeling she wouldn't appreciate it.

"So, leaving makes you feel like you'd be a failure?" She scribbled notes on the back of the file. I'd be reading those later — when she wasn't around.

"Sure." Damned if she was going to psychoanalyse me after I'd let far too much of my life out, already.

"Mm, and you're surprised your bosses think highly of you?" More scribbled notes.

"Laura. Can we get to the point, please?"

She raised her head, studying me with intent.

"Do you have somewhere else to be, Danny? Because until I finish my assessment of you, you're not going back into that office."

"Are you kidding me?" I was a broken record. I rose. Her eyes flashed, following my movement as I stomped towards her — and the door. I waved at it. "You want to tell me how you'll stop me from going up there and finding an assignment?"

"Not me." She smiled sweetly. A tremor started inside my stomach, the same one I always got when the rug was about to be pulled out from under me. "But Cal will. Sounds like he's been a good sparring partner for the last few years. Put you on your ass more than a few times, from what I heard."

She looked down at her notes. Damp, blonde hair loosened from its knot on top of her head, tumbled forward to cover her face. I was sure it was hiding a smile. I gaped.

"You hadn't even read my bloody file when you walked in the door yesterday morning! Don't tell me that's in those damned notes." I grabbed for the file, but she snatched it from beneath my hand.

"How do you know that?"

I couldn't help the sneer from curling my top lip. "Girl, you had no idea who I was when I caught up with you at the lake. If you'd read that file, well..." I flexed, just a little, spreading my arms out from my sides, "I'm a bit hard to miss."

"Miss the point, more like it," she mumbled.

"Whatever you need to tell yourself." I crossed my arms. "So, I'm not going anywhere. Analyse me."

Laura studied me for a moment, aqua eyes staring into what remained of my soul. "Fine. Tell me something that's not in that file. What do you love?"

"Food. Myself." I retorted, just to piss her off.

"What are you scared of?" Narrowed eyes glared at me. Her foot resumed its tapping.

"Heights." I grinned. That was something she couldn't use against me.

"How do you deal with it?"

"Face first." I sighed as she opened her mouth to hit me with more rapid-fire questions. "Is this actually going to do anything to help me?"

She grabbed a remote, flicking it at the screen, and pressed a sheaf of papers into my hand. My file, I noted, she tucked under her arm as she headed out the door.

"Laura, wait. Where are you going?"

"I need to step away. Watch the video, Danny."

Two hours later, I was bored out of my mind. Meditation and breathing techniques I already knew filled the front of my brain with mindless chatter. Laura wasn't the only one with a need to *step away*. Stretching, I grabbed the remote she'd tossed onto the row of chairs next to where I sat and flicked the screen off.

Silence descended on the room, my ears still ringing with all the things I was meant to have learned in the last few hours. Did people actually buy into this shit? Well, they obviously bought *her*, but I hoped Laura had a lot more to offer if I was going to be away from the team for that long. I was already getting itchy feet.

The door creaked. I wondered if I should put the screen back on but decided against it. Maybe she'd made me sit through the thing as a type of sadistic punishment? Micah's head popped around the door, his neutral face splitting into a wide grin when he spotted me.

"Surviving?"

"Barely. How's it going up there." My voice came out raspy from lack of use.

"Alright. There's a job. Finish here so you can be where you need to." His gaze swept the room, a quick assessment, then settled on me. Even with him, it never stopped. None of us did. And being cooped up in an office wasn't helping.

Where I needed to be.

And where was that? Used to the way Micah spoke, usually in short pieces of conversation, I followed his track of mind easily. Only when he was really upset about something, did you get more than ten words out of him. In fact, at that point, it was hard to get him to stop. Inversely, when drunk, the man was basically a mute.

"Getting to it. Just enjoying some downtime." I paired my sarcasm with a grimace, thinking of Cal's comment about Liam, "but the coach seems alright." I winked, just in time for Laura to see it as she squeezed past Micah.

She'd taken her hair out of the knot on the top of her head. Silvery blonde hair hung down her back in a silky sheet, so different from Ally's stiff, razor-edged mane. I grinned, wondering what they'd look like side by side. Laura would outclass the receptionist by a mile — head to head though, that might be something different.

Not that Laura wasn't smart — that she ran her own successful business alone said she was more than clever. As clever as me, and as driven — even putting my ego aside, that was a rarity. But she had something I didn't.

My lips curled, thinking of the way she'd bantered with me during our run. Laura turned between us, hair swaying with the movement. My hands flexed. I wanted to pull my fingers through it.

"He'll be here for a while, I think," she smiled at Micah. "Tell Cal not to worry? I'll send word when I'm done."

She put emphasis on *done* like it was a jail sentence. Micah cast me a curious look and backed his bulk out of Laura's office. The door clicked, locking me in.

"When you're done," I echoed her words, once we were alone. "I don't get any say in my future?"

"Not your immediate one." She tossed her hair over her shoulder, tanned skin showing against her collarbone. She'd taken off her suit jacket, and the tight-fitting black top she wore underneath did nothing to help my state-of-mind. "Danny. Focus, please."

"Fine. Let's focus on getting me out of here and back into my job."

"Which one?"

"Huh?" My eyes dragged from her chest to her face, a deliberate movement meant to be unsettling. Her head canted, but she never broke her stride. I grinned as her barrage of questions continued.

"Which job do you prefer? You seem to be excellent in both hacking and undercover work. You're here to pick a direction. Which one do you want to go with?"

"Why do I have to pick?" I sounded like a whiny kid again. Dammit.

Laura exhaled a sharp breath. "You need to specialise in something. That's what they — Cal and Liam — want.

Cal's happy with what you do, but honestly, this is a long-term game. And there's only one answer to that."

There was? Well, if it was that simple, why the hell was I down here? I spread my hands.

"Enlighten me."

"Undercover work has a shelf-life of two years. Two and a half, max. Once you've clocked that, you're done." She levelled me with a look. "You *know* that. Remember the guy that did six years? How did that turn out for him?"

I pressed my lips into a thin line, considering her words. I'd fallen into that one. She was right, though. Legislation decreed I could only do so many months — or years — undercover. Matthias — the cop she'd mentioned — still had issues with life. Just regular, everyday life. He hid stuff, constantly lied, as though worried he would be found out. Paranoia combined with a strong case of PTSD. Something about reintegration issues and home life. Since I had neither of those, I didn't see the problem.

"I'm damned good at undercover work."

"You're good with hacking, too. Better than good."

"I've never failed an undercover assignment," I countered.

"But your time is coming up, Danny." She said the words in the gentle tone you'd use for a loved one at a funeral. "Specialise in Digi. Work your way through the ranks, get into management."

I barked a laugh. "Are you serious? Can you see this," I gestured down at myself, "parked behind a desk all day?"

I paced the room, which already felt smaller than when I had walked into it. There was no way I wanted command. No way. I wasn't Cal, and I never would be.

"You could have it, Danny. It's all up here." She tapped her head, watching me. "I'm not getting through to you, am I?"

"Nope."

"Okay." She paused, falling into step with me, then stopped. A flush rose in her cheeks as she waved me away. "You said you weren't worthy of being part of the team, but you also said it was something special. Why aren't you worth it?"

My throat dried. I wasn't even going to try to answer that one. My feet planted themselves in the centre of the room, refusing to budge.

"Did you speak to Cal just now?"

"Did you watch the video?"

Our gazes locked. There was no small amount of determination in her, combined with a solid dash of stubbornness. It was like looking in the mirror, to some extent. But she was organised, not just driven. As though all the parts of her life — work, home, love maybe — *how was a girl like her single?* — were perfectly boxed up. Had meaning, purpose.

That was nothing like me.

"I'm not worth it because I've got nothing. No grand plan. No relationships, no real home. Just a rental that changes with each undercover stint, and a stack of boxes that I never bother unpacking." I rolled my shoulders, tension screaming across my neck. At least the pain in my thighs had dissipated with our run this morning.

"That sounds terrifying."

"Which part?"

"No settled home, no routine. Though with family, I get that." She gave a hollow laugh.

Ah, so not so perfect there, after all. Somehow, it made her more human.

I grabbed her hand, squeezing when she made to pull back and drew her into one of the chairs. I took the one next to her.

"Tell me about your family."

She sent me a startled look, though the assessment that was becoming all too familiar wasn't far behind in her eyes. I allowed her a small smile, seeing myself as I worked through a problem on assignment. What to say or do next, to get a particular reaction or outcome.

"My sister is a drug addict. Only one in the family, and we've never known how to deal with it. Her. It's just...honestly, it's a nightmare. We think she's clean, think this time the promises will stick because we're so desperate for them to be true." She leaned her elbows on her knees. Hunching over, her hair swung forward in a shield around her.

I placed a hand on her back. She started, but relaxed while I made light, swirling patterns there. Her body heat soaked into my fingers through her thin shirt. My fingers curled at the hem, lifting it before my senses returned, and I resumed my study of her.

"You can't control someone else's life. If they're determined to throw it away like that, then you won't be able to stop them."

"I know that." The words were muffled behind her hair. "I know, but...I keep trying anyway. Damnit, Danny. I didn't want to talk about this." She scraped her fingers across her scalp, tossing her hair over her shoulders. The silver curtain slithered over my hand. The urge to tangle my fingers in it was too strong to ignore. I let it slide over my fingertips, fascinated with the buttery scent that filled the air.

My fingers twined in her hair, and she stiffened. I dropped my hand.

"Yeah, well, I hated your damned video. Brings out the worst in me." I smiled as she straightened, though there was nothing in it. The energy that had been sapped from me earlier returned in force, the air between us charged. I breathed her in.

Laura caught my eye, fidgeting with the remote. She opened her mouth, hesitating.

"Are you hungry? I need to stay out of this room."

It wasn't the first thing she'd meant to say, I was sure, but I'd take it as a win, if it set me free, even for a little while. I smiled; it sounded as though she hated her office as much as I did, already.

Sunlight hit me with welcome warmth, feeling rather like a worm that had been underground for too long. The pressures of being in the "box" — the office building — fell away. I liked the open air far more than the constant pressure the four stout walls put on me.

"You don't like being inside?" Laura asked, laptop bag on her shoulder. It seemed to be a permanent fixture.

"Fresh air is good. It's why I love..." I trailed off, not wanting to reopen that can of worms now we were out of her office.

"It's why you love undercover so much," she mused, looking at me sideways as we walked. "You really are scared of that desk, aren't you?"

I laughed, startled. She was right. It didn't matter if it was my own desk, or Liam's...the idea of being stuck in that building every day for the rest of my working life was claustrophobic.

"You picked it."

Surprisingly, I wasn't stressed talking about it. Laura made it easy to talk about how I felt, letting things out I'd never said to anyone — sometimes, not even myself. Amazing what the woman had achieved in just one morning. I huffed. Maybe she *was* getting through to me more than I thought.

I should give her more credit.

When I headed down the block towards a sushi joint I favoured, Laura turned the corner. I pivoted on my heel, jogging to catch up to her quick stride.

"Where are we going?"

"You'll see."

She turned down a tiny alley with almost no light. I shuffled behind her, hoping the place wouldn't get any narrower, or I wouldn't fit. She knocked on a door to our left, which opened into another, dim corridor. Standing back, Laura gestured me inside. I ducked beneath the short lintel.

"Uh, Laura..." Red and blue lotus wallpaper covered the long hall, doors lining the sides. The place looked like the entrance to a brothel. "Where are we?"

The only answer I received was a poke in the centre of my back. I shifted my shoulders, my shirt sticking to me. Talk about being stuck between four walls. I strode to the end of the hallway and could have sworn I heard a giggle behind me.

The hall opened into a small foyer area. A short Asian woman in a purple-patterned dress stood beside a tall, black desk, assessing me with narrowed eyes.

"Hi, Sylvie." Laura popped out from behind me.

The woman enfolded her in a hug, peering at me over Laura's shoulder. She said something too quiet for me to hear, towing Laura away into another room. I followed tentatively and found myself in a blindingly-bright kitchen.

The restaurant — if that was the right word — could have sat no more than eight people. A long bench bar set with plates surrounded a large barbeque cooking area with a chef in the centre, chopping and flipping food faster than my eye could follow.

The penny dropped as Laura pulled me down onto a stool next to her.

"It's a teppanyaki bar."

Laura nodded happily, conversing with the chef in what sounded like his native tongue. I only spoke two languages — English, and bad English — and had no chance of understanding a word of their conversation.

The smells that filled the place had my stomach reacting violently. Laura was still chattering away when two bowls filled with some undisclosed dish were slid in front of us.

I picked up my chopsticks and dug in.

"Oh, man. That's good." The chef nodded and left with a small bow as I called out my thanks. "How did you find this place?"

Laura had just put food in her mouth and swallowed too quickly. I grinned, thumping her back, thinking of how she'd poked me in the hall to get me moving. She turned a cute shade of pink and managed to get her food down.

"I helped Sylvie set up after she had some business coaching. She came to me. We worked through what she wanted, she came up with a plan...and this was it."

I cocked my head, considering her words. "Her plan?"

"Yup," Laura nodded, stabbing her bowl, "her plan. I don't give you the answers, Danny. You come up with those yourself."

"So, you open what, neural pathways, and let the ideas flow?" My bowl was emptying, far too quickly. "This is delicious."

The deep pink of Laura's cheeks deepened. She finished her food in silence.

"Do you want to go back the long way?" Her eyes twinkled. I appreciated the gesture and nodded.

"Thanks," I leaned forward, brushing loose hairs behind her ear, the pink still present in her cheeks. I decided I liked it.

Pulling out my wallet, I turned to Sylvie, quickly slipping her my card. Laura was busy collecting her things, and she missed the transaction entirely. She led me out of the kitchen in a different direction from where we had entered. Sylvie reappeared with my card and a plate of mints, beaming.

Laura looked from one to the other of us, then huffed, trotting along yet another corridor. I grabbed two mints from the plate offered under my nose and gave Sylvie a wave. Laura shot down a short stairway and was out the

door as I held back a laugh. When I reached the street, I had
to jog a few steps to catch up with her.

"Sorry." I fell into step beside her.

"No, you're not."

"You're right." I grinned. She looked at me askance,
raising her eyebrows, but never broke her stride. "I'm not."

"You didn't have to do that," she said softly. I ducked
my head to hear her. She tucked her hair behind her ear,
hand fluttering just a bit.

"Of course, I did. You just gave me the best lunch I–
well, I've probably ever had. I was heading for the sushi
bar." I bumped her shoulder gently. "It's me who should be
thanking you."

For more than she thought. The last hour had been a
window into her soul. The more I knew about Laura, the
more intrigued I was. The girl had some serious layers going
on, and I wanted to peel them all back to see who she really
was underneath.

Hair bouncing with her quick steps, the lines of her
suit hiding what I knew was a perfect figure beneath. I
wanted to peel away more than just who she was behind the
career persona — and those clothes could be discarded
along the way, too.

As if she'd read my mind, her head tilted back, white-blonde strands cascading down her back like a waterfall. She smiled; lashes lowered. I would have done anything to know what she was thinking. Her next words put a dampener on my desires.

"Are you ready to get back into it?"

Our office building was only a block away. I sighed, pushing my hair back, my faux freedom already stripped away, and forced a smile.

"Sure, can't wait."

"You wanna get takeout?" I stared at the ceiling of Laura's office, flinging a ball of crumpled paper into the air above my head as I lay on my back across her desk. We were well into the third evening in the office. It appeared my torture extended beyond the usual office hours.

"Focus. Please," she scolded me. "Don't waste both our time."

"Why? You don't have a social life. All those perfectly organised compartments with your life set out in little boxes. Did it occur to make room in one for friends?"

I lifted my head off the desk. She glared at me, jaw hard, and swung her hair over her shoulder and into a bun with one hand. A chopstick-looking hairpin skewered it. It was a skill I'd seen her master a few times. I wondered what else she could do with those hands.

"My social life is none of your business."

I took in the way her eyes tightened at the corners; her lips pressed into a hard line as she turned her back to me. It was a punt, but it was worth it.

"You don't have a social life. Do you?" She shot me a look over her shoulder, eyes wide, and I knew I'd hit the mark. I stepped closer. "I know, Laura, because I'm the same," I said softly. "I give everything for the job."

"Focus," she repeated between gritted teeth, rotating on the spot to face me. "Come on. This isn't about me, and I won't let you get away with any more distractions. Right. So, if you were going to profile yourself, what are the weaknesses? Like you'd do for undercover work."

We had been around the block on this one for days. I knew the answer, but there was no way in hell I was admitting more to her than I already had. I yawned, knowing it would incense her.

Get your rocks off another way, you sick bastard.

"It's eight o'clock, and you're starving me. If you want me to be able to run early tomorrow morning, you need to feed me, woman." I swung my legs around, scooting off her desk. "Starvation isn't good for a man."

I put as much innuendo in my words as I could, prowling toward her. Laura's eyes flashed, her lips parting with some scathing retort I was sure when my pocket buzzed. I held up a hand, digging it out of my jeans. Her mouth shut with an audible snap. I winced and hoped she hadn't broken anything.

Micah's name flashed up with one line of text.

"Ah. Here comes the cavalry, now."

Micah knocked and walked straight in. With no concept of personal privacy, he never really afforded it to anyone else either. Laura had picked up on that, too.

"Boundaries, Micah."

He waved her away, beelining straight for me. "You ready?"

"Any time, brother."

Micah nodded, turned, and exited as quickly as he had arrived. I turned to Laura, who stood with her arms outstretched and a blank face.

"You coming?" I held back a grin.

"Coming where?" A note of caution entered her voice.

"Bonding time. I'm sure we're a case study in action. It'll be fun."

Indecision warred across her clean features. She grabbed her laptop bag and stuffed papers into it in an uncharacteristic rushed manner. Flush rose in her cheeks, and she stood with a stiff spine. Damn, she was hot when she was angry.

"I'd better. No social life, remember? Gotta make friends."

I gestured to her to precede me from the room, closing her office door behind me.

Laura followed us to Micah's place, despite the warnings we gave her of the lack of parking around his warehouse. Micah existed — *lived* was far too comfortable a word for his spartan lifestyle — in a semi-industrial area.

Winning monster truck comps gave him additional income, and he'd purchased an entire warehouse big enough for him to work on his truck, and sleep in the office-cum-loft above. In a single weekend, he'd turned it into a one-bedroom living space, complete with kitchen and lounge.

"This is different," Laura whispered, edging closer to my side in the darkness. Streetlamps were few and far between in this area, and we stood in the shadow of Micah's house — more a garage with a bed, really — the moon and city lights hidden behind the enormous structure.

"It suits him." I leaned on the wall.

Micah had held a spot for Laura with his giant truck, waiting until she could zoom into it. A car yard sat opposite his warehouse, and the street was lined with their excess stock. Parked illegally, but here, there were no local cops who bothered to look, apart from us.

"I suppose so," she murmured doubtfully.

Something boomed in the near distance, then again, and she jumped. I slipped an arm around her, giving her a quick squeeze, listening.

"Roller door." I tilted my head. "Here he comes." Micah's footsteps reverberated through the building's floor as he thumped his way across the inside of the warehouse.

"How did you know?" she asked as the metal door swung open. Micah raised his chin at me and disappeared back into the darkness.

"You couldn't hear him?"

The light flickered briefly as Micah hit the switch then came on fully, illuminating the large, empty space. Empty, that is, except for the hulk of his blue monster parked in the southern corner of the building. He headed up a set of stairs at the far side. I followed him, then realised I was alone.

"Laura?"

"This is huge," she whispered, revolving on the spot, "I'm scared to speak up in case the whole place is filled with sound."

I laughed at that outright, my bellows echoing around the space, bouncing off the walls in a crazy mimicry.

"It's like a cathedral," Laura murmured, reaching out to grip my hand. I started, my fingers curling around her slim, cold ones by reflex. She still wore her work top — and must have left her suit jacket in her office.

"Come on, Miss Starstruck, let's get you upstairs. He's got heating."

"Oh, good."

I towed her into Micah's living space, knowing he opened it to very few people. He hadn't objected when Laura had followed me from the elevator, just gave me a considering glance and walked into the garage without another word.

Typical of him — manners and people first; always himself last. I hadn't received a message from him, though, which meant he'd accepted her into his very tight circle of intimacy. I wouldn't use *friends* with Micah — he viewed the world differently to the rest of us.

"Mama dropped food off."

I grinned — Mama's food was mouthwatering. Italian to boot, she could put any chef to shame. The room looked different — it took me a moment to pinpoint the difference.

"Gina moved out?" I kept my comment casual — it had been a rough few months for them both.

"Yeah." Micah stopped; his head canted to one side. "It's quieter."

He took off for the bedroom. I didn't push further; he'd tell me what happened with his girlfriend — ex — when he was ready.

"Awesome." I headed for the fridge; my hand still folded around Laura's. She looked up at me, her eyes sliding in the direction Micah had disappeared. I took the hint. "Break up. It got pretty nasty. His dad is still trying to fit him into a standard mould and Micah..." I shook my head.

"Doesn't fit," she supplied, squeezing my fingers. I nodded.

There was no way I was letting her go, for now. Unless she pulled away. I hoped to hell that wouldn't happen. She dug a green packet of mint Tim Tams out of her bag, sliding them onto the benchtop. I reached for them, crinkling the edge in a bid to tear the wrapper open. She slapped my hand.

"What was that for?" I clung to the packet of chocolate biscuits. Laura tugged the pack from my fingers.

"Later," she waggled a finger at me, glaring.

Several large boxes filled Micah's fridge. "You want me to heat these up?" I yelled. Though his loft was one only one bedroom, it took up more than a third of the floor space above the ground — and that wasn't insignificant.

Micah's answering shout came from the back of the loft where he slept. I couldn't decipher it but took it for assent.

"Does his mum run a restaurant?" Laura untangled her hand from mine to grab the box on top of the stack as it wobbled precariously. I laughed.

"No, but she easily could. There's always siblings and extended family around. She could feed an army." I grinned; the only crowd Micah was comfortable in apart from at the track was with his family — and even then, it was borderline.

"Oh." Laura was quiet, and I knew she was thinking about her own family; the drug-addict sister she'd mentioned earlier.

"Micah is...different." I cracked some of the boxes open. "Fuck, I'm starving."

Vegetables filled one box, handmade parcels of ravioli and gnocchi another.

"Thanks for bringing me here. Micah doesn't let many people into his private life, does he?" Laura asked.

I started. "Yeah." I grinned. "It took me a lot longer to figure it out."

"There's that emotional intelligence we've been talking about." Laura grinned back.

I exhaled, my chest significantly lighter. Laura was quickly becoming a firm fixture in my life — I hadn't realised her acceptance of my best friend meant so much, until now.

Micah really *was* different, in a hell of a lot of ways. People were always curious about his sexuality, but as a bodybuilder — not pro, though he easily could be — he was expected to behave a certain way. He broke all the moulds — and pretty much everything else he came in contact with.

I tiled my head back, looking at the ceiling. Micah always seemed to be alone — and as his best mate, I didn't want that for him. Sucking in a breath, I looked down at Laura.

"You cook?"

"I can reheat food like a boss." She pirouetted in the middle of the open kitchen — the fewer walls for Micah, the better — and slid bowls of food into the microwave. I applauded, grinning as she took a bow.

"Aren't you supposed to curtsy?" I leaned back on the wall, watching her. There were hardly any curves beneath the black suit pants I knew she favoured, but the stretchy white top she'd worn under her suit jacket all day hid very little at all. Without it, I took the luxury to study her.

A perfect hourglass etched her waist into a tiny thing — but I knew she'd put the hours into working her core tight. I needed to wrap my hands around her and tapped my fingers on the cool wall for distraction.

It did fuck all.

Laura raised an eyebrow. "If you wanted me to be a medieval wench, Danny, you just had to ask." The microwave pinged. She popped the door and swept away with what must have been blisteringly hot bowls in one hand. I grinned, watching her ass as she sashayed away.

I liked this woman.

CHAPTER SIX

LAURA

I carried the bowls to a long, planked benchtop that took up nearly half the floor. Through a small divider, a low-lying bed was visible — similar to a traditional Japanese style. I wondered who had told Micah he needed walls, and why he'd listened.

"For you, Sir."

"Thank you, Madam." I nearly dropped the bowls hearing Micah play along. He grinned, the corners of his eyes crinkling. I shook my head in fake remorse, pointing my nose to the ceiling. He snorted but didn't otherwise drop out of character. "My deepest apologies."

Well, the boy had theatre ingrained in him, if nothing else. I scooted onto a stool beside him. He pressed a button on the top of the bar, which flicked over the largest wall-mounted screen I'd ever seen in a residence.

Cars zoomed around a track, stats popping up faster than I could keep up with them. I squinted, chowing down on the gnocchi in my bowl. Suddenly, the screen was forgotten.

"Oh, my *god*, Micah. I need to adopt your mum."

As soon as the words were out of my mouth, I cringed. Private as he was, Micah might see that as a huge intrusion. Tact wasn't always my friend. Danny slipped silently onto a stool on my other side, his hand squeezing my waist gently.

"Too late." Micah swallowed a mouthful of food, turning to face me. "You're family, now." He turned back to his screen, watching the larger cars whizz past.

I swallowed down a growing lump in my throat. It wasn't Micah who was uncomfortable, after all.

"They're mini monsters," Danny murmured in my ear. All the hairs stood up on my arm. I could feel the *heat* of him. "He watches to see what lighter trucks do; see how they react. Then, he tweaks his to make it better. It's all about efficiency."

"Are you watching the trucks or your friend?" I asked, dipping my head for more. I needed Mama in my life. Right now. I grinned at him. "How often do you do this?"

Danny shrugged. It appeared to be his go-to thing. "Pretty often. I like the trucks. I'm not into comps, but the circuit is pretty cool. I hang out with him a bit at the track when he competes."

"It's amazing you accept him for who he is."

"You know I'm here, right? What's that saying about a room? Man, I need to study this." Micah left his food, walking around the other end of the bar. "That — see, there? The red one. Look underneath. I need that."

I squinted at the screen but never got to ask what it was he saw. Danny clearly did, arguing finer points of fuel distribution. I ate my food, soaking them both in. Slowly, I began to learn — osmosis was an amazing thing.

The two of them together — Danny, leaning so far over the bar to point out things mere mortals would have missed; Micah, with a mind working so fast, only Danny could keep up with him. Used to Liam and Cal, I realised the older guys — closer to my own age — didn't stand a chance. Their next generation would wipe the floor with them. I made a mental note to congratulate Liam for his foresight in headhunting these young guns.

I needed to nurture it; the contract I held with Cal wasn't for Danny, though we'd both let him think that — it covered their entire unit. At some point, I'd expected to do team building. But after witnessing Cal and his old partner work together — and the young pair I was currently ensconced with — I realised it wasn't necessary.

Liam stood apart, necessarily so with the rank he held; there was a ceiling the boys would have to break through before they could reach that level. I could see these two taking on those roles — possibly faster than they expected.

Liam was up for early retirement; he had other things — such as Selena — on his mind while Cal didn't appear to know what he wanted these days after being driven by his obsession with Wayde Logan for so long. But now that was over, he was fishing for direction.

Danny's face was intent, and I could see the thoughts turning behind those liquid dark eyes. He and Cal had more in common than he would ever admit. The more I watched him, the more I wanted to delve inside him — not his head, the career stuff, but to really know him, know who he was beyond the mask. Was I seeing the real him, right now? I cared...I cared.

Put the brakes on.

Why did I care about a client? Potentially a lucrative one, but that really wasn't why I was in the industry. I loved watching people unlock their own potential and discover something about themselves they believed was impossible. Then sit back to cheer them on while they skyrocketed.

Hell, I sounded like a timeshare brochure for career development.

But with Danny, it was so much more. And that was dangerous as hell.

"I'll clean up." I stretched, full as a goog. "You guys chill out–"

The argument started there and lasted far past when I'd wanted to call it a night.

"Okay, okay." I held up my hands, covered with soapy water — Micah didn't believe in dishwashers, though I'd set my case as best I could for water conservation with the right model. "He-man — go, fuel cell up, or whatever," I shot him a dark glare, "while Skeletor and I clean. Got it?"

"Yeah, got it." Danny's voice was suspiciously muffled. He didn't argue about the name-calling either — that was alert number two. I twisted around, spotting the empty packet on the counter.

"What happened to my Tim Tams? My mint ones?" I glared, playing up my irritation.

"You're so cute." Danny swallowed his biscuits, grinning when I gaped at him.

"*What?*"

"Isn't she?" He elbowed Micah, who bore dark stains on his fingertips. "Like a pissed off kitten. Cutest thing I've ever seen." His eyes laughed at me while Micah shook his head, one hand full of chocolate.

I stalked towards him, holding out a hand. "Share." I got one back. *One.*

Micah held his hands up in defence, twisting to focus back on the screen. Not a single mumble left his mouth. I wondered at his thought process, as Danny lunged over me, still pointing out improvements. Micah waved a hand silently, and I dragged my he-man away.

"Let him process," I murmured, collecting as many bowls in one hand and Danny's not insignificant bicep in the other, towing them both to the sink.

"I know he can think," Danny started testily, spinning, so he faced me, and liberated the crockery, placing it on the bench behind me. His hands landed on my waist. "You think I can't see what my best friend is working on?"

"He's not stressed. You are," I whispered, not wanting to draw attention to our domestic — could you have a domestic with two people not in a relationship?

Danny inhaled deeply but didn't release me. The warmth from his hands spread through me, and I leaned a little closer before I could help myself. I placed my hands over the ink on his forearms, resting gently, but not pushing him away.

"I know, I know," he mumbled, "But you've been digging around in my head. There's a lot broken in there. And... I don't share well." His eyes darkened, his words taking on a whole new meaning.

94

I tried to step back, the professional part of my brain telling me to evacuate, but Danny didn't let go of my waist.

And I liked it.

He pinned me to the bar, so it dug into the middle of my back, just below my shoulder blades. My hands hit his chest as my heart raced, recognising Micah was only metres away. I chanced a look over my shoulder, but he was still ensconced in whatever was on the screen. I turned back to Danny.

He was so close. After that, each thought became disjointed. His breath hit my lips. Fingers played with the edge of my top, lifting the stretchy fabric to slide broad fingers beneath. I closed my eyes briefly, trying not to breathe hard.

"Danny..."

I couldn't think, let alone focus. Staring into hooded eyes, I knew I had no chance of backing out of this. A lazy grin spread over his face. He dipped his head.

Eyes closed, I expected him to kiss me. His voice in my ear gave me new delusions.

"I'm nothing like Micah," he murmured, lips brushing my skin. It was incredibly intimate, though contact between us was barely there. He leaned over me, around me, so he was everywhere at once.

I shivered, trying to take smaller breathes to keep from panting. A man that made me pant? Hell, I should be begging. But it wasn't in me.

Danny traced the line from my shoulder to my waist, hands completely encircling my waist. "Your curves could keep me going for a fucking month."

"I don't have curves." It was a statement, and the first thing out of my mouth. He'd hit me with my only body issue — that I was a straight line. Or a brick. Put it whatever way you liked it, there was nothing pear-shaped about me. Apparently, Danny saw me differently.

"What, these?" His hands scraped against my sides. A stray thought bouncing around my mind wondered if fucking him would be hard, and fast, or slow, the way he'd looked at me that first day. I banished it, along with a stack of others, stepping aside, but he came with me.

"Danny," I whispered, letting my hands lightly trace the plane of muscle evident beneath his shirt. I couldn't. *We shouldn't.* My brain and lips whispered it at the same time.

"Shouldn't we?" he murmured; his breath tracing patterns on my throat. My hands drifted to his shoulders, barely touching. I was torn between the desire to cry for wanting him and not having him, and the need to push him away, maintain the relationship we had.

And what was that, exactly?

My hand curled around the back of his head, playing in his hair. I could barely breathe. His mouth brushed mine — or maybe it was his breath. I gripped his shoulder, briefly, tightly, so I had something to remember. He stared into my eyes, his own much darker than I remembered.

His head bowed, the ghost of his lips covered mine, then he stepped back. Cold air sank into the space between us, bringing me back to reality.

The lights were off, and we were alone.

I shivered, wishing I'd taken his invitation — *had there even been one?* — missing his arms around me, already.

Danny walked me back to my car, his hand on the small of my back the whole way, while I argued with him. My skin craved contact with his, but in the end, nothing had changed, and we were back where we had started — fighting.

"I don't need an escort," I insisted, turning to face him in Micah's doorway. His hands circled my waist and lifted me off my feet. He placed me kindly on the pavement while I worked on ways to torture him in the coming week. "Don't pick me up! I'm not a fucking toy, Danny."

Apparently, all that teasing had loosened my inhibitions. I turned my back to him, stalking towards my car. I was almost there when his arm whipped around my waist, pulling me against him.

My back met his hard chest, curving to meet every part of him. I hated myself as I gave in, leaning back, letting my head rest against his shoulder.

"Laura," he murmured, lips teasing the sensitive skin of my neck, his fingers trailing from my shoulder to my waist, brushing the side of my breast. A small gasp escaped my lips, my hands curling into fists by my sides.

I reached one hand up, resting it against his face with a sigh. A deep rumble began in his chest, drawing upwards, along my spine. With a growl, he spun me around, my hands flying to his shoulders, clinging, as he pinned me against my car.

"Danny, what–"

I stared at him with wide eyes, my chest heaving.

He released me; his hands pressed either side of me by his fingertips on the roof of my car. He leaned into me until I could see every line, every crease of his mouth.

"Eyes up here, Laura." His voice was low, taunting. Slowly, with every ounce of control I had, I dragged my gaze upwards, meeting his eyes. Hooded and unreadable, he looked right through me, and his gaze dropped to my lips, then lower.

My heart pounded, but this had to stop.

"Eyes up here, Danny."

His eyes flew to my face, the growl beginning again. I swallowed, and his eyes followed that movement, too. I raised my hand, needing to feel the life that ran through him.

His head snapped sideways, eyes searching the darkness around us. Hairs on the back of my neck tingled, a strong urge to hide in Danny's arms and mimic his reaction brewing inside me. I did neither.

"What?" I dropped my hand, telling myself I was glad of the reprieve. It was a hard sell. He shushed me, two fingers against my lips. My hand covered his — it wouldn't even fit around his wrist. He stared over my head for a few more seconds, then returned a rueful gaze to me.

"Getting paranoid," he apologized. "Cal must be rubbing off on me."

His fingers slid from my lips, leaving them tingling. Danny caught my hand, bringing it to his lips.

"Goodnight, Laura." He murmured against the back of my hand. I closed my eyes, loving the feel of his mouth on my skin. His fingers brushed my cheek, tucking my hair behind my ear. "I'll stay here until you're gone."

He watched me, squeezing my fingers, and opened his hand but I didn't want to move mine. Finally, I slid my hand from his, looking into his unfathomable eyes. "Good night, Danny."

He nodded, stepping back as I started my car and pulled away from the curb. I looked in the wing mirrors for him, but all I could see were shadows.

CHAPTER SEVEN

DANNY

Time passed quickly, working with Laura. In the week that followed, I was head down, bum up, delving through a deluge of memories I'd rather have kept forgotten. Laura harped on a certain few, and we had far more spats than happy times in her office.

Plenty of them were mine. Ironic, really, as I saw my workmates briefly in the hall, rushing around. I knew there was a lot I was missing out on, and I wanted nothing more than to get back into that room with them.

Though I enjoyed running every morning with Laura. It was one of the few times she laughed. With her, as with Micah, I didn't compete against her, only myself. It was one of the few times I was comfortable around other people; less likely to be judged on who I was.

Or who I wasn't.

Other than that, she was a hard taskmaster. I finished every day totally exhausted, and I loved it.

"Are we going to go over the same thing every day, Laura? Because this is getting tiring." My words sounded more like Cal's than my own. I cringed; maybe I was more tired than I thought.

The screen glowed at me, made brighter by the dimmed lights. I'd watched motivational videos for hours. Over the lot, I never wanted to hear someone tell me to breathe when what I should be doing was using my brain.

"Alright. Let's try..." Her brow furrowed; she paced the room with long strides. Face bright, she swung around. I groaned. It was never a good omen. "Okay. I want you to lie to me."

I perked up. "That's something I can do."

"I know." The resignation in her voice riled me.

"Fine," I snapped. "I love your office, and I can't wait to do this with you every day. Satisfied?"

Laura shook her head with a sigh. "Hardly. I want you to tell me three things: two lies and a truth. I'll do the same. You pick which is which."

"Sounds like a Facebook game."

"Actually, I use it as an icebreaker for conferences and larger groups." A blush rose up to her cheeks.

"They say confession is good for the soul," I murmured, tracking the colour as it reached her fine cheekbones. She turned bright eyes on me.

"Mine should be clean, then," she said.

"And what does this achieve?" I mulled over her idea, but I didn't really have an objection. Arguing with her was more a habit now.

"You can read people when you're undercover, right? Body language, all the signs," she trailed off, fidgeting at the hem of her shirt.

"You know that already."

"But, can you read someone in a boardroom? Can you read your boss?" She looked at me, expectantly.

"Of course," I scoffed. Laura stood still in the centre of the room.

"Really?" She gave a faint smile, "What about Liam?"

My lips compressed. "No one can read Liam."

"Wrong."

"Yeah?" I snarled; the sound came out far more aggressive than I'd planned. I slapped my hand against my leg, hard.

"Cal can," Laura said.

That stopped me. "Fine. Let's play your game." I threw on a bored persona. Maybe I could exhaust her with confusion.

"Okay."

I winced at the obscenely-bright smile shining at me. "Right. What do I do?"

Laura pulled a chair to the front of her desk and pointed at it. I waited until she seated herself on the other side, clearing the desktop of stationary. I sat on the small chair gingerly, hoping it wouldn't buckle beneath my bulk.

"Two lies. One truth. You pick which one is the lie."

"Easy." I leaned back, splaying my elbows behind my head.

Laura raised an eyebrow. Her head bowed over her hands clasped in front of her. After a moment, she raised her head with a perfectly calm face — all emotion dropped. I started; it was like looking in a mirror. A niggle began in my belly, realisation dawning that I might have misjudged her.

"I love my job. My sister annoys me. I have a degree."

The words came out slow, all well thought out. She didn't move, and not a single word had an inflection to it. I knew the answer straight up — the sister. Laura was a self-made woman; that ruled out number one. And she didn't have a degree. I was pretty sure of that. Which left the middle answer. But her point was made — if I didn't know her, I wouldn't know the answer.

"The sister," I said softly, releasing my hands from the back of my head. "She really means a lot to you, huh? Which makes the lies harder to accept." I gave her a rueful grin. "Hell, how do you deal with my shit, then?"

"With difficulty." She smiled. "Your turn."

I leaned back, mulling. She wanted to play this like a career thing — boardroom, she'd said. Well, not everyone always told the truth.

"I've been in love."

"Lie."

I raised an eyebrow. "Hold your pony, cowgirl. I get on with my boss."

She smiled. "Lie."

"I know what I want."

"Truth." Her head canted, she studied me. So used to her smile, I didn't like being under her scrutiny.

"Nope."

"Clearly two is out." I nodded. "You've never been in love."

"So sure of that?" I gritted my teeth that she'd picked up on that so fast. Too transparent — I needed a good dose of Cal's brand of paranoia.

"Only with yourself."

I laughed outright. "Well, there's a truth."

"So, it's a lie, then. The last one." Laura smiled in triumph. Damn.

"You're too fast." I leaned back, looking at the ceiling.

"Why are you grinning?"

"Because I lied. To all of them." I tipped my chin down. Her eyes narrowed. "No one tells the truth every time. Or plays by the rules, Laura."

"You're right."

That stopped me. "What?" My eyes narrowed as I studied her. A small smile played at the corner of her mouth, though she tried to hide it behind an impartial mask.

But the victory was difficult to disguise.

"Well, well. You little cheat. You didn't play by your own rules, either." I leaned back, grinning, and laced my hands behind my head.

"Nope." She shook her head, allowing a small smile to cross her face.

I couldn't hold my own back. There was so much to this woman — she was competitive, but not against me; only herself. She was more than a match for my own smarts, had beat me at a game where I thought I was King.

With a start, I realised I was damned close to falling for her.

"Well," I said again, completely floored, but not prepared to show it, just yet. "That was unexpected." I went for cool but managed to miss the mark. By the flare in her eyes, it was by a fair amount, too.

"Disdain doesn't suit you." Her voice held an edge. Patronising, or mocking? I couldn't decide.

"It should. I get enough practice." I jabbed my finger to the floors above her office, but by the growing anger in Laura's eyes, she still thought I meant her.

"Aren't you the sweetest."

"Aw, thanks, babe. Aren't you always right?" I couldn't resist the barb. Besides, she was cute as hell when she was pissed.

She harrumphed, tapping her fingers on the tabletop. "If I were always right, you'd be back at your job by now."

"But you know you're right." Just to annoy her further. "It's your superpower."

"Come *on*, Danny. Stop just agreeing with me! Stop being who you think everyone else wants you to be, and just be yourself! Can you do that for me, please?" Laura's voice squeaked at the end of her rant. I snickered, and she turned on me, eyes flashing.

It was the same thing we'd been edging around for days. The banter dissipated; the relaxed atmosphere suddenly charged with tension.

The problem was, I didn't have a straight answer for her. I slouched back, splaying my knees wide.

"Sure, Laura. No problem. I'll just drop the part that has saved me every time I go undercover. I'll put that away because thinking fast hasn't saved my life fifteen fucking times." I let the edge of a snarl enter my voice but kept it as condescending as I could. "I'll stop agreeing with you because my ability to blend in with a crowd, with people I don't know, is what gains their trust. I'll stop, right now. For you."

Laura flicked her hair over her shoulder, meeting my glare. It was my favourite look of all the ones in her arsenal she employed daily to coerce my ass into gear.

"Do I look like I'm here to waste my time for *you?*"

"Nope. But you look damn sexy doing it."

Laura stared at me with her mouth open. When I thought she might storm off — I loved the way her butt swayed beneath her suit pants — she pushed her chair back and strode around the desk. Once again, she left me feeling nothing more than an adolescent school kid, like I had since the first day I'd walked into her office.

Towering over me, eyes flashing, she leaned forward, placing her hands on my shoulders. I inhaled her — something sweet, like honey or vanilla combined with the saltiness of her sunscreen, reminded me of the sea.

Having her this close was incredibly arousing. I gripped the edges of my chair in case I did something — *what was her word?* — inappropriate. I fought the grin off my face, winning the battle by a skerrick.

"I thought we weren't touching each other. Your words, remember?" I said calmly, and her eyes flashed again.

"And I remember a man who rose to a challenge, not crawled away to hide."

Anger coiled in my chest, and I fought it down with effort. I'd gotten the rise out of her, but she wasn't getting the same reaction from me. The sweet scent hit me again, and my dick twitched. Well, not all of me, anyway.

"If I was hiding, I wouldn't be stuffed into your damned, poky office all week, trying to fix something that isn't bloody broken." I leaned forward into her. Nails dug into my shoulders, but she didn't back away, holding my gaze. Pink flushed her cheeks, matching the colour of her lips.

"You hide in plain sight, and you know it. Danny," she whispered, eyes searching mine, "if you block me out, I'll never be able to help you."

She sighed, honeysuckle breath gusting across my lips. My hand rose on its own, brushing the tips of her hair. I needed to wrap my fingers in it; the urge to pull her against me overbearing. And if she was going to stand that close... I gave her hair an experimental tug. A little noise came from somewhere deep inside her, and for a second, I thought I would kiss her.

Her eyes cleared, and she backed away. Her hands shook as they ran through her hair where I'd touched it, the ends swaying with the movement.

I rolled my shoulders. My skin stung where Laura had dug her nails in, and my hands ached with the need to hold her. Still, I couldn't keep the words back that bounced around inside my head.

"You touch all your clients like that?'

"No!" Her voice was shrill, hair flicking from side to side. "No. I've never touched anyone. Okay, let's start again." She shuffled papers on her desk.

And professional Laura was back. I liked my version better.

"Laura, stop. I'm not starting again." I leaned forward, scratching the back of my head.

"We need you to work out — whatever it is. Let me help you."

"I'm not a rescue puppy. You don't have to save me."

"How do you know?"

"Because I live in me every day! I work just fine. Maybe I'm someone you can't fix."

She sent me a patronising look that told me otherwise, pacing the room in quick steps that moved every part of her body in a rhythm that nearly had me out of my seat. How was she able to be so sexy and so damn irritating at the same time?

I tried again. "Laura. Stop pacing." I waited until she looked at me, almost still, before I continued, trying to organise my thoughts. "I'm not a restaurant owner or an exec at the level Liam works at. Probably never will be." I shrugged at the omission and pretended it didn't ache, deep inside. "I'm not someone else who needs this. There's nothing to fix. If you don't like what you see, then I guess I'm not in the right place."

I lifted my hands, open-palmed, sighing as I waited for the rejection that was sure to come, my heart already layering armour over it to protect against the sting. Her eyes narrowed, but I was too deep in my own pit of nothingness that existed inside me that I couldn't even look at her properly. The wall became an object of study: neutral and bare with few battle scars. Hard. Unmovable.

"If you're not going to help me help you, then I can't do anything else." Bitterness edged with frustration oozed from her across the room. I studied the wall.

"Guess not." I turned back to her, regret filling my heart at the sexy hell-kitten standing in front of me. Her eyes narrowed, breath hissing between her teeth.

"Daniel Elijah Woods. For a man with an IQ the size of his not-insignificant ego, you have the emotional intelligence of a goldfish." Flush rose in her cheeks as she glared at me, looking cute as hell. I held back a smirk, taking perverse enjoyment in knowing I'd gotten to her, letting it cover my own hurt.

Her face flushed, but not with the fury I'd expected. She glowed — almost — in the dim room, eyes bright.

"That's it," she whispered, "that's what I'm missing with you!"

"Ah, what is?" I asked with no little trepidation. When she got that fanatical gleam in her eye, I knew I was headed for trouble.

"It's not smarts. There's plenty of those in your head. Damn, Danny, I've been focussing on fixing the wrong thing." She grinned at me, feet jiggling on the floor.

"And what's brought on this change?" I asked, trying to keep up with her — not something I experienced often. Unless I was working with Liam.

"Emotional IQ. EQ. You– you sort of lack it." She smiled at me apologetically. My eyebrows felt as though they might crawl over the top of my head.

"Are you telling me I need to work on not being an asshole?" I asked, offended. Though she'd pushed enough buttons that I knew she was probably right. At least a bit.

"Well, no. But there are times–" She broke off as I rose. "Where are you going?"

"Back to work." I grabbed my jacket off the back of the chair next to me, aiming straight for the door.

"Danny, wait–"

I spun on my heel to face her. "Wait? I've done more than enough waiting while you played Shrink Laura. I'm going to work. My job. So I can damn well be useful again."

I walked out of her door without a backward glance.

CHAPTER EIGHT

DANNY

I pressed the button for the elevator, but the thing was seven floors away. Pushing open the fire door, I ran the three flights, almost tripping over my own feet. Energy rolled off me as I re-lived our argument, my hands shaking.

Frustrated at the time wasted, it had been nothing but a huge flirting session. I opened the stairwell door, staring into the Incident Room with my chest heaving. Ally perched at the reception desk, typing out something while she spoke on a headset.

Maybe Cal had given her additional work? She filled Steph's spot well — *too well,* I thought, grumpily. Cal looked like he was lecturing Micah and Black about something — a standard day, really.

"Hi, Danny!" Ally chirped as I passed. I gave her a quick smile — one of many I could use at a moment's notice.

She smiled back, dipping one shoulder, looking up at me through her lashes.

The energy I'd had on the stairs deserted me in a wave. Why couldn't it be Laura at that desk, flirting? Driven as she was, I realised that the small workload Ally dealt with would bore her to tears. I grinned to myself — I loved that Laura's brain was as sexy as her body. But she was downstairs, and I was... here. I nodded tiredly in Ally's direction, knocking on the incident room door. My stomach clenched, wondering if I shouldn't have gone for a run or left for the day.

I remember a man who rose to a challenge, not one who crawled away to hide.

Laura's voice echoed in my head. Engrossed in my own brand of self-analytics, I nearly missed Cal waving me to my desk, never breaking his verbal stride. Black, Cal's old partner, lounged in his chair like with a throne, his beard far longer than I remembered.

Micah's eyes tracked my progress across the room. I sank into my own chair with relief.

I tried to focus on Cal's words, but for a while, they washed over my head. I was glad just to be allowed back onto the team. Finally, I managed to zone back in.

"...you'll be able to get a gauge on this group from what I've put together. Black?" The bearded cop jerked his chin. "You're on recon. Be seen, and this job will be blown before it's started. Micah, you're good for demolitions? I'm not sure we'll need you, but it's good to get the practice in. Danny — we need to work on what you're up for."

Cal spun his desk chair, leaning over the back of it. Within seconds he was engrossed in conversation with Black. Theodore Black might be Cal's ex-partner, but he was an integral part of the team. We all were.

The task force wasn't structured like a regular unit. We were modelled on the US Navy Seal team structure — each man had a job and took point under his own expertise as it came into play.

"I got a new toy." Micah splayed his legs, taking up most of the office, as usual. I grinned.

"Yeah?"

"Rocket Launcher. Thought I'd make some changes."

I laughed appreciatively. Micah's idea of "a few changes: usually involved making the *bang* at the end much bigger than it already was.

"Got time for a demo?"

"We can do something downstairs. Or maybe at the range. I don't want to bring the building down."

"Really? Might be doing us all a favour." Out of the corner of my eye, I noted Cal watching us and lowered my voice. "Should get some practice in. Might need it if this is anything like the last job."

Cal's head snapped up. "Danny. If we're using guns, we've already lost." That sobered me. He tossed a file in my lap. "Read." A grin slid over his face. "Welcome to Operation Predator."

For once, I did as I was told.

An hour later, I was engrossed in the profiles of a group of small-time hackers. Everyone else had been given the info days ago, and I was desperate to catch up. I flicked through the files, reorganising it to suit my style. Cal always put Persons of Interest first — but I led with the largest threat.

I studied the picture of a twenty-something, bulky dude. Luke Manning. Small-time thief, organiser of a hacking ring that aimed to remove small roundups of change from banks, online.

All those parts of cents that changed in transactions, moving from currency to currency, alterations in interest rates — it all added up to much more than just small change. Luke Manning was making a living off it. He had written a logarithm that tracked them — and filed them neatly into his own bank account. It was just enough to keep himself, and his ring of mates financial. Each one had their own portion of small change diverted to their accounts, too.

Micah leaned over my shoulder. I knew he wanted something, but he knew better to reorganise my work when I was working through a plan.

"This guy," I tapped Luke's photo. "We need him. He'll open up the whole operation." Micah was silent. I swivelled around to face him. "What?"

"Cal wants you to focus on these two." He pointed to the pictures of two young guys, barely out of high school. "They hack fast. Too fast for the rest of us. You're the only one who can keep up with them."

"They're lackeys."

"Maybe." Micah fell silent for a moment. I waited. "Watch them all. Pick your target."

"Okay. I can do that." I left my hand on Luke's image, drumming my fingers. "But, there's something here. He's the only one with skills to organise these idiots."

"Don't underestimate these idiots." Cal leaned on my desk, grinning. "It's good to have you back. Laura called ahead and cleared you for work, earlier." He gave me a steady look that made me wonder just how much he understood of what had happened this morning in Laura's office. I needed to apologise to her — and thank her for saving my ass.

That didn't stop me from being cranky with her, though.

Cal dropped a manilla folder onto my hand, covering the photo. Micah straightened and wandered over to Black, discussing the best way to bring down a small building in the city centre. I shook my head; the boy was nuts, no doubt about it. When the hell would we ever need to do that?

I brought my focus back to Cal, staring at the file on my desk. "What's this?"

"Could be your new housemate."

"You're putting me back undercover?" My heart jerked in my chest. I fought the smile off my face, but Cal grinned for me.

"If you want it." He watched me, the smile dropping from his face. "If you think you're ready."

Ready? I could fucking hug him. I shrugged.

"Sure. Might have a different focus than what you wanted, though." I pushed the folder aside for a moment — I'd get into that later. For now, I had to start planning. "Micah said these guys are who you wanted me to look into, but this guy," I dug around and uncovered Luke's file, "this is the guy I need to be near. He's key, organising their ring."

Cal stilled, considering. I tried not to hold my breath. The last time I'd spoken to him, we'd argued — again. I really did need to pull my head out of my ass and get the job done right. Hadn't that been what Laura was trying to say? I cringed inside but kept my face blank.

Cal mimicked my shrug. "Run it the way you read it, Danny. Predator is your Op."

"Mine?" I struggled to keep my jaw from hitting the ground.

"Yours. I'll run the office while you're not here, be your backup. I'm here, any time. You get stuck, be a big boy; put the ego aside and call me. I do it to Liam all the time. It's not a weakness; it's smart." He gripped my shoulder. "Read it the way you see it. I trust you."

Well, hell if today wasn't full of surprises.

My afternoon was filled with phone calls to our suppliers, setting up new accounts and making a profile for myself. New name, a new identity. I slipped it on like a fresh pair of boots.

My phone vibrated on my desk. I picked it up without much thought. "Yeah."

"Danny?" A cultured voice on the other end had me focusing in a hurry.

"Marcus? Why are you calling me?" Marcus Lehman was Selena's partner in her law firm. While she helped Liam out as much as possible, we didn't really see much of Marcus. I wondered how he had gotten my number.

"Is Cal about?" His voice was strained. Unease grew in my gut.

"He's in a meeting upstairs." I knew Cal hated the politics of running the task force, but he was filling Liam's role for the time being.

"Ah. We have some issues with the judge on the Logan case."

"What sort of issues?" I gripped my phone too tight. Cal poked his head through the door, and I motioned him over, putting Marcus on speaker. "Cal's here."

"We're going to struggle to get a conviction. I suspect Logan has bribed the system with his — borrowed funds. He's also Michael Armist's employer."

Cal groaned. "Are you fucking joking?" I echoed his sentiment. Michael Armist had assaulted Selena in her own home, and now it looked like there was a lot more to it than a case of stalking. Another can of worms opened. We were drowning in the stuff. Cal leaned forward to nut out legal system details with the senior solicitor. I listened, absorbing every detail I could. Finally, Cal hung up.

"Shit. Liam needs to know." He dialled Liam's number, tapping his foot. Nothing. He tried again. "Keep trying," Cal pointed a finger at me, diving into his terminal to drag up files.

I dialled, but the damned thing repeatedly went to voicemail. I watched Cal try with his phone again, and start speaking. I put mine down with no little trepidation. When were we going to be free of this asshole?

Ally kept the guys in supply with their caffeine habits and my water bottle filled. They left, one by one, until I was alone, and bent my head, glad of the quiet, though Ally popped her head in a few times.

"Want your water bottle filled?" Ally was as perky in the evenings as she was in the mornings. Something in that irritated me, but I didn't want to lose focus to study it.

"You know you're not supposed to be in here…" I squinted at my screen, trying to line up images for my new identity. Cal and I had agreed to resurrect Danny Miller one final time.

"It's fine, Cal lets me tidy the cutlery and things…" She glossed over my objection, but I wasn't really paying attention.

I nodded absently, grateful when she handed it back to me a short while later, along with a small container filled with raw vegetables, neatly sliced. Surprised, I looked up and got an eyeful of tanned leg where her skirt bunched as she settled on the corner of my desk.

"Um, thanks?" I had no idea how to get rid of her when my head was full of organisational flow charts.

"You're welcome." Her ponytail bobbed distractingly. "I didn't know if you were a Keto or Paleo guy, so I went simple. Did I do okay?" She smiled brightly, tapping the top of the plastic box I still clutched.

"You did fine. It's — uh, four o'clock...aren't you going home soon?"

Did I sound harsh? Had to work on that EQ, along with everything else. A little voice inside my head that sounded horribly like Laura told me to tone it down, but I pushed it aside.

"Oh, no. It's for your dinner. Cal said you'd be working late tonight." She gave a tinkling laugh I was sure was fake. Paranoia was already kicking in, and I hadn't started undercover, yet. "Do you want company?" Her fingers slid across the top of the box, back and forth.

Did I want what? Was she propositioning me? An office affair was not on the cards — not now, not ever.

"I have a lot to do." I waved vaguely at the pile of files around me and the three screens I worked across, my head down.

"I'll be at my desk for a little while. You let me know if you need anything." Her heels thumped the carpet as she jumped off my desk.

"Uh, will do. Thanks."

I buried my head back into the files, pulling characteristics and expertise into a funnelling matrix that gave me exactly who I needed to be to work with — and around — the group of hackers Luke Manning ran.

By the time I looked up again, I was the only one left in the office, and Ally was waving at me as she headed for the elevator. Glad to be alone, I launched into their profiles, memorising everything.

The streetlights were on when I finally looked up, ready to go home and study my ass off. There were a few small things that bothered me about the job — for such small change theft, why were we tasked with it?

While it probably amounted to a few hundred thousand, we usually focussed on much larger robberies. There must be something I was missing in the bigger picture. Cal wouldn't waste his time with such small fish, otherwise.

The glass around the office rattled, and I looked up, expecting to see Ally's annoyingly-bright face looking in at me. Blonde hair framed a tanned face — not the fake orange and bleach that Ally favoured, but the fresh, outdoorsy look that had haunted me for over a week stared in at me.

My retort died on my lips as I packed everything into a few folders, never taking my eyes off Laura.

She jiggled a bit as I opened the door to the incident room, her first sign of nerves, or excitement, perhaps. I struggled to keep my eyes on her face as her entire body vibrated with her movement.

Considering how we'd left things this morning, I was surprised to see her anywhere near me. Especially when everyone else had left hours ago.

"Hi," I said softly. Wide, dark eyes stared back at me.

"It's my fault," she blurted. I raised an eyebrow.

"You came up here to tell me that?'

She whacked my arm. I feigned trauma, earning myself another light slap.

"Let me apologise. Please." Her shoulders slumped a tiny bit, dark rings appearing beneath her eyes. "I shouldn't have pushed you, not like I did. It was the wrong way to approach things, and I shouldn't have let myself get so close to you."

The circles were getting darker by the minute.

"It's not your fault, Laura." I studied her. Fine lines that hadn't been there this morning creased around her eyes. "Girl, you need to get some rest."

"Are you telling me I look terrible?" A small smile ghosted across her face, leaving far too fast for my liking.

I took a step into her space. She raised her eyes but didn't move away. A grin curled the corners of my mouth — I loved that I didn't intimidate her.

"You don't seem to mind having me close." I trailed my fingers the length of her arm, holding back the need to kiss her. If I pushed at the wrong time, she'd walk. I realised I'd missed her through the day but covered it with work. Damn, she was a distraction, but a good one.

Her breath quickened; she stood stock-still.

"I wanted to show you something. Something I do when I'm lost — or can't focus." Her eyes never left mine. "This is well outside the scope of work, but I– I wanted to share it with you. Please, Danny."

128

CHAPTER NINE

DANNY

I had a ton of work to do, but I knew I'd drop anything for her. She nibbled her lip. I circled her wrist with my fingers, brushing them over her hand. She clasped mine for a second, then drew away, eyes wider than I could have imagined.

She turned away, fussing with her hair as she aimed for the stairs, playing it cool. But I'd felt the tremor in her hand before she'd pulled away. A grin crept over my face as I watched that fine ass make its way to the ground floor.

Laura stopped in the ground floor foyer when she realised I wasn't following her. I gestured to the carpark.

"My car's this way."

"I'm just there, on the street." She pointed to the sleek, silver sedan she drove, parked out front of our building.

"I'm not going to fit in that." I raised an eyebrow at her. She sent me an incredulous look, eyes drifting down my frame, nodding in defeat. "Not comfortably, anyway."

"Okay. Just let me get something from my car." She returned with an oversized cotton bag that looked as though her life was stuffed inside the thing.

I didn't ask questions as I led her to the underground carpark the boys and I preferred to use — the delivery entrance meant the trucks had easy clearance, and parks were always free.

Even Micah's blue monster made it in. Black usually parked his black import elsewhere, apparently not wanting to be associated with us.

She stopped beside my Gladiator, hands hesitating over the door. I reached through the open cab and turned it on.

"What's wrong?"

"How do I get in?"

I laughed, pointing out a little red lever on the open frame doors. She gave it an experimental tug, looking relieved when the door opened and climbed in carefully.

"Don't worry. You can't break it."

Laura smiled cautiously. "I'll trust you."

"Good to know." I put the truck in gear. "Where are we going?"

"Half Moon Bay."

"What for? It's across town." She smiled, a mysterious thing. I wondered what she had up her sleeve but let her keep her secrets, for now.

We were silent beneath the city lights. When it became too uncomfortable, I reached for my music, just as she started to talk. She flapped at me, shifting in her seat.

"It's okay. Go ahead."

"I just wanted to know how you got on today, after we..." she trailed off, looking at her hands. Her silvery hair streamed behind her, sexy as hell framed against the night sky and city lights. Her hands twisted in her lap, until she noticed my look, and stopped.

"It was good, actually. To be back there." I gripped the steering wheel, not wanting to tell her how relieved I had been to be back working, doing something. Anything other than watching motivational videos and having my ego dissected on her office floor.

"I'm glad." She smiled.

"You are?"

"Yes. If you weren't happy going back, then nothing we worked through made a difference."

I wasn't convinced we had managed to work through anything, but kept that to myself, too. "I didn't want to upset you, saying I liked being at work."

"Why would that upset me?" She turned to me, her curiosity catching my eye. I focussed my attention back on the road.

"Ah..." Feeling like I was about to fall into a pit of my own making, I hedged around the topic. "In case you thought I should maybe be downstairs with you?"

I mumbled the last part, hoping to hell she wouldn't claw me while I was driving. That was probably a worst-case scenario, but I wasn't keen on another argument, not when she seemed so amenable.

Laura laughed, the sound drifting away as we hit the coast road. I took my eyes off the road for a moment, studying her: hair streaming behind her, skin glowing beneath the city lights. She looked as relaxed and as comfortable as I'd ever seen her.

"Glad you think I'm funny," I said, turning into a carpark she indicated.

I parked in the gravel lot against a line of saltbush. Waves crashed in the darkness beyond. Laura hopped out, towing her bag over her shoulder. Her shoes thudded on the passenger seat. I watched, but followed suit, still wondering what she was up to.

Laura walked along the edge of the gravel, seeming completely oblivious to the sharp stones, while I hopped along behind her. She turned down the hill, following a little rabbit track that disappeared over a sand dune covered in saltbush.

The trail down to the beach was a steep incline. More than once, my footing slipped out from under me, while she skipped nimbly from step to step in the residual glow from the city. By the time we hit the sand, streetlights had been replaced by moonlight.

Laura dropped her bag halfway down the beach, where the headland curved into a crescent shape. The water was calmer here; it was a popular swimming spot during daylight hours. As Laura began to strip off pieces of her clothing, I suddenly had an idea what she had in mind.

"Ah..." Not opposed to the idea, but also not completely comfortable with it, my words dried up before the last item of clothing fell to the sand.

Lithe, toned, and completely naked, Laura walked down the sand. One perfect leg placed before the other, she walked straight into the waves. The darkness covered her, but I heard her call from somewhere beyond the light.

The part of me that felt some small responsibility for my coach said I had to go. Still, there was a solid part of me that had far less chivalrous reasons for entering the water.

It was frigid to start with, and I bit back a yelp. No point screaming like a girl, though at the back of my mind I wondered what else might be in the dark water with me.

"Laura," I called softly, treading water. There was no sound except the waves gently lapping the shoreline. A light touch brushed my calf, and this time, I did yelp; a hard sound that shattered the silence.

Motion erupted beside me. Laura's head popped out of the water in front of me before my mind caught up.

"Damn, girl. I thought you were a shark."

"Sea monsters coming to get you?" she teased.

"Maybe. Uh– why are we swimming naked at night?"

Laura was silent, and I wondered if she wasn't going to answer me. Her foot slid against my leg as she swam closer. Light reflected off the small waves around us, the ebb of the ocean continually drawing us together.

"When– when you left, this morning, I stopped. Things got out of hand so fast, I couldn't control the situation." She shushed me when I opened my mouth to object, half her features hidden in shadow. "I replayed that conversation over and over. It brought out a lot of things I did wrong, especially the way I responded to you."

I couldn't see enough in the darkness, but I was pretty sure she was blushing. Over half of the situation she described was my doing, but I wasn't owning up to that, right now. I grinned, showing teeth, and she batted at my arm.

"Stop that." Laughter lightened her voice.

"It wasn't just you, Laura. Today, or any other. I can be a prick." I shrugged. "None of my relationships work out well because of it. Friends, family or otherwise. I did warn you it was my superpower."

There it was. What she'd been trying to get out of me all that time, and I gave the words to her freely. I had a limited shelf-life, and it was short.

"You get on well enough with your undercover marks," she said quietly, her words swept quickly away by the tide, but it stopped me. "What's your longest stint undercover?"

"Eighteen months."

"What's the longest you've had a girlfriend for? Or boyfriend?" she hastily corrected herself.

"Girlfriend." I smiled, "eight weeks."

"Oh, Danny." she sighed, but it hit something raw in my chest.

"It's fine." My smile wasn't much, and I knew she'd see right through me.

"Could any of them have lasted longer?" Laura tilted her body in the water, swimming from side to side. Her movement was mesmerising.

"Maybe. If I wasn't such an asshole." I couldn't take my eyes off her.

"What if it's not you?" She ignored my asshole comment.

"What do you mean?" I kicked my legs to keep from turning numb all over.

"What if the girls you...choose aren't quite right for you?"

"Maybe they chose me."

"Maybe," she echoed, but it felt like she was throwing the words back at me.

"Don't pity me." I twisted in the water, ready to head for land.

"Wait."

She didn't plead or beg, just offered a soft word. I closed my eyes and did as she asked. The water moved around me as she swam closer, but stopped, not touching me though I knew she was right behind me.

Eddies swirled between us as she circled me, a constant pressure; close, but never touching. I tracked her movements, mimicking each of her strokes with my own, twisting and twining, until we were moving in a constant pattern, dancing to the rhythm of the sea.

Finally, she came to a stop in front of me. Her skin glowed in the moonlight. I reached out, very hesitantly, and traced the curve of her cheek, letting my fingers slide beneath wet strands that seemed translucent against the dark water.

"Why did you bring me here, Laura?" I growled softly, my harsh tones clashing against the serenity of our movements.

Her eyes went wide, lips parted just a bit.

"Whenever I come here, it...it brings me peace," she whispered, her words mixing with the waves. "Everything gets left behind, until I'm just me. I wanted you to have that too."

I pressed my fingers against the back of her neck, drawing her toward me. I stopped when she was a breath away, her body not quite touching mine, the water warming between us. My skin tingled, demanding to find out just how soft those pink lips were. I traced thick lashes covering luminous eyes, so deep I wanted to fall into her and never climb out again.

She's your coach.

I cursed myself for crossing that line, running my fingers down her cheek one last time. Her forehead rested on mine, my eyes closed against an ache so close to loss, it threatened to engulf me. She wanted me to find myself, to be stripped back to what I knew was inside me.

"You have."

We made our way slowly back to the beach. For the first time in my adult life, I was near a naked female and didn't want to have sex with her. Not that she wasn't attractive; Laura's body was so perfect, it could have been art. Forever was too short a time to get to know that body — not a rushed fumble of limbs from a girl I barely knew but the slow discovery to memorise each and every curve of her.

I could never have her.

That was a good thing, I told the little heartthrob inside me; I'd ruin whatever this was that we had. That's what I always did. Break something special. I smiled bitterly to myself, the ache back with a vengeance.

A soft bundle hit me in the face, interrupting my pity party. It unfolded into an enormous beach towel. I wrapped it around my waist, the cold air a fresh reminder of how easy it was to go from comfortable to being laid bare.

Laura's towel encompassed her entire frame, the ends dangling in the sand where she had planted herself on the beach. I sat next to her, close enough that our thighs touched through the heavy towels.

I looked out at the dark water, fathomless as the night darkened. Cold air rushed against my chest as a breeze picked up, then stopped, leaving the water eerily still.

"It's a different thing, being laid open," Laura echoed my thoughts. "I don't know what it is about this place. But...it can take a little to get used to."

I nodded, the movement jarring against her calmness. I clenched my teeth, knowing she'd have noticed. Laura leaned against my shoulder.

"Are you okay?" Those luminous eyes studied me like they could see right through my soul.

When did you become a romantic?

The truth was that despite being close to a woman I knew I could easily fall for; I didn't think I would ever be alright, ever again.

CHAPTER TEN

LAURA

Danny's face was full of emotion, flitting from one to the other so fast I could barely keep track. Being out in the water had hit him, hard. There was no magic quality in the water, no spiritual journey in stripping bare and entering the sea at night.

For me, it was the process of stepping away from the city, from the chatter, the rush and being free of any physical restraint that seemed to loosen something in my mind. To utterly let go.

"I'm fine," he murmured, arms loose on his knees as he settled on his usual blank facade, shutting out the world again. The glimpse into him had been amazing — there was so much I still didn't know about him. I suspected Danny had spent so long hiding behind the mask of the big, brawny guy, that he had forgotten who he actually was.

Typical undercover cop — he'd started living the lie. I wanted to jump on him, shake him until the incredibly deep man who had come to the surface briefly settled and stayed there. Instead, he'd sunk back into the depths of a swathe of personas, letting them form a barrier between himself and whatever there was that might hurt him.

I doubted he even knew he was doing it.

"I've never shared this with anyone else." Immediately self-conscious, I wished I could take the words back. They sounded stupid, even to my own ears. Danny's eyes never left my face, the weight of his gaze heavy, but not intrusive.

"Good."

I shifted, torn between wanting to touch him, give him reassurance, and let him find his own way through whatever darkness he was battling inside. My towel drooped at one shoulder. I gathered the ends, tugging at them to retain the warmth disappearing at speed.

Towel wrapped around his waist, Danny must have been freezing. His torso was beyond ripped — even cast in shadow, heavy ridges of muscle decorated every inch of his body, leading to a well-defined chest and those amazing shoulders. I squeezed my fingers into fists, bunching the material tighter.

"We should go–" I started, cutting myself off when his hands drifted lightly across my skin where the towel had fallen down. His fingers skated across the surface of my skin, tracing small patterns. I closed my eyes in bliss, tensions I hadn't known I carried shuddering their tiny release from my muscles.

I let my head rest on my knees as his hands moved higher, deepening their pressure at the nape of my neck, into my scalp. His hands were firm, strong in their motions. I sighed, letting the sensations overwhelm everything else in my life, if only for a moment.

After a time, his hands slowed and drifted lightly back across my shoulders. He tugged my towel back up.

"We should get you dressed," he said softly, retreating into himself. It was an odd feeling — to be sitting next to someone, close enough to touch but to be unable to reach them. He was so distant, tucked away in his own mind.

I chanced a look at him. "You must be frozen solid."

"Have been for a bit." He stared straight ahead. "Doesn't matter."

"Of course, it does." I ferreted around, tossing him what I thought was his clothes.

"Um, this isn't mine." He held up a black, satin bra.

"But you'd look so sexy in it," I replied, snatching it back. Danny grinned cheekily, catching the strap around his finger mid-air. He gave it a tug. My face heated, though I wasn't sure why — he'd seen me walk naked into the water.

There was something a little more intimate about a man handling your undergarments, however.

Mercifully, he released the strap, eyes hooded. With the moonlight at his back, I couldn't quite see all of his face. I shifted, getting dressed as much as I could beneath the towel. Something had changed in the quality of the air around us, and I was far more self-conscious than I had been before.

I'd just got the damned thing clasped at the back when he leaned right over me. For the first time, I felt the intimidating size of his physical presence. Planting a hand either side of my legs, Danny loomed over me, his bare chest dry and smooth. Heat emanated from him.

His cheek brushed mine as he stretched past me, grabbing his shirt. Warmth puffed across my lips in a soft burst, then he sat back, a knowing smile lingering at the corners of his mouth.

"You could have asked," I murmured, realising there was no way I was going to get into my suit from beneath a towel. Discarding the cover, I stood, slipping on my suit pants and shirt as quickly as I could. I stared out at the waves, feeling Danny's gaze on me.

When I finally faced him, he was fully dressed, my beach tote hoisted over one enormous shoulder. I couldn't help admiring the carved quality of his chest, visible even beneath his shirt. How many hours had he put into working for that in the gym? That was some serious determination — and no small amount of pain, right there.

"Eyes up here, Laura." I dragged my gaze back to him, dark hair slicked back from his face, exposing every angle. I swallowed.

"Will you take me back to the office? I need to get my car." I stumbled on the words as he gestured for me to lead the way back to the carpark.

Darkness obscured the small trail that led up the hill, but I scrabbled along the bank until I located it, glad of the climb that burned in my thighs as a distraction from the man following me.

I couldn't deny I wanted his hands on me. But he was still my client, and I'd already bent too many rules for him.

Danny tossed my bag over my head to land on the passenger seat. I spun around, ready to berate him, but he was so close. The odd roll bars that made up his crazy doors poked into my back. He ran a hand through his hair, jingling his keys in the other.

"So...it's a decent drive back to the office." He paused, eyes on me. "I live a few blocks away."

"You drive that far every day?" It was the first thing that popped into my brain, followed quickly by a second thought. "Wait– are you propositioning me?"

"Huh? No! No — I just don't want to be alone tonight." He shrugged as if it was nothing. But if he had asked, it was certainly something to him. "It's not that far."

I blinked, trying to keep the conversation straight in my head, but he made the decision for me before I could process everything.

"I'll take you back to the office."

He reached past me, tugging the door of his Jeep open. I watched him as I climbed up, silent. His mask was back, but I knew there would be plenty of emotion roiling beneath, invisible to the rest of the world.

Danny started the engine, hand on the gear shift. I placed my hand over his, hoping I wasn't about to make a huge mistake.

"Okay."

"Okay?" He raised both eyebrows.

"Okay." I swallowed. "We can get my car in the morning." I lifted my hand off his, burrowing them between my knees. I buried my feet under my beach bag, trying to settle, but nerves jumped beneath my skin, making it impossible.

"It's okay, Laura. I'd just like the company, after…" He stared straight ahead at the road as he pulled out of the carpark, heading in the opposite direction from the way we'd come.

"I'm sorry," I pressed my knees together against my hands. Numbness began to spread from the tips of my fingers.

"Thank you." I looked at him in surprise. He waved one hand. "Truly. It was…mind-opening. I'm just a bit raw now, though." He rolled his shoulders, and I knew he meant inside, not what was on the surface.

"I'm sorry," I whispered again, with no idea what else to say. I hadn't meant to hurt him, but I understood; it was confronting to have to deal with all the backflow of cloistered emotion and accept yourself for who you really were. "It can be a– a disturbing process."

"Just a bit." Danny's voice was rough. He coughed, looking away from me.

"I wanted to see– to let you see what it was like to be you. Without the mask," I hastily adjusted my explanation, stumbling when I nearly confessed I just wanted to see him as himself for me — not for anyone else. But that was a selfish thing, and I wasn't about to admit to it.

The corner of Danny's mouth curled, and I cursed softly under my breath — nothing got past him.

We drove the rest of the way in silence — Danny lost deep inside himself, me panicking and wondering what the hell I was doing with a man I'd met only a week ago. I knew I needed to keep it at a professional level, but with this man, it was difficult not to be swept away in the heart of him. He was like a tornado, tearing through life. Everything — and everyone — around him was caught in the path he wrought.

A few minutes later, we pulled into a side lane, only just big enough to fit Danny's truck. If something came from the other direction, we would be in trouble.

Thankfully, nothing did come at us as we drove past the back of residences. We took two more turns into a rabbit warren of apartment buildings and entered a high-roofed carpark that looked more like a loading dock. He chose a space that had a large, yellow smiley face painted on the wall.

"Your work?" I smiled, shoulders shaking a little. Nerves and stress were a bad mix for me. Danny barked a laugh.

"Micah's. He rarely drinks, but when he does, the results are...interesting." He grinned, grabbing my bag before I could object, stuffing thick files beneath his oversized bicep. Everything about him was oversized. That sparked another thought, but I refused to go there — for now, at least. His eyes darkened for a moment. "Thanks for coming back here with me."

I nodded, tugging my laptop bag out from where I'd stowed it beside my feet, brushing off sand. I followed him into an elevator that barely fit him, covering a yawn. I checked my phone — it was nearly midnight. When had that happened?

The doors dinged open on his floor. He caught my hand in a quick squeeze and led the way down the hall into a small, open-plan apartment. Clean and sparse, grey, and blue manga art dominated white walls. No other personal items lay scattered around. He dropped his keys on a stainless-steel kitchen bench with a dull clang.

"Do you spend much time here?" I asked, setting my bag beside a grey, leather lounge.

"Nope. It's just a rental. I get a new one when I go undercover. Cal sorts storage for me until I'm ready for a new place."

"How often do you move?" I couldn't imagine being so unsettled; I'd owned my home for three years.

"Few times a year. It's just a place."

I bit my lip to keep from replying, but Danny folded his arms, watching me. A grin crept onto his face.

"What?"

"You going to tell me I need to have a place to base myself, somewhere I can put down roots and be safe each night?"

My face flamed, and it was my turn to shrug. "Do you know me so well, already?"

Danny laughed, wrapping an arm around my shoulders. I stiffened at the contact, panic flaring in my chest, as he towed me to the sofa.

"You need to get work done?"

I shook my head, the contact of his arm across my shoulders making my nerves jump like they had in his truck, but for a different reason than before.

"No, I'm done for the day."

"Good." He squeezed my shoulder. "Then I'm shagged from that bloody cold swim. Let's go to bed."

I froze.

"Wait– Danny," I stammered. He drew me around to face him, brushing hair back from my face.

"To sleep. Nothing more." He pressed his forehead against mine, eyes closed. When he opened them, he stared straight through me. A shock ran up my spine. I let him draw me into his chest, his lips inches from mine. "Do you trust me?"

I nodded, barely able to breathe. His eyes held mine for a moment longer before he stepped back, releasing my shoulders.

"Good."

Danny slid his fingers down my arm, reminiscent of what he'd done in the office, clasped my hand, and towed me down the hall. I managed to keep up with his quick stride as he flicked lights off around us, dimming the apartment to almost black.

Only the reflection of the city glow through some of the windows illuminated the rooms with reflected light.

He paused at a doorway off the hall, releasing my hand. His breath hitched. I pressed my fingers to his back, suddenly as uncertain as he seemed to be.

"Danny?"

He exhaled in a gusty sigh and slipped into the room. I followed, immediately enveloped by the scent of him — musky, male sweat. Not overpowering, but all him. He drew a blind open, light slanting into the room. A heap of cloth that smelled like him found its way into my hands.

"What's this?"

"A shirt. Unless you'd like to sleep naked?" I could hear the amusement in his voice and was glad of the darkness as I flushed again. I retreated a few steps, slipping off my clothes and laying them as neatly as I could in a small pile on the floor in a corner. Danny's shirt was soft, and the same as his room smelled like him.

His hand caught my elbow. I jumped a little, lost in my own thoughts.

"You okay? If you're not comfortable with this, I can sleep on the sofa." There was a short pause. "Or I can take you home. But... I'd rather not do that."

Neither did I but admitting that meant I was more invested in this man that I should have been.

Keep bending those rules, Laura.

The little voice in my head taunted me. I nodded, letting him draw me onto his bed. I slid into the spot beside him, every inch of my screaming to walk away, but I couldn't. His arm wrapped around me, and I found a quilt draped over both of us as he pulled me down onto his sculpted — and very naked — chest.

My hand hit hot skin. I inhaled sharply, drawing back but his arm wrapped around me, settling me into his side. I closed my eyes, letting myself sink into his shoulder, immersed in the feel of him.

"Thanks, Laura," he mumbled, his voice already thick with sleep. I yawned into his side, curling myself around the breadth of him, and closed my eyes.

A buzzing near my head woke me. Confused, it took a moment to figure out where it was and to realise it wasn't my alarm — I rarely set one. The mountain of warmth beneath me shifted, and I fell back into a fluffy pillow. I pried my eyes open. Danny arched over me as he fumbled for his phone. Finally hitting the snooze button, he dropped his head, collapsing across me.

"I was comfortable. Damnit." He raised his head. "Morning."

He said it as if it was the most normal thing in the world, waking up next to a woman he'd never slept with before. Maybe it was, for him.

But not for me.

Danny propped one elbow beneath his head, still draped across me. "Sleep well?"

Still lost in a fog of sleep, enjoying his weight over me, I seriously considered his question.

"Yes, I think so. It was comfortable," I admitted. "You were," I corrected myself. I wiggled; one leg bent at an odd angle as the bonelessness of sleep deserted me. I flopped back, still wriggling.

"Laura," he inhaled, "don't do that."

I frowned, trying to get comfortable. "What?" I moved my hips, but he was lying on them. One of my legs started to go numb.

Danny rolled, bracing an elbow on either side of me. Heat rolled off of him onto me. My breath caught; I stared up at him. So close. His eyes were hooded, his gaze intense. I pressed a hand to his chest, pushing back the urge to explore him.

"That," he growled, dipping his head. Suddenly, I was very aware of where his body pressed against mine, with no sheet between us. His breath brushed over my lips, and they tingled in response.

I arched off the bed without thinking, my brain catching up when my mouth was millimeters from his. I fell back to the pillow, pushing at his shoulders, my mind warring between wants and needs. He didn't so much as budge, but very slowly, he dropped his lips to mine.

A gentle brush, his mouth barely touching my lips. My chest rose and fell quickly, but his movement was anything but fast. The pressure of his touch against my lips was perfect, opening my mouth with his, slowly dipping his tongue against mine.

I closed my eyes, tasting his lips, following the rhythm he set, though my mind screamed for something darker, something wild. He settled his weight carefully on me, and I was enveloped in the warmth of him, breathing him in. My hands curled around his neck, into his hair, pulling him deeper.

A growl rose in his throat as it had last night, sending my heart racing. Still so controlled with each movement, each kiss. I arched a little against him, sliding my hands along his shoulders, exploring as I'd wanted to so many times before. The shape of him filled my hands. I splayed my fingers over his back, memorizing every curve of muscle. His kisses turned something inside me hot and molten, and I ached from his hands on me.

He drew back, looking at me with those hooded eyes again. "Laura." His voice a hoarse whisper, he cupped the back of my head with his hand, lifting me up to him. "This has to stop."

His mouth brushed mine with every word. I leaned up, kissing him, but when he didn't respond, I stopped. He still held me up against him, his breath kissing my lips as his chest rose and fell hard.

"I don't want to stop," I murmured, trailing my fingers down his cheek, light stubble brushing rough against my fingertips.

"We have to."

It was said so final, but I couldn't bear the thought of not being able to touch him again. A little noise mewled in my throat. I hated the weakness of it, the begging. His eyes darkened, something animalistic coming alive in them.

He pushed me back onto the bed, pressing his knee hard between my legs. I gasped at the sensation, writhing a little, but he didn't back away.

"Danny–" Eyes wide, I drew short breaths.

"Fuck, Laura." He sank back into me, kissing me deeply. His hands wound into my hair, sliding down my back to pull me hard into him.

Just as abruptly, he released me, standing quickly. He scrubbed a hand over his face, staring down at me, completely unreadable.

"I need a shower," he growled and left the room in a flurry of movement. It wasn't until the door slammed shut that I realized his shirt I was wearing had risen up around my waist.

CHAPTER ELEVEN

DANNY

I never made it further than the hallway. Leaning against the wall, I could have banged my head on it. What the hell was I thinking? Certainly not with my brain, which was how we'd ended up tangled around each other in my bed.

It had been a terrible idea to bring her back to my apartment the night before — but both of us were exhausted; physically and emotionally drained from the day and whatever the hell she'd done to me in the water.

"Danny?"

Laura poked her head out of my bedroom door. She must have dressed in a hell of a hurry because she was back in her work clothes from yesterday, looking as fresh and clean as though she'd slept in her own bed last night. The only change was her sleep-mussed hair and swollen lips.

My hand was halfway up to cup her face, pull her into me and finish what I'd started when she caught the movement, eyes widening perceptively. I dropped my hand.

"Thanks for staying last night." I'd already said that, hadn't I? My voice was rough, and I coughed to clear my throat, managing a small smile. "Ready to go in a few minutes?"

Laura nodded, gripping the doorway with white knuckles.

"Do you mind if I make some breakfast?" She edged around me, heading for the kitchen. I brushed my fingers down her arm, hating that I couldn't just let her go. She halted, slowly swiveling to face me.

"There's bugger all in the fridge. Some protein shakes, maybe." I gestured to the garage. "Get something on the way to work?"

"Okay." Her voice shook a bit.

I wanted to curve my hands around her waist so badly, pull her to me and finish what I'd started in the bedroom. Fuck it, why not just carry on back there? Suddenly, I didn't care if we were late. My hands closed around her arms, reveling in the combination of softness and strength of them.

"Stop this. Now."

It was a command, and like a well-trained dog, I did what she asked. Backing away, I swallowed past a hard lump in my throat.

"I'll go take that shower." I couldn't hold her gaze, lest I break whatever small amount of trust we'd developed.

I left her standing in the hall, trying to figure out what the hell was wrong with me.

We ended up leaving the apartment much later than usual, and my promise of a short drive across the city turned into a backlog of peak hour traffic. Drive-through provided a greasy breakfast neither of us usually ate, though I noted Laura ordered a dirty chai.

"Thought you didn't drink coffee?" I asked, pulling back into the line of traffic amid a mass of honks, and managed to block several lanes.

"I don't."

I clenched the steering wheel, determined to get her to open up. "Special occasion, then?" I aimed the bull bar at a silver Audi, turning as tightly as my truck allowed. The tiny bubble of a car moved significantly.

"When it's called for." Laura stared straight ahead, clutching her takeaway cup.

"And today calls for it?"

"Yep."

I sighed. Laura fidgeted with her cup. When her toes started tapping, I passed her my phone.

"Music's in there. Pick what you like."

Laura scrolled through my music, connecting the slim charge cable I passed her way. I was about to tell her to pick something — anything — the air in the open cab ridiculously oppressive, when a few opening bars had me sitting back. Ed Sheeran's cover of "Chasing Cars" by Snow Patrol filled the air between us.

"Nice pick."

Laura reached across, squeezing my arm. I gripped the steering wheel, trying not to react. "I'm glad I stayed last night."

A grin uncurled across my face. "Yeah?"

"Yes." She sat back, watching the traffic. I tapped my foot lightly on the pedal, running my next words through my head a few times before I ended up blurting them out anyway. "But–" she took a long breath, her cup deforming a little in her hands. I hoped my truck wouldn't be wearing her drink shortly. "Danny...promise me you'll stop the undercover work. Get that career on track. Please."

"Sure."

One day. But not today.

I couldn't say the words aloud. Unease roiled in my stomach, and I regretted my breakfast. Lying to Laura was nothing like lying to myself.

"Thanks." She tilted her head back, smiling.

So fucking gorgeous.

"When this is all over...and we have time. I want to take you on a real date." The words ran out of my mouth. I paused, thinking them through, but they rang true, somewhere deep inside me. What was this girl doing to me? She didn't move, didn't say anything. I squeezed the wheel tighter. "Please?"

I stared at the traffic like I could burn a path between my truck and our office building as we approached, though we still moved forward at a sluggish pace. My stomach dropped when she didn't answer.

Should have waited, you stupid bastard.

I pulled into the garage entrance, searching for a spot, and found one between Micah's monster and Cal's white Ford Raptor. My hand was on the key to kill the engine when Laura spoke.

"Okay."

I stilled, sending a brief prayer heavenward. It was the same thing she'd said last night... and look where that had gotten us. But still — I looked sideways at her without turning my head. "Okay...what?"

She laughed, that tinkling sound from last night that had nearly ripped my insides out with wanting her.

"Okay, a date sounds good." She swung a long sheet of silver-blonde hair around her shoulders like a shield, flashing me a killer smile. She leaned across my seat, sliding out of her seat belt, and placed a perfectly toned forearm on my shoulder. So close, her breath brushed my skin. I held back a shiver. "You can take me out, Danny Woods. But it will take a hell of a date to top this morning."

Her lips brushed my cheek, then she was out of my truck, walking quickly to the elevator banks. I remained in my seat, hand on the key, slightly stunned. By the time I made a move, she was gone.

I contemplated the stairs but running six flights wasn't in me this morning. She was right, though — that had been a hell of a way to start things off. A grin I knew was goofy as hell slid onto my face and was still there when I walked through the office.

"Morning," I greeted the place in general. Ally didn't look up from her work. Cal sent me a hard stare and motioned me into the incident room.

"I've got something for you."

I followed him dutifully, catching movement from Ally out of the corner of my eye. She tapped a tapered plastic nail on her phone screen as she watched Cal with narrowed eyes. Whatever the hell was going on there didn't bode well — for my boss, or the team in general.

I leaned on the doorway as Cal turned to face me. "What's going on?"

"That job — you're in."

"I'm in?" My head swirled as I tried to remember yesterday, but all that came to mind was Laura wearing nothing at all, walking into the water. I shifted uncomfortably and tried to banish the image, but it seemed determined to burn itself into my brain.

"The undercover assignment. You're hungry for it, right?" Cal eyed me with a furrowed brow. I waved a hand.

"Yeah, right."

Cal walked past me, shoving me firmly inside the room and shut the door to the fishbowl. Behind him, Ally stood at her desk, still watching us.

"Danny, what the hell? I thought you wanted this. That's what I sent you to Laura for — to get your act together." Cal ran a hand over his short hair, the shaved look growing out from the dreads he'd sported for nearly eighteen months after his own stint undercover.

"I do, I do. Really," I added when he looked unconvinced. "I've got the profile sorted, all the docs. Worked on it last night. I'll be sweet with his guys."

"Yeah? Where are your files?" Cal folded his arms over his chest. Lean and lanky, he was still one of the hardest bastards I knew. Damned good boss, too.

Hands and arms conspicuously empty, I'd let myself be distracted by Laura. Again. I slipped my hands in my pockets, mind whirling to sort myself out of the mess I'd made without involving her when the glass door at Cal's back shook.

Ally stood on the other side, looking murderous.

Saved by the crazy receptionist, 2.0.

Cal nodded, resigned, and opened the door for her.

"What is it?" he asked, not moving out of the doorway.

The incident room held all of our files, tech, and personal info. No one outside the team got in here. Apparently, Ally didn't yet qualify for the honour. Kudos to Cal for recognising what I had.

Ally held up her phone. Cal leaned forward, straining to read the tiny writing. I was torn between the urge to grab popcorn or laugh at the schoolgirl attitude. The thought that

I'd come close to fucking my professional coach this morning sobered me quickly.

Cal straightened, cursing under his breath, and motioned Ally inside, closing the door behind her. In the reception area, Black stepped out of the stairwell — clearly, he'd felt motivated this morning, and paused, no doubt wondering what the hell we all were doing. He took a seat in the reception area, arms open in a *"what the"* gesture.

I shrugged and turned back to the small drama unfolding before me, coming in part of the way through whatever Ally had led with.

"...and I've been getting messages all night. There are accusations flying — Cal, if this is how you treat your staff and deal with your personal life, then I'm going to have to–" she cut herself off, lips tight. Cal raised an eyebrow. It was the only move he made, and I envied his restraint.

I edged towards the door. "Uh, maybe I should leave you two alone..."

Cal raised a hand, palm out.

"No, this involves you, too."

"Ah, what does?"

Cal stepped back, perching on the corner of his desk.

"Mandy has been messaging Ally. God alone knows how she got the number — that's a breach of privacy right there," he gave me a hard stare, knowing full well the relationship I'd had with his ex, "amongst...other things."

Mandy was a great stirrer — she could invent a story with the best of us, and tried to make it stick, too. I shook my head.

"Not from me, boss. We broke up over a week ago. Before Ally started, or maybe the morning she did?" I wracked my brain, nodding as the week returned to me, "yeah, the morning of the day Ally rocked up here. Why? What's she said–"

I was about to say, "*what's she said now,*" but Cal gave me a hard look, and I let the sentence hang. *Now* implied there were more incidents, and whatever Cal knew, he didn't want to share our previous issues with Ally.

I recalled the memorable night Mandy had cried all over my shoulder, swearing black and blue Cal had attacked her — not that there was a mark to show for it. I had been so easy for her to play; I'd bought into her story without too many questions and ended up punching Cal during a practice spar.

It hadn't been a legal move either, strictly speaking. Frankly, I was damned lucky he'd let me keep my job, let alone stay on his team.

As a result, a very angry-looking Ally faced a dual wall of determination. It wasn't her that was the problem — but there was no chance in hell either Cal or I were going to let Mandy screw with our unit again.

"She's accused one — or both — of you of roughhousing her. Cal, this isn't something I can take lightly. If one of your boys," she shot me a sharp glance, "or you have attacked a woman, I can't just stand back and let that pass."

"No one has hurt anyone, right, Danny." It wasn't a question, and he didn't take his eyes off our receptionist. I could feel the intensity in his gaze from my spot beside him — and I wasn't even the one being scrutinised. I nodded, resisting the urge to fold my arms, knowing it would form a barrier between the three of us. We needed Ally to believe whatever we told her. Cal appeared to be struggling along the same vein; tension radiated across the tight line of his shoulders.

He gripped the edge of the desk behind him with red knuckles quickly turning white. I'd seen Cal lose his shit a few times — usually aimed at me. It wasn't something I'd wish on anyone. And if he let loose with Ally, it'd likely cost him his job. All for a girl who appeared to be intent on screwing us over. God knew why, but it was typical of Mandy.

I should make a profile up of her to use in the future, but right now, I had to step in.

"Ally, there's history here you don't have. Can we sit down, and I'll go over everything with you. Coffee, okay?" I didn't give her a chance to object, ushering her out of the incident room to the lounge seat Black had just vacated. He walked around us like we carried a bomb about to explode.

I grabbed for the coffee machine as the door to the incident room banged shut. The glass reverberated in its frame. I winced. If we kept slamming the door, we'd lose the glass one day.

"Sugar?" She shook her head. "Milk?" A quick nod. Her flirtatious attitude from the day before was conspicuously absent. I had to choose my questions carefully, so as not to incite the proverbial bear further.

"Danny, this is really something I should be talking to—"

I passed her the mug, plucking her phone from her other hand as she took the offering. Eyes flaring, she glared at me as I sat on the sofa. Slightly longer than a two-seater, it left just enough space between us to be comfortable while seated at opposite ends. Ally crossed her legs while I splayed out, watching her body language.

"Mandy is an ex of both Cal and I. Recently." She sat stone-faced; this information was nothing new to her. I waited until she took a sip of her coffee. "Separately. We don't share well."

I gave a one-shouldered shrug while Ally choked on her coffee. I was glad she wasn't wearing white today. Coffee dribbled onto her navy skirt, disappearing into the material without a mark.

Her lips twitched, somewhere between a pout and a grin. Finally, she opted for the latter. Icebreaker achieved. Moving on to step two. An idea of what Mandy was trying to do formed in my mind, and I aimed to head her off before she could cause more damage than she already had.

"Mandy tried to convince me — did convince me — that Cal had attacked her, just after they broke up. The funny thing was, he was out on a date the night she said he hurt her. I didn't listen. Took her words as gospel and punched him. In the face." I leaned back. "I don't know how she got your number, Ally, and I'm just as pissed about it as you. We don't take privacy lightly here. A break with our previous receptionist nearly got six of us killed, last month."

"Three."

"What?"

"Three of you. Not six," she corrected me, a challenge in her eye.

"Six. Mila, Jenny, Ashley," I ticked off the hostages Wayde Logan had taken in addition to wounding Black, Cal and myself. "Plus, the employees he killed at the bank. I count everyone, Ally. While you're here, I count you, too."

A small smile appeared over the rim of her mug as she contemplated my words. Step two, develop trust, success. Now for the interesting part — getting her to open up. Be an ear. I might not get everything I needed right now, but building a foundation was essential to extracting what I might need later on.

So, the hard part. I lifted my mug, pretending to sip a drink I hated. I sat and waited. Ally's gaze dropped to her knees. She fidgeted with the hem of her skirt, one foot jiggling on the carpet. Most people are uncomfortable with silence. If I spoke before she had the chance, there was a damned good chance I'd miss something important.

"The messages started coming through around eleven last night. Almost midnight. Said you were with her, that you were out with her and had an argument. There was some confusion about Cal as well — I wasn't sure if the three of you were, um, together, or..." Her face turned bright red.

I contemplated leaving her to flounder, but that didn't seem a gentlemanly thing to do.

"I was out last night. All night. But not with Mandy."

"Oh?"

I smiled, holding the mug to my lips again. Ally mirrored me. I placed the putrid liquid on the small table beside the lounge.

"Motivational coaching." I gave her a bland smile. "Pretty sure Mila can attest for Cal's whereabouts." I leaned forward, elbows on my knees. "What other information do you need from me?"

Fifteen minutes later, I passed a tepid mug of coffee to Cal in the incident room with instructions for Ally to take a break, preferably outside.

"You did well." Cal placed the coffee on his desk, tapping the handle. "Actually, I was quite impressed. It's not easy to become emotionally detached from something you're so close to."

"Is that your way of apologizing for nearly losing your shit with Ally?"

"Mmm. Keep it to yourself, maybe." Cal sipped the coffee and put it carefully back on his desk with a grimace. "This is shit, Danny. Did you make this?"

The corner of Cal's mouth quirked. I laughed at him. Remembering the files I'd left in my car, I headed for the door to retrieve them. Cal stopped me.

"Danny. Don't ever offer to abandon me again when I need a witness." He waved me out of the room, still laughing.

CHAPTER TWELVE

LAURA

I hesitated in the stairwell outside Danny's office floor, biting my lip. I'd missed him the day after I'd spent the night in his bed — my head still whirled with that one. I'd even checked the garage, but the trucks were all gone by the time I was finished for the day.

Maybe I should have messaged him, though it seemed somewhat intimate, considering I'd have to pull his number from his file. I'd thought about asking him back to Sylvie's teppanyaki bar but decided a run would be better.

It was hot as hades in the middle of the day. We wouldn't be able to do the entire lake, but there were some great shorter paths that ran through a treed area that would give us some shade.

I smiled at the new girl behind the reception desk, motioning toward the boy's office. "Hi, I'm just after Danny."

She smiled, a sharp thing that seemed out of place in their office.

"He's not here."

Nothing was forthcoming as I waited for more information, and my smile dimmed a little. "Oh. I can come back later." The nerves hadn't been worth it, after all. I redirected my feet to the elevator.

"He won't be here."

I turned to face the woman who obviously knew a lot more about Danny than I seemed to, smiling, and raised an eyebrow.

"He's got work to do, and... He won't be back."

"You mean he's transferred?" My heart stopped in my chest.

"I mean he's not working from here, right now." Her face may as well have been made of porcelain. Nothing moved on it.

"Oh." I had nothing else to say. Doubt hit me like a sledgehammer. After yesterday morning, had Danny changed his mind? Was this his way of telling me he didn't want me to contact him? Cal's back was to me in the office, so I couldn't even check things out with him. "I'll, uh..." I waved at the door, retreating.

"You're the motivational coach, aren't you?"

I turned back from the open elevator doors. "Professional development."

"Of course."

She watched me retreat, not taking her eyes from me as the elevator doors closed. A sinking sensation curdled in my stomach that had nothing to do with the motion of the elevator.

I dithered outside my office door, fingers wrapped around the handle, doing nothing. If Danny had been moved departments, wouldn't he have come down to tell me? Surely, he hadn't gone back undercover after promising me he would stop? No, his word was good, I was sure and dismissed the thought. If he'd been demoted — wouldn't *Cal* have told me? He'd been my client, after all. Amongst other things.

I swallowed back a lump in my throat and pushed the door to my office open. Danny's file still sat on my desk. I flipped open the front page — all his details were listed there, including his phone number. I rang his mobile, a knot loosening in my stomach as it picked up.

The number you've dialled is no longer connected. Pause. *The number you've dialled...*

I placed my phone carefully on my desk, lining it up in the centre of Danny's closed file. In a matter of hours, he'd disappeared off the face of the earth, like he'd never been there at all.

I tapped the screen, wondering if I should call Cal. He'd have all the answers. But — if Danny didn't want me to find him, then I shouldn't push. My mind whirled with the mixed messages, from his kisses less than a day past to his promise of a date later on.

I had read it all so wrong — played into it. What the hell had I been thinking? I refused to go upstairs and beg for information on someone who clearly didn't want me.

Leaving my phone on my desk, I went to change into my running gear. Smelly, and disgustingly still slightly damp with stale sweat, I didn't care. It really didn't matter, when I had no running partner, anyway.

I left the building, not looking around, refusing the urge to search for him. The black leather interior was blazingly hot when I climbed into my car, heading for the lake. I slathered on sunscreen and ran the entire circuit, trying not to think about Danny. That regular pace beside me, those amazing shoulders I'd adored.

I was back at my car before I knew it, hands on my knees as I wheezed. I grabbed my water bottle from the driver's side, but the water was almost boiling hot in the sun. I hadn't thought any further than running on my own, sprinting it out. Aircon blasted me as I gulped the nearly scalding water, anyway.

Another dark-haired jogger passed my car. My heart leapt. *Danny.* I waved, but the man just looked at me oddly, moving around my car. My head ran in circles, recalling the way he'd touched me, his mouth trailing over my skin, losing myself in him. I'd never had anyone kiss me that way. Like I was glass, and he was afraid to break me. Like he'd cared.

Oh hell, I'd gone and fallen for a cop who hadn't cared a whit about me.

I leaned my forehead on the searing hot steering wheel and cried.

I didn't bother going back to the office for more than a few minutes to collect my laptop, leaving the building as fast as I could. All I wanted was to head home and wash today away.

Aircon was a welcome relief. Usually, I left everything open for the fresh air that raked the hill, but today, I didn't want to let the outside in. Instead, I closed the house up, setting everything in its usual place. My tights stuck to me as

I peeled everything off, leaving them in a rumpled heap on the bathroom floor. My hand was on the shower faucet when my phone rang.

I looked at it uncertainly — afraid I'd see Danny's name. With how I was feeling, I was scared the first thing I would do would be to rip him a new one. After five rings, I leaned over to see who was calling. Belinda's name flashed on the screen. I sighed and picked it up.

"I'm about to get in the shower." It was a standard greeting; my sister and I hadn't used hello and goodbye in years. "I'm filthy."

"You're always filthy," she giggled on the other end, slurring her speech a little. It wasn't even dinner time, and she was already drunk. Or high. "Filthy bitch."

"Did you call for an actual reason?" My voice was as cold as the bathroom tiles, and my muscles were beginning to seize. I needed to get under the hot water.

"Just wanted to see you," she hummed part of a tune afterwards, off-key. I winced.

"Bel, I don't think that's a good idea."

"Come *on*," she whined, "I just want to go out."

"I can't tonight." I was shattered — physically and emotionally. Plus, I had gotten limited sleep last night, as I caught up with work. "Maybe over the weekend."

"Okay!" she agreed brightly. I held back a groan. There was an offer I was going to regret.

"Okay. Well, I'm going to have my shower, now..."

"Okay, bye!"

I pressed end, placing the phone on the vanity, wondering what sort of torture I'd signed myself up for this time.

The shower may have been the best thing that had happened to me in the afternoon. I curled on my lounge, flicking through Netflix, and settled on a random rom-com. Halfway through it, I began berating the girl for her stupid decisions, remembering why I hated romance films. I flicked through sports, but there was nothing decent on. Finally, I turned the TV off, lying in the dark.

My mind drifted back to waking in Danny's arms, the weight of him wrapped around me. I'd loved every second of it — hell, I'd just loved *him*. The tears threatened again as I lay surrounded by a harem of pillows, and wished I had a dog, or something living to cuddle. Anything for the company. The emptiness of my house ate at me, and exhausted as I was, sleep refused to come.

The week passed in a blur, though I berated myself a thousand times for caring about someone who apparently hadn't cared about me, and that I couldn't bring myself to move on after such a short time. That I'd been taken in by his flirting told me how desperate I must be for love and attention, and I hated my weakness just a little more.

On Friday evening, I closed my laptop, sure I was the only person in the office building at eight pm. Belinda would be waiting for me downstairs. I rolled my eyes at yet another message from her, replying quickly as I powered down my laptop and began to pack up for the evening, typing back a quick reply.

Belinda: I'm freezing down here. Hurry UP.

Me: I'll be a minute.

Belinda: We're meeting people. Be faster.

We were? I groaned. I should have known there was a reason she wanted me to go out. We rarely socialised, and it never ended well, though I kept trying. The definition of insanity, Einstein said that, right? Or someone equally clever, which I clearly was not.

I changed my work shirt to a clingy black top that sparkled under the fluorescent office lights and added an extra layer of mascara and red-tinted lip gloss. It was the best I could make myself do.

Unenthused, I ignored the messages zinging my phone, slipping it into my pocket and headed for my car. When the elevator doors pinged open, I was surprised to see Ally. She mirrored my expression.

"I thought I was the only one left," I murmured politely, my mind a million miles away. She patted my arm, and I flinched at the unexpected contact.

"It will pass, babe."

What will pass? And since when was I *babe?* Danny had called me that once. My stomach lurched with the elevator.

"Okay..." I frowned, letting the thought drift away as my pocket vibrated again.

"These things take time. But you shouldn't be waiting around for him like this." She smiled, eyes pitying, condescension rolling from her in waves.

"I *what?*" I stared at her as the penny dropped. "I'm not waiting for Danny. I was working." My mind caught up, and I wished this almost-stranger would butt out of my life and business. It felt like high school all over again.

"Of course, you are." That same, sugary smile, dripping with sarcasm. "Good night." She gave a jaunty wave, disappearing into the foyer.

I shook my head in disbelief, wondering why she'd been around so late — she shouldn't have been in the office without one of the boys around. I was tempted to check the carpark for Cal's truck, but a cough drew my attention back to the doors that bordered on the street.

Belinda leaned against the window beside the door, waving her phone in my direction. Red stockings matched the colour of her hair — that was new. Her skirt and midriff top warred in a battle for who had the least material.

"You took soooo long," she groaned theatrically, opening her arms for a hug. I hesitated, hating myself for it, then leaned into my older sister. She didn't smell or appear drunk — though that was no guarantee. My older sister could hold liquor like a soldier.

"I was finishing up for the night."

Faded, over-treated red hair flipped over one shoulder. "Why do you work so hard?"

"Because I have my own business, and I want it to be a success?" She waved her arms around her head in circles, shoving my reasons away. I sighed. "What are we doing?"

"I *told* you; meeting some people. They're nice. You'll like them." She fidgeted with her phone, tripping over her feet as she turned. Was she swaying? I frowned but wrote it off as paranoia.

I trailed her to my car with serious misgivings. Belinda hoisted a look over her shoulder, rolling her eyes at my obvious reluctance.

"I'm telling you; you'll like them."

I seriously doubted it.

Half an hour later, seated around a sticky table covered with assorted remains of cocktails and shots, I knew I'd been right. I'd parked where my sister had pointed out a dirty vacant lot behind an equally dirty club. The potholes were so large, I'd nearly sprained an ankle just making it to the front of the place.

Now I stood around a table with four men I didn't know but who all appeared to be intent on ogling as many of my sister's assets as they possibly could. The interior of the place hadn't improved from my first impression.

Thumping music blared, though the dance floor was empty. I winced as lights strobed in my eyes yet again, missing the solitude of my home.

Wasn't it just last week you were keening for any company at all?

Last week didn't involve a frat party pounding in my head.

I could hold a conversation perfectly well, all by myself. No additional presences required.

"You want a drink?" A sweaty hand covered mine. I removed mine politely, covering the top of my glass with it as an excuse. *Lame, Laura.*

"No, thank you."

"Don't say much, do ya?" The man leered over me, and I fought the urge to back away. I shuffled around the table discreetly — I hoped — putting a little distance between us and tried not to inhale his body odour.

"Difficult to talk when it's so noisy," I said, watching sweat run down the inside of his shirt where it hung open.

"WHAT?" He leaned closer and yelled in my ear.

I sighed. This had never been my scene. Belinda held court — albeit a sleazy one — with her admirers. I tapped her shoulder.

"I think I'm done. Work in the morning." I gave her a strained smile. She frowned.

"We just got here."

"I know, but...I'm not feeling it tonight. Sorry," I apologised, though it wasn't aimed at her. I hated that she came to places like this, and if she didn't leave with me, she'd end up with one of these guys, or more. "Come with?"

"Nope." She pasted a bright, completely fake smile on her face.

I sighed again. "Which one's the dealer, Bel?"

She gave me a wide-eyed, vacant stare. My sister had brains; she just tried very hard not to use them. I snorted. Like someone else I knew. I grabbed her arm, towing her away from the table.

"Back in a minute!" I called cheerfully to the disgruntled men clustered around the small table.

Belinda yanked her arm from my grip. "What the hell are you doing?"

"Saving your ass. They aren't good people, Bel."

"I. Don't. Give. A. Fuck."

"No, but I do. Come on. You can't stay here. This isn't a place to get a hit." That sounded like I was condoning her habit. "It's a place to catch an STD. God, I can't stay, Bel. I need real air." Determined to at least save her for one more night from some dreadful, self-induced fate, I towed her behind me.

Clouds of smoke billowed around the DJ's table. I tried my best not to cough. It didn't work, and I turned away, hacking my way through the haze.

Eyes watering, I found myself on the other side of the dance floor. Gasping slightly for breath I looked up and froze. Danny sat with a group of men who looked just like him — all buff, wearing singlets, slick-backed hair.

Every one of the four guys around him had at least one scantily clad girl on their lap. I swallowed as a girl in a white tube dress perched on his knee, bleached blonde hair falling forward as she leaned into him. He said something to her, and she laughed as I watched them, a voyeur to a scene I would have preferred never to witness.

Fucking liar.

The words screamed in my head. Danny was nothing like I'd thought he was — where was the healthy, intelligent, *career-focused* man I'd fallen for? Here he was, drinking and doing God knew what drugs with the rest of his group.

Just like them.

Just like Belinda.

Liar. Liar. Liar.

The girl on his lap sat back, playing with his shirt. She gave a wiggle, pulling his arms around her. A broad grin on his face, he pulled her against him. One, large hand clearly outlined on her tiny, pert backside, his phone jiggling in his other hand.

He hadn't lost it after all. I vaguely became aware of someone calling my name, but I was rooted to the spot. His fingers made tiny circles on the girl's ass, reminiscent of the way he'd touched me that night at the beach. He gave it a hefty squeeze, and pushed her away, spreading his arms across the back of the chairs either side of him, laughing at one of the other men.

I choked on a dry throat, wondering if it was possible to vomit up nothing at all. The lines on Danny's face creased as he laughed, eyes crinkling at the sides. A pang that quickly became an ache tore at my heart. His head turned my way, his gaze sharpening as he spotted me.

The smoke machine belched clouds around me as sharp nails stabbed my wrist and yanked me mercifully into the noxious mist.

"What are you doing, staring at those guys like a goose?" Belinda started as I marched her toward the exit. "They aren't guys you mess around with. What are you doing?"

"I'm taking us both home. Now." I reversed her grip, holding onto her, my tenuous lifeline.

"But, my drink–" She scrabbled at my hand, but I held on as tightly as I could.

"Forget it."

I strode out of the club, glad to be breathing fresh air again. I'd be even better after yet another shower to clean off the grime and stench of the place, and safely inside my own house.

I am never dating again.

It was a petty thought; I knew that as soon as it popped into my mind. But I couldn't go through this again, not any time soon.

"Wait," Belinda puffed after me as I rounded the corner at the back of the club. "Why were you staring at those guys?" Her eyes begged me to answer, to turn around, and I stopped.

"Why?" I unlocked the car, shoving her unceremoniously inside, and slammed the door. I got to my own side to find she hadn't moved. "Put your belt on. Please?"

"They're dangerous. Really bad news. You're not involved, right?"

"Why would I be involved with anyone like that?" If I was lying, it was only to the shade that haunted me.

What the hell was Danny into in his spare time?

I put my car in drive and backed out of the carpark, heading for the lonely security of my home.

CHAPTER THIRTEEN

DANNY

I strode outside the club, scanning the carpark, but it hosted only a few beat-up sedans — no sleek, silver coupe. I ran my hand over my head, guilt from not contacting Laura before I began my assignment assailing me. But there hadn't been time — a perfect opening had come up, and I had to take it.

Shattered glass crunched over gravel behind me. Instincts screaming, it took all I had not to swing at the guy who emerged from the shadows.

Sporting a scar from a knife fight that trailed into the depths of his singlet, Luke Manning had served time for a few menial crimes. Driven, smart, and an excellent hacker, like me. For the time being, he was my landlord, too.

And a key suspect in the undercover case Cal had assigned me.

"You okay, man." It wasn't a question, and Luke's hand gripped my shoulder. I didn't shrug it off; that wouldn't fit the profile. Instead, I shook my head, sulking.

"Thought I saw my ex. Bitch owes me." I cringed internally at the act, hating that it really was Laura I was talking about.

When I'd spotted Laura — or thought I had — in the haze that filled Shandy's, I'd frozen. Forgetting my cover story, everything dropped away. I'd chased a ghost out of the club and stood on the pavement alone, wondering how I was going to salvage the night.

"I was worried 'bout you." Luke hadn't removed his hand, and it was a heavy reminder that one fuck up could cost me severely. "You know. Not being big into the girls — fuck, man. I know they're skanks, but get some, yeah? Gotta relax, unwind. Take one home. Hell, take 'em all."

He sounded like a brochure for a timeshare, but there was a glint in his eye that told me not to let down my guard.

I shook my head. "Nah, too fresh. Another night, eh?"

Luke surveyed me, a bone-deep assessment I knew better than to walk away from. Damnit. Laura — whether she had really been here, or not — had become a distraction. Again.

Get your game on, Danny.

I'd managed to steer clear of the drugs in the house so far, but Luke was competitive and liked to push. Naturally, I pushed back, but I never went full throttle with him. There were times to lose quietly and being undercover wasn't about winning.

Not yet, anyway.

I rolled my shoulders back. "You done?"

I held his gaze, letting the challenge settle in. Finally, he grinned, dropping his hand.

"Don't wanna lose you to some old girl now, alright? We've got work to do. Not tonight, though."

I followed Luke back into the club, knowing I'd have to fend off every girl he threw my way for the remainder of the evening. I hadn't been interested before, but now — now, with Laura on my mind, they all paled against the phantom of her in the smoke.

I needed to call in, tell Cal to give her a message, but I wasn't game to do that in the house I shared with the boys.

It was just a different team. I looked around the room, picking out each man — Luke, leader, organiser. Clever, but still...this whole thing didn't feel like his style. He was a balls-out, bust-down-the-doors man, and this job they worked, taking change from banks...it was subtle. Maybe a little too subtle. I had to find out who he'd gotten the idea from.

My eyes narrowed as I worked it through, stretching to cover my discovery time.

Justin had the smarts, and he kept up with the guys, physically. But like Cal and Liam, he had a lean build. There was no way he'd ever bulk up like Luke or me, without some sort of help. I hoped he wouldn't turn to drugs just to be one of them.

He was a speedy hacker, but there was little drive to work big jobs. More the typical university grad with an entry-level job, happy with breaking his little corner of the system.

Zahn was a mean prick. A little mini-me, revelling in the excess of power and influence rolling off Luke. He was who Cal had picked out for me to work with, but I knew the real power lay elsewhere. He met my eyes across the table, slugging down a beer.

How he managed to sneer at me the entire time was a small miracle. Pity his skills didn't extend much further. I laughed at him. I knew he hated that Luke had brought me into their circle. He wasn't someone I could turn my back on — none of them was.

McKenna Smith was the odd one out. Laid-back and quiet, he worked his keyboard fast and hit the gym hard. Played hard, too. Drugs, girls, grog — he fit the perfect profile for the job. Never bragged about it, though. It made him unique amongst Luke's crew.

But these guys were all small fry. I was still trying to work out what Cal had sent me in here for.

I kept the broody persona up for a good hour, letting them cajole me back into a 'fun night'. A girl who hadn't already been around the group — tonight, at least — settled herself beside me. Dressed in jeans and a sparkly top, she appeared a different class of girl than what the boys usually took home.

With the money they threw around, I was surprised they didn't frequent a better type of establishment. But they were comfortable in the dingy club — which had pretty relaxed standards when it came to drugs — so that's where I was, too.

"You taken?" she asked, leaning back with her eyes closed. Soft, auburn curls twisted lazily around her face. If Luke wanted "proof" I was into his scene, this appeared to be the best option for tonight. An image of Laura flitted across my vision: her hair splayed across my pillow, toned body wriggling beneath me. I'd lost control, then. Hell, I'd wanted her so badly, it hadn't been a stretch to pinning her beneath me.

Stopping before I fucked her right there, had been.

I shifted, adjusting myself through my jeans, and lied through my teeth. "No."

She turned her head sideways to face me, still leaning back.

"I haven't seen you here before."

"I've been around." I looked into her dilated pupils and wondered what she'd had. And how much.

"You don't look like it. You're fresh meat. That's why the girls are all over you. They want a taste."

"Yeah?" Is this what it felt like to be a girl in a bar, with guys crawling all over them? One of the local girls — Mindy? Sounded a hell of a lot like Mandy — ran her fingers through my hair on her way past. My skin prickled, and I tried not to show the disgust that pulsed through me. The girl beside me gave a knowing glance.

"Who was she?"

"Who was what?" I played dumb for the hell of it — anything to pass the time until the boys were ready to go. If they continued on their usual habits, I had five or more hours left to endure their shit.

"Your girl. Saw you looking for someone before."

"Yeah?"

"Girl in black. She yours?"

She *had* been here. And I'd missed her. Then reality came crashing in. Of course, it hadn't been Laura — she wouldn't be caught dead in a place like this. I didn't blame her.

"No. Once, maybe."

"Mmm." The girl turned back to studying the ceiling, eyes closed. I kept an eye out to make sure she was still breathing.

"Not this one." A familiar hand clapped my shoulder. The urge to punch him rose to the surface. I fought back with effort.

"Yeah?"

I tilted my head back, looking up at Luke. My mind screamed against exposing any part of myself to this man — he was a predator; I'd read that right from the outset — and smiled. The big, brawny guy smile I'd been using for years that immediately reduced my IQ to single figures for most of the room. But not to this guy.

"You waiting for me to kiss you, pretty boy?"

"Want me to punch you, stud muffin?"

The girl beside me snorted. I grinned with appreciation, not taking my eyes off Luke as he dipped his head. Maybe he *was* going to kiss me. Well, first time for everything.

"She's my ex," he whispered, breath hot and moist on my skin. I held back that punch. Barely. "And she's out of fucking bounds for a slick bastard like you. You got me?"

I didn't move, just kept the easy smile on, everything relaxed. I yawned in his face.

"Yeah, dude. Now fuck off out of my space."

A smattering of laughs came from the guys around us. Luke nodded as he straightened. I sat up, rolling my neck from side to side to work out the kinks from having it in such an awkward position. The boys watched us, waiting for the next round, but I wasn't up for putting on a show. I stood.

"Gotta piss."

Fuck, I hoped the next five hours weren't this torturous.

My phone buzzed, lifting me vaguely from a deep sleep. I'd organised a new prepaid number when I'd signed the lease for Luke's house but kept my phone. Cal stored my two boxes of stuff in his apartment. There wasn't enough of it to bother hiring a storage space. He'd find me a fully-furnished rental when I finished this job.

I slapped my phone, but the buzzing continued.

"The fuck." I flipped it off the table beside my bed, narrowly missing falconing myself with it.

Luke's number came up a swath of times, despite that his room was just across the hall from mine. Flicking through the messages, I groaned. He'd picked up three girls from last night's session. Apparently, photographic evidence was required.

I dropped my phone off the edge of the bed. Who knew what time we'd gotten home last night, but it was too early to bother getting out of bed — especially if we still had excess company in the house.

The house Luke had inherited was small and unnoticeable. Needing a fresh coat of paint and some weeding, it looked just like any other rental property.

The boys weren't showy, except with their toys — cars, bikes and the like. For their demographic — young, dumb, and just out for fun — a party image kept them off the radar. The cover was well thought out. Still, I kept wondering if Luke had the brains to plan something so intricate.

My door rattled on its hinges. I groaned again, closing my eyes.

"Get up, bitch. Gym's calling," Luke yelled through the door.

"Later." There was nothing that would get me out of bed. Nothing.

"We're leaving. Get the fuck up, or I'll pull you out of bed."

"Baby, if you come in here, you cop a thrashing," I croaked a second time, attempting to swallow. My throat stuck together, furry. I gagged.

Luke laughed from the other side of the door. I glared at it and got up anyway.

Shucking on a fresh singlet and running shorts, I opened my door. Luke leaned against the wall opposite my room.

"Creeper." I eyed him suspiciously. He grinned.

"Been called worse."

"I'll bet. You said we're going?"

Luke nodded, heading for the front door. His navy Cobra sat in the covered drive. I eyed it with contempt.

"I'll bust the suspension in that piece of plastic." I headed for my truck before he could cuss me.

Raw Iron Gym was where guys — and a few hardcore women — actually worked out. While there was a lot of testosterone flying about, generally good-natured ribbing went on. Most of the guys worked out in silence, focussed on sculpting muscle definition.

Luke and the boys started on their favourite machines. I stretched a little longer — more than I should. I knew why, though I hated that I took time away from my own workout — as it turned out, Raw Iron was also the gym Laura favoured. I'd been hiding from her for over a week but couldn't help setting myself up to where I could watch her, but she couldn't see me.

Who's the creeper now?

I shushed the voice in my head and began my workout. Less than ten minutes later, sweat was pouring off me. I worked hard on keeping my physique the way I wanted it, but Luke and his crew pushed limits I usually didn't — permanent body damage wasn't my goal. The only person in the room that I wanted to beat was *me*.

"Keep up, man." Zahn, Luke's mini-me, poked me. I didn't let go of the bar. Mostly because if I did, I'd tear something.

"Don't do that. It's not good," I grunted.

"You know our new boy doesn't like contact. From anyone." Luke looked me over lazily, though his comments rang alarm bells. I was dropping my cover. Damn, I had to get Laura out of my head. Hard to do when she walked through the doors of the gym to the cardio room.

I looked away from those perfect legs encased in dark purple tights and a black crop and caught Luke's eye. "Only 'cause pretty boy here tried to jump into my bed a few times." I grinned amongst the catcalls, showing teeth. "Claims he was drunk, but I don't know..."

I flexed, checking myself out in the mirrors opposite the weights equipment. The catcalls increased, and a blonde ponytail swung around in the corner of my eye.

I dipped my head, hands clenched on the bar and prayed she wouldn't see me. Luke stood in front of me; his bulk blocked out the rest of the room, and me from Laura's line of sight. He took a step closer — which I wasn't grateful for — my head was at the level of his hips. He glared at me. I'd had enough of his testosterone. I released the bar with a clang that raised heads and stood up, right in his space.

He backed up a step.

"Get outta my face, pretty boy." I moved around him, but he put an arm out. "What?"

"Something about you isn't ringing bells, Danny. I let you into my home. My crew. You see us dealing...but you don't do any of it — not the girls, not the drugs." He stopped, and I could see him reigning in whatever he'd been about to say. He surprised me with a grin. "Don't be so fucking clean, man."

He clapped my shoulder, leaving a mark. I didn't flinch.

"Watch it. Your dirty might rub off on me," I grumbled at him, my mind whirling. If I didn't pull my act together, I'd screw up this case. Any chance I had of Cal trusting me after that would be pretty low.

Luke flicked a hand, bringing me back. "Sluts seem to like it."

"Nah, it's your stunning personality."

Luke guffawed, and we got lost in our training. I finished up early and headed to the showers, keen to wash the taint away, but I had a feeling this time it would stick. The steam did clear my head, and I resolved not to let Laura distract me again.

Still berating myself for losing focus, I stepped out of the showers, towel wrapped around my waist, and came face-to-face with Luke and Zhan. They both leaned against the wall, arms folded.

"Ahh, Peewee Herman and Pretty Boy. Back together again." I started to dress, despite the unease that rolled in my stomach. What was Luke up to now? "Creepers," I muttered again.

"Hurry up." Luke jerked his chin in my direction.

"What's up?"

"We got a job."

"Yeah, what sort of job?" I dropped the towel, dressing as I faced them. Luke sneered.

"The sort that'll get you in shit and earn you some respect."

Could this conversation be any more pathetic? I played along — had to amuse myself somehow.

Focus. Laura's whisper filled my head.

"With whom."

"With me."

I ran a hand over my hair, pulling my gym bag onto my shoulder with a sense of foreboding.

"Lead the way."

"The way" turned out to be my truck. The boys piled in, filling the thing. Luke set an address into the GPS.

"Gonna tell me where we're going?"

"Nellie's."

The backseat giggled. I grit my teeth. "Okay."

Nellie's was a drop house. I'd heard Luke talk about it when he thought I wasn't listening. I hated drugs, the lack of control it took from a person. Undercover, I'd been in situations where I'd had to try some things.

I hoped today wouldn't be a repeat occasion.

The house appeared to be the standard in its neighbourhood. Paint peeled from weathered boards, glassed windows looking as foggy from the outside as I suspected they were on the inside. I killed the engine and got out of my truck, hoping no one would steal it while I was gone.

Luke stared hard at me, jerking his head toward the house. "Let's go."

My hand clenched around my keys. I shoved them in my jeans pocket, giving my truck a small pat as I followed Luke and his mob up the overgrown drive. Something crunched under my boot as we reached the door. I scuffed shards of glass into the grass that tickled my ankle.

"Leave it." A tiny woman stood in the door frame, dressed in a rainbow of striped tights and shirts. Bright scarves adorned her shoulders. A mass of frizzy, grey hair stuck out from between the scarves at crazy angles. She nodded at Luke. "He's out the back."

"Thanks, Maisie." Luke wrapped the woman in one arm, gesturing us all passed him. When I went to follow them, he held up a hand. "Maisie helped me through a tough time a few years ago. Could have left me to die, but she helped clean me up. I'm grateful to her, and I protect her. No shit in her house, you got that?"

I ignored Luke's grandstanding and reached past him for Maisie's hand, squeezing gently. "Danny, Ma'am. Lovely to meet you." I smiled, and she returned it with kind eyes.

When it all came down, Maisie would likely be one of the key witnesses against Luke. Her son, Nellie, used to run the drug trade through her house, but since his apparent demise a year ago, the trade seemed to run itself. If I got on her good side now, I might be able to convince her she was doing the right thing for Luke later, when I asked her to betray him.

Luke nodded slowly, flicking a hand at the door. I entered the house, trying not to think what a jackass he was.

Focus, Danny.

The main living area was covered in shawls. Colourful material decorated every mismatched chair that ringed the walls, all occupied with men I didn't know, and one girl with faded red hair. Zahn went straight to her, lifting her onto his lap.

She giggled — a thin, high-pitched sound that rang alarm bells — the tension in her voice didn't seem right. I made a note to watch the small, blonde man a little more closely. Peering surreptitiously at the girl, I saw shadows beneath her skin that could have been old bruises. Likely as not, she'd been passed around, paid by getting high. Something about her was familiar, but I couldn't place it.

A dirty coffee table with two bongs sat in the centre of the room. I resisted the urge to crinkle my nose — the smell of weed curdled my stomach.

Luke slapped a hand against my back. I clenched my teeth, biting back a surge of temper.

"So, boys. This is Danny. Does some little jobs for me." I winced at his reference to the few errands I'd completed in the last week — mostly money handling. It was his test to see if I stole anything — cash, drugs. So far, it'd been simple enough.

Today might not be as easy.

I nodded to the room at large, a few "hellos" mumbled from shadowed corners, but mostly silence reigned as they weighed my worth.

"Danny's going to help set up the next drop," Luke's voice boomed around the room. Frowns appeared on faces as Luke stepped in front of me, presenting his back to the room. "We talked about a job, yeah?"

"Yeah."

"You said you were good with computers. The two guys in the back — they're hackers." I kept my eyes on the back wall, taking in as much detail as I could: two men in their late twenties, dirty shirts, greasy hair. "My competition. If they get jobs before I do, our income suffers. You get them out the back. It's quiet. No one will say anything."

I kept the surprise and a decent dose of disgust off my face as I processed what Luke was asking. He wanted me to take these two out the back and beat the hell out of them as a deterrent? Motorcycle clubs had classier moves.

I'd known he didn't have the skills to run his little circle all the way, but this? It wreaked amateur.

I shook my head. "No."

His hand came down on my shoulder, squeezing hard.

"No?"

I smiled but kept all emotion out of it. Soulless. It was a look I knew scared the hell out of most of my marks.

"Trust me?"

"Not a fucking ounce." Luke's eyes narrowed.

"Good." I nodded to the two guys at the back of the room Luke had indicated. "Let's go."

I wandered through Maisie's house. Bakelite statues and plates filled every surface. The kitchen was just as cluttered. A collection of unrelated mugs and plates — mostly dirty — filled the laminate benchtop. Scarred lino curled at the edges covered the floor.

I found a slim blade on the bench and tested it against my thumb. Not a steak knife, it had a smooth and very sharp edge. Footsteps followed me into the cozy space.

Luke filled the doorway opposite, shielding the room from view much as he had done in the gym, waiting.

"Luke says you boys wear black hats?"

Black Hats were hackers with malicious intent. They stole money and identities, destroyed systems, and generally did as much damage as they could. Luke's team was more specialised, targeting specific information — which was where I came in.

The younger-looking of the two crossed his arms over his chest.

You're a fucking pig, yeah?"

I grinned, nodding in Luke's direction. "Think I'd be hanging out with this prick if I was?" The more ambiguous the answer, the better. Less to trip myself up with, later on.

The skinnier of the pair cracked first. "Prometheus." He thrust a thumb to his greasy-haired mate. "Holo." The thumb went to himself. I resisted the urge to roll my eyes. They evidently felt they were high enough on a hacker's scale to rate a mention, but if they weren't on my radar, they weren't important.

"Surprised you didn't name yourself after Ninja Turtles," I poked, trying to get a rise; having a reason to go head-to-head with them would make this part of the job that much easier. Still, I needed Luke's commitment to me.

Neither of them moved. I sighed.

"My boy here says you poach his jobs." They made a small uproar. I twirled the slim blade between my fingers — a trick Black had taught me. The weight of Luke's gaze made it that much heavier. "I'm here to make sure it doesn't happen again."

I leaned against the counter. Relaxed outwardly, I hoped like hell I wouldn't actually have to injure one of these poor bastards. The skinnier one — Holo — smirked.

"All those muscles and you gonna rely on a knife? Fucking joke." He turned to his mate. "This fool won't do shit."

I smiled back, emotion draining away. Still smiling, I let myself feel nothing as I slowly turned the knife in my hand. Reversing my elbow, I pressed the tip to the door of the fridge, driving the blade through the metal, tearing it apart in a controlled movement straight down. I kept my eyes on the two hackers the entire time, zoning out to everything else.

When the handle snapped off, I walked over to the guy who'd spoken, placing it in his open hand while I palmed his wallet. There was bugger all in it, but I tossed the few notes to Luke with a nod.

"For the fridge." I placed the wallet on top of the busted knife handle, making a neat pile. The guy stared open-mouthed at me. "We won't be hearing from you, Holo. Isn't that right?"

Both men shook their heads, mute. I nodded; my mouth still stretched in my dead smile.

"Good."

Luke shifted aside as I approached him, eyes hard. I walked through the house and out the front door, switching my mask to a kinder one for Maisie. She nodded to me, looking around for Luke.

Being outside was a welcome relief. I inhaled slowly, leaning against the house with folded arms where I could see my truck. Tension from the altercation began to dissipate, but something inside me died a little more every time I acted this way for people I had little true interest in.

Five minutes later, Luke and his entourage reappeared. I pulled my keys out of my pocket, more than ready to leave.

Luke slapped my shoulder, but I'd had enough of his manhandling. I whirled, my hand in the centre of his chest, and slammed him against the house. Something cracked. I hoped it was his skull, not the wall.

"Don't fucking touch me again."

Luke didn't move or say a word. I knew I hadn't scared him — but I'd drawn a line. We'd see what happened from now on.

I stepped back, jingling my keys across my fingers in a jaunty dance, and repeated his earlier command to me.

"Let's go."

CHAPTER FOURTEEN

LAURA

My office was empty. It wasn't just Danny's bulk that I missed, filling the space with his presence; it was his personality. However snarky he might be that day, the room lacked something, stark in his absence.

I burrowed into my work — keeping up with old clients and working with some new ones, though they were all smaller cases. And nothing like the challenge Danny presented. I was so engrossed with my notes that I missed the knock at my door the first time.

"Hey." Cal's head popped into my door at the same time as he rapped on the wood, and I realised it wasn't the first time he had knocked.

My head snapped up. "Uh, hi? Oh, Cal!" I stood, then stopped. I was acting like I was starved for human company. Which maybe, I was. But I hadn't seen or heard from anyone in Danny's unit since that morning in his bed. I closed my eyes briefly, trying to banish the image and failing magnificently.

"Laura." He smiled, taking a few steps into my office, and stopping just shy of my desk. "How are you doing?"

I waved a hand over papers scattered haphazardly across the surface of my desk. Hardly my usual style, but some things had changed in me.

"Busy."

"Yes. I can see that." Cal cleared his throat. "I meant, how are you doing without Danny?"

I swallowed, willing myself to breathe and not cry. Neither happened. I hoped I wouldn't turn purple.

"I'm perfectly able to cope without him around, Cal," I snapped, then lowered my head a little. The breath finally went in. "I'm sorry. That was rude. I just hadn't heard from anyone."

"He's doing well." Cal nodded, sympathy in his dark eyes. He ran a hand over his scalp. "I'll keep you up to date."

"Okay," I whispered, but Cal was already out of the room.

"You should have stayed. We had so much fun!"

My stomach clenched as I considered exactly what constituted as *fun* to Belinda. Bodily fluids and fine powder came to mind.

"It wasn't my scene. Sorry." The only thing I was sorry for was that I had agreed to go in the first place. Again. This time, she'd had other female company, and I'd been less concerned about leaving her. Perhaps I shouldn't have been so blase. Sickness bloomed in my stomach.

She's not your responsibility.

Which was silly, really. She was my sister. Which made her both my responsibility and not my responsibility.

"We met some nice men. Well-muscled. The sort of man you like." She looked at me from her slouched position over my breakfast bar, dark circles decorating her eyes beneath several layers of day-old foundation. I pushed a bowl of salad towards her. She wrinkled her nose but took the fork I proffered.

"There's more to men than just good muscles," I murmured into my own bowl, thinking of the way Danny's shoulders had felt beneath my hands. Or so I'd thought, anyway. I squeezed my fork.

213

"You'll never date someone who's not fit," she squawked at me. I placed my bowl on the sink.

"I won't be dating at all."

"OOOh, who broke your heart?" she asked in a singsong voice that raised hairs on my arms. I swallowed back a wave of anger at myself for letting her into my head.

"No one. I have work. Look after yourself."

I'd closed my office for the week after seeing Cal. The sympathy in his eyes had squashed my heart just a little more, and I was terrified I'd dash madly upstairs, begging for Danny's new contact details.

That, and I didn't want to have to deal with their aggressive new receptionist. But it was time to get back to burying myself into work and living through someone else's life goals.

Belinda announced that afternoon she was staying for several nights. I suspected all her worldly goods were packed into the overcrowded duffel bag stowed beneath my dining table, though she used very little of anything in it, raiding my cosmetics and clothes.

"You don't mind me staying, do you?" She twirled in front of my full-length mirror like a child playing dress-up.

"Only if you manage not to destroy my house again," I reminded her, trying to rein in my judgment, but I knew it came across as sour grapes.

"Oh, I won't do any drugs here. Not again. I promise!" She dropped my black dress in a puddle on the floor, reaching for the next one — a lace sheath I had worn once. I put my hand out, stalling her.

"That's my date dress. Hands off." Despite my earlier declaration, I hoped I'd feel like it again one day.

She grumbled but moved along the line, pulling things from my cupboard into a growing pile on the floor.

"What about this one?" It was a red tube dress I'd let myself be talked into buying but had never worn, and likely never would. It was far too short for my comfort.

"It's yours." I waved down her squeals of delight. "Please, tidy up when you're done?"

"Of course, sis."

I nodded, heading out to the verandah for fresh air, setting up my laptop and notes. The sun was sinking by the time I decided to run — I'd traded my morning jog for an evening one, where Danny's shade couldn't chase me down with every step.

Belinda was asleep on my lounge, an empty bottle of whiskey next to her. I covered her with a blanket, binned the bottle and went to change. A pyramid of clothes populated my room.

Liar, liar, liar.

I sighed at yet another empty promise from my sister.

The lake sparkled under an early-risen moon as dusk settled in. It was odd — while I could run in the barely-there dawn light with no worries, running in the evening used to bother me; the constant worry I'd be mugged.

Now, I just didn't care.

I pounded the path, setting a pace far faster than I usually did. Maybe if I was completely exhausted, I wouldn't dream of him tonight. I woke every morning with the smell of Danny in my bed, despite the fact he'd never been in it.

But I still want him there.

I refused to let the tears come, exuding the salt through my pores instead. Footsteps reverberated through the path beneath my feet, and I choked a little, remembering Danny when he'd caught up with me the first lap around the lake. He was a hopeless flirt, but I'd loved being with him, had given him a part of me I'd never shared with anyone else.

It was my own fault for letting anyone get so close.

The jogger approached, my pace slowing a little. I could almost feel Danny's presence behind me. I blinked away my desperation. The runner passed me, long strides taking him around me in quick steps. Physically, the man was fit, but I had zero interest; only a broken desire that I wanted it to be Danny, every time. Even when he wasn't here, he haunted me.

I had to find a new running circuit.

"Bel? Are you awake?" I called into my house, flicking lights on. I'd stopped for sushi on the way home, reminding me yet again of Danny. I had to get a life. Get away, or something. Tomorrow, I'd hit the gym again, try to work out the panic eating me slowly from the inside out. "Bel?"

I checked the sofa, but it was empty. Belinda's tote was missing from its usual spot beneath the table, too. The bedrooms were also vacant. An ache began in my stomach. I dug around my bag for my phone, pulling up her number as soon as it was unlocked in my hand, and pressed call. It took a long moment to connect before the ring tone came through.

My lounge buzzed. I dropped my phone, digging between the cushions and extracted Belinda's phone. Clutching it tightly, I sat on the lounge, numb, wondering when everything in my tightly-organised life had gotten so out of my control.

Eventually, I moved off the sofa, tossing my sushi in the bin. My appetite was long gone. I really did need a dog. Where the hell had Belinda gone? I leaned my forehead against the cold of the fridge door, mind racing. I didn't want to go back to the club she'd taken me to, but for now, I had no other concept of where she might go.

I picked up her phone and tried a few passwords, but I locked myself out. I sighed. A trip upstairs to Cal in the morning would be in the offing, though I knew I shouldn't bother them with small stuff, and it was outside of their scope. No, I wouldn't be going upstairs after all. It was the club or nothing.

Think, Laura.

I tried her name, mine, mum's. Hell, if I had to call my mother. It would kill her. Dad wouldn't say a word, I knew. He cared — he just couldn't talk about it. No, I should wait. Belinda would come back. Wouldn't she?

What if she doesn't?

Missing my sister, and needing Danny so damned much, the tears finally started to fall.

I walked into my room, suddenly bone-tired. The short, black dress Belinda had left on the top of the pile of clothes stood out. In a haze, I fixed my makeup and hair, slipping into a dress that brushed the tops of my thighs.

I'd put my hair up, but when I looked in the mirror, I'd thought of the girls around the circle of ripped guys where I'd seen Danny. Resigned, I let it fall down my back in a sheet; even its brief stint up hadn't made a dent in my straight hair.

God, I hoped he wouldn't be there. Or, maybe I hoped he would. I brushed my hair out, letting it cascade down my back, and added a slash of dark red lipstick from the bottom of my makeup case — nothing like what I usually wore out.

I puffed out a breath, wishing I could call for company, but Danny had been right — I didn't have a social life. Maybe I could call Micah? But reaching out to someone I barely knew sat oddly with me. Besides, he'd likely want to involve Danny. No. My only options were to go alone or not go at all.

I had to find Belinda.

The carpark was as dingy as before but darker. The single security light was out. Shattered glass scattered the gravel in dark, glittering shards. I skirted around it, smoothing my dress, and wished I'd chosen something longer.

As before, there was no doorman. I walked into the club, peering into the haze of smoke that permeated the large room. Claustrophobia rose in my throat, but I forced it back.

Find Belinda.

My gaze was drawn to the same group of guys where I'd seen Danny. Their table was populated with exposed muscle, but no dark head of hair was amongst them. No redhead, either. I scanned the room, heading for the bathrooms I knew were on the other side. Having a destination reduced my misgivings of the place significantly.

A few of the men stared overtly at me. I fought not to wrap my arms around myself, smiling as though enjoying their attention.

"Don't be so rude, sweetheart." Hands wrapped around my waist. "Give me some of your company."

Greasy hair clung to the man's face. *He must be twice my age.* My stomach clenched, but I smiled blandly. "Off to powder my nose." I tried to extract myself from his grip, beginning to panic. My skin crawled at his touch. "Ladies room," I added when I realised he hadn't understood the reference.

His hands dropped away, and my smile became genuine. The rest of my trip across the room was unhindered. I opened the bathroom door and spotted a head of frazzled, red hair at the basins.

"Oh, my god. You scared me. I thought I wouldn't find you–"

Belinda turned to face me, and all the air sucked from my lungs. The skin around her eyes wasn't dark from lack of sleep — it was black from bruising. I caught her face in both hands while she smiled at me woozily.

"What happened to you? Who did this?" My voice rose several octaves as I surveyed the damage. What the hell had happened to her in a few short hours? Thank god I hadn't waited any longer. Belinda's pupils were almost completely dilated, and her breath stank of booze. I checked her arms — two fresh puncture marks sat in the crook of her elbow. The combination of a potential overdose. "We're leaving. Right now."

I gripped her arm tight, towing her out the door, and came face-to-face with a wall of muscle. At first, I thought it was Danny. Relief blossoming, I began to smile, but hard features registered; a sneer he'd never use — certainly not with me. I pulled up short.

"Excuse me. I thought you were someone else."

Arms as thick as tree trunks blocked my way. I tightened my grasp on Bel, putting her behind me.

"You're taking my fun away."

What the hell? I squinted at him.

"What?"

He nodded over my shoulder. "Red. She's mine." A slimy grin. "Tonight, anyway."

"She's my sister. And we're leaving," I said firmly.

"You can leave." Hulk reached behind me, plucking Belinda from my hands like a wilted flower.

"Stop!" I grabbed for her. Belinda's head lolled. I hoped she'd only passed out. I grasped her other arm, the one bearing track marks, holding tight in a bizarre game of tug-o-war.

It was briefly lived as Belinda was taken from my grip yet again — but from someone behind me, this time. I tried to whirl around, flailing, but the man in front of me gripped my arms, hard. I stared into his suddenly-close face, the hairs on my arms rising as fear replaced panic.

"I've got her, Luke," A man spoke behind me. My eyes widened — I knew that voice, had dreamed about it. A hand on my chest flattened me against the wall before I could call out to him. I sucked in a short breath, my heart hammering. A dark shape moved away down the hall, carrying my sister.

Danny.

I knew it was him. It had to be — or I'd just lost my sister.

"You don't come back here. Ever." My cheek stung as he slapped my cheek lightly. "Look at me."

I dragged my eyes back to the man — Luke — in front of me. He gripped my chin, squeezing where he'd slapped me.

At least I had a damned good idea of who'd attacked Belinda. Fire ignited in my belly, overriding common sense and any laws of self-preservation I possessed.

"You bastard!" I launched forward, scrabbling at him with hooked fingers, hitting nothing but air. He pressed harder on my chest, arm straight, putting him out of my reach.

"Usually, I like a feisty bitch, but you're trouble, girl." He nodded over my head. "Get her out of here."

Broad arms wrapped around my waist, lifting me off my feet. I shrieked — terror for my sister and rage at my total lack of control of anything ripping from my chest in an animalistic snarl.

My hands fit around the arms at my waist, and I stopped fighting.

"Danny?" I tried to twist my head back but couldn't see anything as I was towed into the carpark.

Every inch of me went cold. If I was wrong, then I was in a very dark place with a hellishly strong man I didn't know. Instinct finally kicked in. I began to struggle, thrashing my fists against an immovable object.

I was set down gently on my feet. Frowning, my car was right in front of me. I spun around, desperate. "Please, you have to– " Hands shoved me forcefully into the driver's seat, keys landing with a soft clink in my lap. "Danny–" It came out as a choked whisper, the loudest sound I could make.

The door slammed shut, and he walked away without a word. I swallowed, barely able to breathe with the mix of panic and heartbreak tearing through me. My hand was on the door to go back in — I still had to find Belinda. There was no way I was leaving her with them — and Danny was clearly one of *them*.

A soft moan turned my head. Belinda lay curled in the passenger seat, belt secured across her. One hand on her chest to check she was breathing, I fumbled the keys in the ignition. After two false starts, I managed to get the car moving, suddenly desperate to get away from the place. A shadow stirred against the wall. I paused, wanting — needing — to talk to him, but Danny's actions tonight clearly said he wasn't interested in me.

If it even had been him.

Tears pricked the corners of my eyes as my mind caught up. I was alone.

Again.

Fingers beginning to tremble and cheek stinging, I let the ache in my heart bloom. Not waiting to see if the shadow was the one who haunted me or someone I'd blanketed in Danny's likeness, I put the car in drive, and took my sister home.

CHAPTER FIFTEEN

DANNY

Walking away from Laura may have been the hardest thing I'd ever done. When she'd called my name, I'd gripped the brick wall behind me, slicing my fingers open with the effort not to turn back and hold her, bury my face in her hair.

But I had a job to do.

I watched her car from the shadow of the club until the taillights disappeared into the deepening glow of the city. Traffic moved steadily around me as I made my way back inside, entering through the kitchen door I'd used to bring the sister outside. When I'd seen Laura pairing off against Luke, I'd had to grab her to stop myself from flattening him right there.

Not something Cal would have been impressed with. I grit my teeth in a humourless smile. I needed to call him sometime, catch him up. Luke worried me in more than one way — drugs, domestic violence, the threats — that was all part and parcel of his lifestyle. The usual, small-time criminal.

But there was something more about him that bothered me — something brewing beneath the surface.

I needed time to find out what that was. If Laura kept turning up, I'd never get the answers I needed to close this case up.

"Your girl's a problem," Luke seethed, spit coating his lips.

I waved a hand. "I sorted her. She won't be back." *I hope.*

Tonight should have been a wake-up call for her. Although her sister insisted on making an appearance, there was no way Laura belonged in my world. *My world.* This dark, rotten underside of people I flitted in and out of for work. But it was becoming more than work. I spent more time with crooks than I did at home. I clenched my teeth, turning the ache in my heart to anger.

"You're right." His tone held an element of victory, and I looked at him sharply.

"What'd you do?" I grinned, though putting his head through the wall behind seemed like a good option.

Hold your shit together, Danny.

Luke shrugged. "Slapped her 'round a bit. Her sister was easier to deal with."

Because you stuck a needle in her arm while she was flirting with your crew, you sick fuck.

His words finally sank in. I kept his gaze as rage boiled in my chest — I hadn't even checked Laura for damage. This assignment was taking more from me than I'd dealt with in prior cases. Somehow — and I wasn't sure when — this job had become personal.

I kept my stance easy. "Like I said. It's sorted."

"What'd you do, fuck her outside?" He leered at me. The boys gathered around us, the tension in the air thickening to choking point.

"Nah. Next time I see her, I'll take my time with her." I gave him the same soulless smile I'd used at Nellie's, but I wasn't lying. The next time I was alone with Laura, I swore I'd have her seven ways from Sunday — if she let me anywhere near her.

After tonight, I doubted it.

Luke watched me, considering, then clapped my shoulder, despite my earlier warnings. "Let me know when you get bored. I'll show her what a good fuck really feels like."

I rolled my eyes as the boys erupted, punching his shoulder. It was like being in an inebriated kindergarten.

Time blended and I'd clocked over five months on assignment. I hadn't spoken to Cal in over a fortnight. Luckily, Luke had given me a few drops for the day, and with some miles left to go, I made the call. Cal picked up on the second ring.

"Only got a minute."

"Go." Cal's short response was perfect for the situation.

"Luke's done almost nothing. Money, drugs, girls — it's all the same shit. No people trafficking, no hacking. J fucking squat."

Cal was silent for a moment. I squeezed the steering wheel.

"Alright. Try for some hacks. He had a job that involved banks. Who set that up?"

"He did. Mentioned it once, never again. Dunno who, yet, 'cause it sure as hell ain't Luke."

"Push him on it, make some ground. Otherwise, we've got to pull you."

"Like hell. There's more to this. I want to see what's going on."

"Hurry your ass up. Liam's taking heat. And there are issues with the judge and L—" Cal cut himself off, swearing.

"On it. Gotta go."

I turned onto Luke's street, hanging up. The open cab of my truck afforded little privacy, but it was the best I had, for now. I checked the thing most days for bugs — hadn't found one, yet. Or anything else that said I was under surveillance. Still, I couldn't take any chances.

I pulled into the drive, making sure I blocked Luke in. He hated it, and it had developed into a power play. Petty, but it served as an excellent distraction from what I was really doing.

I walked in without a word, tossing a wrapped packet of money his way, and nearly knocked out the girl giving him head while he lounged on the sofa.

"Shit. Sorry, babe."

A blonde I'd never seen before raised her head, but Luke wrapped his hand in her hair, muffling her reply. A sea of white tumbled over his fist, reminding me forcibly of Laura. I wondered if he'd chosen her on purpose.

I sank into a recliner across from him while he counted the cash, nodding as he reached the end.

"It's all there." I raised an eyebrow.

"You wouldn't be breathing if it wasn't."

"Quit grumbling, old man."

Luke grinned, showing teeth. "Good little errand boy, aren't you?"

"Pay's alright. Boss is a bit shit." I grinned, splaying my legs out, flicking through my phone.

"You want something better to do?"

I stilled. It was only for a second, but I knew the big bastard would have caught it. He groaned, gripping the girl's hair tight, his hips flexing. I went back to scrolling through messages on my phone — all the fake accounts Micah set up. Poor guy spent most of his day commenting on inane activities he had zero interest in. There were some coded messages in there, too.

Mickey D: *Boss' pissed with me.*

Me: *What'd you do?*

Mickey D: *Took too long on a job. Fucker ripped me a new one.*

I ground my teeth. Cal was right; Liam was covering for us. The girl got up, leaning forward to kiss Luke, but he pushed her away. Pouting, she sashayed her way up the hall, ostensibly to clean herself up.

Luke grimaced. "Not the best."

"Where'd you find her?"

"Want one for yourself? Have her." He cocked his head. "Looks like your girl."

"Keep telling you she's not mine." Hell, not after the way I'd treated her.

"So you say." Luke's eyes never left me, hands on his knees. I didn't bother looking at him.

"What's the job?"

Luke leaned back, zipping himself up. "There it is."

I didn't answer, scrolling through more fake messages.

Brad the Dick: *New IT guy's an asshole.*

Me: *You fight with everyone? It's a wonder you still have a job.*

I closed my phone, sliding it onto the coffee table, and followed it with my feet.

"Whatever."

"You hungry?"

I stilled again. Intentionally, this time. Luke wasn't talking about takeout. "Always."

Luke inclined his head, standing as the girl came back out. She gave me a wan smile, eyes shifting to Luke. He peeled five notes off the wad of cash I'd given him, slid three to her and pocketed the rest.

She flipped her hair over her shoulder, eyeing me speculatively. I stood, and she smiled. It dropped quickly as I opened the door. She glared at me, flinging her hair again. I grinned, closing the door behind her.

Luke laughed, gesturing me into his room. I paused, leaning in the doorway.

"Hitting on me, bro? Thought you got some already."

"Told you she wasn't any good."

He gestured me inside, flicking open his laptop and began typing in command prompts. I watched his progress, working through what he was doing in my head before he got there. Every excess part of my brain switched off as I focussed on the new job in front of me.

Three hours later, my stomach growled. My concentration broke as I scrolled through lines of script, trying to work out where the error in my coding lay.

Luke thumped my back. "Good work. Take a break, alright?"

I waved him away. "Just give me a few..." I found what I was looking for and dived back in.

When I emerged from Luke's room, rubbing tired eyes, the boys cheered. Seated around the small, low table in the centre of the living area, they each held a hand of cards. Small piles of poker chips sat in front of each of them.

"Welcome back, bro." Luke leaned back, beer in his hand. I ignored him.

"Who's winning?"

"Justin. Little shit's been taking us each turn." Zahn sat back, tipping his head up. I looked behind him. The glass windows reflected his cards perfectly. I grinned at Justin and let it ride.

These guys played nothing straight. If Justin managed to get one up on the bigger guys, I wasn't going to take it from him. Youngest in their team, I knew what it was like to be uncomfortable and to have to fight for your place.

Like I was doing now.

I sank into the chair next to Zahn's and filched his cards. He looked down after a moment, staring at his empty hands. I knew I'd done the lift well — he hadn't felt it for a few seconds.

Red suffused his neck, climbing upwards at a steady rate. With a mini war-cry, he turned, slamming his fist towards my face. I blocked it lazily — alcohol and drugs had slowed his reflexes — and his timing was off-kilter. I knew I shouldn't poke the drug-filled bull, but it was too easy. And in a place like this, I had to get my jollies somehow.

He glared at me and stormed away. A moment later, a door slammed in the back of the house. The boys erupted in laughter.

"He's not the man you want to enrage." Luke fixed me with a steady gaze when the ribbing settled, echoing my sentiments. I gave him a sloppy grin and played dumb. Luke kicked my shin.

"Ow?"

"Listen, you stupid fucker. You've got brains. Use them." When I said nothing, Luke sighed, shaking his head. "He'll take it out on your truck. Probably."

That got me sitting up. You didn't screw with me that way. Luke laughed, eyes mean. Well. I'd walked into that one.

"Gimme some more work like today, and I'll fix it every time he trashes it."

"Shit, Danny. Get your head out of your ass. We need him."

I snorted.

"Why? He's an ignorant son of a..." I dropped the conversation as Zhan returned, a glass filled with dark gold liquid in his hand. He dropped into the seat he'd vacated earlier, dealing himself in. I swapped my cards for his before he noticed. He squawked, but I flicked the backs of the cards in his hands.

"Made them better."

A broad grin spread over his face, and he laid them on the table with a flourish like he'd done all the work himself, scooping in chips to cries around the table.

Luke caught my eye with a jerk of his chin as I tossed in the shitty pair Zhan had dealt himself.

"Nicely played," he said softly, beneath the chatter of the other men. His stare settled on me, assessing. I wasn't sure if I'd just had a win, or if I'd given away too much.

"You up for something bigger?"

I didn't look at Luke, slugging water. They'd ordered pizza, and I'd eaten far too much. The other three had called it a night. I made a point of being last to bed most nights — there was opportunity in the quiet hours.

"You're throwing jobs my way damned fast."

"You've earned it." A one-shouldered shrug accompanied his comment.

"Have I?"

Luke was playing a different game — his attitude ever-evolving — like he wore a mask. Too close to mine for comfort.

"I worked out a way to get into the Reserve Bank. Think you can handle it?"

"You want me to rob the Reserve Bank of Australia?" It was our biggest bank, controlling interest rates, and inflation. Generally, it ran our economy. I leaned forward, pretending to consider it, cheering internally. At least I'd have something to tell Cal. Now I had to set it up so we could pull the sting off. "Shifting decimal points like before?"

"Bit more than that."

"Yeah?" I twirled my water bottle in my hands, studying the ridges. Waiting. Always waiting.

"We change the interest rates — fluctuate it that tiny bit — a fraction of a fraction. The window will be less than a minute — less likely to be noticed."

"You think they won't notice you stealing what, a few million?" I sat up straight. Luke shook his head, holding out a hand.

"As we leave, we drop it a few points — something significant. In the fallout of sorting thousands of home loans they're losing to, arguing with customers and the media to rectify mistakes, we just...disappear."

"You want to close out operations and walk away?" *Not likely.* That was the problem with hacking or theft. It was hard to break the habit. You got caught up with taking more and more, every time you escaped scot-free.

"It's enough to make your boys happy, dude. But you know they'll want more. That cash won't sustain you. What do you do when you run out?"

Luke tilted his head back, not answering for a moment. "Then I get a new crew. Or I walk."

You'll never be able to stop.

I turned it all over in my head, working through what was needed to pull the job off. I was missing something. I ran a hand over my head. Luke's eyes tracked the action. "Sounds like a plan. I'm shattered, going to bed."

I stood, rolling my shoulders. Several things popped. Luke hadn't moved.

"So, you in?"

"Yeah. Why not?"

CHAPTER SIXTEEN

DANNY

Beneath me, Luke strained — dude had the largest biceps I'd ever seen. Well, that wasn't strictly true — Micah would easily top him in size — but outside the unit, this guy rated as enormous.

His hands wrapped around the bar, pressing slowly upwards. Around us, machines clanked, Raw Iron bringing in its usual clientele of executives and pro-bodybuilders. There was just a smattering of guys like us — too much money and enough testosterone to train with the big guys.

Luke hissed out a long breath. Veins popped on his neck, tendons standing tall as he strained. Sweat pooled on the towel-covered bench beneath his head. Fortunately, he managed to hoist it high enough to roll it onto its stand without too much assistance.

Breathing deep, he slowly rolled to a sitting position. I patted one sweat-slicked shoulder, letting him know he'd done well.

"Sure you could catch that if I dropped it?"

Luke grinned over his shoulder at me, running a hand over his freshly-shaved head in a gesture I found all too familiar. Best friend and betrayer. That was me. Over the months I'd lived in his house, our relationship had developed. I'd worked hard for it.

Of course, I wasn't really mini-hulk's best mate — but he didn't know that. I smiled back genially — I hoped — and slapped his shoulder a little harder.

"More worried about you dropping the damned thing, slicked up with your pretty-boy baby oil."

He grunted, standing to stretch out his legs after his time on the bench. Zahn leaned forward.

"You gonna have a turn? I'll spot you."

There was no way I'd trust the guy with anything heavy over me. While I'd nurtured a relationship with Luke, I hadn't bothered with Zahn. I wasn't going to get along with everyone, and the tension was normal in a group of guys — though he had more bitch factor than I'd initially thought.

The guy was likely to carry a grudge. There was no way I was going to give him the opportunity he was searching for.

"You can't keep up with me, Mini-me."

A shapely pair of black-clad legs appeared in my peripheral vision, striding confidently through the gym.

Laura.

I moved around the bench, the padded floor springy beneath my trainers, and leaned against the equipment behind me. Safely out of her line of sight, I flicked Luke's towel at him.

"Ready to go?"

"You quitting already?" Luke quirked an eyebrow my way.

"Nah, just sick of watching you check yourself out in the mirrors."

As we headed toward the showers, I kept Luke between me and the cardio room where Laura worked out, making sure she hadn't seen me. I needn't have worried — she sat with her back to me on the rowing machine, keeping a strong rhythm. Watching muscles bunch and tighten across her shoulders beneath golden skin was mesmerising, much as she had been the first day at the lake.

"Not bad."

I jumped. Luke was already at the door that led to the changing rooms, watching me gape at a girl I'd been actively avoiding with a dopey grin. I shook my head. Laura was a distraction I couldn't afford, especially now Luke was planning a bigger job.

Focus.

I couldn't help a last glance over my shoulder in her direction and hurried to catch up with him. We were halfway down the hall when Luke started.

"You've never shown interest in any of the girls before."

That gave me pause. He knew I'd been sweet on Laura, especially after the debacle at the club — but it was doubtful he'd remember her, especially in a different setting.

My cover profile was as a gym buff — which should have included regular perving. And the honeys at Raw Iron gym were exceptional. It should have been right up my alley. I didn't think he'd identified her as the girl he'd accosted the night I'd rescued her sister and hauled her ass away from him. Her calling after me still broke my heart.

I rolled my shoulders, trying to brush it off.

"You've been watching me *not* watch anyone else?"

"Didn't want you coming in for a cuddle at night." Luke grinned, stepping into a shower cubicle.

I shook my head. Working out six days a week, partying every night...it sounded like a dream job. But there was a normalcy I missed. Laura said she had a house of her own — I'd never even thought to buy one, content with hopping from assignment to assignment. I thought of my life, boxed up in Cal's spare room.

I rubbed my thumb over the ink on my arm — a black queen and a white king in check — as I upped the water pressure of my own shower. Leaning forward to let the close-to-scalding water pound my back, I recognised the time undercover was getting to me. Heat soaked into muscles gone cold, loosening everything up.

I rolled my shoulders, recalling Laura on the rowing machine. Still so fucking gorgeous. I missed running with her every day — watching her ponytail bounce as she pushed herself, with the most incredible ass I'd ever seen. Missed her banter, the determination in her eyes when she fixated on a problem.

Hell, I even missed her damned motivational videos. I thought of her, that night in the club, dolled up in a dress that only just covered what it needed to — though I'd already seen her naked, had her beneath me in my bed.

That fast, I had a hard-on. Damn, I'd never get the girl out of my head.

I missed her. God, I missed her. This assignment had come up, and I hadn't had time to say goodbye. Working my way into a tight-knit group usually took months of planning

— and I'd walked in only twenty-four hours after I'd received the file.

Luke thumped the cubicle door.

"Coming, princess?"

"Hold your horses," I grumbled. "Gotta fix my makeup."

Luke hollered with laughter on the other side of the pink door — *who the hell chose salmon paint for the men's locker room?* — while I pushed Laura as far to the back of my mind as I could. Stuffing my towel into my gym bag, I hoisted it onto my shoulder before I followed Luke out of the bathroom and into the corridor leading to the carpark.

Clearly, I hadn't pushed Laura back far enough, as I walked out the door and straight into a mass of damp blonde hair, wet from her own shower.

Sparkling aqua eyes met mine, perfect pink lips open in a little *o*. I had a quick vision of her mouth open like that for an entirely different reason.

She bounced backward and my hands wrapped around her purely on reflex, though I held her for a moment longer than was strictly necessary. I bent to check she was okay. Or so I told myself, as I pulled back from almost kissing her right there.

Breath hissed between my teeth, lips tingling. I resisted the urge to wipe the back of my hand across my mouth as I straightened. I placed her back on her feet — and a good metre away from me.

Luke leaned against the opposite wall; arms folded with a knowing smirk decorating his face. He'd grill me about this later.

Laura blinked, mouth open to apologise, I thought. A flash in her eyes tightened her features, and I knew she'd recognised me. Her hand lifted, drifting upward, and I anticipated her touch, had dreamed about it for months. Her slap came completely unexpected, the crack echoing down the empty hallway.

Blue eyes blazed from a tanned face.

"Where the hell have you been, Danny Woods?"

Well, fuck, if that wasn't my cover blown, right there.

My cheek stung as I faced off against the sexiest woman I'd ever seen. Being close to her again made my heart pound. I covertly wiped sweating palms on my legs. We'd been on mostly okay terms before I left, but that night in the club might just have screwed up everything I'd thought we had.

Plus, I'd asked her out — tentatively — before I'd been put on assignment. By the wild look in her eyes, I could bet no one had told her I was undercover — especially not when she'd been prying me away from it. And I hadn't even called.

Shit. No wonder she was cranky.

Laura huffed, scraping wet hair back into the sexy mess on top of her head. A flush rose in her cheeks. Okay, make that more than cranky. Truth be told, she had every right to be. I resisted the urge to touch my face — I was pretty sure she'd raised a welt. But that would be the least of my worries.

A quick glance at Luke confirmed my suspicions — no longer leaning against the wall, arms still crossed over a barrel chest, he watched me through narrowed eyes. Not only would he now likely recognise her, but I'd also signed the lease under my cover name — Miller, not Woods.

"Don't look at him for help!" Laura's voice rose, panic rippling beneath it — either at seeing me and not knowing how to deal with it, or seriously angry I'd stood her up, and never called. She drew herself up, reaching just above my shoulder and planted both fists on her hips.

The latter, then.

I raised my hands in an attempt to placate her but never got further than opening my mouth.

"Don't. You. *Dare* make excuses. Ghosting me is one thing — walking away from the last of our developmental sessions is completely another. I won't waste any more time with you, Danny. It's sad, I really thought we were making progress..."

She trailed off, momentum draining away. She still looked mad, but I sensed disappointment in her, too. A tiny glimmer of hope bounced in my chest.

"I didn't– I got–" Hell, how did one explain to one's crush they'd been sent on assignment in front of their key mark? "Things got...busy," I finished lamely, knowing it had been an error to try to explain. Laura's eyes flashed, confirming my assessment.

"You– I don't want to see you in my office ever– I don't *care* what Ca–"

She stumbled over her words, stuttering in anger. I didn't have time to think before she not only blew my cover but named and shamed my boss in the same breath. I snagged her waist, pulling her into me and kissed her before she could finish the sentence that could have ended my task force career.

Cold air hit me as she gasped, resisting only for a moment before her lips softened, her slim frame leaning into me. Tangling my hand in her damp hair, I held her mouth against mine, sweeping my tongue across the line of her lips.

She parted them with a sigh, hands pressed flat to my chest. God, she tasted exactly as she had that morning in my bed. Honeysuckle with a hint of vanilla.

Part of me remembered Luke was watching us, but right now, I didn't care. I lost myself in the feel of her, fitting her against me.

Whatever she'd washed her hair with was berry scented, mingling with her own, sweeter flavour. I drew back, satisfied with her dazed look beneath dark lashes. I had only a moment to enjoy it before a second crack echoed down the hallway, announcing her slap on my other cheek.

At least the welts would match.

Laura's chest was still heaving when Luke tapped my shoulder. I dragged my eyes away from her, trying to ignore the stinging in my face.

"Work your shit out with your girl, man. Talk later, yeah?"

He sent me a hard look and swaggered down the hall to where his car was parked. That was a screw up I'd salvage later — Laura hadn't completely ousted me, though I knew it would be a hard sell with Luke later on.

But right now, I had to fix the hot mess in front of me.

I waited until the door shut behind my housemate before I opened my mouth. Laura's eyes narrowed, but I held up my hand to stall her, speaking softly from the corner of my mouth.

"I'm on a case." The words came out a little more harshly than I'd intended, but from the surprise that flared across her face, Laura got the point. Time to fix this one. "Let's go somewhere more...private."

Her eyes flashed. "Danny, I'm not going any–"

"Please," I murmured. "I brought your sister back."

"That *was* you," she whispered, eyes wide.

"Yeah." I swallowed past the lump in my throat. "I missed you, Laura."

The omission crumbled the edges of my heart a bit. For a moment, I thought she'd slap me again, and make it a hattrick. She nodded, relenting. I captured her hand, squeezing it tightly, and raised it to my lips. She followed the movement with her eyes all the way, leaning forward just a little.

I hoped to hell I could repair my mess now because I suspected there was only ever one chance with a woman like her.

Laura drew her hand back, twirling her cup on the table, a frown creasing symmetrical features. Cinnamon from her dirty chai drifted amongst the dust motes around us. Her hair dried in a messy knot on top of her head, silver shining against the glowing tan she sported.

"Why wouldn't Cal tell me you were on assignment?"

I thought of my boss. "You know what Cal's like. Focussed and unstoppable — on one subject at a time. Don't try to burden him with more than that."

Laura gave an unladylike snort, emptied her cup, and flagged the waitress for a refill. She smiled as the girl returned with a fresh cup, switching it out for her old one.

"I wish he'd told me — that anyone had told me. I thought– Ally made it sound like you'd transferred. And your phone was disconnected." She broke off, lifting her eyes to mine. "I'm sorry I slapped you."

"Shit, I forgot to pay the damned phone bill. And I'm the one who should be apologizing." I grinned, raising an eyebrow. "But you *did* slap me. Twice. That's battery, you know."

"You– are you–" she caught the glint in my eye, the corners of her lips twitching. "Am I the one saying sorry, then?"

I raised an eyebrow, playing it up. "Maybe I shouldn't have kissed you."

Laura's cheeks reddened. I grinned despite the glare she sent my way. It hadn't been the right thing to do, but I'd needed a distraction. And hell, I'd enjoyed it. By the looks of her, she had too.

"I'm glad you did." Her hands clenched around the cup.

Smart, sexy as hell, and driven, she matched me in every way. But she had a serious edge where I played everything down — it never paid to let anyone know you might be the smartest guy in the room, especially in my job.

Laura looked at me, and I could see her trying to piece together my new life.

"So, you live in the house with them?"

I'd brought her up-to-date on the walk to the cafe, only a block from the gym. She'd chatted with the cafe owner. It no longer surprised me that she knew everyone's name when I hadn't even known who owned the place.

There was a current trend of having your beverage served in an avocado shell, but I'd opted to take ours more traditionally.

"Danny?" Laura looked at me, expectantly.

"Yes, I live with them. Eat with them, workout together. Party." It was her turn to raise an eyebrow, and I looked away.

"Plenty of fun times then," she murmured.

"I don't take any of them home. The girls."

"In a place like that club, you wouldn't have to. Your housemate is terrifying, by the way," she added, conversationally.

"He hurt you." It was a statement. I recalled Luke bragging about it and covered her hand with mine. She jerked a little but didn't pull away. "I'm so sorry it came to that."

She shook her head. "It's not your fault, Danny. Belinda was there. I had to– to find her." She looked at me with wide eyes. "If you hadn't been there that night, I don't know what would have happened."

My lips pressed together in a hard line. I did — I'd seen Luke force himself on a girl, take her out the back of the club. Afterwards, they limped away — often for more than one reason. I wanted to haul his ass to the local station, but that wasn't the job. I drew small circles on the back of her hand with my thumbs. Her eyes tracked the movement through lowered lashes.

I didn't say anything about Luke, not wanting to scare her. What he'd done to her sister was proof enough that he was a threat to any girl alone.

"He thought I was gay — hadn't perved enough, apparently." I huffed a laugh, determined to make her smile. "Until he found out about you. So, you needn't worry."

It came out harsher than I'd intended, but regardless how much I'd missed her, the thought that she'd nearly blown my cover — twice — however inadvertently, niggled. I was sore about it, but fixing things with Laura was my first priority.

I was still working on how I would get my ass out of the shit-fight that was sure to occur as soon as I went back to the house.

"It's okay. You do what you have to do, I guess. For work." She studied the tabletop. It took me a moment to work out what she meant.

I reached across the table, curling my fingers under her chin. They met with slight resistance, but I was determined.

"Laura. Look at me," I spoke softly, but it was a command, none-the-less. Slowly, she raised her head, eyes meeting mine. I brushed the back of my hand over her cheek, swept stray strands of silver-blonde hair behind her ear. "I don't do the drugs unless it's critical to the job. I never sleep with any of the girls. No kisses, no other perks." I dropped my hand before I did something else stupid in a public place.

Just you.

Eyes wide, Laura nodded. She swallowed, tried to speak several times, but kept closing her mouth. I needed her to speak, some notion that she accepted I wasn't lying to her.

My teeth clenched; I pressed my hands to the table. What little patience I had left deserted me, and a rejection from her was more than I could handle.

"I understand if you don't want anything to do with me. It's a rough world I'm living in. You don't belong there."

I rose, grabbing my gym bag, and headed out of the cafe. The sunshine outside was sickeningly bright. I stamped my way towards the water, too angry to drive. How could I have fucked that up so badly? I could have sworn she was okay with everything I was saying. Unless she didn't believe me about the girls.

Damnit.

I kicked at a large pinecone. It ricocheted off the path, smashing against a tree trunk. I stared out over the water, running a hand through my hair.

"Danny."

I whirled. Laura ran up to me, panting. She placed a hand on my chest, but I couldn't respond.

"I'm so sorry, my laptop bag– I tried to chase after you, but it got all tangled, and I–" bright blue eyes stared into mine, searching.

My heartbeat slowed, the ache spreading into a warmth that filled the bare spot where my heart should have been. My hands slipped around her waist, but I held her back when she leaned into me.

"I promise you I didn't touch any of them."

Confusion crossed her face. "I saw you with a girl on your lap. At the club. Your hand was on her..." Laura dropped her hand from my chest, trailing off.

I frowned. The girls had stayed away after I'd made it clear I wasn't interested, and I hadn't been near them when I'd rescued her from Luke. But I'd thought I'd seen her a week earlier, thought my mind was playing tricks. If she'd been there that night...I groaned, squeezing her waist.

"I was still getting to know how it all worked, settling in with Luke's crew. I thought I saw you — but then you disappeared. I followed you out, but you were gone." I swiped at my face with one hand. "I'm explaining this badly. I've never been with them — with any of them. In any way. All I want is you."

CHAPTER SEVENTEEN

LAURA

I managed to keep my jaw closed, barely.

I can't trust you because you lied. Did you?

"Thanks," I said softly, "I thought you might tell me to go to hell," I mumbled the last part, not looking at him. Danny's hands squeezed tight around my waist, and I gave a little gasp, shocks of electricity racing beneath my skin. He released me, rubbing the back of his head.

"Sorry." He gave me the dopey grin I suspected was all him. "I'd never tell you to go to hell."

"That's good to know." I cautiously fell into step with him as he started walking one of the paths that rambled into the deep foliage of the park. He was silent for a few steps.

"I'll have to work a miracle with Luke this afternoon."

I frowned as I caught up with our prior conversation. "What mess? And how could he possibly think you're gay? You turn the flirt on high at the first sign of a female."

I sent him a cheeky grin to take the sting out of my words, but his features tightened. He rubbed the back of his neck again.

"I signed the lease as my cover profile. He thinks my surname is Miller. You ousted me pretty fast, right before you slapped me — the first time. He noticed, and he'll have recognised you by now. You're pretty memorable." He looked at me sideways, a muscle ticking in his cheek. "I'll have to spin some fast shit to save my ass — and my case."

'Oh." I touched his hand, fingertips tracing the ink that ran along his left arm. "I'm really sorry, Danny. I hope you can fix it. I can speak to Cal–"

"No."

I looked up, fingers pausing on his arm. "What?"

"Don't say anything to Cal. Or the rest of the team. I have enough bridges to build after... Don't give me that look."

I dropped my gaze, a warm flush spreading over my cheeks. "Sorry." I knew exactly what he meant. Turning off my professional side was difficult — impossible, sometimes. I needed to fix everything. That didn't work out when other people wanted to sort out their own problems, and I jumped in their way.

"I won't say anything," I replied softly, "But how are you going to fix things with Luke? If he suspects you of– won't going back be dangerous?"

He shrugged. I knew I'd hit a nerve. There was always an element of danger in his job — but it was the sort of pressure he thrived under.

"Not that big a deal." He played it down, but I could read the lie in his words. "I'll think of something. At least we got our date in."

My eyes widened, and my mouth dropped open. Danny covered his mouth in a suspiciously unrealistic coughing fit.

"Danny W– Miller. If you think you are going to get away with it that easily, you have another thing coming. I want a full-service date as an apology."

"Full service?" He stopped fake coughing and raised an eyebrow. "I hadn't picked you as a high maintenance girl. Ah, what sort of full service?" He stopped altogether. I would have paid well to know what was running through his mind.

"Concerned?" I caught his gaze with mine.

"What could a gi– woman like you want?" he corrected hastily. "While the thought of you in a floor-length ball gown doesn't ring quite true, I can't deny the image is enticing."

His gaze heated, drifting lazily down my body and back to my face. The grin that creased his face was undeniably sinful.

"I just meant — time away from here. From work, and..." I stuttered, wishing I hadn't put him under pressure. He liked a challenge far too much. His hooded eyes held a dark promise, and I shivered in the shadow of the thick trees that lined the path. Danny took a step closer to me. I didn't move — I couldn't have if I'd wanted to.

His hands slid around my waist, along my sides as he drew me into him. My heart pounding, I took long breaths, battling to stay in control of my senses, but he was everywhere around me. His lips brushed my cheek. My hands curled around his arms, tracing the ridges of muscle, heat radiating into my hands.

Danny's mouth brushed over mine, hesitating a breath away. I swayed in the circle of his arms, relaxed for the first time in months — since the last time he held me.

A shrill noise accosted us at ankle level. Iron bands wrapped around me and I was lifted away, deposited on a patch of grass just off the path. The bands loosened, and I could breathe again. Danny swore profusely, dancing a quick step as a fluffy, white cloud yapped at his feet.

"I'm so sorry," an elderly lady puffed her way up to us, "He likes bright things." She sent an apologetic grimace to Danny as she collected her dog. Danny waved her apology away, bending to connect the lead for her.

I held back giggles as he made his way back to me. The little dog bounded ahead of the woman on a lead much longer than she could control.

"I warned you about those trainers." I smiled as the cloud launched at a flock of pigeons, dragging his owner after him. "I thought of maybe getting a dog," I looked up at Danny, "when I couldn't reach you. My house was so..."

"Empty."

I nodded. "Yes."

Danny cocked his head, silent. I tried not to fidget. Maybe he hated dogs? But he'd handled that one well. Though what I had in mind was something just a little larger.

"Living in Luke's house, I've been thinking of you. A lot." There was that sideways, dopey grin again. "My entire life is in a few boxes in Cal's spare room. When this assignment finishes, he'll set me up in a new place. I don't even bother to unpack them, anymore." He stared into the trees, distant. I brushed my hand against his, and his fingers wrapped around mine, like a reflex.

"It must be hard," I murmured.

Danny looked at me, surprise creasing his features. "That's the thing — it's not. It never has been. I've never thought about having a place of my own until I remembered something you said."

"It's a relief to have somewhere to go when things don't always work out. A sanctuary," I finished, biting my lip. I was still ridiculously embarrassed that I hadn't thought Danny might be undercover or that I'd taken Ally at her word — the insinuations had been all too easy to believe. Cal and I needed to have a conversation on several levels.

"Maybe I need that." Danny looked straight ahead, and I didn't know if he was talking to himself or to me. I didn't question him. The path narrowed as it turned back on itself. Danny let go of my hand and slipped his arm around my shoulder, pulling me into him.

I leaned my head lightly against his shoulder, enjoying the comfort he offered. His arm trembled and I started — had I missed something or misread the situation terribly? It wouldn't be the first time, I thought darkly, remembering Ally's comment in the lift the night in the office.

But when I looked up, a broad smile lit his face.

"Is something funny?"

He shook his head. "No — it's just that we usually run together, or we're on an urgent mission for lunch. I don't think I've ever just walked with you."

I smiled. "I guess not."

"I'm used to moving a bit faster."

We reached the edge of the park, the noise of the city rushing to break the serenity of the oasis in its centre. The carpark came into sight. I sighed, the tensions of the morning returning all too fast.

"When will I see you again?" I asked quietly.

"This isn't enough to tide you over for a bit?" Danny grinned.

I slapped his stomach lightly. He *ooffed* theatrically.

"Don't you get your cheeky on with me. We still have a few sessions left to tidy up loose ends." His smile faded, and I choked on the stupidity of my words.

Got foot-in-mouth disease there, Laura.

I stared straight ahead, wondering how I could bring back the moment that I'd lost. I could feel it fading away, and I didn't want to lose it entirely. Danny's hand tightened on my arm, and he directed us away from the path that led past the cafe toward the carpark.

"Where are we going? My car's just there." I raised my arm to point it out, but Danny swung around in front of me, batting my arm away.

"I'm sorry, Laura. Try to act natural."

His hand released my arm. Sliding it around my back, he yanked me against his chest and kissed me — hard. His mouth crashed down on mine, his hand moulding itself to the back of my neck.

How can I act natural when he's kissing the hell out of me in a very public place?

My mind screamed the questions, but my body didn't care. My hands slid up the front of Danny's shirt, around his shoulders. I dug my nails in, just a little, the way I'd imagined so many times. His tongue lashed against mine, a growl vibrating from somewhere deep inside his chest as it rose toward the surface.

Every inch of me tightened as I sank into him. His hands slid down my sides, over my ass, and he pulled me against him, leaving me in no doubt that he wanted me. A small noise tore from my throat, and he swallowed it, softening his hold, trailing kisses across my jaw. Nearby, someone coughed, but I didn't care. I could stay in his arms forever.

Danny's lips brushed my cheek, the sensitive spot between my ear and my neck.

"Luke's watching us." His hands tightened on me. "Keep your eyes closed. Enjoy it." His teeth grazed my throat, and it was all I could do not to moan in pleasure.

"You had better make sure you do something about this, Danny. You're driving me crazy," I murmured against his lips as he returned his mouth to mine. "This whole situation is crazy."

"I know. Get in my truck, and make it look like you want to fuck me the whole damned way. I won't have him following you home."

I'd been about to say it was no problem, but my blood ran cold at his words.

"Belinda is at my place. Will he hurt her if he finds her?"

Danny raised his head, looking straight into my eyes. My breath disappeared, and I begged myself not to panic.

"My truck. And when I get you alone again, I *am* going to fuck you."

My heart raced again, my mind whirling. "Tell me you said that so I wouldn't be so terrified." I leaned up, nipping his lip lightly as he started walking again, towing me along. It was playacting, right? Just all play-acting, I reassured myself. His hands ran across my back with a delayed urgency, pulling me closer into him.

At his truck, he picked me up, lifting me over the roll cage door. I shrieked as I plopped into the seat. The seatbelt wouldn't cooperate, my trembling hands fumbling on the strap, and then the clasp.

Danny stepped into his truck and reached around me, pulling the belt tight against my chest. Then his mouth was on mine again. He gripped my knee, fingers sliding quickly upward, following the line of my tights, until he had his hand almost completely wrapped around my upper thigh. I couldn't help the moan that built up in me, tearing free against his mouth as he wrenched my legs apart.

"Danny, he can't see us here?" It was a question — I had no idea where Danny's crazy housemate was.

"Fuck him. I want you." He palmed my stomach, pressing me back into the seat, his thumb stroking my inner thigh.

"Not here. Danny," I placed my hand over his, holding it against my leg. His relentless gaze captured mine, his thumb flicking out, brushing over the core of me. I gasped, gripping his wrist tighter against the whirl of sensation and emotions rioting through me, "please," I whispered.

I wasn't even sure what I was asking. If he'd told me to strip, I knew I would, without question.

Danny rubbed circles on my inner thigh, then drew back, brushing his lips over mine. Eyes hooded, he paused a hairbreadth from me, and I stopped breathing.

"Gods, you're testing me, girl." He gave my seatbelt a final tug, and leaned back, slapping the steering wheel lightly, and started his truck. "I don't even know where to take you."

"My place?"

"Hell, no. I won't have him following us back there. I can't take you to the office either." He put the truck in gear, and stilled, then grinned. "I'm taking you home."

"I thought you just said you can't–"

"Not your home. *My* home."

I looked at him, more confused than ever. Was he taking me to the house he shared with Luke? The thought of being near him sickened me. How could he even concentrate? My heart was still racing from the way he'd touched me.

Everything ran about in my head until I couldn't focus on anything at all.

"How do you deal with this– this life?" I whispered.

I pressed my thighs together, wiping sweaty palms on my tights. Danny glanced over, following my movement, and grinned. He dragged his gaze along my body. I took a shuddering breath that did nothing to calm me. My nerves jumped around, haywire from the entire situation.

His hand wrapped around mine, squeezing tightly. "You'll be okay."

I nodded, biting my lip, but I doubted it. Something had changed, and I couldn't work out where anything was headed right now. Danny shifted, pulling me closer across the wide vehicle, and drove in silence.

CHAPTER EIGHTEEN

DANNY

We drove for half an hour to reach the edge of the city. I took a smattering of extra turns, checking my rear vision mirror constantly to ensure no one followed us. Laura never said a word, sitting quietly, lost in her own thoughts, her hands clenched tightly in her lap. Finally satisfied that we were off Luke's radar, I turned away from the city limits. Skyscrapers and residential apartment buildings fell away into a smatter of agricultural farms and larger homes.

I turned onto a dirt road, flicking on the radio. Laura leaned back in her seat, the picture of relaxation, though her fingers remained tightly entangled in mine.

"You okay? Laura?" She didn't respond, staring straight ahead. I flicked the indicator on and pulled off onto the grassy verge. I squeezed her hand, pulling her to face me. She was pale, and her fingers tremored just a bit in mine. "Babe, you gotta tell me."

"You live like this, all the time." Her eyes lifted to catch mine, filled with unshed tears. "You must be exhausted." She placed her fingers gently on my cheek, running them gently down my neck.

I shivered, staring at her in wonder. Here I was, thinking she was terrified out of her mind from what had just happened — what *I* had done — while the whole time, she was worried about me.

"It takes getting used to," I acknowledged. "The first time I was under was only a few days. I had a headache the whole time and ran on pure adrenaline. The guys thought I was on speed, I talked so damned fast." I laughed at the memory, but Laura's face never changed.

Her fingers slipped inside the neck of my shirt, sliding against my skin. I stirred at her touch.

"This is why they want you to change," she murmured. "They want you to have stability, a future. A home." Laura smiled. I mulled on her words and didn't like the taste they left in my mouth.

It seemed like every time I turned around, someone was trying to change the way I lived, the way I saw things. It irritated me to no end.

You were thinking the same way.

I put the truck in gear, heading up the familiar road. I might have been thinking the same way, but it would be nice to get there on my own, first.

The house was white and freshly painted. I hadn't been around to help look after it for months, thanks to being on assignment, but that was pretty accepted around here. I killed the engine, sitting silently, appreciating the quiet away from the never-ending chatter of the city.

Here, the only engine was the cherry picker, working the orchard in season.

"They're trying to look out for you." Laura was still working through my career when I had left it behind at the city limits.

"I know. And — I understand. We're family. I'm just feeling...pushed."

Laura nodded as the front door opened. I was out of the truck, leaving my keys in the ignition, before the dark head of hair that matched my own cleared the front step.

"Daniel!"

I engulfed my mother, picking her up to kiss her cheek. Tiny and birdlike, I was always terrified I'd break her. She fussed as I set her down, brushing at my shirt.

"It's good to see you."

"You should have called," she scolded, "and maybe wear more clothes."

"I was at the gym."

Soft footsteps on the gravel reminded me. "Mum, I brought– uh, this is Laura."

I stumbled over the introduction, with no clear idea of how to present her. Which was better: *this is my professional development coach who I've been fobbing off and flirting with mercilessly,* or *this is the girl I nearly fucked in the front seat of my truck less than an hour ago?*

Neither was something I could ever say to a mother. Not mine, at any rate.

"Hi, Mrs M– Woods," Laura corrected herself hastily, glancing my way with wide eyes. I smothered a laugh, and those aqua blues narrowed. I may have overdone the fake cough thing on our walk.

Mum smiled broadly, catching Laura's arm. "Hello, Laura. Come along, Daniel. We have lots to catch up on." She towed Laura towards the house, and added in a whisper, "you must tell me where my boy has been for the last six months. I don't hear anything from him when he's on these assignments. He worries me."

"You know I can hear you," I called, shaking my head.

They disappeared into the house. I grabbed a bag of washing from the back of the truck. I'd meant to do it but now seemed as good a time as any. Luke's place had a laundry, but I liked my things cleaned separately from everyone else's. I didn't have many personal hang-ups, but that was a firm one.

Getting my own place was looking better all the time. Maybe I really should listen to my boss. I looked up at the large, two-story country house. Beams of Jarrah ran the length of the verandah, their pinkish hue standing out against the white of the house.

I missed the place. Living in the city was handy for work — for everything I needed — but the quiet out here was something I lacked at– well, maybe *home* wasn't the best choice of words.

Mum was talking Laura's ear off when I found them in the kitchen, both pouring over a cookbook. Laura flicked from page to page while mum scurried around, locating the ingredients she called out.

"You two made friends fast." I was a little disturbed by the speed with which my mother seemed to have attached herself to Laura.

"We're fine here." I had to look up to check it was Laura who was speaking to me. "You do whatever your plan was."

I had a plan? It was news to me. I leaned against the door frame with my arms folded. There was no chance I was leaving these two alone together. "What are you up to?" I asked Mum as she whizzed past, hands full of vegetables.

"Your father is out in the yard. Take him these." She placed a large plastic box full of old corks in my hands, liberating my washing as she shooed me out of the kitchen. "I'll get this done. Off you go."

I stared after her, catching Laura's amused expression over her shoulder. I grinned ruefully. Maybe I had bitten off more than I'd expected; the two of them together were a formidable team — and they'd only just met. Perhaps I'd have more luck with Dad.

I headed out across the yard, aiming for the shed, but that was empty. I left the box of corks on his workbench — whatever he was using them for, they'd be safe there.

A yell echoed from the depths of the orchard. I jogged across the open paddock, glad of the dense shade the old trees afforded as the heat rose from the well-mulched ground.

"Dad?" I yelled. A muffled reply came from several rows back. I wound my way through to find Dad crouched on the ground, poking at the base of a cherry tree. "What are you doing?"

I joined him on the ground. A dark knot oozed thick sap. I looked into the canopy — the leaves of this tree were wilted compared to its neighbors. Dad sighed.

"This one will have to go."

"Rot?"

"And something else. Can't let it take hold."

I nodded — Dad hated "killing" his trees, but ultimately was a pragmatist. If it had to go, he would do it.

"It's only one tree."

Dad looked at me like I'd suggested sacrificing his sister. I smothered a grin.

"Mum sent you a box of corks."

"Thanks." With no other explanation, Dad rose, dusting dirt from his already-grime-covered jeans. "Haven't heard from you in a while. Your mother gets antsy."

We walked back to the work shed, the sun beating down.

"On assignment." Dad didn't say a word, staring steadfastly across the paddock, bright green with new growth. "I brought someone with me. She needed to get away."

"You left her with your mother?" A grin spread over his face. "We'll know all the state secrets before dinner then."

I groaned — Mum was the queen of interrogation. Killed you with kindness and food, until you opened your soul to her.

"Damn. I didn't think of that."

"How's work?" We reached the workshop. Dad popped the top of the box I'd brought down that contained the corks, lining them up neatly on the scarred bench. Tools went out next.

"It's okay. Had some issues with the boss. Laura — the girl I brought with me — has been coaching me, career development. Assignment's a bit wonky. Need to work on a new angle." I couldn't say more, and he knew that. "What the hell are you doing?"

Dad made a cut in each of the corks with a small blade and began running lathes through the centre.

"It cleans them. Nothing works well if it's coked up. Gotta clean it back so what's there is useful." He rubbed the tools until they came up much cleaner than before. "So, they want you to...what, move departments?"

I shook my head. "Cal wants me to specialise. Laura thinks I should be aiming for Liam's job."

Dad worked in silence for some time. I looked around the shed filled with a random assortment of tools and car parts; it was the collection of a lifetime — Dad's lifetime. I picked out a few old items Micah would have loved.

"Sounds like a smart girl."

"Smarter than me." I grinned. Dad put the corks down, lining the tools up in their holders above the workbench.

"Maybe you should take the advice."

"Management isn't for me. I can't sit still for that long. You know that."

"Might get you what you want."

"What I want is undercover assignments. Getting into someone else's head, working through strategy."

"Is it?" Dad pushed his hands into his pockets, walking towards the house. I stared at the neat row of tools. I couldn't help thinking he'd been trying to send me a message without actually telling me — Dad's typical way of communicating.

I had no idea how Mum put up with him — I'd left home at seventeen, and we got along a lot better, now. I followed him down to the house, the smell of something incredible led me by the nose. I never usually deciphered his meanings until well after I needed them.

The kitchen was clattering with plates and chatter when I walked in — Mum and Laura debating what best to serve steaks and roasted vegetables on. I stared — surely, we hadn't been out in the orchard that long. I checked my watch — it was nearly dinner time.

"What did you make? It smells amazing."

Laura looked up with a smile. "Your mum has been too scared to use the settings on the oven. I told her to blame me if it all went haywire."

I looked at the oven. "She's had that for five years."

"And has barely used it. She's terrified of all the new buttons."

"I'm sure it came with an instruction manual," I muttered, running a hand through my hair and came up with an assortment of twigs and cherry leaves. "I'm going to wash up."

Laura nodded, intent on counting out portions of roasted parsnips. I wandered down the hall, breathing in the smells of being home. I paused with my hand on the bathroom light, the contrast of my small, boxed life versus the warmth of the home I'd grown up in hitting me in full.

Laura had tried to tell me. Liam and Cal had both given me a heads up that the undercover work I'd been doing wasn't sustainable. They tried to give me a prod in the right direction, not just my career, but my life. Hell, even Dad had brought it up, in his own round-about way, and probably had been for a long time.

I hadn't listened to any of them. The thought of heading back to the house I shared with four other men I didn't know or like filled me with a pang for something I didn't realise I'd been missing — some sense of home or belonging.

I didn't even bother to organise my own rental properties. It was like I suddenly didn't belong anywhere — and I definitely didn't belong in either Cal's or Liam's jobs. I thought of Laura, so contained and organised. She knew exactly where she belonged in her world, while I didn't even have a world to belong in.

I washed in the dark, unable to look at myself in the mirror.

CHAPTER NINETEEN

LAURA

I felt him the moment he walked into the room. Glad his mum had left me to set the dining table several rooms away, as my body instantly responded to his presence.

I kept my head down, concentrating on dividing vegetables across the plates, too used to feeding only myself or my sister. Mostly, I ate out, and cooking with Danny's mother was something of a luxury.

My parents never cooked — both academics, they either both ate out or didn't eat at all. Belinda and I had both been black sheep on our family tree, filled with mathematicians and professors at various universities around the world.

Neither of us held a degree, but enough determination to achieve whatever we wanted — for me, a successful business; for Belinda, her next high.

"Last of the potatoes — do you want the extra few?" I addressed Danny, though I hadn't acknowledged him yet. Largest in the family, I guessed he'd take a fair bit of filling up. A seed began to sprout on what I'd like to do on our date.

"How did you know I was here?" He was closer than I'd expected.

I whirled around, waving a serving spoon threateningly. "Let me finish up."

Danny's hands landed on my waist, pulling me against him, and pressed his lips gently to mine.

I melted.

He caught the spoon as I dropped it, deepening the kiss for a moment before pulling away. I mewled softly when cool air replaced the warmth of his mouth. His eyes were dark, but not with the desire of this morning. More... Haunted. I ran my fingers across his cheek, lightly scraping through his hair to his scalp. His lids drifted shut for a brief moment, and when they opened again, his mask was back in place.

"What's wrong?" I whispered, checking over my shoulder, but there was no one else in the room.

Something in the way he held his shoulders — wound tight like an over-tensioned instrument — said he wanted to keep whatever ran around his head to himself. I prayed I wasn't prying too much, seeing as it was only this morning that I'd slapped him, twice. My hand returned to his cheek, gently this time.

"I missed you," he murmured, kneading his fingers into the back of my neck like he had that night at the beach. I arched into him, my head tipping back with the bliss that spread across my shoulders. Heavenly. My eyes snapped open, and I flicked my head up too fast.

"Stop distracting me." I tapped his shoulder with one hand, the other pressed to my temple. "Ow."

Huge arms engulfed me, and I was pressed hard to his chest, the steady rhythm of his heart beating against my cheek.

"Glad to have you back. Honestly," Danny added as I extracted myself to look him full in the face, unconvinced.

Nancy bustled in, smiling at us. I broke away from Danny's embrace, embarrassed — physical contact was frowned upon in my family home. She shook her head, waving us away as she collected plates. Danny hooked his arm around my waist, drawing me back to him. I loved that he needed to touch me, filling some void I didn't know was empty.

"She won't mind — she'll be glad I've met someone worth bringing home."

I frowned. "But you've had plenty of girlfriends."

"I've had plenty of flings," he corrected me, sliding his fingers slowly down my arm to capture my hand. I wondered if he would take as much time in bed.

A shiver passed through me at the thought of his hands on my bare skin, and my cheeks heated under his knowing gaze.

He leaned in, brushing his lips over mine. "I've never brought a girl home before, Laura."

The way he said my name, full of meaning and promise sent my senses tingling. I barely processed his words.

"Oh," was all I could manage as he drew me to the dining table.

Danny stopped, a hand on my shoulder, "Dad–"

"We've met." Trevor smiled at me, nodding to his son, "while you were off doing your hair."

A giggle escaped me. I couldn't help it. Danny rolled his eyes good-naturedly and pulled out a chair. I sat, unused to the old-fashioned values he often displayed, so at odds to his minimalist outlook on life.

Dinner passed in a blur of childhood stories and escapades, many of which left Danny red in the face. I hugged Trevor and kissed Nancy's cheek as we left with promises to return soon.

Danny's truck roared to life, ripping into the silence of the settled farmland.

"Thanks for bringing me here," I murmured, waving goodbye. Danny gripped my hand briefly, then dug around in the back, finally tossing me a zip-up hoodie.

"You'll need that." He grinned, and I could just see his face outlined in the glow from the dashboard.

He was right. Frigid air rushed into the open cab as we drove back to the city. The quiet countryside slowly filled in, and a sense of loss filled me as the chatter returned. I managed to get the jacket on beneath my seatbelt, snuggling into the feeling that he was all around me. Danny still sat in the gym singlet he'd worn since this morning.

"You must be freezing!" I exclaimed, trying to give the jacket back. He shook his head firmly, retaking my hand, his thumb rubbing over my knuckles.

"Nah, I'll be alright."

"Fine, Hulk," I grumbled, squeezing his fingers. His grip tightened, and for a moment, I thought he would say something, but he subsided into a dark silence I didn't dare break.

The city lights came into full view before he shared his thoughts.

"When this is over — this job, I want to do two things. First, I'm taking you on that date I promised." He looked across at me with mischievous eyes. Heat flared in my cheeks, and I was glad of the darkness.

"And secondly?"

"Second, I want to– Laura, will you help me find somewhere to live?"

I swivelled in my seat, wide-eyed. "You're settling down?"

He shrugged, and I could see the offer sat uncomfortably on him. This was not a man used to asking anyone for anything — let alone requesting assistance for something that was evidently quite intimate to him.

"Just a rental, for now. Cal usually picks them. I've never cared before what they looked like, where they were. But I'd like to find out what I want," he squeezed my hand tightly, "and maybe one day I'll buy something. When I know where I'm at."

His voice was rough and raw. I squeezed back, my heart warming.

"I would love to help you."

"Thanks." He glanced briefly at me then back at the road. "I've got no idea what to look for."

"We can work on that. Danny, does this mean," I hesitated, hating to drop into work-mode while he was laying his heart out, "that you're going to drop undercover work after you've finished this job?"

I held my breath. Then, his head jerked once.

"Yeah."

I bit my lip so that I didn't launch out with a victory scream, but sedately squeezed his hand and smiled into the darkness, proud of my restraint.

Danny asked for directions to my house. I frowned but gave them anyway.

"What about my car?"

He gave me a sideways glance, jaw tight.

"I– uh, got Micah and Ally to collect it hours ago."

"How did Micah fit in my car?" Danny didn't answer, seemed to be waiting for something. The penny dropped. "Wait, how did he start it? Did he tow it?"

"No, he would have, uh, hotwired it." Danny shifted uncomfortably. My eyebrows rose.

"He hotwired my car." I sat quietly for a moment. "Is it always going to be like this; you doing things without asking me?" My emotions ranged from outraged at his high handedness to amused. I shook my head. "You could have asked. There's a spare magnetised to the underside of the chassis."

Danny's lips twitched.

"You're kidding."

"Nope."

He burst out laughing. I grinned ruefully.

"We have to fix that." He stopped laughing, shaking his head. "That's a huge security risk. You know that."

"Probably. But Belinda has needed the car, and it seemed safer to do that than give her a key she'll lose anyway."

"Aren't you scared she might wreck the car?"

"She's my sister. I'd prefer she were safe and able to walk away from a situation, rather than be stuck there, unable to get away. Like you, with Luke. What are you going to tell him?"

Danny shrugged. "Dunno. I'll make something up."

"Are you scared?"

A pause. "No."

"Worried?" I pressed.

"Yeah. It'll be fine."

Danny pulled up the front of my house, leaning across me. My car was parked tidily in the driveway. Micah had done well, I thought, considering my car was an eighth the size of his monster truck.

"Nice place." He leaned an arm across the seatback, surrounding me in a wall of muscle. He smelled faintly of salty sweat and a smokey sort of flavour.

I started to shrug out of his jacket. "Here. You'll need this back. You must be freezing." He shook his head, pulling it back onto my shoulders.

"Keep it. It looks good on you." His face in the shadow, he rested his forehead against mine. "It'll be a while before I see you again. Be safe. If anything happens, call Cal, or Micah. Or Black. They'll look after you." He traced the line of my face, winding my hair around his fingers.

"I don't need–"

"Please, Laura," he brushed his fingers over my lips, "You know what Luke's capable of — I don't want you anywhere near him. Let me finish this job."

"I will, but–"

His lips pressed against mine, his tongue brushing my lips. I sighed, letting him in. Every time I let my guard down with this man, something happened to bring it back up again. I wanted — needed — this time to be different. His arms wound around me. There was a click as my seat belt was undone and he pulled me closer, deepening the kiss. Bolts of liquid pleasure raced through me.

I memorised every line of his face with my hands, traced the shape of his shoulders. I sank into him until the world disappeared around us.

He drew back, the gap between us widening as he began to shut down, retreating behind the mask he lived in. He kissed me once more, squeezing me tightly.

"Promise you'll come back to me." My breath caught, I stumbled on the words.

His eyes dark, he didn't move for a moment.

"I'll see you soon."

"Laura, got a minute?"

Cal's head popped in at my office door. I nodded, typing notes frantically before I lost my train of thought. Cal waited patiently until I finished.

"Sorry. Had to get that out."

Cal nodded. "Danny called last night. Was everything okay at your place? Your car?"

"Perfectly," I smiled. "Nothing damaged."

"Tell me if that changes, please. We're family here, Laura. You're a part of that, now." I nodded. Danny had said something similar last night, but I hadn't really known what it meant. Cal rubbed his hand over his head. "And...I wanted to apologize. We didn't keep you in the loop, all assuming you knew from each other. We didn't look after you. I'm sorry."

It was a genuine apology.

"Thanks, Cal. It was a mix-up, that's all. But..." I trailed off, not wanting to seem bitchy with the next part. Cal raised an eyebrow, so similar to Liam. I hid a smile. "Your receptionist, Ally, she made it sound like Danny had left me — as a client and more...more personally, too." Cheeks flaming, I outlined my encounters with the blonde, hoping I hadn't misread the entire situation in my distress.

Cal listened carefully, nodding. "Thanks. Danny noted a few things about her as well. I'll speak to her."

My relief must have been obvious, as Cal crossed the room, hugging me. I squeezed back.

"If Luke contacts you, or you feel anyone watching you — call me right away. Here are all our numbers." He placed a handwritten card on my desk with all their numbers listed.

I picked it up, nodding. Something in my chest grabbed, and I couldn't breathe for a moment. No one else ever looked after me — and knowing how much Danny cared after last night, this was almost overwhelming.

"Thanks, Cal," I whispered, my voice straining.

"Put the numbers in your phone and destroy the card. Black's is a burner phone for a case, but he'll take the call if he sees your number come up. It's got Danny's new number for when he's back." He gave me a long look. "You've been good for him. Last night's call was a...revelation." He grinned, knocking his fist on my desk, and left, the door closing with a soft click behind him.

Tears trembled on my lashes as he left. I blinked them back furiously, confused. I wanted to bury myself in my work, but I also wanted to bury myself in Danny's chest, to feel his arms around me, and never let go.

I dug around in my tote beneath my desk, extracting his jacket. The all-male scent of him enveloped me. I breathed — my chest loosening — and managed to hide in my work for a few more hours.

CHAPTER TWENTY

DANNY

I sat outside the front of the rental house I shared with Luke for a full minute after parking my car — any longer, and he'd know something was up. That was one of the first rules of undercover work — never let them see your emotions. Not the real ones, anyway. Only let them see what you wanted them to see.

Luke saw far too much for my liking. Maybe Cal was right — he 'd warned me last night to play it cool and walk away if I deemed it necessary. I was grateful for the leniency, but I was unlikely to use it.

I'd been lucky when I'd come in last night. The house was empty, and no one had crawled out of their beds until well after I left for a run and to hit the gym. It was time to face the music. Luke wouldn't wait forever for an answer, and regardless of the care we'd taken in moving Laura's car, I was worried he'd managed to follow us. I didn't want a repeat of what had happened in Cal's apartment during Operation Niffler, especially with a woman I cared for so much.

But she was a temptation, a distraction. And right now, I needed my head set well on my shoulders if I was to convince Luke I wasn't a threat.

There were no other vehicles in the drive, but that didn't mean no one was home. I opened the door, listening for telltale sounds of habitation as I entered the small house.

The air conditioning was set to *blizzard* when I walked in — a sure sign Luke was home. Had he parked his car out the back to keep me on edge? Something in my gut had me worried. Hell, I was getting as paranoid as Cal, back when he was chasing Logan.

The bugger about that was that *his* gut had been right.

Luke leaned with his back against the kitchen counter when I entered, an open beer in his hand, half-empty even though it was only eleven in the morning. An unopened one sat on the bench beside him, condensation pooling around its base.

His eyes tracked me as I slapped my gym bag down on the table, extracting my sweaty clothes.

"Sorry I dashed off on you, man."

"No problem." He swigged the beer, and I could feel the weight of his gaze, assessing me. *Shit.* I was going to have to get my story straight. He nodded at me. "Girl gave you some nice facial decorations."

I grinned, knowing there were no marks on my face. I'd made a point of checking this morning, though I'd definitely earn any stripes she'd wanted to deal out. "Yeah, she's got a good swing on her."

"Good ass, too."

 I sent him a mock glare.

"Hands to yourself, bro. Girl's mine."

Luke snorted.

"Sure about that? Bit of a love-hate relationship, huh. You straighten your shit out with her?"

"Yeah." I nodded, still digging around in the bottom of my bag for nothing at all.

Come on, motherfucker. Stop making me wait.

Luke straightened. "So, Woods. Not the name I see on my lease papers."

I ducked my head, pretending to fidget around in my bag. This had to come out slow, or he wouldn't believe the lie.

"Bad family. I kept Mum's name. Don't wanna talk about it."

I bundled my clothes under my arm, slinging my gym bag over my shoulder. Luke held out an arm to stop me as I tried to get to my room. I realised he'd planned the move, setting himself between the front door and the hallway I had to access to get to my room. The big bastard was definitely smarter than I gave him credit for.

He levelled me with a look.

"You know what goes on here, man. I don't give a fuck if it's a long sob story. Tell me."

Convince me.

I held his gaze that told me the truth of his words. He didn't care for the sob story.

"No sob story, dude. Just a father that beat the fuck outta my mother each night 'til I was big enough to send him to hospital and drive away with her and my sister afterwards." I gave him a tight smile, shifting my bag on my shoulder in an uncomfortable shrug. "What can I say, my Mumma cooks good."

A grain of truth in every lie, though I borrowed heavily from Micah's history.

Luke paused for a moment, holding my stare. This dude's control issues were out of this world. He and Cal should have a showdown.

"You never changed it? Legally."

I laughed at him, but his face never changed. *Hard ass.*

"Did you just use that word around me? Seriously, dude, I'm not good at keeping track of anything, let alone doing something that permanent."

I stopped myself before I said any more. The key was to keep the lie alive, and not embellish past what it needed to be believed.

Luke was still for a moment longer, then he slowly nodded, rolling his shoulders as though nothing important had just happened.

"Yeah, right. Listen, that job we talked about — I wanna jump into it. Get the framework started tonight, work out what we're up against. You still in?"

I shrugged, easy. "Yeah, I could use the money."

"Good. 'Cause Zahn's going to eat you alive. You're lead — we'll work from your plan on this."

"My plan? I thought this was your job?" I let him see my surprise — it was completely genuine.

Why would he want me to take point on this?

The only thing I could think of was so if it all came crashing down, I'd take the heat and go to prison for it. That wouldn't happen, but he didn't need to know that.

"You got the skills. After what I saw the other night, you could give me a run for my money." He smiled with thin lips. I returned it, but worms wriggled in the pit of my belly. *Something's not right here.*

"No worries, man. Give me the info; I'll start working on it."

Luke nodded and removed the arm that barred my way. I headed down the hall, wondering how deep the rabbit hole went.

"Okay, here," Zhan pointed at the screen, lines of code scrolling through as he noted the changes I'd made out to Luke. "Stop. That one won't work." He folded his arms across his chest, glaring at me smugly.

I'd worked on the hack for three full days, and my butt was numb.

"Really? Hundreds of lines of original code, and you pick on that." I leaned forward, making sure it was right before I dug myself a hole I couldn't climb out of, looking for a distraction. Zhan *had* managed to pick out the single function I'd added in to track the money they would remove. This was going to get tricky. *Time to use the scapegoat.* "Wait — isn't that the portion Justin gave me? I thought he said half of it was yours."

"Sort your shit out. It's not a fucking kindergarten," Luke growled. Seeing as it matched my sentiments precisely, I stepped back, leaning on the doorframe to crack my back. Zahn started at the noise, and I sent him a sharp grin.

"Looks good," Luke muttered, running his finger down the screen. It flickered for a second, then he sat back. I frowned.

"What the hell did you just do?" I looked at Zahn, but he wasn't paying attention. No help there. I studied the screen, my mind racing, trying to figure out what Luke had done — and how he'd done it. "This— you added that in. Where did that come from?"

Luke folded his arms and leaned back, tight-lipped. I read through the code several times, my mind whirling. There was a lot of new stuff in there, and it could get the job done, completely untraced. I memorised as much as I could on the spot — something flickered in my memory. I was sure this had been used before, and I needed to take it back to Cal, though I didn't like the look of some of it.

I knew Luke hadn't been smart enough to pull this off alone — just as I was sure my code would work — but leave a stack of telltale markers that would alert security bots of the hack. How had he gotten it on there without me seeing it?

"This," I jabbed at the screen. "Where'd you get that? You're not smart enough to write it."

He stared at me, unmoving. I knew I wouldn't get answers now — I had to get Zahn out of the room. The whole thing felt wrong — and the last time I'd ignored a feeling like this, I'd woken up on Cal's foyer floor with a serious headache.

"Zahn, get me a beer."

"You don't drink beer, fuckhead."

"Then get one for your boss."

Zahn looked like he might object, mouth opening, likely thinking I meant me. I shook my head, indicating to Luke. Luke nodded without looking at him, and the little mini-me left.

I sat back in the chair I'd been in all day, my glutes protesting at being squashed out of shape for the fourth day in a row.

"Tell me."

Luke leaned back, examining the ceiling. "Tell you what."

"Where'd you get it?" Luke said nothing. "Who from?" I insisted, angry I hadn't worked this through earlier. I'd lost a lot of Luke's trust, thanks to the incident with Laura, and I wasn't sure he'd tell me bloody anything now. I held my foot from tapping as I waited, outwardly calm.

He has to speak first.

"It's just a job," he said finally, still staring at the ceiling.

I let it ride for a second, knowing I had to hit him where it hurt to get the answers I needed. My pocket buzzed, but I ignored it. *Not now.*

"Who's pulling your strings, Luke?" I asked softly.

He straightened in a hurry, glaring at me, though there had been no threat, no judgement in my tone. A simple statement of fact.

And he'd reacted to it.

He rolled his shoulders, but I knew he was unsettled. He didn't like the idea that someone else was in control of him. It was all too easy to read his body language — I wished getting inside his head was as simple.

Luke was all about personal freedom — but I knew there was something I was missing, here. I held back a smile. Prison wouldn't suit him well, but he'd have to get used to it. I had a file as thick as my wrist on him — there was sufficient evidence to ensure he wouldn't have personal freedom for a very long time. But for now, I needed to get this from him.

"Name, man. I want to know who I'm working for."

No one moved. My pocket buzzed again; I ignored it. Luke scrubbed a hand over his face, his foot tapping. I tried not to hold my breath as I waited — but patience in this arena was something I had in spades.

Finally, he nodded, leaning forward, elbows on his knees.

A can came flying through the doorway, and I caught it by reflex. Another launched over Luke's head. He didn't bother to lift a hand, letting it hit the chair on his other side. Zhan swore, scrambling through the doorway and crouched down to collect it, muttering darkly.

A strange glint in Luke's eye told me I wasn't going to get the name from him tonight — possibly not ever. I growled as he stood, muscles popping across his shoulders. He sauntered out the door, plucking the beer can from my numbed fingers as he passed. Zhan came up with the other beer, looking around.

"Where'd he go?"

I shook my head, extracting my phone as it vibrated again. Micah's message trail was a mile long as I caught up, reading the bottom line several times to be sure of the meaning.

Mikey D: Fucking got fired. Gotta to move back in with the olds. See you when you're free.

I held back my reaction, not wanting Zhan to see a change in me when inside, I was seething. But it wasn't Micah I was cursing.

I was off the case.

CHAPTER TWENTY-ONE

DANNY

I crossed my arms as tightly as I could, shaking my head as Cal gestured at an empty chair in the incident room.

"I was doing fine," I spoke through gritted teeth, clenching those hard as I tensed the muscles across my back.

Cal nodded, eyes on me. Where I once would have felt the urge to move away from his stare, now I held my ground. I needed answers.

"You were. And it's good work."

"But?"

"But, you know the answer."

"Laura." Her name left my mouth in a hiss. Cal's turned down, and he gave a sharp nod.

"Yes."

"I had it fixed. You should have given me a chance to—"

"Did you?"

I canted my head, considering. "What do you know that I don't?"

"Ha. Not going there with you." But the corners of Cal's mouth lifted from their scowl. "You were made. If Luke hasn't figured it out by now, he will, soon. I'm not putting you — or Laura, now she's on his radar — back where the odds are against you."

My hands clenched into fists on my biceps.

"There's more going on there. I still don't know who Luke is working for—"

"I thought you said Luke was the top dog in this," Cal asked flatly, though it wasn't really a question. I'd filled him in on everything, to the smallest detail, but we hadn't got to the night he'd pulled me off the job. My patience with him hadn't lasted that long.

"The job I was working when Micah messaged me," Cal opened his mouth, and I held up a hand, "Luke wasn't planning it. He was working through someone else, and you pulled me out at a critical point."

I didn't share with Cal that the point had been critical because Luke wasn't going to tell me squat. I wanted back in, and I was sure this was my window.

Cal held his silence for over a minute. His eyes never left my face. I tried not to watch the seconds tick by on the wall clock behind him.

"Would he have told you who he was taking direction from?"

I ground my toe into the floor. *Damnit.*

"No."

"Then you're out," Cal sighed, standing. He had a few inches on my six feet. "You did good, Danny. Put the report in tomorrow. Get some rest; hit the gym. Do you need to take leave?"

"Nah, don't wanna end up like Liam."

Cal grimaced, and made his way to the door. He paused, one hand on the frame. "Do you need a place to crash? Your boxes are in my apartment."

I thought about those two lonely boxes in someone else's house, the conversation with Laura returning with a vengeance. I'd made do with what I had in my truck for the past six months at Luke's; I could survive one night with the bare minimum.

"I'll crash at Micah's."

"He's competing this weekend."

"Yeah?" My face finally cracked into a grin. "I might hit the track, then."

Cal nodded. "He could use some support. Don't stay late." He left the room, hustling Ally from her desk. I glanced at the wall clock — it was past eight. Ally was pulling long hours, but maybe she felt she needed to stay as long as any of us were in the office to secure her new job. Though she'd been here for six months now, I realised, scratching my jaw.

I had so much to catch up on. Maybe Cal had done me a favour, pulling me out early, though frustration still boiled in my chest. I might hit the bags downstairs before I left for Micah's. Pulling out my phone to text my best — and only — mate, the six-month hole in my life suddenly loomed very largely indeed.

Micah's place was locked when I knocked. Scuffing around with a loose brick in the footings, I withdrew a key wrapped meticulously in foil. Careful not to tear his neat work, I let myself in, making sure to replace everything just as it had been.

I walked across the expanse of the warehouse in the dark. I'd been here so many times, I could have found the stairs with my eyes closed.

The space felt enormous without Micah's truck dominating it. I was halfway up the stairs before the sense of home hit me, followed by a small wave of nausea. The only place I felt at home was in someone else's home. My offer to Laura hung in the air. I didn't regret it — but I wasn't entirely comfortable with it either.

My lungs constricted at the thought of her. I wasn't sure I would be able to face her without yelling at her. Even cold disdain. Not after today. I rolled my shoulders, but they were tight from too many fast rounds at the bag, and not enough cooling down. My knuckles burned when I clenched my fists. Maybe I'd gone a little too hard. I bounced on my toes, jogging to the top of the stairs.

I dumped my bag on the bench, still thinking about Laura. We'd just gotten back on track — was I really going to let my ego screw this one up? I decided I was, and to add to my pity party, I flopped onto the sofa — which would have been fine, if there hadn't been someone already on it.

A small shriek and a wriggling octopus of limbs flailed beneath me. With a curse, I stumbled back to my feet, tumbling into the railing of Micah's loft as I tripped on the edge of the shag-pile rug.

"Who the hell are you?" The high, thin voice was vaguely familiar. I scrounged in my pocket for my phone, lighting up the torch. Vibrant green hair surrounded a narrow, pale face in a short bob, which matched equally-green pyjamas. Eyes squinted, and a pillow lifted to block my view.

"Jimmy?"

"Yeah?" The voice returned muffled, and a laugh bubbled in my chest.

"Are you hiding behind a pillow?" I peered into the oddly-dark space, removing a pillow from the mousy young woman curled on Micah's sofa.

She nodded, brilliant green hair swaying around her face, bluntly cut at cheek level. Named Jacomina by some long-winded parent, she'd applied online at the track for a hydraulics engineer position as "Jimmy."

With qualifications off the chart, the mechanics team had been astounded when she'd walked in. Less than an hour later, she'd added to the efficiency of every truck on the track, and firmly ensconced herself into the tech team to boot. She and Micah had worked together since.

She wrapped her arms around herself, and I cursed, leaning over to flick on the overhead light.

"Oh. It's you."

She settled back on the lounge, pulling a thin blanket up to her neck.

"Aren't you freezing? And where's Micah?"

"He took the truck out with a few new guys on the circuit. I'm fine. It's colder at my place." She yawned, settling back.

"Ah, okay. I heard he was competing tonight."

Jimmy squinted up at me. "Uh-huh."

"So..." I wanted to dig around in her head as to why she was here, with the other part of my brain still trying to figure out where the hell I was going to sleep. I eyed the floor. The garishly red shag-pile rug was starting to look good.

"In case he breaks it. Can you turn the light off, please?"

"You're on his lounge in case he breaks his truck?" I echoed.

"S'what I said," the blanket mumbled, and I flicked off the light.

"Well, I'm– just, ah, going to crash..."

Where, exactly? I wasn't taking the big man's bed.

I flicked out my phone, checking my earlier messages to Micah. He'd definitely been fine for me to crash and hadn't said anything about Jimmy being in his house. I lay on the rug, twisting my back a few times, though it did nothing for the tension pinching in my shoulders.

Damn. I should have taken Cal's offer up for a bed. He was always happy to put me up for a few nights until there was a place ready for me to move into with my meagre belongings.

A wave of exhaustion washed over me as I lay in the dark, the day catching up with me, or maybe me with it. I shook my head. Laura's face floated across my vision, and I remembered kissing her in the park.

Sure, I'd played it up under Luke's eye — *fucking stalker* — but her response had been worth every moment. Her hands had curled around my shoulders almost possessively, and I'd wanted to lift her onto my hips, feel her legs wrapped around my waist.

But she'd also gotten me taken off the case. I sighed, adjusting myself. I could still taste her — a mix of the cinnamon from her dirty chai and something like vanilla. Guilty, I turned my mind from the sexy blonde in the presence of an — albeit sleeping — mechanic and turned my thoughts to Micah.

He rarely socialised, not really needing regular contact with other people. He was far from an introvert, just secure in his own skin. He knew who he was and what he wanted from life.

Lucky bastard.

Maybe that's why our friendship had lasted; I wasn't around enough to bother him. I cringed at the thought. Jimmy's earlier comment niggled though — that she was here in case he broke his truck.

Micah rarely damaged his monster. Even then, it was only in the toughest of competitions. What the hell was he doing that might involve breaking it — to the point he had a mechanic sleeping on his lounge?

I let exhaustion drag me deeper as the blanket began to snore.

A murmuring from somewhere below woke me. It took a moment before awareness — and feeling — rushed into me. Groaning, I rolled onto my side, trying to stand. Pins and needles stabbed my toes. It took three goes to get my legs working, and even then, they wouldn't cooperate with my stiff back.

My phone slipped out of my pocket, bouncing on the rug. I cursed. The voices stopped.

"You're awake," Micah boomed up to me, his voice echoing across the space. I peeked over the rail to see the blue roof of his monster truck parked in one corner.

"Want me to start on breakfast?" I yelled back, already heading for the fridge.

"Yes!" piped Jimmy, her high voice reaching me in both pitch and range.

I smothered a laugh; if they were talking trucks, the whole world could bypass Micah. I slugged water — my mouth felt like a critter had crawled in there overnight and died — and cracked half a dozen eggs into a bowl, hunting for a whisk.

By the time they came upstairs, I had toast and scrambled eggs laid out on plates.

"You're almost as efficient as me," Jimmy joked, managing to hop onto a stool before she inhaled her eggs. I piled mushrooms on her plate, and she grinned. Micah didn't bother sitting to eat.

"I'll take that as a compliment." I grinned back at Jimmy, then turned my attention to my friend. "Where were you last night?"

Micah raised his eyebrows. "Checking on me?"

I cringed. Making Micah uncomfortable wasn't quite the same as badgering anyone else — he never showed much emotion; it was just the way he was. Any reaction meant he'd taken the comment to heart — or was up to something. But it was his place, not mine, and I had no right to pry.

"Sorry." I filled my face with food to avoid stuffing my foot back into it.

"It's alright, man." Micah continued eating. His plate emptied quickly, and I refilled it with the last of the mushrooms and toast. He nodded his thanks. "I tried a few new things. Didn't work out." He sneaked a glance sideways. Jimmy kept her eyes on her plate, not reacting at all. My brow furrowed.

"What do you mean, didn't quite work out?" I asked slowly.

Micah lifted one shoulder.

"Ah, I sort of–"

"Broke his truck." Jimmy glared at him through a blunt curtain of seaweed-green hair. Micah had the grace to look sheepish.

"Well, yeah."

I looked between them as the air turned brittle. They'd never fought, or even bickered before, so far as I knew. The two were so close in how they worked, everything seemed to run smoothly.

Until now.

Studying Jimmy, I noted dark circles that hadn't been there the night before beneath her eyes.

"What time did you get back last night?" I asked casually.

"Bout two," Micah spoke around a mouthful of food. Considering how much was jammed in there, I was impressed he could speak at all, let alone contain its contents.

"Mm. You been up since then, right?" I directed my question at Jimmy. She nodded at the remains of her food. I removed the empty plate from her as soon as she finished and pointed to the lounge. "We're gonna leave you alone up here. Get some rest."

"But I've got to–"

"You have all day. We can take my truck. Fix the monster when you're more awake."

Jimmy caught my eye and gave a quick nod, slipping under the blanket. She rolled onto her side, turning her back to us. I gestured at Micah.

"Five minutes, and we're outta here." I eyeballed him.

The big guy nodded silently, following me down the stairs in less than the time I'd allotted both of us to get back to the office.

I could see the damage to his truck by the time I'd made it down the stairs. Scratches marred the bodywork, and there was a dint of the roof. Had he rolled the damned thing? I kept my thoughts to myself until we were out of earshot of Jimmy. The girl clearly needed to get some rest.

As soon as we hit the end of his street in my truck, I let loose.

"What the hell were you thinking? She might be a techie, but hell, man — she needs sleep."

"I'm sorry Cal dragged you off the case."

My teeth ground together. "That was a low blow." Micah didn't look at me. "What the hell's going on?"

"Just trying some new things is all."

"New things that wreck your truck."

"It's my truck." For the first time, he sounded like a petulant child.

"I'm nagging, huh?"

"A bit."

"I'll stop."

Micah laughed at me. I fought my own grin, glad as the tension dissipated into the pre-rush hour traffic of the city. Melbourne wouldn't wake for another good hour or more, the crisp air around us a testament as to why we rose and worked late.

"How'd I get taken off the case?" I asked casually.

The smile faded from Micah's face. "Cal didn't say?" He twisted in his seat, rubbing his shoulders against the back of the chair when I shook my head.

"Not really."

"Shit." Micah turned away from me, and I held back an urge to thump him. Just.

I hissed my breath through clenched teeth, knowing the answer before I asked the question.

"Laura?"

"Yeah."

"He go to her, or did she come to him?"

"She came up to see him."

She'd fucking blindsided me. I slammed my hands on the top of the steering wheel. "Fucking hell."

Micah turned to face me — no mean feat for a dude his size. "She cares about you, man. Just looking out for you."

"I was at a critical point," I growled.

"Yeah, and we can use what you got. That code you brought back — that's something else. We can get the answers through that."

"Yeah, and if we don't?" I ground my teeth together. "I was that close. So close to getting what I needed."

"What you needed for what?"

I snapped my head to the side, earning myself a cricked neck. "What?"

"Did you want to close it off to finish the job, or to earn Cal's good opinion of you?" Micah's eyes were clear, and no malice rested in his face. I snorted softly, turning my attention back to the traffic. He really was the Luna Lovegood of cops.

"Am I that transparent?"

Micah nodded in my peripherals. "Maybe to me."

"Wish I could see the world your way."

"No, you don't." Surprised at the sadness in his voice, I glanced back at him, but he stared ahead at the road, already beginning to clutter with cars. "Are you going to see her?"

I remembered the feel of her beneath my hands, the urge ripping through me to spend hours memorising every curve on her. She was a world-class distraction, and she'd already cost me far too much.

"No."

CHAPTER TWENTY-TWO

LAURA

I stopped a block from my office to get another dirty chai and a few bento boxes for lunch. It would be a hell of a day with few breaks if I followed Cal's plan. He'd called last night and laid out what he had in mind. It had kept me awake through the quiet hours, my brain turning over with possible avenues to explore.

And he'd let me know Danny was back.

"Thanks, Hiro." I waved to the old man who had run the sushi train for as long as I could remember. He nodded, smiling close-lipped as I headed off, snuggling my collection of boxes. I couldn't be bothered moving my car, and a block wasn't far to walk.

I stepped lightly into the foyer of the office building we all shared and aimed for the elevator. The stairs were too risky with my tower of bamboo trays. The doors opened quickly, and I was glad not to have to wait.

As I waited for the doors to close, Micah strode past the open doors. He turned his head, spotting me and sent a quick grimace and a wave before he was gone, my greeting dying on my lips. Danny followed, mirroring his friend's actions almost to the T, but his eyes were filled with anger when they met mine.

"Danny," I called, as the doors began to close, but he disappeared from my view. I frowned, moving back as the elevator filled, floor to floor, and very nearly missed mine, lost in thought. He'd glared at me — I couldn't think of any reason, unless something had happened with Luke, because of me. A lump rose in my throat.

I unlocked my office, mechanically setting up for the day, my mind anywhere but on my job. I grabbed for my phone charger as it tumbled from my handbag. It skittered across the top of the desk and over the side. Walking around the back of my desk, I nearly tripped over two large boxes stacked one atop the other. I yelped, backing into the sharp corner, rubbing my backside as I studied them.

"What are these?" I peeked at the tag on the top. *Woods* stood out in large, heavy handwriting. "Are these...?"

"Mine."

Danny stomped into my office, tossing a pair of files onto my desk. Papers scattered the surface, and I scrambled on instinct to catch them before they followed the charger over the edge.

"I'm glad you're back. Four days have been too long–" I halted mid-sentence as I rose from my half-crouch. Danny stood close, his arms crossed over his chest, glowering down at me. For the very first time, I recognised how intimidating his physical presence was when he chose to use it.

"Why?"

I frowned. "Why what?"

"Why did you go to Cal?" he growled, not moving. I traced the chess pieces inked into his forearm arm with my eyes. The queen leaned on her side, defeated, a knight standing in the shadow, behind her. But the King stood tall, off to the side, almost insignificant, despite the sacrifice the queen had made. I'd never noticed it before. "Laura?" Danny prompted impatiently.

"Oh, Cal, I–" my train of thought was totally disrupted by him, and I found myself backing away. Danny's hand shot out, catching my elbow. I froze at the contact, tiny shocks sparking beneath my skin. His hold was firm; not the intimate way he'd touched me before, but not painful, either. I swallowed, trying to remember what he'd asked. "I went up to see him about your program. I hope you don't mind, but after seeing you at your parent's farm, I knew there was more to work through with you. To get you ready for, well," I gestured upstairs, "Whatever they have in mind for you."

"You got me thrown off assignment."

"What?" My jaw hung open. I squinted at him. "Are you sure?"

"Whatever you said to Cal, that was it. I was off the case after that. And I was this close, Laura," he held up two fingers, less than an inch apart, "this fucking close to finding out what the hell is going on." He ran his hand through his hair, leaving the short ends sticking up straight.

"And now you're off the case," I echoed softly, my mind racing. What had I said to Cal? I wracked my brain, but nothing stood out. Danny stared at me, face tight, eyes unforgiving.

"Now I'm off the case." His voice was low, and I knew whatever he felt towards me, it was well reined in. A shiver ran over me under the intensity of his gaze. I had to regain some control of this conversation.

"Danny, I'm really sorry," I stepped sideways, tugging my elbow from his grip. He released it, but tracked my retreat across the office, "I have no idea what I said. I never told him about seeing you, or Luke, or anything!" My voice rose a notch. I clamped my teeth together and bit my tongue.

"Fine. So, you're why I'm back here," he growled, sweeping the room with his arm. I massaged my tongue on the roof of my mouth to regain some feeling.

"Yes. There are some things you need to work through, and I thought we could start with–"

"You're not a shrink, Laura." Danny paced the room in long strides.

"No, but I–"

"So, you don't get to be inside my head. There's no room right now. Hell, I don't even know who I am outside of work!" His voice rose with frustration, his palm slapping the top of my desk, hard.

The slap resounded in the small space of my office, pages slipping from the files to tumble onto the floor.

"Did Cal send me your boxes?" I asked softly, beginning to piece together what Danny's boss really wanted from me. Danny rubbed a hand over his jaw, obscuring his face.

"Yeah."

I nodded, pushing one out of the way so I could sit at my desk. I flicked open my laptop and gestured to him. Danny stared at me; brow furrowed. I sighed.

"Grab a chair."

I brought up a stack of browsers, all listing different types of rentals around the city. Scrolling slowly, I dropped down menus, drawing ranges for price and suburb. After a moment, Danny slipped his big hands under mine with remarkable ease, turning the keyboard his way.

Typing faster than I would have given him credit for, he set the parameters for his new home, scooting his chair closer to mine so we could both see the results.

"That one's nice."

"Nah, too close to the pubs. Be rowdy as buggery on a Friday night."

"Okay...how about that one?" I pointed out a townhouse with a Victorian facade in the middle of the city. Danny grimaced, and I let him have control of the mouse.

"That one." He clicked on an apartment near the river that looked surprisingly well-priced for its location. I pursed my lips, scanning the photos the estate agent had provided.

"Does it have parking?"

Danny grinned, bringing up a picture of the undercover garage. "Looks like it used to be a loading dock. She'll fit." He grinned happily.

"Do you want me to make an appointment for you?" I didn't look at him as I asked, holding my breath. Danny had settled into the idea of finding a new place very quickly —

especially considering how angry he'd been. Asking him to set it all up for himself was a big step for a guy who had been almost shouting at me less than half an hour ago.

Danny didn't answer, and I risked a look at him, my stomach tight. To my surprise, he had his phone to his ear, waving me away when I opened my mouth. He paced the room slowly as he set up the appointment; not the long, angry strides of before, but a more considering pace.

I opened my calendar and started sorting appointments for myself, ready to free up time — if he wanted me to come with him, that was. He ended the call, and I brought up some documents quickly, pretending to read through them. He hovered at the corner of my desk, and I looked up.

"How'd you go?"

"He'll take me through tomorrow morning, just before lunch." He fidgeted with the edge of my desk, tracing patterns into it.

"That's great," I smiled, "This is a huge thing, Danny. I know–"

"Will you come with me?"

Danny stared down at me with worried eyes, capturing the edge of my desk in a death grip. I nodded, still smiling.

"Of course." I placed my hand over his, stiff with tension. "You can let go now."

"Oh. Sorry." He released my desk and stepped back, fingers twitching at his sides.

I'd seen him angry before, and dead calm when he was completely in control of something, but never nervous. All the plans I'd had to work through his PTSD — what I'd spent time working on the night before — went straight out the window. I'd become something of a minor expert on the topic, and I didn't need my notes if he was still happy to work with me. I took in his jeans and black muscle tee with a speculative eye.

"Do you have gym gear here?"

Danny stilled, eyes alight with curiosity. "Yeah. Why?"

"Let's go for a run."

I made no qualms about taking his truck, familiar by now with its personal brand of eccentricity. Danny was silent on the drive to the lake, reaching out once to grip my hand. He released it quickly before I could respond, but the tension which held his shoulders so straight drained visibly every few minutes. He flicked through music and put Jake Owen on.

"I wouldn't have picked you for a country boy," I mused, staring at the city rushing by, greenery growing closer.

"Good to know I can still surprise you."

"Are you still angry with me about..." I closed my mouth with a snap, careful to keep my tongue out of the way this time, cringing that I'd opened my mouth at all.

A muscle ticked in his jaw, but he shook his head. "Nah."

"Don't bullshit me, Danny Woods."

"Would I ever?" he said lightly, not looking at me.

I just shook my head, grinning.

He parked the truck quickly, snavelling a spot in the carpark that actually fit his truck.

"Got the parking fairy today."

"Must be the company. Don't you always get the one out front of the office?"

I smiled, but my heart was heavy, knowing he was still upset with me over whatever had happened with Cal. I needed to talk to him, but right now, I had a much larger

331

problem to tackle. In more ways than one — Danny's size still showed, even in the space his truck afforded.

He faced me, his arm sliding along the back of my seat. His fingers brushed my bare shoulders, exposed in my racerback singlet, and coated liberally with sunscreen. Just the proximity of him had me already on edge. The contact sent my skin into party mode, nerves jumping around everywhere. I unbuckled, sliding away from him.

Warming up quickly, I ran through in my head what I wanted to say — how I could get him to open up and work out for himself the issues being undercover was causing him. Plus, there was a good deal of self-worth he needed to come to terms with.

"You ready?"

I blinked, returning to the man in front of me, a light sweat already spreading a sheen across his shoulders. It was as though his body anticipated the workout.

"Sure," I returned, a glint in his eye telling me this wouldn't be an easy run. As long as we had time to talk — but in ten kilometres, who didn't have time to talk?

"Good." Danny strode away, and I trotted to keep up with him. We hadn't even reached the lake when he broke into a full run, and for a brief moment, I wondered if I'd be able to catch up with him. The soles of my shoes slapped the pavement as I got into stride, any lethargy dissipating with my quick steps.

Danny set a punishing pace, but my competitive side kicked in, and soon I'd fallen into step with him, my mind still a blur. By the time we were halfway around the lake, dodging other mid-morning runners, I'd given up trying to talk, keeping myself focussed on keeping in stride.

I risked a single glance at Danny, his body pouring sweat as it worked — a finely oiled machine. His brain was in as good condition, I knew, but the part of his mind that dealt with a sense of self and self-esteem needed retraining.

Somewhere in his many stints undercover, he seemed to have forgotten who he was and replaced it with the mask he wore more easily than his own identity.

I wanted to bring him back.

And that meant taking a step back. I wouldn't be able to see the big picture properly if I was too close.

"You doing okay, princess?"

I shot him a quick look, surprised to see we were already done. My chest heaved as we slowed to a quick walk. I checked my watch — we'd completed the circuit in an hour, flat.

"Not bad," I murmured, covering my loss of breath by smoothing non-existent loose hairs from my face. Sweat dripped from both of us; Danny's shirt clung to his body, outlining every ridge of carved muscle. I dragged my eyes away, wondering where to start.

"Good run," he filled the silence, though it was far from uncomfortable.

We'd fallen back into our usual rhythm — somewhere between comfortable and intimate.

"You needed that, huh?"

"Yeah. I did." Far from looking exhausted, Danny appeared more energised, though less on edge, than before.

"Shower?"

"Lunch."

I shook my head. "Nu-uh. I am not going anywhere, apart from your truck to shower at my office, smelling like a gym shirt."

Danny stopped, facing me with his back to the water. "Doesn't smell bad from here." He took a step closer, into my space. I resisted the urge to touch him, to push him away, scared I'd jump him instead.

"You're my client, Danny," I said firmly, sidestepping him as I had in my office. It had worked well for me, then. "I can't mix work with..."

"Pleasure?" he murmured, his arm shooting out, his hand wrapping around my elbow. He didn't draw me into him but held the contact. I swallowed, realising this was the same place he'd kissed me last time I was here with him.

"Yes." I couldn't pull away from him — or didn't want to.

"Yes what, Laura?"

I blinked, my senses returning. "Yes, I need to keep work separate. For now," I added, uncomfortable under his assessing gaze.

His eyes moved down my body in an incredibly slow once-over, as though he was memorising every part of me. Breath hissed from between his teeth. He dropped his hand and resumed walking.

My eyes closed, I took a deep breath. Somewhat settled, I followed Danny to his truck. The line of tension across his shoulders was back, and I sighed, seeing the mask returned to his face. Despite the good the run had done us both, we were back where we had started.

The drive back was quiet. I tapped my toes on the mat beneath my runners, unsure how to break into Danny's thoughts without being invasive — or setting off his defences further. He was already resistant to me — or my work — he'd shown that many times.

But we *had* made progress before he'd gone on assignment. I recalled the night at Half Moon Bay. My mind slipped to the morning after — waking up next to him, the weight of him settling on me as he kissed me.

I started to banish the images and stopped. Why not use a good thing?

"Remember that night at the beach?"

Danny's hands tightened on the steering wheel. "That's not something I'm likely to forget," he said sardonically, his voice laced with innuendo.

I slapped his arm. "Not that part — being in the water; when we were swimming. How you felt afterwards." Silence emanated from the driver's seat. It hit me like a wall. Maybe not *quite* the right approach, then. "What if you could feel that way all the time? About yourself, your work, your focus..." I let the thought hang, knowing I'd hit a sweet spot with him. For someone with no life, work *was* your life.

I used myself as a prime example.

Danny still didn't speak but gave a single, jerky nod. I held in a smile. Screeching a victory cry at the top of my lungs seemed a little inappropriate.

It was a small concession from him, but one I could work with. Ideas swirled in my head, a plan — not the one Cal had outlined, but one I had a good idea would work, began to fill out in my mind.

"You're plotting. I can see it."

I considered objecting, but there was no point. "Guilty."

336

Danny snorted a laugh. "Fine, Ms Miyagi. Do your worst."

"You're mangling your movie quotes," I reminded him.

"I'm good with it." But the corners of his mouth hinted at a smile. Half of me wanted to reach out, to see if his smile was real, while the other half despaired how I'd get through the afternoon without kissing him.

I started with meditation, and predictably, Danny objected — loudly.

"You've got to be kidding me," he grumbled as I turned the lights off, and placed a little bell on the floor beside us. Cross-legged, he looked incredibly uncomfortable.

"I thought you'd be more flexible. Maybe we should do some yoga, first."

"I'm not stretching on your office floor," Danny yelped. "I'm clean!"

I smothered a laugh. "I hadn't taken you for someone so pedantic," I grinned.

"Let me tell you who's ped–"

I turned on music from my phone, cutting him off. Deep sleep music with a circadian rhythm, it was a baby sleep app, but the effect was the same.

"It's cyclical," I explained, as Danny squinted suspiciously at my phone.

"Are you going to turn me into a hippie?"

"No," I laughed at him. "It helps to have a focus point to bring yourself deeper. This time I'll talk you through it, but after that, we go together." I grinned to myself as Danny's eyes closed in resignation. There were plenty of things we'd be doing together — if I played this right — and most of them were going to take Danny right outside his comfort zone.

"How do you feel?" I asked him half an hour later.

Muscles rippled over his shoulders as he activated them in sequence across his body, waking them up. He rolled to his feet, quite agile for a guy who'd been on his backside on my carpet for a decent period despite his earlier objections.

He bounced lightly on his toes and settled. "Good," he said softly, holding out a hand to help me up. I took it, not wanting to admit my own feet and backside had gone to sleep. I flexed my ankles, wincing as pins and needles assailed the nerve endings.

"We're done, for today." I pressed my lips together, hating that I felt uncomfortable in my own office. "Will you work with me on this? See if it makes a difference?" My words were tiny echoes of what I'd said to him in our first week together, and he'd objected then. I wondered if he would, now.

"If you think it will get me back to work sooner, then yeah, I'll work with it." He didn't release my hand, brushing his thumbs in small circles on the back of it.

I smiled, pretending calm while my heart rate increased. Danny smirked as though sensing my reaction to him and pulled me closer.

"Whoa. Wait just a minute." I pressed a hand to his chest, moulding slightly to the defined muscle beneath. "First, I need something."

"What?"

"That full-service date." I grinned. He gripped my hand tighter.

"I thought you said no work and pleasure...together," he growled the words softly, drawing me into him.

"This might not be what you think it is," I warned, digging my fingers into his chest a little.

"If I get to spend time with you," he paused, waving a hand around my office without breaking my gaze, "then I'll do whatever you want."

"You might regret that." I smiled, mentally running a victory lap around the office.

"I doubt it." Danny's eyes were full of dark promise, and I remembered what he'd said in the park the day Luke had followed us, wondering if I hadn't just got more than I bargained for.

CHAPTER TWENTY-THREE

DANNY

Laura let me out of her office, waving to me at the door to the elevator, arms laden with work to take home. I leaned against the wall opposite as the doors closed, feeling a little bad for not helping her as the door closed, knowing she was parked down the next block.

As soon as the doors closed, I hit the stairs — heading up, not down. Cal often worked late — and it wasn't that late, just yet.

I peered into the office from the landing. Ally sat at her desk, stiff-backed, typing quickly. I never remembered Steph doing as much work as she seemed to — but maybe we were behind in filing. I made a note to ask Cal what her job entailed, out of curiosity.

"Hey, Ally." I patted the top of the reception counter as I passed, spying Cal at his desk, surrounded by open files through the glass wall.

"Hey, Danny," she replied, not looking up.

I continued through to our shared office, hanging my head around the wall.

"Boss, got a moment?"

Cal looked up, his features smoothing as he came out of whatever he'd been focussed on. "Danny. Sure." He shuffled papers into piles as I pulled up a chair.

"I'm looking at a place tomorrow."

"That's great." Cal leaned back in his chair. "How did things do with Laura?"

I bit back a grin; he'd hit the issue straight up. Typical Cal — there was no bullshit with him.

"That's what I wanted to talk about. What did she say when she came in?"

"Are you asking why you got taken off the case?"

I shrugged. "Both."

"She talked to me about you as a client. You got pulled because you were made."

Damnit.

"She tell you that?"

Cal stared at me, tapping a pen on his knee. "You came up here to ask me how to deal with your personal life."

"No! Well, not entirely." Caught off guard, I floundered.

"Danny, get your head out your ass. This wasn't about your home life — you're meant to be working on your *career.*" Cal stressed the last word, and I fought back anger at his condescending tone.

"It became personal pretty quick," I snapped. "What did you expect with her digging around in my head every day?"

"That's fair." Cal stopped tapping the pen. "Has it helped?"

"Yeah. Maybe. I dunno." I threw my hands in the air, kicking my legs out. I pedalled backwards until I hit the opposite desk. Four walls became four too many.

"Letting someone else in your head...can be intimate," Cal said carefully, not avoiding my gaze.

"Are you seriously gonna give me the birds and bees talk?"

Cal laughed. "Nah. But I watched Liam work through PTSD with Selena. Even as close as they are, it was... invasive."

"Noted." I looked down at the files on Cal's desk. Luke's picture peeked at me from beneath a manilla folder. "How'd you find out? Tell me you didn't bug me."

"No need." Cal shook his head, tapping the pen again. "That little scene you made with Laura in the park was pretty visible from where I was having lunch. Luke didn't look impressed either."

"Fuck."

"Yeah. Who do you owe an apology to?"

"I'm taking her out tomorrow night. After we look at a place."

Cal nodded. "See you in a few days then."

"The building was designed in the early twentieth century and overlooks the Yarra River. There have been notables who lived in the street in the past century..." The estate agent wandered through the apartment, flicking on lights as she went.

Laura and I trailed her heavy perfume from room to room as she spouted historical information I couldn't care less about.

"Are rental inspections usually like this?" I whispered to Laura. She shook her head, lips pressed together in what I suspected was an attempt to withhold laughter.

"What do you think?" she asked quietly as we stopped at a larger, arched window overlooking the water. A rowing scull raced past, the rowers working together in a neat rhythm.

"I like it. It's open; I don't feel suffocated in here. Plus, I guess it's short term..." I rubbed the back of my head, uncomfortable with the idea of thinking of the future — my future.

"It's okay to be nervous," Laura said, her voice still low, pressing a hand on my arm. I smiled down at her, my palms itching with the need to feel her bare skin beneath them.

A fake cough behind us turned us both around. The agent looked at us expectantly, raising a thin line drawn onto her face that attempted to pass for an eyebrow.

"Well?"

"It's nice, but we'd like to have a look at–"

"It's fine." I caught Laura's hand, squeezing gently. "How do we do this?"

The agent provided me with a digital contract and a stack of clauses, explaining each one in detail. After what seemed like an hour, I'd transferred the bond to her and signed for my new home.

Two sets of keys were presented to us, Laura pressing the ones given to her into my hand with a red face. I grinned.

"Guess I'd better get my boxes out of your office, then," I said as the power suit trundled her way down the hall to the caged elevator.

"Yes," Laura replied, clutching the strap of her handbag with one hand and mine with the other. "Oh." She began to unclench her hand from mine, but I held tight. She looked up with questioning eyes.

"Thank you," I said softly, pulling her around to face me. "I wouldn't have been able to do this — had never even thought of it — before you."

Her smile was nervous, and near on the cutest thing I'd ever seen. Her fingers interlaced through mine. "It's the job," she gave a self-deprecating shrug, looking down. I was glad, as she would have missed the coldness that washed through me at her words.

"The job," I repeated dully, withdrawing my hand. I was still just a *client* to her. "That's great." I slipped my mask back, careful to cover the painful swelling in my heart. I couldn't work out if it was going to explode or complete its transformation into stone. Still, I didn't want anyone else near me when it happened.

"What?" Laura looked up at me, confused.

"I'll grab my things from your office later."

"Okay..."

I propelled her to the door, some false, inane smile plastered across my face. "See you later."

"Danny?" She turned on her heel as I opened the elevator grill, my fingers wrapped through the intricate pattern like I was strangling it. "Will I see you tonight?"

The date. Damn. This would be the second time I stuffed her around. But how the hell could I go on a date when she clearly saw it as some sort of team-building exercise?

"I might spend tonight settling in." I closed the door firmly, pressing the button to send her to the ground through the grill. Laura backed to the rear of the cage, hurt flickering in her eyes as the cage began to descend.

I sent her away from the home she'd helped choose, my heart sinking heavily in my chest.

Stone it was, then.

I managed to fit a cheap, two-seater sofa into the back of my truck, and a second run got me a bed frame and mattress with promises of other furniture to be delivered tomorrow. A borrowed trolley helped fit everything into the lift, which was easily large enough to accommodate it. I moved it around the open living area that split up a step to an equally-open bedroom that looked out at the river.

Once I'd moved the sofa to every spot in the room I could see, I conceded defeat and left it facing the water. At least I'd have something to look at.

Micah turned up with my boxes — a quick text had gotten me my boxes, without having to deal with Laura again. A large tray of warm chicken wings and rice sat on top of it. Micah grinned.

"Mama cooked for you. Knew you wouldn't have a fridge or anything."

Fuck. I'd forgotten the fridge. And a microwave. Looked like tomorrow was another shopping day. I grinned back. "Thanks for looking out for me."

"You want company?"

"Nah, I'm good. Gotta get my head around a few things."

"Anytime you need."

"I know. Thanks, dude."

He knuckle-bumped me before frightening the street as he revved his monster away from my new home.

I had a home.

I grinned, trundling the boxes back upstairs, wondering who my neighbours were. Each apartment took up an entire floor, so I wasn't likely to meet them. The rent wasn't exorbitant, but it gave me a sense of self while I worked out what the hell I was doing with my life. I'd never had to worry about what came "next" before.

I emptied the tray of food quickly — Micah's mum cooked almost as well as mine — watching lights come on along the river as dusk fell over the city.

Placing the empty tray on the counter, I added a bin to my mental list of items to get tomorrow. I shot a message to Cal saying I wouldn't be in until later, and he sent a winking emoji back. I groaned — I'd told him tonight was my date with Laura — he thought I was having a late morning because we'd hooked up.

That was something to deal with tomorrow, though — I wasn't game to try to explain that one via text messages when he was probably having a great night in with Mila.

Suddenly, my new apartment seemed very big and very empty. My thumb hesitated over Laura's name on my phone, but her words this afternoon still drove a spike through me. If I was only a job to her, then our relationship — if we even had one — really had nowhere else to go.

I spent the rest of the night unpacking the bed and putting it together. It wasn't until I'd ripped the plastic wrap from the mattress that I realised I had no sheets or blankets. In the end, I lay on the bare mattress and pulled a few bath towels I'd extracted from the bottom of one of my boxes over me.

I had almost everything I needed to furnish my new home either in my truck or on its way before my conscience caught up with me. I dialled Laura's number, fully expecting the call to ring out, but she picked up almost instantly.

"Hello?" I said cautiously when there was no sound from the other end. "Laura?"

"You're an absolute asshat. You know that."

"I do," I agreed, but a smile curled the corners of my mouth.

At least she was talking to me.

"I barely slept," her voice was muffled. Was she crying?

Guilt hit me twice over — I'd both stuffed up her sleep *and* made her cry? "I'm sorry."

"Are you coming into work?"

"I went shopping."

"Oh."

My brain froze — I'd called to apologise, and now that was done, I had no particular plan in mind.

"Uh, can I take you out tonight? If you want to go. With me. To make up for..." *Stop. Extract foot from mouth.* "I'm rambling."

There was a small hiccup on the other end. I winced.

"It's good rambling." I could hear the smile in her voice.

"I can keep it up," I offered.

"Tonight would be great." Her voice was soft. "See you at six? Don't wear anything fancy."

"Where are we going? Wait, are you going to be finished with work by then?" I joked.

"Yup. Danny...what did you tell Cal?"

"Ah." *Shit.* I hadn't fixed that up. "He thinks we, uh...I'll fix it."

"That would be great."

I hung up feeling much better — but I still had to deal with the fallout from Cal. I fired off a message to him and began to haul my furniture upstairs.

Finding places to put things was a novelty — I was almost done when the phone rang. I picked it up without looking.

"Couldn't wait for tonight, huh?"

"I'm not your booty call, Danny."

Cal.

"Uh, about that..." Why was I constantly on the back foot? "Laura and I never–"

"It's her birthday. For god's sake, Danny. Get her something nice and make up for whatever you did to piss her off and get your ass into work tomorrow."

"Will do."

It was her birthday? No wonder she had been crying. I put the rest of my shopping down and headed out to get my date something. I pursued rows of jewellery but wrote them off as too fancy, too impersonal. I needed something for Laura. She wasn't a fancy girl, by any means. Classy, yes. Fancy — definitely not.

I laughed at myself, alarming one of the salesgirls, who skittered away. Made a girl cry on her birthday — I *was* an asshole.

She wouldn't expect anything, and I didn't want to be encumbered by a bulky bunch of flowers. She was an active woman and driven — and I wanted to get her something she'd use.

I had a lot to make up for. Whatever I gave her needed to be appropriate — but also something she knew came from me.

I left the store with a small box that would fit well in my pocket and went home for a shower and a shave. Half an hour later I was dressed in jeans and my favourite Under Armour, black tee Liam had designed for us.

Micah was so damned big, almost everything had to be custom-made for him, and Black and I weren't far behind. Liam had done us all a favour and sorted a type of uniform for us.

I spent the afternoon unpacking the rest of my things and trying to sort in my head where the hell I was with

Laura. I cared for her — more than I should. Probably. She wasn't the piece of work that Mandy was, by any means, but I still wondered if something was holding her back.

The day I'd kissed Laura by the lake — regardless of who was watching — had given me a view inside her. The girl was full of passion — I could have sworn she was ready to jump me right there. And when I'd said I'd fuck her the moment I'd had her alone...that little intake of breath, the way her eyes widened... my cock twitched at the thought of her wrapped around me, her bare skin pressed to mine.

But that wasn't what tonight was about, I promised myself. Tonight was to make up for the hurt I'd caused because of my own hang-ups — not hers.

Pulling up outside her house deep in Melbourne's inner suburbs, I took a deep breath. I held onto the steering wheel a moment longer than necessary, hoping I was doing the right thing. Laura and I had great tension together before I went on assignment, and after; the way she'd responded to me, I knew nothing had *really* changed.

She was so driven, so focussed. I didn't want to drag her into my uncertain world. Hell, I didn't even know what my world looked like.

Patting my pocket to make certain the little box was secure, I bounced up the steps, full of nervous energy. My knock echoed inside the large townhouse, and I didn't have to wait long before the door opened.

Laura wore her trademark tights and tank. Small, sparkling studs decorated her ears, exposed from the high ponytail she'd used to draw her silvery hair away from her face. My fingers brushed the small bulk in my pocket, but I didn't dive in just yet. I wanted to time it right. I smiled, leaning down to brush my lips across her cheek, the scent of berries and honeysuckle assailing me.

"Happy birthday," I murmured in her ear, breathing her in.

Her eyes widened as I drew back, her chest rising quickly.

"I didn't want to say anything."

I grinned. "You didn't need to." I didn't add that it had been Cal who had told me.

"Mmm, perks of being a cop, huh." Her smile was slightly crooked, and I held back the urge to touch her face. *Take it slow.* She wouldn't appreciate me barging in, actually behaving as bearish as I looked. I grinned internally. Well, not just yet, anyway. Maybe later. I was happy to play tonight by ear.

"Ready?" She nodded, confidence suddenly fading from her stance. I sucked in a quick breath and took her hand. She started, then her fine fingers closed around mine. I opened the car door for her, wondering if she'd balk at the help, but she climbed into the truck with no issue. I didn't bother to try not perving on her gorgeous curves.

355

"You'll have to give me directions. I don't know where we're going," I reminded her.

A small smile graced her face.

"Urban Central."

With each turn, I wracked my brain for what the hell my girl had planned. When we turned onto a dingy side street populated with clubs and some dodgy hostels, I was more confused than ever.

Urban Central was a building much like any other of its ilk. Laura was out of the truck, hugging the doorman before I could get around the front of my vehicle. His hand lingered far too long and way too low for my liking, though his eyes told me he knew exactly what I thought of him — and of her.

Laura tossed me a throwaway look over her shoulder, stepped away from the man, and disappeared between tinted doors. I gave the guy a hard look as I passed, the smirk on his face irritating me to no end.

The elevator door pinged behind me as I joined her in the lift. Laura hit the button to the top floor. I stood facing her, still unsure what I'd gotten myself into. Her smile was all cat-got-the-cream.

"Still wondering?"

The elevator shot skyward, and unless there was a hidden, rooftop bar at the top of the building — very possible in Melbourne — I had a good idea what she had in mind. I didn't like it.

"Laura..."

The doors opened out onto a brightly lit expanse, the edges of the building melding with the evening sky. Two pulleys were set up along the far side, a cluster of men in matching black shirts huddled beneath them. Lengths of rope coiled neatly on the ground, carabiner clips glinting beneath the floodlights.

"Laura–" I started again but couldn't finish the thought. I swallowed, turning to face her, but the words wouldn't come at all. My chest closed tight, and I masked the rising panic as best I could, but I knew she saw through my pretence.

She stepped into me, one hand on my chest, and for a moment, I forgot how much I hated heights.

"You remember what you told me in our first session?" Her eyes were a deep aqua, starlight sparkling in them. I fell deeper into her. With effort, I took myself back to the first day in her office.

I did remember.

I'd been a bag of nerves, much like right now, and I'd covered it by flirting with her, just to piss her off. It seemed like an age ago.

The corner of my mouth lifted. "That I deal with fear face first."

"Then that's what we're doing."

I opened my mouth to object that her birthday might not be the best time to face my greatest fear, then closed it, looking closely at Laura. Her eyes were just shy of wide, and she had drawn one side of her lip into her mouth.

This *was* something typical of her — facing your fears was one of her favourite ways to communicate with someone.

In a sense, this was her apology. I needed to make it mine, too. I folded my hand around hers, squeezing, certain she could feel my pulse increase.

"Then let's do it."

Her smile was reward enough, bright enough to light the darkness beyond the rooftop. She led me to the tribe of instructors, who engulfed her in a group hug. My teeth began to grind before I could stop the reflex. I was *really* tired of other men touching my girl.

The thought gave me pause, even as Laura approached me, reaching out with a tentative hand. When had I started thinking of her as mine? Tonight, I couldn't seem to think of her any other way.

"You've done this before, for work, right?"

"Yeah, but it was quick, and a while ago."

"Ever done it face first?"

Hells, no.

Liam had sent us on a team-building trip up the Grampians where we were faced with a small measure of orienteering and abseiling down the local mountain which, truth be told, wasn't all that tall. The guide Liam had equipped us with had seen my fear straight up and partnered me with Micah — the biggest adrenaline junkie I'd ever met.

The man's veins were filled with adrenaline, I was sure, and competition was his jam. He and Laura would get on just fine. I grinned at the thought. We must have climbed that mountain and rappelled down it twenty times before he was ready to stop.

He'd given me what I needed — a challenge. It had changed my focus, and that's what I needed to do now, except — no Micah. And competing with Laura wasn't us — even running with her, I was still pushing myself, breaking my own limits, not hers.

Laura was my company, not my competition, though she had my deepest respect for keeping up with me. There weren't a lot of people who could do that.

Now it was time for me to keep up with *her*.

She towed me to the edge of the roof, positioning me beneath one of the pulleys. I eyed it with no small degree of trepidation, cold sweat prickling my skin as I leaned forward to peer over the ledge. A large hand gripped my arm. I jumped, huffing out a quick breath.

"Whoa, mate. Step back from there while we string you up, right?" Not waiting for an answer, he tugged ropes around me, measuring me with first one harness then another, until I was as trussed as a Sunday roast.

Every time he tightened a strap, my stomach gripped. I breathed in with each one, trying to bring myself back to the centre of calm the way Laura had taught me. The instructor in front of me was talking, but I could only see his mouth moving. My head was a fishbowl of information swishing aimlessly in a soup of brains and synapses that weren't firing the way they were supposed to.

A light touch to my hand startled me, but it wasn't an instructor this time.

Laura's thumb pressed on the queen chess piece inked over my wrist.

"Remember," she whispered.

I jerked a short nod, focussing on the task before me. Thinking back to our last session together, my eyes closed. Quiet emptied my world of panic and noise. My heartbeat slowed back to its regular rhythm. My breath was hollow in my ears. I opened my eyes, squeezing her hand.

"Ready."

The instructor looked at me doubtfully, glancing sideways to Laura, who nodded. He frowned, evidently still worried about me, and led us to the edge.

After all the build-up and worry, it was over in seconds. Standing there, waiting, was the worst part. My hands gripped the rope in a familiar position, muscle memory pitching in. As I leaned forward over the edge of the building, I glanced at Laura.

Completely relaxed, she stared at the ground from a position far higher than a cat could survive if it jumped. Or was pushed. I grinned. Her breathing was steady, back straight. God, the girl was strong and not just physically.

It was sexy as hell.

This was not the time to start thinking with my dick. She turned a brilliant smile on me and released the tension on her rope.

I was less than half a second behind her. Cold night air slapped my skin, and in seconds I was hovering above the ground, legs shaking with the adrenaline hit from running face-first down the side of the building.

Laura flipped the right way up, feet gently touching the pavement. My own landing was far less elegant. I leaned against the wall while she fussed at my waist, unclipping me. My heart raced — not from fear this time, but exhilaration. For those few moments, I *had* looked my fear right in the eyes; and dismissed it.

Laura released me from my harness, giving both ropes a good tug. The harnesses disappeared back to the top of the building, awaiting their next victims, I presumed.

"Like it?" Laura asked shyly.

I grinned. "Hell, yes."

"Do it again?"

"Fuck, no."

She laughed appreciatively, towing me down the street, away from my truck. Two doors down, she turned into a narrow, dark alleyway.

"Uh, where are we going?"

I might be a big guy, but even I wasn't stupid enough to go wandering around dingy alleys at night.

Laura threw an enigmatic look over her shoulder and rapped on a peeling door just a few meters into the lane. It opened quickly, warmth and light flowing out, giving life to the darkness. I stepped into a narrow corridor painted orange, spicy scents wafting around me.

Famous for its hidden gems in the city, Melbourne hosted a plethora of boutique restaurants and bars that remained unknown to most, some seating only a handful of people at a time.

A short, round woman who reminded me of my mother greeted Laura with a hug, chattering quietly in her ear, and tugging at her clothes in mock disapproval. I realised she was allowing me another glimpse into her private world.

These were obviously people she regularly dealt with, either in a professional or personal capacity — though I suspected from the depth of the relationships they displayed, it was the latter.

The woman motioned Laura past her, stopping me with a look I recognised well. Fists on her hips, she surveyed me with a critical eye. I stood silent, knowing better than to interrupt her study. Finally, she jerked her chin in the direction Laura had taken, but I shook my head.

"After you, mama," I murmured, holding out an open hand.

She grinned broadly, bobbing, and led me to a table at the side of a small space, filled with tables and the low chatter of diners. Laura was already seated, and the stout woman tapped her head.

"A good boy," she pronounced in heavily-accented English. "I will get your food." She bustled off before I could object to not having ordered any yet. A look from Laura told me not to interrupt the evening's process.

I slid into the small booth as a fresh beer, and an enormous bowl of paella slid onto the table. The tiny woman fixed Laura with a beady eye, waggling a finger. She turned to me.

"Make sure she eats."

I nodded, a small smile creeping along my lips. "Yes, mama."

The woman nodded, apparently satisfied, and returned to the kitchen.

"That smells amazing."

Laura grinned. "Bettina may be the best cook in the world."

"Over Micah's mother? You should see what else she can cook."

"Will I get the honour?"

"You will, at this rate."

Laura smiled, reaching for the ladle, but I beat her to it. Her hand landed on mine. I raised my eyes to meet hers, and her fingers flexed a little, tracing lines down the back of my hand.

Her tanned fingers looked good, contrasted against the black queen tattooed there. She hesitated a second, then drew her hand back, settling quietly on the other side of the table.

I kept my smile to myself as I piled her bowl high with paella, despite her protests. Poking the bowl toward her, I decided to test the waters a little.

"Face first down a tall building, huh?" I nearly moaned aloud at the first mouthful — it was at least as good as it smelled. Laura blushed at my question, stuffing a spoonful into her mouth. I suspected it was to avoid answering me. "So, did I pass your test?"

She choked. I slid a glass of water her way.

"I wanted to do something with you that was more important than just a movie, something that wasn't just superficial."

I raised an eyebrow.

"And making me face my deepest fear fit that criteria?"

"Heights aren't your greatest fear."

"No?"

"No. Failing to protect those you love is."

It was my turn to choke. Laura slid the glass of water back toward me with a small smile, but sad eyes. I ignored it and downed half my beer, instead.

I wanted to make some smart-ass remark, but as usual, she was right. I ate in silence, mulling over her words.

I looked up to see she hadn't touched the rest of her food. Bettina would be angry with me, and there was no way I wasn't coming back to this place if she cooked like this every night.

"I'm jealous of how easily you read people." I nodded to her bowl. "Eat."

She took a small bite, her head tilted to the side. Blonde strands fell loosely across her face. I resisted the urge to brush them behind her ear, but I hated the idea of being intimate in front of a crowd of people — tonight, at least.

It cheapened the moment for me, somehow, and something told me tonight was important. More than her birthday, we — *I* — had the chance to start again, to get it right.

By the time we had finished, my stomach was stretched beyond its usual capacity.

"God, that was good."

"Mmhmm." Laura chewed her last mouthful of miguelitos — a tiny cube of moist chocolate wrapped in layers of crisp pastry.

"Foodgasm?"

Laura made the same muffled sound again. I grinned, reaching for her hand across the table. Bettina returned to clear our plates, and I tried to slip my credit card into her hand as I had at the teppanyaki kitchen, but she wouldn't have it, flapping at my hands. She rattled something off in Spanish, and I shook my head.

"Thank you." Laura stood, embracing the smaller woman, who turned a dusky shade of pink all over. She gave Laura a gentle push, shooing us both off like a pair of lost ducklings, both of us thanking her many times.

The night air was frigid after the warmth inside Betina's restaurant. I leaned against the brick wall, folding my arms as I sent her a grin.

"What just happened?"

"Oh. She, um, knew it was my birthday." Laura flushed darker, ducking her head.

"You're something special to a lot of people. You know that, right?"

Laura studied the ground as we walked. At my truck, I put my hand over hers as she reached for the door, turning her to face me. The doorman behind me coughed not-so-discreetly. I ignored him.

I trailed my fingers across her cheek, through her hair.

"Laura," I caught her chin, lifting her eyes to meet mine, "you mean something pretty special to me, too."

My mouth brushed hers, the barest touch. She breathed in sharply, pink lips parting, and it took all the restraint I had not to take her in my arms right there. My lips tingling, I slipped my arm around her, clicking open the door to my truck. Her gaze held mine as she silently climbed into the passenger seat, the air around us charged.

I walked around the driver's side door, leaning in to switch the ignition on before I sat down, drawing in a deep breath before I was in an enclosed space with her. I didn't want to rush her or push her, but by god, it was going to take everything I had to keep my hands off her.

The doorman caught my eye as I climbed into the truck, his mouth curled in a sneer. I didn't let my expression change, though my hands itched at the thought of the way he'd touched Laura when we'd first arrived.

Stretching my arm across the back of Laura's chair, I curled my fingers around her shoulder, tracing light patterns into her skin as I pulled away from the curb.

"What's the best way to take you home? Unless you had something else in mind?"

Laura shook her head, nibbling on her bottom lip. "Home is fine," she murmured, programming her address into my GPS. "Now you can find me whenever."

A blush rose in her cheeks, deep enough it was visible in the darkness.

"Thanks for... hell, everything, tonight." I kept my eyes on the road. Laura shifted closer to me across the open cab, sliding her hand down my leg. I clenched the steering wheel tighter.

I checked the GPS — eleven minutes left before we would reach her house. I wrapped the arm across the seatback around her, praying I'd manage to keep control of the urge to find a spot off the road.

"You're welcome," Laura answered. I had to concentrate on remembering what I'd said in the first place.

Stop thinking with your dick, Danny.

It was becoming a mantra. Difficult with a fucking gorgeous woman beside me. Laura ran her fingers along the inside of my knee. Even through my jeans, I could feel the trail her nails left as they drew upwards. I desperately wanted to feel them digging into my back.

The ten remaining minutes of the drive to Laura's house took an age. I pulled up, scoring a parking spot directly out front. Her hand slipped from my leg. My foot on the brake, I left the truck running. No matter how I felt, I didn't want to put any more pressure on Laura. If she didn't want to take things any further, I refused to push her.

I turned to her, unsure where to start, but she unclipped her seat belt, not looking at me. My heart took a dive, but I fidgeted with the denim material of my pocket.

"Laura, I–"

"Would you like to come in?"

Our words ran together.

Laura grinned, winding her fingers through mine. "Please?"

I nodded, killing the engine. She gave my hand a squeeze, slipping out the other side. I followed her up the short path to her door, resting my hand on her waist as she fumbled her keys in the lock.

Inside, she flicked lights on, illuminating a thin hall with white walls and a red cedar floor. The theme continued throughout the house, opening into a broad living space with bi-fold glass doors that overlooked the city.

"It suits you." I turned in a circle, for once, not feeling like I took up the entire space with my bulk. Laura grinned,

waving a bottle of white wine. I nodded, and she retrieved
two glasses from a collection that dangled above her white,
stone bench.

"Thanks. I spent a year fitting it out after I bought it."

Having looked at house prices recently, I had an idea
what she'd paid. My respect for her grew — she worked hard
with her own business, her organisation still blowing me
away, when she couldn't be more than a year or two older
than I was.

"You renovated it yourself?"

She nodded. "Most of it. The place was pretty
decrepit when I walked in. My parents were horrified, but...
It's mine."

"I love it."

She handed me a glass of wine, which I placed on the
counter, digging into my pocket. I slid the box onto the
bench beside the wine, across to her.

"Happy birthday."

Laura stared down at the little box, then back at me,
brow furrowed. "You didn't have to get me anything."

"I wanted to."

She nodded, not moving for a moment, then slowly
lifted the lid. Inside sat a small, leaf-shaped slice of wood,

with a fine stripe of rose gold curving around its side. She picked it up carefully, exposing a white leather strap beneath.

"It's a tracker — sleep, wellness, breathing rate. It has meditation programs built-in and music." I flipped it over and showed her how to attach it to the band. It slipped easily around her wrist. I tried to hide the tremors in my hand — I couldn't remember the last time I'd taken so much care in buying a present for a woman.

She looked up at me with luminous eyes. "I love it." Her words echoed my earlier ones.

Placing her glass next to mine, Laura stepped into me. My hands wound around her, but I held back from pulling her into me, restraint pounding in my ears.

Her hands slid up my chest, the bracelet glinting on her wrist. I watched her, running my hands beneath her shirt, stroking the skin at her back lightly.

Stepping up to her toes, she pressed her lips to mine, open-mouthed. I groaned, kissing her back as her hands linked behind my neck. She tasted sweet, her tongue stroking mine slowly. This was nothing like when I'd kissed her at the lake — I knew tonight, I would get as much time with her as I needed.

CHAPTER TWENTY-FOUR

LAURA

I drew back from Danny's kiss, barely able to catch my breath. He reached for me, but I caught his hand, drawing him along the hall to my bedroom. I didn't object to utilising the rooms in my house, but the bed was by far the most comfortable.

He caught up with me in the doorway to my room, his hand covering mine before it flicked the light switch. The blinds were wide open, and there was plenty of ambient light in the room, while still leaving it dark enough to afford privacy. His arms wrapped around me from behind, one hand palming my stomach, dragging my shirt upward. I shivered as the cool air hit my skin.

His head dipped, mouth leaving a trail of nips and kisses across the sensitive place where my neck met my shoulder. I tilted my head back, heat flushing across my chest to my cheeks as his stubble brushed my skin, his mouth travelling along my jaw to meet mine. He tasted smokey, with a tang of something spicy. I arched back, pressing my mouth up to meet his.

He pulled my shirt over my head, breaking the kiss for only a moment, then his hands were running over my skin like he was trying to memorise every part. I turned, tugging at his shirt. He shucked it over his head with a grin.

He stood still, letting me trace each muscle as I circled him — I'd seen him naked that night at the beach, but never touched, never been allowed to explore him.

Every inch of Danny's incredible body was carved and honed to perfection. The muscle was hard and firm beneath my hands as I completed my circuit, running my fingers down the vee from his hips to his belt buckle. I slipped my fingers inside the edge of his jeans, just holding there, and pressed up to kiss him.

His mouth caught mine hungrily, his hands sliding over my ass, lifting me, and splitting my legs open to wrap around his waist. He carried me to the bed, his mouth never leaving mine.

I ground down against the hardness of him, my thin tights affording little barrier between us. He lay me on the bed, hooking his fingers under the top of my tights, peeling them slowly down, and over my ankles. My knickers quickly followed. Danny tugged at the clip of the leather bracelet, and he collected it when it fell free from my wrist, placing it on my bedside table.

Propped on my elbows, I unclipped the back of my sports bra, sliding it over my shoulders. Danny pushed me back a little, propping both of my feet on the edge of the bed, far apart from each other.

He stepped back, slowly removing his belt, his eyes never leaving me.

"You're perfect," he growled, shivers running haywire across my skin at the dark promise in his voice. He dipped his hand into his pocket with a crinkle. I rolled my shoulders, arching my back as his jeans hit the floor. Every single part of him was in proportion — well-built and finely crafted, and his cock was no exception.

Under his intense gaze, I felt more exposed than I'd ever been. He took his time, feasting on me by sight alone as my heart pounded, my core clenching. I gripped the bed covers as he walked between my legs and leaned over me, bracing a hand either side of my head.

He dipped his head to kiss me, the only part of our bodies touching were our lips and tongues, stroking and dancing together. He stood, gripping my wrists, and pulling me with him.

"What are you doing?"

"Bathroom." He stepped back, still holding my wrists. I led him into my ensuite, unsure what he had in mind. Danny reached around me, flicking on the shower, kissing me while the water heated.

He dragged me under the water, steam filling the air around us. Pressing me against the cold tiles, his skin already hot to the touch, he lifted me onto his hips, pausing to unroll a condom onto himself, and lowered me. Sliding into me in a single, smooth motion. I gasped, my body aching around him in need.

"Are you okay?" he growled in my ear, nipping and sucking the skin at my neck. Water pounded his back, drenching us both. I nodded, unable to make more than base sounds as he began to move within me.

My hands found his shoulders, nails digging in as I clung to him. I'd thought he'd go slow, but his mouth claimed mine, his hips slamming into me. I arched into him, my orgasm ripping from my throat, but he was far from finished.

Danny didn't slow but brought me again and again, my climaxes rolling over each other until I couldn't recognise my own screams.

His head buried into my shoulder, digging his fingers into my hips, he roared his orgasm against my skin.

I hung over Danny's shoulders, my cheek pressed to the back of his neck, my breaths matching his heaving chest.

Water rained down on both of us, rivulets pooling in between the places where we joined.

Which was everywhere.

Danny stirred, lifting his head. I moved so he could straighten, but kept my legs wrapped around his hips. His hands framed my face, kissing me gently, deeply. He rested his forehead on mine as our breathing slowed, matching each other.

Pressing gentle kisses to my cheeks and lips, he lifted me off him, ignoring my mewls in protest. I couldn't form proper words. With slow, firm hands, he washed every inch of me, hands slippery with soap, one pressed flat on my chest between my breasts to hold me up.

When he was finished, he turned the shower off, still unspeaking, and dried me. He held me against him the entire time. Lifting me in his arms, he carried me back to my bed.

I had no objections — I suspected my legs wouldn't work, anyway. I curled into Danny's chest, my mind caught somewhere between whirling with the way he'd fucked me, and sleep. Pulling the sheets back, he lay me on the bed.

Completely boneless, I sank into the mattress, barely registering his movements as he slid his hands between my knees, drawing them apart.

"What are you doing?" I asked drowsily, trying to sit up, but energy deserted me. He pressed a hand to my stomach, sliding his tongue along the insides of my thighs.

"Shh," he murmured, sliding his hand along my leg, holding it back. He dipped his tongue inside me, sliding up to my clit and back, slow, gentle strokes that built pressure in me faster than I would have believed possible after what he'd just done to me.

I laced my fingers into his hair, tugging gently, but he ignored me completely. Continuing in his rhythm, he alternated licking and flicking my flesh with his tongue until my hips bucked beneath his mouth. Small cries rose from deep inside me, lifting me from the bed. I sank back onto my pillow in a tangle of damp hair. Danny lay beside me, pulling me onto his chest, wrapping his arms around me.

I fell asleep listening to the steady beat of his heart.

Light flared against my closed eyes as I woke in my bed, alone. I snuggled my pillow, breathing deep — and opened my eyes with a start.

Danny.

His scent was everywhere — on me, in my bed — and I loved it. Until I realised he wasn't in my bedroom.

"Danny?" I croaked unsexily, my mouth furry. I grabbed a water bottle off my bedside table, sucking on the top as I looked around. He wasn't in the shower. I stood —

and sat back on the bed again, my legs not behaving. Surely, he hadn't left? Doubt hit my chest — he'd done so much for me last night, and I hadn't done anything for him in return.

My heart racing, I trotted up the hall, halfway there when I realised I was naked, clutching a water bottle. Which really wasn't much of a defence — but seeing as I expected I was alone in my house; I didn't really care.

I was wrong — on two counts.

I hit the end of the hall as Danny came around the corner, carrying two large cups he must have scrounged from the very back of my mug collection, filled with chai.

"Whoa," he halted, steaming liquid sloshing in the mugs. He extended one arm to prevent spilling anything, muscles bunching beneath his skin. Dressed only in his jeans, I could follow the way every part of him flexed at the slightest movement, absolutely in love with that finely-honed body already.

Danny coughed, bringing my attention back to his face. Heat rose in my cheeks as his gaze travelled down my body, but I refused to hide from the man who had given me so much of himself last night.

He'd conquered his fears for me, walked out of his comfort zone into mine, and given me the most incredible night I'd had with anyone, let alone on my birthday.

The least I could do was let him look.

I dropped my arms to my sides, not preening, but stood tall. Holding his gaze, I returned his smile, shyly.

"I made you breakfast." He nodded back towards my bedroom. "Shall we?"

I nodded, turning on my heel and walked back the way I'd come. Danny set the cups on my nightstand and disappeared back into the kitchen. He returned with bowls of fruit and muesli topped with yogurt. I sat comfortably on my bed, cross-legged, facing him.

Normally, after the first night with someone, I would have required clothes, but with Danny, I didn't need them.

Sunlight streamed in through the window as he sank onto the bed beside me, balancing the bowls.

"You're like a heater," I mumbled around a mouthful of yogurt. "Oh, my god. What did you do to this?"

Danny pulled me over one leg, so my back pressed to his chest. His jean-encased legs framed my nude ones. I leaned back against him in the sunlight while his fingers trailed over my skin as he ate.

"Nothing. It's just you." He dropped a kiss to the top of my head. I snuggled back against him. "Hell, girl. Don't do that," he groaned.

I grinned into my muesli. When he was finished, I collected our bowls, exchanging them for the mugs of chai. Danny's arm snaked around me.

"Don't you spill that on me," I warned, only half-joking.

"I won't," came the muffled reply.

"We have to go to work," I sighed, wishing we could stay in my bed all day. I flexed my toes, experimenting. "At least my legs work, now."

Danny guffawed, his chest vibrating against my back. I watched his mug with no little consternation as he drained it, then liberated mine, placing them both on the side table. I had only a moment to recognise the glint in his eye before he was on me, kissing, licking, biting. I wriggled beneath him, but he held my hip, pressing down.

"Danny, last night, you–" his mouth covered mine, cutting me off. I tangled my fingers in his hair tugging as I gasped for air. "I need to give you–" But his hands were everywhere. His mouth covered my breast, tugging lightly on my nipple with his teeth as his fingers stroked the wetness of me, sliding up and down in the same rhythm as his tongue last night.

"Danny–"

"Laura?" He raised his head, releasing my nipple with a soft *pop.*

"Yeah?"

"Shut up."

I glared at him in mock outrage, and he sent me a wicked grin as he slid two fingers deep inside me. I cried out, then his mouth was on mine again, his fingers and tongue working together. His weight pressed over me, pinning me to the mattress. I writhed beneath him; hands curled into his back as he brought me again.

I lay panting beneath him, flexing my fingers as they unfurled from his back. Hooking my legs around his back to draw him into me, I pulled him down to kiss me, but he pulled away.

"What?" I asked, my brow knitting.

He grinned slowly in answer, winding his fingers through my hair, drawing me up with him as he sat. His other hand went to the button of his jeans, tugging them over his hips. He wore nothing beneath. Danny leaned in to kiss me again, slowly, deeply, before he broke away, pushing me down, his hand still fisted in my hair.

I kissed the tip of his cock, sliding my lips and tongue across it while my hands acquainted themselves with his legs, the width of him. I slid my mouth over him, letting him guide my movements until he groaned above me.

Pulling me up, Danny kissed me hard, a foil packet crinkling in his hand. I took it from him, rolling the condom down the length of him.

He pressed me back on the bed, one hand square on my chest. I wriggled, wanting to be on top, but he kept his weight over me, sliding deep inside me. I arched off the bed, crossing my ankles behind his back. He growled, a hand curing over my hip, driving deeper, but so slowly.

Every inch of me tightened, and he rose onto his forearms, watching me. I pulled him down to me, sliding my tongue across his lips, tangling with his. His control broke, slamming into me, again and again, until our bodies curled and arched around each other. He roared my name, seating himself deep inside me, and the rest of the world disappeared.

The drive into work was a quiet one. We'd opted to take Danny's truck, with the thought of him dropping me home afterwards. However, he'd gathered a random selection of fresh clothes and undergarments and presented them proudly to me. I just shook my head and repacked an overnight bag.

His fingers remained wrapped possessively around mine the entire drive. After a while, I closed my eyes, staring at the backs of my eyelids. *Work.* How was I going to make this work? Clearly, I couldn't work with Danny any more — but together, we might be able to sort through some of his PTSD issues. Especially if Cal did as he had promised me, and took Danny off undercover work permanently.

We pulled into the underground carpark, taking the spot adjacent to Cal and Micah's trucks. Black's sleek coupe sat next to Liam's platinum one. I still struggled that the two of them drove coupes. The trucks fit the boys, but Liam and Black appeared to have fallen off that wagon.

"I don't know how long I'll be, and I have to get some deliveries sorted at midday." Danny looked at me, apologetically.

"It's fine," I pretended to be miffed, "go, sort your home without me."

Danny was around the truck faster than I would have expected, his hands squeezing my waist.

"I wouldn't have a home if not for you," he growled softly, his mouth covering mine.

When he pulled away, I wrapped my hand around his shoulder, holding tight. I didn't trust myself not to fall.

"If you keep kissing me like that, we'll never make it into the office," I warned him.

"I'm good with that." Eyes hooded, his gaze raked over me before he stepped back, taking a breath. A shiver ran along my back, setting every nerve ending humming. "I'll see you this afternoon."

He squeezed my hand, pausing for a moment, and I wondered if he would kiss me again. The corner of his mouth curled, his eyes positively sinful, and he strode away. Quickly.

I heard his feet pounding the stairs as I waited for the elevator, with a box of things and my overnight bag. My mind drifted back to last night, the feel of him holding me up in the shower, to falling asleep wrapped around him. I smiled, nudging my box of paperwork into the elevator.

"I'll get that."

A flash of bright white hit me. I recoiled a step as Ally pushed her way into the elevator, hoisting my box over the door tracks.

"Um, thanks?"

"It's no problem." She pressed the button for my floor and hers with more energy than was socially acceptable at this time of the morning. I grinned — usually, I'd have run the lake by now, but a night with Danny was a workout on its own. I was sure my smile was indecent and toned it down.

"I'm sure he's lovely," Ally said to no one in particular, facing the door. I looked at her from the corner of my eye, once again uncomfortable around the white-suited woman.

"I beg your pardon?"

"Danny." She turned to me with a smile that didn't quite reach her eyes. "He's very nice."

Ally faced the door again. What the hell was going on? I hated to rise to the bait, but clearly, she wanted something from me.

"But...?" I sighed at the petty games. It reminded me of high school — and I'd hated that with a passion.

"He may not be working here much longer. I just don't want you to be let down." She sent me a condescending, and completely fake, smile. I recognised it from one in my mother's repertoire. "Well, bye!" She waved as the doors opened for my floor, making no move to assist me as I nudged my box into the corridor that led to my office.

I stared at the closed elevator doors. What the hell had that been all about?

"Want lunch?" Danny knocked on my door after he poked his head around it.

"Wrong order," I called, not looking up from a screen I'd been staring at for hours and getting nowhere.

"What?"

"You're supposed to knock, first."

"Oh, yeah. Micah's with me. You want to take a break?"

I nodded at my screen, shutting it down, and joined the boys in the hall. Micah sent me a small grin, focussing on his phone. Danny's hand closed around mine as we left the building. Micah opened the door, making room for Ally, who was coming back in. He didn't raise his head.

"What's going on with him?" I whispered, catching Ally's eye as she passed, looking pointedly at our joined hands. Danny gripped mine tighter. "Danny?"

He stared after her, not speaking, and a pit of uncertainty opened in my stomach. She looked a lot like me, I knew — the blonde hair, the tan, and she obviously worked out. I bit my lip as Danny towed me out of the building, Micah trailing us.

"Come on," his voice was harsh. I jolted out of my thoughts in surprise.

"What on earth is going on?"

"I don't know," Danny admitted, looking down at me. The pit grew bigger, and I began to withdraw my hand. Danny refused to let go. "No. She does *not* get to come between us when I've just found you again."

"She said something odd in the lift this morning, about you not working here much longer."

"Did she?" Danny stared straight ahead, his mouth a thin line.

I closed my mouth, my mind whirling, but I couldn't make any sense of it. From what little I knew, Ally had been sent down to Cal to replace their old receptionist. Maybe she'd been a PA, and felt she was worth more? I knew Cal wouldn't stint on her pay — he paid me perfectly well.

We ate at the sushi train, both boys lost in their respective thoughts while I worried for them. Micah ran up the stairs, leaving us well behind. I walked slowly beside Danny.

"If Ally– um, if she's–" I couldn't get the words out around the knot in my stomach.

"Stop," Danny ordered.

I froze. He turned me to face him, squeezing my arms. I watched him with wide eyes, my heart speeding up. Was this the part where he said goodbye? Tears pricked the corners of my eyes.

Horrified, I blinked rapidly, too stunned to pull away from his hand. Danny stroked his thumb across my cheek, his eyes softening.

"There is nothing going on with Ally," he said softly, stepping into me. I blinked, barely taking in his words as he tipped my head back, pulling me against him. "I couldn't care less for her — I don't even like her." He grimaced, "You think she looks like you — right? Wrong. Her hair isn't as gorgeous as yours, and she looks nothing like you — not to me."

I nodded, still catching up with his words as relief flooded me. Danny caught my face between both hands. I nodded.

"Fine. It's fine–"

"Damnit, Laura." With a groan, Danny dipped his head, capturing my lips. He dropped his hands lower, pulling me tight against him. My hands found their way into their familiar place around his shoulders as he deepened the kiss. His hands slid beneath my shirt, pressing against my skin. A door somewhere along the stairwell slammed, and we jumped apart. I ran my hands over my hair, flustered.

"I should get back to work," I whispered, unable to take my eyes off him. I needed a hormone check or something. I eyed his exposed forearms — definitely something.

"You okay?" Danny walked beside me, neither of us touching the other. *This is why office affairs don't work.* Damn, I knew better than this. I looked sideways at Danny. Lines crinkled the corners of his eyes.

"Are you worried?" I asked, not answering his question. I had no idea if I was okay. By his half-grimace, neither was he.

"A bit," he murmured. "I'll straighten it out." He opened my door, tucking my hair behind my ear. "See you in a few hours." The door closed behind me, and he was gone.

CHAPTER TWENTY-FIVE

DANNY

I waited until I couldn't hear Laura's footsteps, then pounded the stairwell back to the office. I ignored Ally's chirpy greeting, seeing as I'd seen her downstairs and she'd never said a word there. *Fake.* It was all so fake.

The office was full — as I entered the room, I realised it was the first time we'd all been in the same room together since before I'd gone on assignment. Cal passed me a file. It wasn't a formal briefing, but he expected us to at least listen as we worked, depending on what needed to be done.

I flicked open the folder, immediately confronted with a mug shot of Luke, a few years ago, by the look of it.

"What's going on?"

Cal's mouth was a hard line. He tapped the picture, then pushed it aside. Luke's stats were underneath: his height, weight, relationships, where he'd served time. I shook my head.

"I know all this. By heart."

Cal didn't say a word but pushed the photo across the page. I stared at a name it uncovered, wondering how in the hell it had been missed. I turned the file in my hands; I knew Luke's file by heart, and I knew I hadn't missed this. Flicking through, I saw pages of data that hadn't been in my copy.

"This isn't the file you gave me," I said in a low voice. "Where did you get it?"

"Upstairs," Cal said quietly, leaning over me.

"Liam's office?" I half expected him to deny it.

"Someone else's."

I stared back at the name — Joseph Andrew Logan. Wayde Logan's fucking younger brother. Luke had shared a prison cell with Joey for two damned years. My day had gone from amazing — waking up with Laura tangled around me — to the shit-fight at lunch, and now this.

I made to move back; even big guys need their personal space, but Cal gripped the back of my chair, preventing me from going anywhere. I caught Black's eye across the room, where he leaned with his back to the glass, speaking loudly to Micah about engines for his monster truck. Where Cal leaned over me, he completely obscured the view out of the office.

He was obviously as concerned about Ally as I was — or he thought the office was bugged. Again. A few years back, when I'd first joined the team, Logan had managed to bug our office. Then there was the memorable case last year which had brought him face-to-face with Cal.

"Will this asshole ever go away?" I groaned. Cal nodded sympathetically.

"Probably not." His hand gripped my shoulder tight. "We'll get this. But I've got to ask you–" Cal cut himself off as Ally walked straight into the room without knocking, holding mugs of coffee. There was silence in the office as Cal liberated the cups and shooed her back out the door.

"Can we sack her, too?" Micah asked, hopefully. Black kicked Micah's chair. Cal frowned at them both.

"Forget Ally. We need to focus. Here." He tapped the file still clutched in my hands. "Danny, will you go back in? You don't have to."

Cal watched me, as though worried I might *not* actually want to go back undercover. Yeah, I had a place to live now, and Laura — but she'd understand, surely? She knew I lived for this. After all, she'd been in my head for months.

I leaned back in my chair, playing it cool.

"I'm good."

Cal gave me a hard stare as I tried to hide my excitement. *Give me something real to do.* I'd begged him for work months ago, and here was my boss, handing me just what I needed.

"It'll be a couple of days before we can send you in," Cal warned, "We'll have to set you back up, and you need a damned good excuse for why you fell off the radar."

"Laura."

Her name rolled off the tip of my tongue. Cal's eyes narrowed.

"What about her?"

"She's my excuse. Luke knows her — had a run-in with her sister, roughed her up a bit — it's fine, I sorted it." I held up a hand as Cal glared at me. He could rip me a new one later. Black snorted, draining one cup of coffee and reached for mine. I waved him away. "I've been shacked up with her. I'm a fucking gym junkie, cheap hacker. He thinks I'm little more than an errand boy. Spending a week fucking my girl is believable."

Cal pointed a finger at me.

"You don't let Laura get pulled into this."

"Hell no, I won't put her in danger." I glared back, letting my outrage simmer to the surface.

Cal nodded, looking around the room. He didn't say anything until he had agreement from Black and Micah. "Okay. How are we going to do this?"

Two hours later we had the bones of a decent plan — assuming nothing had changed in the week I'd been away from the house. I snorted.

"What's funny?" Cal yawned, stretching his arms over his head.

"Bloody Big Brother House." Cal looked at me in askance with raised eyebrows. I pointed to the screen where Luke and his team were displayed. "Someone's always watching."

Cal grinned. "You ready to call it a night?"

"Yeah. Gotta take Laura home." I hoped she was still up for a night at my place. But if she wasn't...*she's a distraction.* I wanted to punch that damned voice, though I knew it was right. *Focus, first.*

I gathered all the files together, pinning various parts with giant bull clips. Cal collected mugs abandoned on the boy's desks, dumping them in the sink.

"They can wash up tomorrow. Bunch of ferals," he grumbled under his breath, "Ally. Time to go."

Ally's head popped up from behind the reception desk. "Sure, Cal."

I raised an eyebrow as she disappeared again. No one except Liam or Black used Cal's name. He rolled his eyes heavenward.

"At least it's not the Great Dane," I grinned. Cal glared at me.

"Don't you *dare*–" he threw a punch at my shoulder. I dodged him easily.

"Damn, old man. You're getting slow." I saw the glint in his eye at my barb. "Well, you've always been slow..." I ducked the next one, too, laughing. "We haven't sparred in far too long."

"Make it a date for tomorrow?"

"Morning? I'll drag my ass outta bed for you."

"Don't stay up late."

Ally appeared, clutching a handbag as she watched us. Cal ushered her out of the office, and into the elevator. I pressed Laura's floor, avoiding Cal's sharp look. With Ally in the small space with us, he didn't say anything, and for once I was glad of her presence.

I waved goodnight, slipping through the doors as soon as they opened. Cal grimaced over Ally's head, and I held back a laugh. Still grinning, I knocked on Laura's office door.

There was no answer. I tried the handle and found it unlocked. Inside, the office was dark. I stepped inside, wondering where she'd gotten to. I checked my phone — there were no messages from her. My thumb hovered over her name until I saw a glow from the side room off her office, where she kept her extra things.

I poked my head into the room. The glow came from the floor. Laura sat cross-legged her black suit, jacket nowhere to be seen, working on her laptop.

"Hey," I greeted her. Laura's head snapped up, a flush crawling up her cheeks.

"Hey!" She flicked her laptop closed, jumping to her feet. The laptop stowed safely in her bag, Laura crossed the room quickly, standing on her toes to wrap her arms around my neck. I buried my head in her hair, breathing her in.

"God, you feel good." I crushed her against me, brushing my lips lightly over hers. She leaned up, seeking more contact, but I drew back. She frowned. "Girl, if I kiss you here, I'm not gonna be able to stop."

Her smile set her whole face aglow.

"Home?" she asked, collecting bags and hoisting them onto her shoulder. I lifted a box of files.

"Home," I agreed. "Do you take these home every night?"

"Oh. These are different ones from last night."

I sent her a sly look. "Do you plan on doing any work tonight?"

Laura slapped me with a manilla folder. "You're intolerable. Did all your deliveries get sorted?"

I nodded, filling her in on my day, but leaving out the part about having to go back undercover. That could wait until tomorrow. She bumped my shoulder, grinning at me through her hair as she followed me down the stairs to the garage.

I managed to keep my hands to myself until we were inside my apartment. The moment I closed the elevator grill, my blood heated. I placed the box full of Laura's things on the floor, striding to where she stood by the new kitchen table, placing her bags in a neat pile on it as she looked around at the newly decorated space.

"It looks awesome, Danny. You've got great taste." She turned a brilliant smile on me, which faded quickly as she watched me stalk towards her. One hand reached back to grip the chair behind her, but to her credit, she didn't retreat.

Pink lips parted, her chest rising quickly as my hands closed around her, and my mouth crashed down onto hers.

Her hands tangled in my hair, tugging gently, then she drew back.

"We just walked in the door," she protested.

"I've wanted you since the office, but I thought it might be...inappropriate to fuck you on your desk." I watched the idea take seed, the way her chest rose, a flush rising in her cheeks.

"Just a little inappropriate," she echoed softly, though her eyes were bright. I smiled against her mouth.

Her tongue flicked out against my lip, her eyes still on mine. I dipped my head, kissing her deeply, reaching behind her to lift her things from my table. She looked over her shoulder.

"What are you doing?"

"What's inappropriate at work is completely acceptable here." Her laptop bag slid onto the floor as I spun her around in my arms. I slipped my hands around her waist, unbuttoning her black pants. They slithered to the floor while I ignored her protests.

She bent forward over the edge of the table, my hand on her back, pushing the chair out of the way. The lines of her legs were smooth. The lacy scrap that passed for underwear ended in a heap on the floor with the rest of her clothes.

I unbuckled my jeans, extracting a condom from my wallet, playing with the wetness of her. Regardless of her protests, the girl was ready. My girl.

I slid against her, teasing to draw a moan from her before I plunged in all the way. Keeping one hand on her back, I worked her slowly. Laura's hands clenched on the tabletop, bracing. Low cries tearing from her throat with every thrust.

Making tiny circles on her clit with my other hand, the table wasn't the only thing she was clenching. I drove faster into her as she came, shouting my own release soon after.

I trailed kisses along her back, cupping her cheek, so she rested on that and not the hard surface of the table.

"Danny," she murmured, "It might be inappropriate in the office, but I still want to try it."

My dick twitched inside her, beginning to harden again.

"I thought you kept work and play separate?"

Laura giggled, wriggling beneath me. I let her up. She eyed the length of me: my shirt open, jeans around my hips. I stood as still as she had when I'd studied her this morning, naked in her hall.

"Obviously not," she said softly, collecting her clothes from the floor. Finding her overnight bag, she headed towards the bathroom. I watched her leave, her hips swaying with more emphasis than usual, I was sure.

I grinned, cleaning up and rearranging my furniture. The table had been a great find — a dark wood with a scratch on the end that didn't bother me complemented a large, brown, faux-suede lounge.

"What do you want for dinner?" I asked as Laura appeared next to me dressed in tights and a racerback tee, damp hair tangled into a knot on top of her head. "Hey, share that shower," I protested mildly, trailing a finger down her spine.

She shivered, pressing against me. "Maybe in the morning," she yawned.

"You can't be tired. We didn't even run today." My hands fit perfectly around her.

"You wore me out." She snuggled against me, digging into her laptop bag.

"You really are going to work all night, aren't you?" I hoisted her bag, plopping everything onto the lounge.

"Mhhm. You forgot to buy groceries, didn't you?" Laura asked with a grimace.

"Got the fridge, though."

"That's handy. Chinese?"

"Huh? Oh, yeah. Sounds good." I scrolled through on my phone while she set herself up at one end of the lounge.

"You need a coffee table," she called over her shoulder.

"Add it to the list," I pointed to a notepad pinned to the fridge by a niffler magnet. "Spicy?"

"Please."

Working together on the lounge was comfortable — far more than I had expected. I sorted through notes on Luke's file, memorising all the details about Luke and Joey's time together. Laura had several calendars running on her laptop, with print outs she constantly referred to.

"How many lives do you run?" I asked, stretching tight shoulders from hunching forward. One of the calendars was blue and by far the most blank. "What's this one?"

Laura snatched it back, blush rising in her cheeks. "Nothing," she mumbled. The corner crumpled, exposing a name at the top. I raised an eyebrow.

"You schedule your sister?"

"No, I– Okay, yes. Sort of." Laura looked up at me with wide eyes and took a deep breath. "It's how many times I see her and when. I haven't heard from her since she left that night after we saw Luke, and I have no idea where she is. This is the only way to try to find her. My parents don't want the police involved."

Still red in the face, she tilted her head forward, letting her hair fall over her face. I brushed it back behind her ears.

"Why don't your parents want the police involved?" My voice was sharper than I meant it to be, and I cringed, softening my tone when she didn't answer. "Laura?"

"She's an embarrassment to them."

"So, they won't look for her? Just leave her with drug dealers — men like Luke? Do they have a clue what could happen to her?" My voice rose. What the hell sort of parents did she have?

"They know." Laura wouldn't look up. "To them, she's a failure. Well, a reminder of *their* failure, and they can't face it. Her."

I nodded, silent as it all processed. "How do they feel about you?"

Laura gave a self-deprecating laugh.

"I'm on the safe list, but only because my business is a success. They still don't talk about me because I don't have a degree. Academics, remember?" Laura shook her head, pain evident in her eyes. "Not everyone has the perfect family you do, Danny."

I held her gaze as she gave me a bitter smile, reaching out to pull her against my chest. She leaned her head on my shoulder, wrapping her arms tight around me. A suspicion niggled in the back of my mind.

"How long has it been since someone held you?" I asked into her hair.

Laura huffed into my chest. "Last boyfriend? I– I'm not sure."

"When was the last boyfriend?" I stroked her hair. She was silent for a long moment.

"A few years ago, maybe?" The admission seemed to scare her as much as it did me. I pushed the files I'd been working on onto the floor, letting them fall into disarray, not caring where they landed.

Pulling her along the length of me, I lifted both of us onto the lounge, her legs tangling with mine. I reached back for the TV remote, flicking on sport, but I wasn't watching it. Tension drained from her as I stroked her hair, her breath becoming even and deep.

It was full dark when I woke beneath her.

Her breathing was deep and regular, her limbs as boneless as they'd been the night before. I slipped my arms around her and carried her to bed. I shucked my clothes onto the floor, sliding carefully into my bed — this time with a full complement of blankets and sheets.

Laura rolled toward me, reaching out, and I gathered her into my arms. She sighed, still more tension leaving her — the woman could give Cal lessons in control. I grinned, settling back with her head on my chest, and slept.

And overslept. A faint beeping alerted me well after the sun had risen. I frowned, flapping at the nightstands I'd placed beside my bed, and only succeeded in knocking over a bottle of water. Swearing, I rolled out from beneath Laura, already missing the intimacy of her against me.

I found my phone in the box of Laura's files in the lounge — all our things were still scattered across the floor where we'd left them the night before. I began piecing Luke's life back together into the file, separating my work from Laura's.

Belinda's calendar lay beneath the sofa, and I scooped it up with my things. If she'd printed it, it was on her computer, so I wasn't taking her only copy. I shuffled it back into my pile as footsteps reverberated along the wooden floor. I wanted to have a look at it later, in the office.

Laura's arms slipped around my shoulders, resting her head on my back.

"Morning."

"Morning," she whispered, her breath warm on my bare skin. "Thank you, for...everything. Last night."

"You're worth it." I reached around, pressing my hand to her back, holding her against me. After a moment, I sighed.

"We have to go to work. Don't we?" Laura spoke into my back.

I swivelled around, pulling her onto my lap. Nodding, I swept strands of soft, silver-blonde hair away from her face, kissing her gently, then more deeply. She wound herself around me, a perfect fit. I broke the kiss, pressing my forehead to hers.

"Yeah."

I left Laura at her office, lingering in the doorway for a last kiss. The file beneath my arm was heavy — I worried I wasn't as prepared as I needed to be. Laura's hands drifted across my chest as she tossed a look over her shoulder, toward her desk.

"Maybe I can mix work with pleasure, after all." She sent me a cheeky grin that quickly became a frown. "What's wrong?"

"I have to go back undercover." I ran my hand over my head, forestalling her objections with a finger lightly pressed to her lips. She nipped at it, and I grinned. "This case is turning out to be bigger than I thought — there's a lot riding on it. I can't say more. Cal or Micah will give you a lift home if that's okay." I smiled apologetically.

She nodded, and I expected her to argue after all we'd been through with my coaching.

"I get it, Danny. Do what you have to do. I'll still be here."

My hand cupping the back of her head, I crushed her mouth beneath mine. When I drew back, we were both gasping for breath.

"I'll keep an eye out for your sister."

Laura's eyes widened. I tapped the door frame with my fist, walking away with a lump in my throat.

I had no idea when I would see her again.

CHAPTER TWENTY-SIX

DANNY

It was still early, and the building was quiet as I walked toward the stairwell. Due to my change in routine — my nights and mornings with Laura — I hadn't run in what felt like ages.

I flexed my ankles and calves as I opened the door to the fire escape, and sprinted the four floors to the office, taking the steps three at a time. Even for a guy my size, it was a stretch.

I hit the landing covered in a light sheen of sweat, gripping Luke's file in one hand. Stretching my legs and shoulders out, I waited until my breathing evened out before I opened the door, checking my watch.

I'd be the first one in by a good hour — even Cal didn't get up this early. I grinned. Mila had softened him a little. I strode through the reception area, intent on compiling the notes I'd made last night in preparation of this morning — Cal was sure to grill me before I was allowed back undercover — and stopped.

A pert ass clad in her trademark white suit was stuck in the air inside our office. I stepped quietly up to the door, watching Ally as she rifled through Cal's desk. Logan's picture lay on the floor, alongside a stack of files on his previous robberies. Was she one of his?

I shook my head; I'd known something wasn't right about her from the start — and I'd ignored my gut.

Fail, number one. I patted the back of my jeans, but I wasn't carrying. We rarely did — Cal was right. If it came to using guns, we *had* already lost. It was time to use the intelligence I tried so hard to hide.

"Whatcha' doing?" I slid the file into the back of my jeans, folding my arms over my chest and leaned casually against the door frame. Effectively blocking the only exit to the room, I still wanted my hands free if this came down to what I expected.

Ally shot up, banging her head on the edge of Cal's desk. She clutched her head as she rose, facing me. Her eyes darted from me to the doorway behind me, and I read the moment she realised she'd have to talk her way past me.

"Ouch," I said conversationally and fell silent. Waiting.

"Danny! Hi, I was just– sorting some things for Cal..." I caught the hesitation before she glossed over it, smoothing her hair where it was mussed. Flush coloured her cheeks — the only time I'd ever seen her off-kilter.

I shook my head, smiling. "No, you weren't."

"I wasn't what?" She still looked longingly at the doorway behind me, but there was no chance she was getting that option.

"Sorting something for Cal. You don't come in here. No one but us does." I took a step toward her. The room was already tight for space with our desks; with me standing in the centre of it, there was no way she could get past me to the door. She looked unnerved but held her ground. "And you're not one of us, are you, Ally?"

Ally opened her mouth, thought about it, then closed it again. I waited, unwilling to put words into her mouth that she could latch onto as a scapegoat.

She dipped her head, coming back with a smile that set everything on edge. She even took a step my way, halting when I raised an eyebrow.

"Maybe you don't know everything about Cal...and I." She swung her hair, looking at me through her lashes.

"After all, we have some very late nights together, and you haven't been here that much."

Oh, the seeds of doubt. I knew my boss well, just as I knew she was full of shit. She played it well, though; if I hadn't seen her in action, it would be an easy play to believe.

"Ah, don't go there, babe." I sent her my soulless smile, and she retreated a step. My smile got bigger. "I'll call him right now, right?" *Fuck, I sound like Liam.*

"No! Please," she begged, eyes wide, searching behind me for a way out. "I– I don't want Mila to know."

"Bullshit. I'll ask once more. What are you doing in here?"

Lips pursed, Ally looked straight at me, apparently coming to some sort of decision. Her hands went behind her back, but I shook my head, and she dropped them in resignation. Just because I hadn't spotted a weapon on her, didn't mean she wasn't carrying concealed.

"If you put your hands back there again, I'll have to arrest you."

She smiled, a hard-edged thing, and I realised I'd made a mistake. Ally straightened, flipping her blonde hair over her shoulder, the attitude she wore so well returned in full force.

"You can't arrest me, Danny. I'm Internal Affairs."

"Fuck me." I sat through her quick rundown of her investigation, running the key points around in my head. Liam didn't know who she was, and neither did Cal, nor any other member of the team.

We'd done some questionable things in our last operation — and Ally was here to check over our process. Any fuck up on our part meant Logan could be released back into the wild, like a fucking fish. And lastly, I couldn't say a word to anyone.

Not Micah, not Black, certainly not Laura.

Not Cal.

I slapped my hand hard on top of my boss' desk.

"This is bullshit," I groused as Ally jumped. She smoothed her hair again when I glared at her, and she had the grace to look discomforted.

"Tell anyone, and you lose your job." The smug expression suited her all too well.

I shook my head as she finished tidying the mess she'd made on Cal's desk. It was so tempting to tell her to shove it. I pressed my lips together, pissed at myself for not spotting it earlier. It was so obvious when I looked back: the comment she'd made about Cal not touching Steph as he escorted her out on the first day, fishing for information on Liam's ulterior motives.

"You all have it so fucking wrong," I growled at her back, digging my phone out of my pocket.

"Really? There's a lot of questionable practices in this office, and you all took your sweet time locating Wayde Logan," she snapped back.

"Are you kidding me? Cal barely slept for five damned years trying to find Logan, to fix the stuff-up for letting him escape in the first place! Liam's only bloody *agenda*, as you put it on your first day, is looking out for all of us. Yeah, I remembered," I remarked caustically at her surprised look. "The funny thing about being part of a task force team and doing undercover work is that we remember *everything*. That's what gets us through."

I yanked my phone out of my pocket, my skin prickling. I had to walk this off if I was going to be able to face Cal today, and convince him everything was normal — and I hadn't decided if I was going to do that, yet.

"What are you doing?" She grabbed my phone, alarmed. I snatched it back.

"I'm messaging Micah to set up my undercover messages. You *do* know all the things we do to make these cases work, right?" I snapped pettily, "and I thought you said not to touch anyone."

Ally glowered at me as I kept typing. I *was* setting up more messages with Micah just in case Luke or one of his minions got into my phone. Yet there was another purpose to the coded message, too.

Danny M: Watched the game last night. Bloody shitfight.

Dots appeared while Micah read my message. I didn't usually bother with them until after I went under — I was gambling he'd recognise something was off.

Brad the Dick: You watch it at home? We win?

Danny M: Nah, lost like fools. Idiots upstairs fucking with their strategy. The new cheerleader was a bit off.

More dots appeared and disappeared. I assumed he was messaging Cal. I tapped the phone on my leg, leaving the screen open for Ally to see. I sent her a vacant, meaningless smile.

"The usual bullshit set up. Makes it look like I woke up with a hangover or lost money. Both things this group would assume." Assume, though Luke knew I didn't drink.

Ally nodded, glancing at my phone and away. It vibrated in my hand, and I blacked the screen until she moved back out to the reception area.

Brad the Dick: Ah, too bad. I'm sure we'll catch them in the next round.

I hid my grin, glad he'd understood. Liam would know by now that something was wrong. With him and Cal looking after everyone, I could go back undercover with no other concerns than finding out what Luke's arrangement was with Wayde Logan.

Cal walked in, talking with Black. He tossed me a file, completely ignoring Ally, who watched us all from behind her desk with a bright, fake smile. I flicked the top of the file, looking at Cal speculatively.

"Today?"

He nodded, stopping in the middle of the reception area. "If you're ready."

"You know I am." I grinned; this was a conversation we'd never usually have outside the incident room.

"Liam might come down later. He wants a word about your coaching before we lose you again."

Ally snorted, and all three of us turned to stare down at her. She coloured, mumbling something and buried herself in work I was sure had little to do with our office. Cal winked at me, gesturing to the office, Micah bringing up the rear as he arrived.

Cal closed the door, leaning against it. Micah joined him, and between the two of them, they formed a barrier between Ally and us, assuming she could lip read. If the office was bugged, we were probably all screwed anyway.

"Is Liam really back from leave?"

Cal nodded. "And Selena has a new case to work on."

"She's tough to get around." I grinned. Cal nodded.

"Liam will keep her in check." His expression sobered. "*Are you ready?*"

"Yeah. And I might have something extra." I outlined the relationship I suspected had developed between Luke and Belinda, and how I thought we could use it to extract Laura's sister. Not involve the cops, be damned. If the girl was there, I was getting her out. My estimation of Laura's parents sank with every moment.

"You two right to set up?" Cal looked between Micah and me.

Micah waved his phone in my direction. "Already started."

"Good. Get the rest sorted. Anything you need taken care of while you're under?"

It was Cal's standard question, every time. He'd look after everything I needed — but I was mostly organised, this time.

"Rent's set up for direct debits — if I'm there longer than a month, I've emailed you my utilities' passwords. Pay those?" Cal gave a single nod. "And can someone take Laura home tonight? She spent the night at my place, so she doesn't have a car."

Micah grinned. "I got her."

"Thanks, dude. Appreciate it."

And that fast, I was back on the job.

Luke wasn't as easy to convince as I'd made out to Cal, nor had I expected him to be. I was waiting outside his house with an overnight bag when he and his crew rocked up; the sly bastard had changed the locks.

"Well, fuck me. You got balls."

He opened the door, and I followed them in, ignoring the glares.

"I was gone for four bloody days."

"You didn't say you were coming back," he countered. "And it was for six days."

I nodded. "That's fair."

"Surprised you didn't break in."

I grinned at that one. "Couldn't be bothered."

Luke grinned back, nodding — but not to me. Three sets of hands grabbed my arms, pulling me down — or tried to. I just stood there, and slowly extracted my arms, folding them over my chest.

"Good show guys." I shook my head at them, laughing. Three disgruntled faces glared at me, but I ignored the lot. "You want a shot, go ahead. Might take one back, though."

Luke considered me, eyes assessing.

"You with the blonde?"

"Every night. And some mornings," I added, thinking back. I brought my attention back to the present as Luke stepped up to me. Of a height, we were literally nose to nose. The grandstanding was a bit much, even for me, but I waited, the urge to head-butt him growing stronger with each moment.

"I tell you about a job, and you fuck off three nights later. Don't call, don't let us know what you're doing. Doesn't look right, yeah?"

I looked him straight in the eye.

"If I break your nose, will we still be friends?"

Luke laughed, stepping back. He'd made his point, and I'd gotten away with it cheaply — though I expected this to come back to bite me at some point later on.

The boys partied, as usual, that night — and the next, and the one after that. Three days after they'd sent me back in, I knew nothing more than I had at the end of my last stint. I sat in the hazy club, pretending to be interested in the frazzled, underweight blonde beside me, trying not to cough my lungs up.

And missing Laura like hell.

I mulled over Luke's deal of the night — a small drug stash, but nothing I'd bother busting them over. Once the bust was done, that was it — I wouldn't get any more from them. And Logan had never bothered with drugs — this was just pocket money for Luke.

I leaned back, raising my hand to a group of guys who'd been in the club the last time I was here. Sweaty palms slapped mine, and I resisted the urge to wipe it on my jeans. Instead, I draped it across the seatback.

The girl beside me preened. Luke caught my eye, looking pointedly at the girl. I snorted. He wasn't likely to

care if I cheated on Laura — which I wasn't going to do —
but it didn't fit with the image I'd presented before.

I leaned over the girl, whispering in her ear, letting my
hand trail down her side. She gave me a cheeky grin, rising. I
slapped her rump, sending her off in Luke's direction. He
laughed openly at me, grabbing the girl's head, and directing
it to his crotch. I looked away as her fingers got busy.

"You still got that truck?"

I turned my attention to one of the low-life thugs who
had greeted me earlier.

"Yeah, she's still running well."

"Sweet, who did you get those rims from?" I sighed,
coming up with some bullshit story about stolen parts I'd
gotten cheap, and the hours rolled on.

I was ready to call it a night when a familiar mop of
frazzled red hair stumbled across the dance floor. I
interrupted a bloke telling me about his latest fling, who was
into whips.

"Gotta piss, dude."

"Yeah, yeah." He waved me away, turning to a guy on
his other side who had passed out. He talked to his dozing
form, anyway.

Once I was out of the main room, I broke into a jog, catching Belinda as she tottered toward the lady's bathroom.

"Hey." I grabbed her arm, turning her carefully, lest she spewed on me.

Belinda wobbled on her spiked heels, lifting her face to me. It took everything I had not to recoil. Dark circles hung beneath her eyes, yellow bruises fading around the eye sockets in an uneven row — like she'd been hit multiple times.

"Jesus," I swore, scooping her up. I carried her down the dark hall, away from the boom of the club, and kicked the back door open. My truck was parked on the kerb at the front, but it was only a short walk through the carpark. I had one foot in the clear when Luke appeared around the corner, trailed by Justin, McKenna, and Mini-me.

I sneered at Zahn.

"What the fuck do you want?"

"Following the big man." The little shit preened like a fucking peacock.

"Yeah, never one to think for yourself."

Zahn flipped me the bird. Luke shooed him back.

"Stop bitching," he frowned, turning to me. "What are you doing?" He nodded to Belinda in my arms, who had passed out judging by her snores, and was becoming heavy.

"Just looking after my girl's sister."

"Yeah? 'Cause one of the boys in there says you're a cop."

"You get whatever he was smoking? Sounds good." I stepped forward, but they refused to part. Shit. The hard way, then. I kicked Zahn in the shin. "Move, dickweed."

He grunted and smiled cruelly, removing his hand from his pocket. Light flashed on the metal beneath the streetlights, and he gestured for me to back into the carpark. I moved back just far enough to put a little distance between us. I wasn't worried he'd win — unless someone had a gun, which was always a possibility. But I couldn't fight in the dark — and the carpark had death written all over it. Plus, Belinda was likely to end up getting hurt. Damnit, Black was the knife fighter, not me.

"We're going to do this here? Fuck me." I didn't look away from Luke, but I spoke to Zahn. "You are as stupid as you look." I hoisted Belinda's inanimate form. "Would you?"

Luke's lip curled as he took her gingerly, holding her facing out. I sympathised.

"Make it quick," he advised quietly.

I raised an eyebrow, then kicked Zahn in the balls. He howled, bending at the waist and swearing in fragments as he clutched himself. I caught him twice on the side of the head with a wheel kick, and he dropped. It was a showy move, and completely unnecessary, but it sent a message. I collected Belinda from Luke, who eyed me.

"Maybe I should've put you in the cage."

"Fuck outta the way," I snarled, hefting Belinda.

Mini-me groaned, puking on himself. I nudged him with my toe, hoping I hadn't damaged the poor bastard. He was small-time, and always would be, living in the shadow of a crook like Luke.

Likely to share a jail cell with him, too. Which brought me back to the point. They were into cage fighting as well? And now, Luke knew I could fight. This night just kept getting better and better. I strode past him, strapping Belinda into the passenger seat.

I walked back to Luke, who watched Zahn stumble to his knees.

"You and I need to have a conversation," I growled. Luke nodded, not looking at me. "About Joey Logan."

Luke's head whipped around. I held his gaze, letting the emotion drop from me as fast as I'd dropped his mate. He stuck his chin out, nodding. I held back a sneer — riled as I was, punching him would be easy right now. Too damned easy.

Stay on the right side of the line, Danny.

I strode back to my truck, expecting to hear footsteps crunching the gravel and a knife in my back, but no one followed me. I checked Belinda was okay and drove to Laura's house.

Laura let me in, wrapped in a slinky robe that did nothing for the fact that I couldn't stay with her.

"Danny? It's three in the morning. I think." She yawned blearily, peering at the bundle in my arms. "Wait– is that–?" Her face cleared of sleep with a speed that surprised me. She stepped back from the door, pointing me to the couch.

"She's okay," I shushed her. "I've checked. I've also called a doctor. He'll be here in an hour or so. I don't think she's OD'd, but you probably need to keep an eye on her."

"It's okay," Laura dropped to her knees, "I'll sit with her."

I squeezed her shoulder, wanting to kiss her, but the grime of the club still clung to my skin. I was too dirty for her clean house, her clean life. She glanced over her shoulder.

"You're not staying?"

"Nah, gotta get back, sort some shit out. Keep in touch with Cal. He'll make sure you're up-to-date." *He'd better this time.* I headed up the hall, but she called me back.

"Thanks, Danny."

I sat in my truck without a jacket, freezing my balls off outside her house. It wasn't until I pulled away from the kerb that I saw another vehicle behind me mirroring my movements. Within a block, I knew I was being followed. Which meant they knew where Laura lived.

Fuck, I was an idiot.

Sighing, I dialled Cal.

"What's up?" he demanded. He sounded wide awake for the wee hours.

"They know where Laura lives. I need someone there, now. I have to get back to the house."

"Shit. I'll call Black — maybe Micah. They'll look after it."

"Thanks." A toilet flushed in the background on Cal's end. "You guys okay?"

"Yeah, Mila's been sick. We were up." Voice gravelly, he spoke low and away from the receiver. Mila answered, soft and weak.

"Okay." I was unconvinced, but I couldn't help him, right now. "I hope she's alright."

I hung up, wishing I hadn't bothered my boss. Taking a few more turns, I drove past the club and lost my tail. Had to have been one of Luke's.

I headed back to the house to wait it out.

CHAPTER TWENTY-SEVEN

DANNY

I leaned back on the sofa, wondering if I should have raided Cal's firearm cabinet. My head ran with scenarios, but I waited, head back, eyes closed. Resting. This could be an opportunity or a shit fight, but I'd need to be as wide awake as Cal to get through it, either way. Passed out, I was only a danger to myself if I wasn't coherent when the boys dragged Zhan's ass in.

Cars pulled up along the drive, and I shot Micah a message. He'd stayed with Laura while the night doctor attended her sister and hung out until Cal could relieve him. I let the information slide from my mind — that wasn't the headspace I needed to be in right now.

Danny M: Saw the girl. Bit of a crowd happening.

Brad the Dick: Hanging out if you need.

Danny M: Good for now.

Knowing I had Micah as back up helped. He and Black would likely be within spitting distance of the house, trying not to be obvious. Black could blend — he had a rough edge the rest of us lacked — but Micah had no chance. It was something he thrived on.

I grinned, putting my phone on my knees. Luke walked in, trailed by a mute crowd carrying a half-conscious Zahn. His head lolled on his shoulders. A small pit of concern ignited in my stomach, but I buried it deep. Danny Miller wouldn't give two shits if he'd killed the sucker. Luke nodded my way.

"Surprised you're here." Justin and McKenna took Zhan into his room. "Not your damage."

I looked at him in surprise. "Didn't think you'd care."

"About him?" Luke huffed a laugh, pouring himself a shot of whiskey. He offered it to me, but I shook my head. "Nah. Bout you — yeah." He eyed me as he sat, the boys scampering down the hall, then tossed back the shot.

"Why the fuck you care about me?"

Luke tapped the shot glass on his leg. "Well, for one thing, you're a fucking liar. How'd you know about Joey?"

"What'm I lying about now?" I didn't look at him, hoping I could scrape this if he thought it was something small.

"Your girl — sister of the junkie slut you keep saving — lives in a pretty nice area. Works in one, too."

"Yeah?" I held his gaze, this time.

"Yeah." Luke placed the glass on the small table between us. "Her office is in the same building that houses police task force operations. You remember that friend who told me you were a cop?" He changed tact quickly. I knew I was in deep shit. I called Micah with my thumb, sliding the phone between the lounge pillows, microphone up.

"Never met him," I yawned.

"Mmm. Reckon you might. Little weedy guy, glasses. Bit of a techie — knows less than he thinks. Ringing any bells?"

"Nope."

But it did — Mila had described a guy just like him, from when she was held up in a bank by Wayde Logan, six years ago. We'd never found him. If he was talking to Luke on Logan's behalf, he was my way in.

"Really. Seems to me that Daniel Elijah Woods is a hot-shot career cop, moving up the ladder."

"Fuck, no. That's my boss."

Luke laughed. "Man, you got some balls."

"I've been told."

Luke nodded, sobering. "Sorry about this, man."

"What's Logan giving you? Apart from the code to break into banks for more cash flow?" Luke shook his head, mouth tight. I grinned. If I was in, I was all in. "C'mon, dude. We both know you didn't write that."

Luke sneered. "But I'll use it. Set us up nicely — though I needed a scapegoat. Was gonna be you," I nodded at his concession; I'd suspected as much. Luke's head canted. "Might throw Zahn under the bus instead."

"Mini-me? He'll be crushed." I grinned.

"Feel good to get a shot in with him?"

"A little too good."

"You really just gonna sit there, in my house, and think this is gonna turn out all right? I can't let you walk out that door, man." Luke leaned forward, planting his elbows on his knees.

I nodded as his movements became more erratic. First came the calm, the jokes. Then he'd try to convince me, and finally, the anger would hit. That I'd betrayed him, that he wasn't in control.

But if he was working for Logan, he hadn't been in control for a very long time.

"I know." I relaxed my shoulders and pasted a dopey grin on my face.

"Shit, man. I liked you." *Past tense.* I needed to get him to the point before he tried to kill me and it was all over. "Drop the cop thing. You can make a shit ton of cash with me. We walk away, never have to worry about anything again. Few jobs, a few years, you and your woman can do anything you want." His eyes glowed with a vision of a future that was never going to happen.

"You working for Wayde Logan, Luke?"

His head jerked as it had outside the club when I'd given him Joey's name. He leaned closer, pointing a finger at me.

"You don't get to do this, the cop thing. That's not who you are!" He stood, pacing, a lion in a cage. A bump outlined against his back as he moved. I needed to get this done, fast.

"What's he promised you, beyond riches? A place with him? He's going away for a long time, dude. He's got no power from where he'll be sitting."

Luke laughed — a dark, deep laugh that made my flesh want to crawl off my bones. "You got no idea — no fucking idea what he can do, do you?" There was a manic gleam in his eye as he reached back beneath his shirt. "His reach will never be broken by your *system*," he spat the last word. At least he was true to his hacker tendencies.

"How's he contacting you?" I stood before he could draw the weapon. If I stayed on the sofa, I was dead.

"He found me," Luke almost yelled in my face, "knew from his brother what I could do, set us all up for life."

You'll get life, my friend, but it won't be the one you think.

"He call you? Or he hack you?" He would have saved it. And there'd be a trail. If this was how Logan was contacting him, I could trace it. All I needed was his computer.

Luke's face went blank, and I almost laughed. The hacker had been hacked. I wanted to grin, before he jerked his arm free, bringing the gun from his back around in a wide arc.

I dived for his arm, getting inside his range before he could aim the bloody thing my way, a roar filling my ears.

Suddenly, there was a lime green motorbike in the living room, and the door lay in splinters on the floor. I took the opportunity to punch Luke in the face, disarming him quickly.

Black leaned over the front of the bike, staring at Luke on the floor, then back to me. "Sounded like you needed some help."

"Where the hell did this come from?" I surveyed the bike, glad the conversation had been audible from my phone.

"Been taking tips from Cal."

I laughed, kicking away Luke's hand as he grabbed at my leg. Zahn appeared in the doorway to his room, pasty as he stared at Black. He produced the knife, again. I sighed for the poor bastard. Some souls never learn.

"Who the f–"

Black lashed out with his boot, kicking Zahn in the ear. I winced as he went down for the second time.

"Gentle with that one. I already got him."

"Didn't do much." Black paused as two figures appeared at the end of the hall. Justin and McKenna paused, surveying the room and its new occupants, and bolted back the way they'd come. Black spoke into a wrist mike. "You got them?" He nodded, and I knew Micah was on the other end. He looked at me.

I held up a hand. "I'm fine."

"Did you get what you need?"

"I got enough."

Which was true — I had enough to lock these guys up, with Selena's help in court — and I could link them to Logan. That was the pinch. I just needed access to Luke's computer. I nodded to where Luke rolled on the floor, blood pouring from his nose. "You got him?" Black nodded, drawing his own weapon.

"Yeah."

I retrieved my phone from the lounge, checking when Micah had ended the call. Ten minutes ago. Shit, had he even hung around to hear the end of it? Probably not.

I dialled Cal's number, but it rang out. I frowned — Cal always picked up. I was about to call Liam when my phone rang.

"Cal?"

"Yeah?" Cal's voice was rough.

"Were you asleep?"

"Yeah, Danny. What's up?"

"We got him." A grin crept up my face.

"Yeah?" Cal sounded more awake. "Where are you? Are you okay?"

I gave him a rundown of the situation. The other end was silent for a minute while Cal processed the lot. I knew he was already picking loopholes in the case. He'd come back at me with what I could do now, to prevent any problems with processing the arrests.

I thought he had gone back to sleep when he finally spoke.

"Logan's got his finger in everything. You did good, Danny. Good job. Get your ass together there, whatever you need to work on, bring it back. Come home."

"Thanks, boss."

From Cal, they were high words of praise indeed, but I wasn't happy with how it had closed off. I still wanted to interrogate Luke, though I wouldn't be given a chance. Cal would handle that — he was too invested in cutting Logan off from the rest of the world. As I mulled through everything I'd gotten from Luke — which wasn't much — I knew we'd only cracked the tip of the iceberg.

CHAPTER TWENTY-EIGHT

DANNY

I trawled through all the information on Luke's computers with bleary eyes. We'd hauled in everything useful from the house, and I'd planted my backside firmly in my chair, spreading paraphernalia around the office. Micah had helped me with a bit of it, but this wasn't a strength of anyone in the office but mine.

Instead of taking up their office hours, I'd stayed through the day and overnight. After the first few times I'd snapped at them for broken concentration, they'd left me alone. Not in peace, exactly, but quiet enough that I could get the job done. After that, well, if Cal wanted my head on a platter, he could have it.

Ally had departed with a high head and the rest of the team, Cal escorting her from the office much as he had with Steph on the first morning our new *receptionist* started. I could bang my head about that one all day, but in the end, Cal knew who she was, though he'd not yet shared that information with her. He'd let her know he was onto her when it suited him — which was likely the day he knew he held her job in his hands.

The glass rattled around the office, and I snarled, regardless that it was seven in the morning.

"If you bastards keep leaning on that bloody wall, it'll shatter."

Being awake all night had not improved my disposition, though I had cleared the final file. I had everything Cal needed to put Luke away — and, more importantly, link him directly to Wayde Logan. As usual, Joey had just been a means to an end for Logan — and I suspected yet again that the brothers didn't get on, at all.

"It's good to see you, too, Danny."

My head whipped up. I blinked, trying to reconcile the voice and the person hanging from the office door.

"Liam!" I stood, planting my fists on my desk as Liam attempted to skirt around the computer drives and cords I'd rearranged our office with. "Sorry about this. I'll get it sorted once I..." I gestured to the mass of papers and notes I was working through.

Liam inclined his head, crisp in a charcoal suit, regardless that the sun hadn't risen, yet. His short, dark hair streaked with early greys; his elegance was almost indecent at this hour. "Not a problem. Been here all night?"

"Yup."

"Got what you need?"

"Yup." I shifted my fist, pressing it to the top of the file. "Everything Selena needs is right here."

Liam nodded, leaning on the edge of Cal's desk. "Good job. You took a big risk going back in just to get this for us." He let a small smile slip. "Selena had bail denied."

"For Logan?" My head wanted to explode. Liam nodded.

"Thanks again."

His words were casual, but this was Liam — there was never going to be a smarter guy in the room — not even me, no matter how Cal might pander to my ego. There was always more to it.

I inclined my head. "It's the job."

"Is it?" Liam reached for the file I'd put together on Luke. I handed it to him. "This is in good order. Selena will be appreciative. As am I." Liam finished flipping through the file.

"You're welcome?"

Liam smiled. "I'm sure Cal is glad to have you as part of his team. Keep it up. But no more undercover, Danny. You have a life now. Don't waste it. Can I take this?" He indicated the file.

I nodded, unsure what to say, torn between pride at his praise and sadness that welled at his words. *No more undercover work.* But he was right. And I knew he fought his own demons — Liam's words came from the heart.

"Sure. Thanks for coming up this early."

"Oh, I'm going down. You're not the only one who's pulled an all-nighter." Liam grimaced, scratching his chin. A salt and pepper shadow framed a sharp and intelligent face. "I'll get this sorted for you and off to Selena's office."

"Appreciate it."

I watched Liam leave the office. For a man not yet forty, he had a serious physical presence. I guessed that's what a decade of special ops work got you, and a solid police career to boot. I'd never be as hard as him. As I settled back into tidying up remaining loose ends, I realised I wasn't competing with him and Cal any longer.

I flicked off the laptop as the sun crested the city, blinding me. I turned away from the window, rubbing my eyes and wondering if I'd had retina burn from the stupid thing — working in the dark hours was far faster. I didn't miss the chatter that cluttered my day. But as the stairwell door opened, I realised I had missed my team.

They trooped in, much fresher than me — but then, they had gotten sleep. Micah and Black bantered their way through the office, trading jabs, while Cal brought up the rear. Dark circles hung under his eyes. I took in his haggard appearance — shoulders bowed, crinkled shirt as though he'd slept in it — or tried to. Liam and I weren't the only ones in need of a shave.

He hadn't looked this bad since we'd been chasing Logan.

"Morning," I chirruped. Three bodies halted, peering at me with suspicious eyes. "What?"

"You high?" Black made a show of checking me over. I batted away his hands, laughing.

"Nope."

"Got laid?" Micah grinned, and I rolled my eyes.

"He's done." Cal circled my desk, flicking through my notes. I nodded, sliding out of his way. "Where's the file?"

"Liam took it earlier."

"Liam was here?" Cal looked surprised.

"Yup. Ready to go to Selena."

Cal's haggard outlook broke into a genuine smile. "You connected the dots?"

"Every one."

He clapped my shoulder. "Well done, Danny. Well done."

My grin matched his. I couldn't help it — his praise meant the world. More than Liam's, and that was a pretty high standard — no one could match him.

Micah fist-bumped me, grinning from ear to ear. Even Black patted me on the shoulder, bestowing a rare smile of his own.

"How's Jenny and Ash?" I asked. Cal seated himself, flicking on his terminal. My notes lay on the corner of his desk. "What's up with the boss?"

Black leaned back. "He'll be fine. Girls are good — Jenny sleeps better knowing Logan isn't free. Don't think she slept much before we put him away."

I grinned at his words, realising I was several days behind in news — another reason to drop the undercover stints.

"Jenny's a special girl," I said the words casually, watching his reaction.

Black's face closed, and he spun to get into his own work. I hid a grin. Jenny had her work cut out breaking the hard bastard down, though I didn't doubt she was up to the task. Black was stubborn as hell, but he had a protective streak, and Jenny and Ashley had fallen right into his path.

Two sets of high heels slapped the floor, and every head in the office raised as we watched two blondes enter the office. Laura smiled at me, breaking away from Ally quickly as she made her way to the office door, but didn't come in.

"Come in, Laura." Cal waved her in before I had a chance. "Pretty sure you know nearly everything about this case anyway. How's your sister?"

"She's fine. Sleeping at my parent's place."

"They took her in?" I was surprised, given the stories she'd told me about them previously. Laura raised her hands in an exasperated gesture.

"Not really. She's going into rehab for a hundred days. We'll see what happens."

I nodded, making my way across the office. She looked up at me, lips parted, then dropped her eyes, squeezing the strap of her laptop bag. She mustn't have even gone to her office first before coming up to see me. Warmth spread in my chest. I caught the tip of her chin, tilting her head back, and kissed her softly.

A soft cough caught my attention, and I looked around with a frown. After Cal's display with Mila during the last case, there was no chance he should be able to have a go at me. But it wasn't Cal.

I followed the line of his gaze to where Ally sat, sitting straight up at her desk, lips pursed as she stared at me. Laura made to step back, but I wound my arms around her, pulling her to my chest.

"Stay," I murmured into her hair.

Cal sighed, running his hand over his head.

"Get it over with," Black's voice echoed from the back of the room. Micah began to rise.

"You want us to go?"

"Stay. This is your office, not hers." Cal raised his eyebrows until he got nods around the room. He stopped at us. "You're always welcome here, Laura." His heavy gaze lit on me. "As are you, Danny. Damn fine job."

Cal pushed his chair back, striding across the office. He shed his exhaustion as he walked, straightening to his full height. Bearing energy I would never want to be aimed in my direction as he approached Ally's desk. She scooted back a little, trying to school her features, and failing miserably.

"What's going on?" Laura twisted in my arms.

"Ally's about to find out all the things she never knew about Cal and this team."

Laura's brow dipped, and I explained everything I knew about Ally's real job. I'd done some digging; my findings were in the reports on Cal's desk.

Apparently threatened by Liam's intent to promote Cal, some of the politicians upstairs decided Cal was getting too big for his britches and were going to take him down a notch. I snorted — that wasn't happening any time soon.

Ally stood as Cal spoke, never raising his voice, though the colour of her skin soon matched the bleached-out tone of her hair. She glared once in my direction, her lips a tight line, then stormed to the elevator, pressing the up button.

"E.T. phone home," Micah squeaked.

I snorted; Laura laughed into my chest.

"You okay?" I asked Cal as he leaned on the door, a hundred years older in an instant.

"Yeah," he croaked. "That's gonna bite me, later." He nodded to where Ally had disappeared in a swish of white.

"Gonna have to deal with more of that shit if you move upstairs."

"You're not getting my job, Danny."

"Fuck, no. Keep the damned thing." I grinned. "Seriously, though. What's going on? I haven't seen you this tired since Logan."

"That's not a good omen, then." Cal paused; head down. After a moment's silence, he looked up to find us all watching him. He sighed again, running a hand over his head, grumbling under his breath. Black never moved, arms crossed over his massive chest. Whatever this was, he already knew about it.

"Boss?" I prompted. Even Laura stilled in my arms, her head canted to one side.

"Fuck's sake, man. Tell them," Black growled from the back of the room.

Cal looked around, eyes settling on Laura with a small smile.

"Mila's pregnant."

Shouts bounced around the room, Laura wriggling like a new puppy. She launched at Cal, hugging him tightly as she spoke into his ear. Cal nodded, grinning tiredly as he returned her hug. After a moment, I stepped forward.

"Alright, enough." I tugged Laura back to me with a grin. She slapped my shoulders. "Ow?" I asked, "Congrats, dude."

Cal nodded. "Thanks, Danny. Now clean up your shit —I don't have time to worry about a second child."

EPILOGUE

LAURA

Fading sunlight fell across the city outside my open window. I closed my laptop, checking my watch. We'd all knocked off early with so many things going on. Both Danny and Cal — and Liam, by the sound of it — needed rest; the other two boys hit the gym while I was packing up.

Content to work from home, I closed Danny's file, satisfied with the feedback I'd had from Liam and Cal. Danny had achieved more than I could ever have hoped for — and I truly doubted I had an inch to do with any of it. It was inside him, all this time. We'd all known that; he just had to start believing in himself.

I checked my watch for the umpteenth time — he'd said he was going to be around shortly after we'd left the office at midday. Now late afternoon, I was running out of ways to distract myself from missing him.

My phone buzzed. I frowned at his message but went to the front door. He stood on the stoop, trying to hide a cheeky grin that crept onto his face, regardless of how hard he tried to hide it.

"What are you up to?"

"Lounge. Now." He pointed. I rolled my eyes, following the dramatic plan he'd obviously laid out in his head. One thing I'd learned with Danny — I wouldn't find out what he was doing until he was good and ready to share his plan with me.

"What are you hiding–" I turned in the centre of my living room, cutting myself off as I was accosted at thigh height by a large barrel of fluff that launched at me. A bright red lead trailed the animal as it lapped the room, slipping and sliding around.

Danny appeared at the end of the hall; a goofy grin plastered across his face.

"Danny...?"

He kneeled, and the furball launched at him, snuggling upside down at his feet. He rubbed the dog's belly, and I saw it was a girl.

"This is Tilly. She's a rejected working dog, just hit her juvenile period. Belgium Malinois. Completely trained — but wouldn't take to the bite. Likes cuddles too much, and she can smell toast at two hundred metres." He unclipped the lead, coiling it around his wrist. The dog slithered to me, wrapping herself around my ankles as though she was a cat — a metre and a bit long pretend cat.

I slid my fingers through her fur. "She's beautiful."

"She'll run flat out for nine hours of the day, and cuddle for the rest. She'll protect you here — but more than that, she's company. Whether I'm here or not, she's yours." Danny stepped back, clenching the lead until the leather creaked in his huge hands. "If you want her."

Almond-shaped, soft brown eyes stared at me from a tan face, her long snout black as though she'd dipped it in tar.

"Tilly," I said softly. She bounced over my lap, flattening me to the floor. God knew how many kilograms of dog suddenly curled on my chest, trying to nap, apparently. Laughing, I let Danny help me up. "She's gorgeous."

"You like her?"

I grinned. "Yes! I like her. I'll keep her." I stood on my toes, kissing him. Huge arms engulfed me. "Can I keep you, too?" My words were muffled, but his chest rumbled with laughter as Tilly plonked her huge body across our feet.

"I'm never leaving," Danny growled in a low voice, sending shivers along my spine. He threaded his fingers into my hair, pulling me hard against him.

If you liked Danny & Laura's story, please leave a review for BLINDSIDED here:

www.books2read.com/Blindsided-BBB2

ACKNOWLEDGEMENTS

Danny's story has been my favourite story to date to write (who am I kidding, they're all my favourites!)

As always, there is a massive team who help put a book together. It all starts with a few ideas and knocking around some thoughts with some writer friends, then I dive into the research.

Biggest, biggest thanks to Damian Marret for all the help with undercover work, PTSD, operations, and other cop culture. Danny wouldn't be who he is without you, and I wouldn't have a story to give you!

Coutney Zatz Moebe - thanks for some amazing stories on your time undercover. They blew my mind, and it gave new depth to relationships and expectations.

My amazing Beta and ARC teams - you guys constantly amaze me with the effort you put into helping develop the story to its best and help me get it out there.

Rozie, for formatting and doing all the pretties for the series.

Sam Eckford, my most incredible critique partner who doesn't seem to mind what time of day we discuss things and lets me know exactly where I've missed the mark.

My local writing friends - Jacinta, Jo & Neen - thank you for the virtual coffees over COVID and here's to actually having a real over together very soon!

My R S Wilde girls - OMG you guys are my sanity. I would never have gotten into half this writing stuff without you.

Ashley, thank you for editing my books. Short notice, long term, and there are always more coming. These books shine ONLY because of you. Eternally grateful.

And you, reader, because you made it all the way through. If you have time, please leave a review. They mean the world. I truly hope you enjoyed Danny's story. The rest are coming.

Sofia xx

ABOUT THE AUTHOR

Sofia is a romantic suspense author from Brisbane, Australia. She started writing romance when she couldn't find the books she wanted on the shelves in her local bookstore and became addicted to storytelling. She exists on a diet of coffee and champagne and routinely kills her collection of tortured orchids.

Join Sofia's newsletter & get a free Blue Blooded Brothers short story:

https://dl.bookfunnel.com/xxyzuy8z4k

Follow her on BookBub:

https://www.goodreads.com/author/show/20210299.Sofia_Aves

Find her on Amazon:

Stalk Sofia in her reader group:

BLUE BLOODED BROTHERS SERIES

Collision - Blue Blooded Brothers

www.books2read.com/Collision-LQP

Politics & Paperwork

www.books2read.com/politicsandpaperwork

Sentinel

Coming in 2020

Impact

Coming soon

Reckoning

Coming soon

Keep reading for a sneak peek of Politics & Paperwork...

POLITICS & PAPERWORK

LIAM

I opened the door feeling like the devil had slept in my skin the night before, then discarded it for greener pastures.

"You look like shit."

Selena's brow furrowed as she stood on my doorstep, sexy as hell. Dark hair curled over the collar of a button-down shirt that hung loosely over her jeans; her laptop and a collection of other bags slung over her shoulder. She wordlessly passed me a giant takeaway cup, striding down the hall.

"Good morning to you, too."

Cool notes followed her through my house — vanilla, mixed with something that reminded me of a rainforest. Combined with the dark ambrosia in the cup, it brought me back to the land of the living with every step.

"Is it? I thought it was afternoon, Liam."

I felt distinctly underdressed in the grey sweats I'd passed out in last night. Not expecting visitors, I was bare-chested as well. Selena headed straight for my fridge, digging around with her pert little ass in the air.

I bit back the urge to smack it, thinking how damn good it would feel beneath my hand. A packet of bacon came sailing over her shoulder. I emerged from my reverie about my handprint on her pale skin just long enough to catch my breakfast.

A packet of bagels followed. I fervently hoped she wouldn't do the eggs. As though reading my mind, she grinned over her shoulder, passing them to me carefully, one at a time.

"Did you have dinner last night?"

Had I? I scrubbed my chin where it itched. I needed a shave, too. That's what days off did to you. I was well out of sorts without the regular structure of my workday.

"I think so?" I offered.

Selena turned to me with a glare that had levelled courtrooms. I, not liking her scrutiny, courtrooms not being my thing. I suspected being a cop added significant bias to my discomfort. She stepped up to me, poking my chest.

"Your coffee rights have been revoked. Sit."

She whisked my coffee away with one hand, pushing me into a chair at my own breakfast bar with the other. I raised an eyebrow but didn't comment on her high handedness. It felt good to have someone else fill my house with life.

"Yes, Ma'am."

A mix of delicious aromas filled my kitchen, and my stomach rumbled in anticipation. Selena flew around the benchtop with incredible efficiency. If this was how she conquered breakfast — I looked at my wristwatch — make that brunch, being cross-examined by her must be excruciating. If you were guilty, that is.

"You're off today?"

"Paperwork. All admin." She spoke over her shoulder, white shirt rising up to display a toned midriff as she grabbed pepper from the shelf above her head.

I groaned in sympathy.

"Don't you have an assistant for that?"

She laughed at me. I held up both hands in defence.

"What? You fancy lawyers have secretaries and interns for that sort of pleb work, right?"

"Solicitor," she corrected me with a frown, "and no, I don't have someone to do that sort of work."

She placed a plate full of the greasiest breakfast I'd ever seen before me. Eggs, bacon, and sausages I hadn't realised were in my refrigerator filled the plate.

"I can't eat this," I protested, "I have to be fit, healthy. This is a heart attack waiting to happen."

She slid two pieces of toast and a small portion of wilted spinach beside the bacon. Oil pooled beneath everything. I lifted one of the eggs, watching yolk surround the toast in a swamp of sunshine. The coffee cup dangled in front of my nose. I reached for it, but Selena snatched it back, fixing me with another steely glare.

"Eat."

I sighed and picked up my fork.

Minutes later, the plate sat empty before me. I'd been more famished than I'd thought. Rewarded with my now-lukewarm cup, Selena seated herself beside me with a bowl full of grains and greens.

"Why couldn't I have had that?" I studied her bowl, swiping a cube of avocado covered in quinoa. That was definitely something she'd brought with her.

"You need to take care of yourself. Someone has to." She plopped more avocado onto my plate.

"Feeding me a plate of cholesterol does that?"

"Always. Have you heard from work?"

I shook my head, leaning back as my food coma hit me in full. I definitely didn't deserve to have this woman in my life.

"They gave me ten extra days of leave. *Must take*, I believe the email said." I grimaced. "The case has stalled — again — and I have too much leave bulked up."

"They didn't call you?"

"Nope."

"They must want you out of there pretty badly. Hmm. I wonder why." She surrounded my cup with slim fingers, turning it in quick circles as she watched me. A twinge of doubt started somewhere on top of the bacon in my stomach, and there really wasn't room for that there right now.

"What's up?" I stretched back, arms over my head. My stomach protested, and I groaned. Returning to the table, I placed my hands over hers, stilling the movement. She started, lifting her eyes to meet mine, but didn't withdraw her hands. "You didn't drive across the city just to make me breakfast, right?"

She sucked her bottom lip into her mouth, biting it. I desperately wanted to pull her into me and kiss her. But that couldn't happen, not yet. Stress showed in the lines of her face — perfectly proportioned, she had a classical beauty. Dark hair tumbled over her shoulders in waves, contrasting against pale skin; it matched dark eyes that held a tinge of violet.

Keep it in your pants, Liam.

She opened her mouth, and for a moment, I was certain I was going to get some smart-ass remark or a brush off. She released the coffee back to me. I accepted it, not taking my eyes off her.

"There's been some vandalism. My street. The typical stuff; street tags, some stuff about cops. My house got done. It's a pain to get it repainted."

"I can fix it for you," I offered. Selena nodded and took a breath.

"And it's the Wayde Logan case."

The words came out in a rush, as though it would be easier for me to hear if she said them quickly.

I placed the cup on the table, collecting my plate under the pretence that I *wasn't* on high alert at her words.

"Yeah? What's going on with it?" My mind screamed to grill her for more information, but she'd let out what she wanted to tell me at her own pace. Pushing her now wouldn't achieve anything but to freak her out.

"Other cases are reemerging. Old ones that were pushed away as something else. Insignificant. I think...Liam, this is bigger than we originally thought."

My pulse quickened. Cal's unit had been chasing Logan under my direction for the best part of five years. I placed the dishes in the sink, stacking them slowly into the dishwasher to give her time to put it all together. When she didn't elaborate, I straightened, looking out the window into the row of trees that lined the suburban street.

"What makes you think that?"

My voice was distant, but all I could see was the last time I had missed something important in an operation. Something that very nearly got me — and five other special ops soldiers — killed. For that moment, I was back in Afghanistan; in the dryness of a dead desert. Pink dust motes swirled around me, obscuring the mark in the sights of my rifle.

Selena was talking, and I came back to her, trying hard to pay attention to what she was saying.

"...Marcus pulled up some older cases, ones that never had a conviction. Same MO, the same line of hostages. Hit a bank in the middle of the morning, just like he did at Central. Only, he looked different. We think that's why he wasn't picked up — why it got missed." She hesitated, and I heard the words she didn't say echo quite clearly in my head. *Why you didn't figure it out.* She shifted on her chair. "Something was done to his face; like it wasn't quite...him. But it's got that same Logan stamp to it."

www.books2read.com/politicsandpaperwork

Go back to where it all began with book 1 of Blue Blooded Brothers series...

COLLISION

Chapter 1

MILA

Tiny feet pattered the worn carpet, glitter coating it with false splendour. The little girl wended her way between patrons. Some were blessed with stars, some with promises of happiness and love; others became apples and bananas. Too much *Ben and Holly*, I recalled from when I'd been forced to babysit for my best friend.

I tried not to look over to my left, the red shoe that– I spun away, and refocused on my task. The man behind me shuffled his feet. I flinched as he dug the pistol into the small of my back, and shivered — skin prickling.

The small office of Central Bank was being held up, and no one outside had noticed. Business operated as usual in the main street through the broad, glassed front as it did every day.

"Oooh, sweetheart, you cold there? I'll warm you up." Foetid breath beneath a rough growl assailed me. I repressed the urge to turn away or vomit, knowing it would only provoke him further. Clammy warmth rubbed my side. My stomach clenched, fighting the numbness that spread through me until I was ice.

A beep sounded at my last keystroke. It was a welcome distraction from my self-analysis. As the thug moved away, I squinted at a screen I'd never seen before.

"It's asking for a password." My voice was husky from lack of use, or maybe it was from screaming silently inside.

"What? No, ...Oi! Nerd! You never said nothin' 'bout no flamin' password!"

Black wire glasses appeared above the divider between the teller cubes. A tuft of dark hair wobbled above a brow furrowed in concentration.

"Seriously, already? Hang on, how far has she got?" Glasses grimaced at me theatrically from his seat at the opposite counter, rolling eyes in the direction of the stale-breathed thug. I returned the sentiment, if only mentally. There was no way I wanted any of these aggressors believing I sympathised with them.

"I'm as far as the login for the manager's screen," I snapped, short breaths puffing through a clenched chest.

Get it over, quick and easy; then they'll be gone.

It was the mantra that had been running through my head for the past twenty minutes.

Get it over, over.

Behind the partition, another patron was being turned into a banana.

We thought we'd been well prepared for an armed robbery. The thin booklet on personal safety was required reading. Give them what they want, and they will leave. Sound the silent alarm behind your terminal.

Karen had tried to do that.

I refused to look at her desk again, my stomach heaving. HR's strategy hadn't worked this time. Maybe I should send them a memo on it, come Monday.

If I was still breathing then.

"Only the login? That's disappointing." Glasses' brow furrowed deeply. "She should have passed that, already. I gave you the codes for those, before...well," he waved a hand behind himself, where a body lay: Karen — the teller who had manned the desk where Glasses now sat before she was yanked from the line of hostages. A swell of emotion blurred my eyes. I blinked tears away angrily.

Don't think, don't think. Over. Get it over and done.

Focus.

Tapped the keyboard, wiggled the mouse. Breathe.

Don't engage. Don't.

"Passwords?"

I was proud my voice didn't shake. My logical brain informed me it was shock and nothing that was under my control. The emotional part didn't answer; it was as numb as the rest of me.

Glasses raised his eyebrows.

"Yes, ma'am."

He flicked a brief salute. A scrap of paper fluttered from his fingers, landing beside the keyboard.

"*Fluffy22?* Really?" I couldn't help commenting. "Cat or dog?"

"Likely the goldfish. Some people have no idea, truly," Glasses responded with a roll of his eyes. We shared a look. I realised what I was doing and quickly returned to the screen: Staring, willing tunnel vision.

Don't, don't.

Heavy footsteps reverberated behind me where the bank manager's office sat. A heavy hand clapped down on my shoulder. Too hot, too overly familiar. His thumb rubbed the sensitive spot on my collarbone, forcing an unwelcome shiver through me.

I willed myself still, to not react, desperate to return to the blank nothing that had consumed me only a moment before, though the urge to jerk away lingered when he spoke. Deep and cold. The same voice I had heard beside Karen.

Before.

"How're we going, we in yet?"

"Not yet, boss; gotta put these in," Glasses indicated the passwords, "Then we should have full access."

I still couldn't believe it. These guys were going to bungle their own robbery. My screen had no way to access the electronic locks for the safe, and anyway, it was such a small branch, surely nothing they held would be sufficient to risk years of incarceration. Reflex had my mouth open to say as much until my brain kicked into gear. My mouth closed with a snap. The three men turned to look at me, and I started guiltily.

"Something you'd like to add, lass?" The question was delivered with some small humour and a touch of annoyance. I shook my head mutely.

"Right, let's get this show on the road."

I chanced a glimpse up at the man behind the robbery: tanned skin, longer-than-average dark hair, hard jaw. Tall and lean. You were supposed to remember details like that for the police, right? His face swivelled my way, displaying ice-cold eyes, unsuited to the rest of his handsome frame.

The devil within, I thought numbly. That wasn't a face that would be easy to forget. I'd have no trouble describing him later, I knew. With hands beginning to tremor from the proximity of the man responsible for the death of my friend, I entered the passwords as the prompts came up. A tiny box popped up in the centre of the screen that I had never seen before.

"...And we're in." Glasses leaned over the divider, meerkat style. "Thanks, love." He winked at me, tapping furiously on a portable keyboard he'd rolled out on the desktop. "Ta-daa."

With a dramatic flourish over his head and the tap of a final keystroke, my screen winked, flickered to blue, and reopened. The little cursor moved around with a mind of its own, opening areas, changing settings. Glasses was manipulating my computer remotely.

More tapping, a little head bobbing, and a clunk came from the rear of the office space — *the safe*. The lights flickered briefly, and I looked around. The three men moved away in a synchronised motion that made me wonder if they'd practised it. Suddenly left alone and grateful for it, I exhaled a long breath that left me more empty than before. One of the men sauntered back out, standing beside the last person in the row of hostages.

Every one of them tensed, and I wondered if they were thinking of the same sound as I did as it ricocheted around my head. Clangs and swearing came from the rear of the bank. I realised I knew less about the bank I'd worked in for three years than I had thought.

Distracted by a swirl of glitter, I looked over at the rows of patrons lining the wall opposite my station: the little girl tracing invisible pictures on the neutral carpet with a sparkling princess wand; a lone, glossy, red shoe, involuntarily discarded upon impact. A stockinged foot, partly visible, protruding behind a cubicle. I dragged my gaze away.

Sit still. Don't think. Don't.

A shadow flitted across the windows that looked out onto the street from the front of the small bank. From their positions on the floor pressed against the wall opposite the teller stations, customers — hostages — shifted uncomfortably, attempting to appear insignificant. Up top, I was exposed, the downlights above me driving sweat around my collar, though it ran down my back cold. I wasn't sure if it was fuelled by fear or heat.

My water bottle cooled my palms, and I slugged down water like a thirsty camel, placing it back on the desk. I shuffled pencils in their holder, ordering them neatly by height. It gave my hands something to do. I took a long, deep breath and tried to settle, to be calm. Letting my eyes close out the rest of the office, I focused on my breath, trying to ignore the sounds behind me. It took a few tries, but I almost had it down, the panic beginning to recede, until I remembered that Karen was the one who had taught me the technique.

My heart pounded anew as I tried to erase the image. Numb fingers fumbled my water bottle, slipping on the condensation coating the clear plastic. It spun in the air, too fast for water to escape, though its movement seemed slow enough to me.

I almost had one hand — who was I kidding; it was the tip of my finger — on the bottle when a loud clang startled me. I fumbled the bottle a second time, wide-eyed as it hit the floor, emptying its contents. I jerked as a small, black wooden box appeared in the corner of my vision and slid forward.

Tanned hands attached to thick forearms reached across my desk. I would have loved them if I hadn't known who they belonged to. I was a sucker for well-muscled forearms, but not at this moment. Fine, white linen sleeves, rolled to the elbows, looked so out of place — an involuntary glance once again gave the impression of a wealthy businessman, not a bank robber.

Murderer.

Gaze fixed, he cradled the box, caressed the lid. It was such an intimate gesture; it felt as though I was intruding on a personal moment. I inched away discreetly until the edge of my chair bit into the backs of my thighs.

Fear permeated the thickened air — from me, and the gallery on the floor. The man behind the robbery stared at the dark, little box with greedy eyes. Glasses appeared, hovering in my peripheral vision.

He annoyed me, and I wanted to bat him away. A twitch in the robber's shoulder left me thinking he felt the same.

Stop sympathising with them.

Reluctantly, one tanned hand released its prize, extended in a beseeching gesture. A tiny tremor quaked through the limb. With no small amount of ceremony, Glasses produced a minuscule key, placing it into the hollow cup of his upturned palm.

The little, silver scrap glinted dully — antique looking — until the tip. I squinted and leaned forward, trying to discern the markings at the bottom of the filigree blade. The end curled upward, screwlike. The inserted key would have to be twisted or wound, like an old music box.

Reverently, the key was lowered to the lock, almost touching. Silence reigned; within the little cluster, no breath escaped.

The moment shattered abruptly, along with the glass of the large, street-front window. A dark shadow blasted through, into the foyer of the bank, showering everyone in glittering shards. Scarlet and indigo lights reflected in the glass littering the carpet. Voices cried out — a high, thin shriek piercing above the rest.

"Daddy!" A little sob accompanied the cry. The group surrounding me broke up, the small, black box forgotten in a surge of movement. The two men who had held the hostages at bay accompanied their leader toward the mess of glass, weapons fluidly drawn as one.

These men have worked together before.

www.books2read.com/Collision-LQP